OUT OF THE BLACK

BY LEE DOTY

ISBN: 1-4196-9685-8

ISBN-13: 9781419696855

Visit www.booksurge.com to order additional copies.

For my wife, Amber. Without her faith and patience, this book would still be an idea I wished I had time to write down.

For little Dek Kerhin, the first (of many, I'm sure) baby to be named after a character in this book.

Special thanks to the people who read this book when it was a word doc, and then a sheaf of poorly bound eight by eleven. Thanks for all the suggestions, encouragement, and especially for the criticism.

Lynne and Brian Kerhin
Matthew and Jen Doty
Anna, Elaine, Bob and Carolyn Doty
Giovanna Doty
Chris DeGreef
Scott Knowles
Larry Stuart
Craig Puhala
Tim Park

Thanks to the muses who inspired me during hours of writing and revising: Delerium, Curve, Etnica, Pleiadians, and the touchsamadhi.com crew— especially SOT, Kri, and DJs Dragon and Derby. These folks make the music I imagine on the movie adaptation's soundtrack.

And a big, resounding thanks to anyone with enough fortitude to make it through all those thank-yous. With great admiration, I paraphrase *The Kentucky-Fried Movie* on your behalf: "You are a fighting force of extraordinary magnitude!"

PROLOGUE: OUT OF TIME

The impact spread slowly across his back, straining his tightly set muscles and driving the air from his lungs in a long, slow groan. Then, the sound of success—the sound of the end—like a large boot in deep, wet snow, the crunch of parting glass broke out all around him and he kicked out hard one last time. The window crumbled away around him and he flew backwards, away from the death in the hallway and into the night air high above Chicago's deserted streets.

Then his world was a tumbling storm of rain, glass and the wind of increasing velocity. The gathering roar of the air around him promised that this would end badly eighty-two floors down. He'd made his choices, fought hard, and would now die on his own terms. Small consolation, considering that he was only about a second and a half into the fall and he'd already had enough time to count to infinity twice and take a nap. It would be a few more seconds before he stopped accelerating, then a few more before the final splat. He wished in passing he'd brought a good book. He was all for the idea of having time to meditate and ponder the eternities or whatever people were supposed to do in their final moments, but he'd only need the time a bullet took from barrel to brain for that kind of thing.

He watched the light from the building's windows bend and refract through the rain and the shards of the broken window tumbling around him and tried to Zen out for a bit. It was really a beautiful scene, now that he took the time to look. From time to time, the glass would tick off his clothes or skin, pressing then fading like tentative teeth in the chill of the embracing rain. He was going out in style.

Going out in style maybe, but he was the last one off the stage. Everyone he'd cared about was dead or worse, and when he finally hit the concrete in a handful of seconds at his own, personal terminal velocity, the stage would go dark. Then the world around it would go dark, too—apocalyptically dark. He'd failed his family and they'd died. Now, because he'd failed again, it was going to be everyone else's turn.

He fell through the hollow air, remorse and inadequacy burning through his ancient heart.

And then a dull radiance below drew his eye. As he watched, a few random points of light pierced the mist, then grew and elaborated into the familiar lattice of the city's streets. Then he tumbled from the low clouds and the city erupted around him. There, feeling small and naked before the blazing urban panorama that seemed to stretch from horizon to horizon, he had his epiphany. The black would always be there, hesitating at the edges of the light, but it would never win. Without the light, the black wasn't anything at all. The storm would rage and bluster, but it would eventually pass from the city, and then from memory.

Sure, it was over for him. Sure, his was a brutal, bad end, but these desperate moments were only the last page of his long and satisfying biography. Death stung only because he'd lived so bright. Loss hurt only because he'd loved deep and true. In some insane way, the sheer unstoppable momentum of his unfolding tragedy suddenly made him feel grateful.

Work to do. With a mental shrug and a mood swing that would make any psychiatrist reach eagerly for the prescription pad, he got back to work. Precious time had passed in reverie, and more passed as his limbs slid into position. Air flowed and tugged at him, and his legs finally extended below him, his arms stretched wide. He wasn't going to survive this no matter what he did, but he was going to get a 9.5 from the East German judge if it killed him.

He passed the twenty-ninth floor positioned like an Olympic gymnast and grinning like an idiot. He cocked his head slightly and scanned the ground, not knowing exactly what he was looking for, maybe a flatbed truck loaded with mattresses or a large bucket of water. Three people were on the rain-swept street below, but none of them looked burly or quick enough to catch him. A heavy woman in a blue sweater walked almost directly below him, head raised and eyes squinting into the downpour. Being a human of a more normal variety, she couldn't yet see him, but he could see her just fine. Her mouth was partially open, lips stretched, her teeth slightly exposed—though there was sadness in her eyes and frustration pinching her brow, she was laughing. He wondered in passing what was so funny, but he knew that whatever it was, neither of them would remember it in a few more seconds.

Not too far off, two men in improbably white clothes stood, looking expectant, like they were waiting for a very white bus. Though he couldn't see their faces from this angle, the men in white were apparently engaged in an energetic conversation. One was gesturing in the direction of the dark car parked at the edge of the street just ahead of the laughing woman.

Looking at the woman again, he realized that without further adjustments, he'd land directly in front of her. "Blood linkage" echoed from his recent memory and a desperate plan began to pull at his mind. Then he decided—he was going to go out fighting, right on through the final second. He might have saved the world when he went out that window a few seconds back, but he really didn't think so. He was pretty sure his enemies could get their precious key from his corpse.

Eighteenth floor: Geometry and aerodynamics blazed through his diamond-hard mind, his sluggish limbs moved, and he rode the altered slipstream into the air over the car just ahead of the woman. With luck, the car's roof would deform enough to allow him to live for at least a few seconds after the splat. Luck, he thought with the first tightness of a smile pulling at the corners of his mouth, the way things were going tonight, that car was probably packed with dynamite and rusty nails.

Sixth floor: His legs were bent slightly, his muscles tensed for the landing. He was as ready as he was going to get. Below him, the woman had taken another step toward the car, her weight slowly shifting from left to right foot as she slogged through the rain at what looked like her best speed. With a start, the falling man realized that now she was alone on the street. His eyes flicked around quickly—the two men in white had disappeared.

Impossible. It had only been about three quarters of a second since he'd seen them last, and they hadn't looked like they were in a hurry. If he had time, he would have shrugged. He'd seen so many impossible things in his ninety-one years that a couple of disappearing strangers didn't even rate an exclamation point in his diary, especially not on a night like tonight.

Second floor: nothing to do now but wait... and think about the shape of the stain he'd make.

Hanging in the air a meter above the car, he wondered if he shouldn't just give up and let the ground have its way with him quickly. At the speed of his focused thought, he knew the next second would draw out before and behind him forever. He'd already lost everything, so why should he force himself to experience every crunching, bursting instant of his death? Why strain and compensate as bone shattered and muscle and tendon were torn apart? Why experience every nanosecond of the coming impact, just for a chance at a few seconds of consciousness afterward?

And then he saw them again, the two men in white, maybe only four meters away now, they were staring directly at him. Their familiar faces were filled with something between joy and sorrow, between grief and pride. Their eyes burned with an intensity that reached past the pain and loss, finally piercing his heart. They knew he could do this, and so did he.

Right through that last second.

With only centimeters left, he tried to yell, just to relieve the tension. He tried for more of a skydiving "woohooo!" than the "aaaaaaaaagh!" of final misadventure, but there was no time for sound before the violence of the impact consumed him.

DARKNESS

AFTERMATH

With a sigh of resignation, Ping Bannon opened the sedan's door and stepped out into the night air. The sandy-fresh smell of the newly departed rain on the concrete pushed his grim agenda aside and brought a small, unexpected smile to his face. Sometimes in the conditioned air of the car, in the heart of the city, it was easy to forget the simple pleasures of nature. He breathed it in, gazing up at the dim stars resolving out of the clearing sky.

Clarity. His job demanded it, and sometimes moments like this could bring it. He had never mastered the professional detachment that made some in his line of work seem cold. Though he liked to think of himself as a tough guy, his mom liked to remind him that he was too sweet to be a cop.

Mothers, he thought, shaking his head.

Shorter than average and slight of build, Ping wasn't an imposing figure. Kind eyes and a thoughtful manner didn't add to his intimidation factor. Though he excelled at most aspects of his job, and sheer intensity could, on occasion, bring a sort of hardness to his face, he'd never played a successful "bad cop" role in an interrogation. He winced as he thought about his last attempt—he'd been the last to start laughing. His partner and the murder suspect had laughed harder though. Perhaps it was a holdover from his first career, but he was much better at putting people at ease than trying to frighten them. He had to admit that he preferred it that way.

His on-the-job suit was a crisp featureless black and though clean and comfortable, it wouldn't get him any dates. His clunky black shoes looked like grandpaware, but were built for support, agility, and traction. They were the preferred footwear of beat cops, but most other detectives had moved on to more stylish shoes. His only jewelry was a platinum holo watch on his left thumb and matching titanium lock rings on his index fingers. Hidden beneath the suit he wore the tools of his trade: detective's badge in his left lapel pocket, secure tablet collapsed in a minimal holster at the small of his back, and matching 2mm issue needle guns in shoulder holsters. The lock rings on his fingers unlocked the guns when he held them, which was mostly on the shooting range these days.

Finally admitting that the time for reasonable stalling was long past, he closed the car door and heard the lock tone as he stepped away. Moving around the back of the car, he saw the red-blue corona of flickering light over the guardrail at the edge of the road. A few reluctant steps brought him to the edge of the downward slope behind the rail, and to his first view of the crime scene.

The police cruiser waited about forty meters away, silently spilling red and blue strobes across the damp street. It was parked near the ruins of a dark luxury car, which had apparently crashed into the wall at the edge of the highway underpass. Ping stopped and spent a few seconds examining what was left of the luxury car—though the frame looked, largely intact; the top of the car was completely gone. Twisted fingers of metal and glass jutted from the points where the roof had once been attached. Around the car, the pavement glittered with broken glass and was littered with larger debris. Maybe someone in the back seat hadn't listened to mom about playing with the pin in the family grenade.

Curious, he moved nimbly down the embankment through the shin-high Otu weeds. The Otu smelled greener and fresher than plants should. They had been engineered to create oxygen and eat carbon dioxide at phenomenal rates, but he wasn't sure if the fresh smell was intended, or just a pleasant side effect.

About halfway down the embankment, one of the two officers on the scene spotted Ping. The officer was huge, perhaps two meters tall and a hundred twenty kilos, with a florid face and bright red hair beneath his patrol cap. The redhead spoke quickly to his partner without taking his eyes off of the new arrival. Ping was acutely aware that the officer was probably wondering what an Asian kid in a suit was doing skipping down from the freeway at this time of night. This gave him a nearly imperceptible flash of annoyance, followed by a much larger sense of amusement. He looked far younger than his thirty-nine years, and he loved to whip out the badge for officers he didn't know. Without slowing down, he fished the badge out of his lapel pocket.

As he approached the edge of the sidewalk, still about ten meters away from the police tape that enclosed the crime scene, he noticed the redhead's hand on his weapon. Ping couldn't tell from this distance if the holster was still locked to the weapon, but from the cop's body language, he guessed not… in fact the guy seemed tense enough to draw on him with little or no provocation. The other cop was also giving Ping his full attention from a position just behind the patrol car. Ping couldn't see his hands, but he could read his face—these guys were spooked and ready to get decisive about resolving their fear.

"Not a good sign." Ping muttered, putting on his smile. He crossed the street and approached the redhead at an easy pace.

"Lieutenant Bannon, homicide. What've we got here?" he said smoothly, attaching his badge to his jacket's exterior pocket. The officer's apprehension didn't dissipate immediately. Instead of the embarrassed relief Ping expected, the redhead raised his tablet and entered a few commands. The cop continued his hard appraisal of Ping until the tablet chirped, verifying his credentials. Then the officer's face softened into a mix of poorly concealed relief and more than a little professional embarrassment. Though the big cop's delayed reaction was both expected and somewhat satisfying, Ping could tell that this guy was not used to letting his game face slip, certainly not to reveal fear.

The cop's game face now portrayed amusement: "Bannon eh? And a solid Irish cop too."

As a social ritual, Ping had always been intrigued by the relationship between fear and banter. "I prefer the term 'Chirish American.'" he said affably.

"Why'd you drop the 'O' Mr. O'Bannon?" The officer continued with an easy, likable smile crossing his weathered face. "Y'know, ya can't hide the Irish... it's written all over your face."

Ping had heard all this before. Though he looked entirely Chinese, he was one quarter Irish. His Irish granddad had met grandma in Hong Kong while attending school. The school had grown into a way of life for him and he'd stayed. Dad met mom at another school in Beijing. Ping had heard all the Irish cop jokes.

"My parents Americanized the name when we immigrated from China... didn't want to sound too ethnic, I guess." he said with his most serious face.

The officer's smile widened,   "Sergeant Malloy O'Flannahan at your service..."

"You're kidding."

The sergeant raised an eyebrow and hooked a thumb at his nametag. Still smiling, he turned toward the destroyed car. "Come on, let's get the unpleasant part over with and we can get back to discussin' the green isle of our heritage."

Ping followed. "Is that music?"

The sergeant nodded without turning. They moved closer and the rhythms of Bob Marley began to shift and flow around them through the cool night air. "You like reggae, Detective Bannon?"

"I prefer the modern stuff... better produced."

"Uh-huh. What we've got here are two extremely dead bodies in the car, eight to twelve more on the street under the bridge, and…"

"Eight to twelve?"

"How many potatoes go into a bowl of stew?"

Ping was still chewing on that when he saw the first potato. It was part of an arm, lying at the end of a bloody radius that emanated from the car. It looked as if it had been burnt black.

Suppressing a "What the…", he bent to examine it. He noticed that the arm looked more than burnt; it was the color of a deep pond on a moonless midnight—shiny and wet.

When he was fifteen, he'd gone to camp with his brother somewhere in Virginia. After they'd gone canoeing, the camp counselors had surprised them by checking their feet for leaches. The real shock was the black, oily flesh they discovered between Ping's toes. The counselor had used a smoldering punk to burn the leech off. It didn't hurt, but it was unbearably gross to his 15-year-old mind: sharing a bloodstream with that *thing*. Now, 24 years later he stared down at the same oily flesh in the shape of an arm. "What the…"

"Yep," said Malloy, interrupting from above. "Come on. The fun's just begun."

As Ping stood to follow, he couldn't completely shake free of his walk down memory lane. He found himself thinking about how the world had shivered and lost focus as all his thought compressed to the glistening dark spot between his toes. He'd woken later to the teasing laughter of his brother. "You okay kid?" the camp counselor had asked through the fog of returning reality.

Malloy was staring expectantly at him. "You okay?" he repeated.

"Sorry. Just thinking."

Malloy gave him a resolute nod "We've done a lot of that, too."

"All the bodies like that?" Ping asked, glancing back over his shoulder.

"No two alike."

"Any ID?"

"We haven't touched anything," Malloy checked his tablet, "forensics should be here in fifteen."

The other officer joined them as they reached the front of the destroyed car. He was an efficient looking black man in his twenties. An ugly pale scar crawled from the bottom of his left ear to his collarbone— Ping wondered how he'd survived whatever had caused that, and why he hadn't had the scar removed. The patrolman's arms were so corded with muscles that he looked like he could crush the black maglite he held. Black points and curves mostly hidden by collar and short sleeves suggested a hidden mosaic of tattoo beneath his shirt. "Rodriguez" was on his nametag.

Like his partner, he didn't look like he was used to being afraid. He glanced at Ping's badge and gave a nod of recognition. "Welcome to the twilight zone," he said with a tight grin.

"I hear it's a dimension of mind," Ping said, glancing at the strings of interlacing automatic weapon craters in the concrete wall behind the car. Bob Marley continued to wail from the damaged car's powerful speakers. The music seemed to resonate in every molecule of the chilled night air. It filled any pause in the conversation, slid around each word. "Let's get together and feel all right."

"You notice this?" Rodriguez used the maglite to illuminate a spot on the overpass above the car.

What Ping could make out looked like pieces of the car's roof, mangled and fused to the infrastructure of the bridge. Dark viscous liquid dripped from several protrusions.

"That's not…" He stopped as he made out the shape of a twisted leg protruding from the wreckage above him. Its black shoe was untouched by the destruction.

They moved through the minefield of physical evidence, skirting piles of biology and destroyed metal. At last, they reached the car, approaching the driver's door from the front. The roof had been blown off from the back, but about ten centimeters of damaged metal clung to the windshield's upper frame. The windshield was spiderwebbed with cracks, most of which emanated from the roughly horizontal cigar shaped hole directly in front of the driver. Jagged shards at the bottom of the frame were all that remained of the car's side and rear windows.

At the driver's door, the interior of the car appeared for the first time. The first glance revealed two bodies: the driver and a passenger in the back seat. The driver was buckled in, but the passenger was on the floor of the back seat, mostly hidden from view.

"What's wrong with this picture?" Malloy asked with a sideways glance.

"What isn't?" Ping answered, but then he noticed: "This wasn't an explosion."

"Something blew off the top without destroying the interior of the car," Rodriguez said.

There were several slashes in the seats and blood everywhere, but no burn or shrapnel damage. The passenger side airbag had deployed and now lay spent over the empty passenger seat. The driver's airbag hadn't deployed, but that was likely because the steering wheel was gone.

The driver was indeed "extremely dead"—slumped forward and to the right in his harness, his head was mostly missing. From the pattern of... tissue... on the passenger's door but not the deployed airbag, it appeared that he had died before the car hit the wall. In his left hand, the driver clutched the detached steering wheel. Upon closer inspection, the wheel was deformed as if it had been wrenched off.

Ping blinked and shook his head, "Looks like the driver died before the car hit the bridge."

Malloy nodded, "The shot probably came through the window. What do you make of the steering wheel?"

"Souvenir?" Rodriguez said around abbreviated breaths. The air was tinged with the smell of the butcher shop.

Ping blunted his visceral reaction to the carnage by pulling his tablet from its holster and getting to work. He expanded it to notepad size and switched it out of standby. He detached the stylus and brought up a new incident report. He used the tablet's three-dimensional scanners to record the contents of the car. He paused occasionally to scratch notes and diagrams, linking them with the images. "I'll need a download of your raw reports."

The two officers entered the necessary commands on their tablets. Ping's tablet chirped twice in acknowledgment of the inbound data feeds. He would review and incorporate them into his report later.

"We already did the full survey," Rodriguez said.

Ping nodded absently from behind the shelter of his tablet as he finished surveying the front seat and moved on to the rear.

When looking from the front, he hadn't noticed the damage to the back seat—four holes in a tight configuration at about chest level—definitely bullet holes. They were probably fired from outside the driver's door, from about where he was now standing. On a hunch Ping turned around and looked down. He stood at one end of another bloody skid mark radiating away from the car. At the far end was what might have once been a body—so much for the shooter.

He snapped some images and turned his attention to the car's second occupant. Not much to see there; at least not much to want to see. Patterns of blood on the seats implied that the victim had probably been standing when he was killed, but whoever had done it had stopped to make very, very sure that he was dead. Ping gritted his teeth and documented. He hoped that he would never get used to stuff like this.

When his tablet contained all the information he could get about the car, he turned toward the bullet-pocked wall. He was documenting the placement of the shots when Malloy spoke. "We got here 'bout twenty minutes ago. Traffic dispatched us to check out the intersection's Big Brother. It went offline about an hour before and wouldn't respond to remote diagnostics.

Ping nodded, "Just coincidence, I'm sure."

"Yeah... Someone didn't want to show up in the background of a traffic violation video. The Bro' took a round powerful enough to scrap it. You'll find a link to its logs and a scan of the scrap in the feed I gave you."

"Witnesses?" Ping asked, knowing the answer.

Malloy bit his lip, shook his head.

"We saw something..." Rodriguez said, eyes lingering on the car's interior, "something fast."

Ping looked up from his work, giving Rodriguez his full attention; he left the question unasked.

After a pause, Rodriguez continued, "I didn't get a good look..."

"Just a good scare, hey?" Malloy interrupted, looking amused, his game face nearly impenetrable.

With an effort, Rodriguez looked away from the car and faced his partner. "You know, your terror squeak was quite... distracting." His game face was back too.

"I got a touch of the asthma, Junior!" Malloy came back.

"Children..." Ping eased into the friendly sparring with the patient-but-firm voice he'd perfected while counseling troubled families. His gaze settled on Rodriguez.

"Yeah... well, we'd found the bodies there," Rodriguez said, pointing to a ragged crater in the concrete behind the patrol car.

"Mortar round?" Ping said, staring at the raised lip around the destroyed concrete.

Rodriguez shrugged, but his eyes better conveyed the extent of his confusion.

"Not unless the mortar fired people," Malloy said, shaking his head.

Ping was about to ask him what he meant, but Rodriguez continued, "So we were already... concerned, you know? I had the flashlight and pistol out—sort of easing up on the back of the car. Then there's this sound... and like a blur of motion, and something explodes out from behind the car."

"Explodes?" Ping stopped scribbling on his tablet in mid-note, "What exploded?"

"Not like 'boom,'" Malloy said, "but moving like it'd been shot out of a cannon... It really freaked him out." He pointed to the overpass, "Rod here took a shot at it—see the hole way up there in the bridge?"

"What freaked me out was that 'asthma' of yours." Rodriguez said as if re-explaining a math problem to an eight-year-old, "I thought maybe you were dyin'. You sure that wasn't the terror squeak?"

"Asthma." Malloy droned.

"Terror squeak." Rodriguez's smile broadened.

"So this guy flew up to the bridge?" Ping asked, unimpressed.

"Nah," Malloy smirked, "he went off south. Rod here just shot up."

Rodriguez shook his head, "It was between the car and the wall. It bolted out just as I looked down into the car. I'm seeing all this blood, and there's this blast of sound like a flag in high wind, and I see something jet out from behind the car, out of the corner of my eye. I bring my gun up quick, but then there's this really unsettling 'asthma' coming from the chief here," he gave Malloy a mischievous glance, "Anyway, I lost my footing on some kind of stuff I really don't want to think about…"

"…and the bridge gets what's coming to it." Malloy gave a knowing nod.

"You keep saying 'it' and 'something'," Ping said, "do you mean 'he' or 'she'?"

"All I saw was a blur." Rodriguez shook his head.

"I just saw a blink," Malloy said, "dark and fast. It coulda' been a man…"

"Except men don't move like that." Rodriguez finished.

Untouched, Unknown

The storm was coming.

Face turned down against the light rain, Anne plodded homeward under a black canopy of lowering clouds. The tops of the surrounding buildings were already lost in the lowering sky and light showers had darkened the pavement. Nature's latest prank at Anne's expense was all set up and it was almost time for the big, wet punch line.

When she woke late in the afternoon, the day had been cool and bright, but deep clouds had moved in with the night. By the time she arrived at work, the sky was filled with the promise of rain. Now, walking home in the fulfillment of that promise, Anne trudged through the thousand small aches that any exertion cost her. Her blue sweater, though perfect for the early evening chill, was completely ineffective against the early morning rain. Socks wet, feet itching, she felt just a little sorry for herself. Usually she tried to be positive, but sometimes the funk crept in and ruined her day.

Normally she didn't waste a lot of time focusing on her long-term issues: like being single at thirty-nine, like having a face only a mother could love—not her mother, but maybe someone else's mother—like tipping the scales at two hundred forty pounds with her lungs full of helium. Thank heaven for metrics! A hundred and ten kilos sounded positively slim compared to her imperial weight.

Ok, so maybe she thought about the big issues a bit, but right now her most pressing problems were the five blocks between her and the train station, and the sky full of water above her. On the bright side, she didn't have to worry about the rain smearing her makeup—she just didn't wear the stuff. One time in college she'd made an abortive try, but the sight of her round face staring back at her from the mirror with the first hint of blush inexpertly applied made her feel like an inexpertly polished turd. Makeup and designer clothes were for some jet set, days-of-wine-and-roses, dating, frolicking-in-front-of-the-cameras subphylum of humanity to which she did not belong. Hospital scrubs and a clean face—this was her lot in life.

She grinned, part humor, part exasperation. She was big enough to admit her life sucked, but tonight had been something truly special. It had started out as usual with an over-snoozed alarm. She'd missed her train and been late to work, but the most unpleasant part of the commute was the grizzled eastern European cabby that had hurled a stream of poorly assembled insults at her for crossing the street legally in his presence. The part that stuck with her was something like, "box be on your family"—box? She'd probably be dreaming about "the box" tonight.

She rolled her eyes and let the smile spread across her face as she considered the hundred small frustrations in the workday of a professional vampire. Seriously, she couldn't see how Count Chocula had done it all these years without getting fed up and taking a stroll in the sun—that cartoon bloodsucker had the heart of a champion. Despite her most bubbly bedside manner, every patient at the hospital was not happy to see Anne and her little tray of needles and tubes. She had it worse than most phlebotomists since she worked the graveyard shift. No one liked to be in the hospital, no one liked to have blood drawn, but it really got personal when they had to wake up for their bloodletting.

Then there was her main occupational hazard: the plague of Harms that started showing up around eleven every night. The ER got between five and ten a night. They were restrained by the time they reached the hospital, but their incoherent verbal assault was always a treat. Eyes dilated before an incomprehensible hallucinoscape, they shrieked and cursed and wept. They were unpredictable, moving from pathetic sobs to merciless violence seamlessly. The police and paramedics who brought them in required first aid as often as not.

The ironic part was that Harmony was sold as a mood-elevator with mild hallucinogenic effects. It was the first and most effective connectivity drug on the illicit market. Though there was still debate on the subject, the prevailing wisdom was that connectivity drugs affected the areas of the brain that governed empathy and the sense of community. Many starry-eyed psychedelic types believed Harmony was the first scientific step toward telepathy, but Anne knew that speech, writing, and television had already blazed the pre-telepathy trail.

Harmony had been hot among the party crowd for maybe a decade now, gaining wide popularity with the post-psychedelic subculture. The psychotic incidents hadn't started until a few months ago in New York, but within three weeks, Harms had made their Chicago debut. In another two weeks, there were Harms in every major city in the world.

Anne understood the desire to escape, to feel like you belonged in a group of strangers, but she was completely mystified why anyone would continue to take a drug once it started leaving people in a state that came in second only to demonic possession in the creepy Olympics. From the number of Harms she saw at the hospital, she didn't need to see any disturbing statistics to know Harmony was a serious problem.

Drawing the blood of these nuts was the most unsettling part of her job. She usually got to wait until they were sedated, but even pumped full of sedatives powerful enough to tranquilize a carload of game show hosts, a Harm might still wake up cranky. A properly motivated Harm could even break the "unbreakable" plastic cuffs cops used. A month ago, the hospital had received new restraints just for the Harms, but she still didn't feel safe.

The crown jewel in her work night came at three this morning. She'd been relieved to take a break from the ER and its swarm of Harms to draw blood from a slightly disoriented 84-year-old inpatient on anticoagulants. Carol was the archetypal granny: thin and fragile, with an easy disposition and plenty of stories of kids and grandkids.

When Anne woke her up, she had been sweet, "You just do whatever you need, Dearie."

As Anne applied the tourniquet and sterilized Carol's arm, they'd had a pleasant conversation about Carol's grandkids. As Anne prepared the needle, she was smiling and laughing. She never saw it coming.

When the needle went into Carol's arm, she made a small surprised sound. Anne's next clue that something was amiss was the clutch purse that smashed into the top of her head. The old hag was screaming incoherently and repeatedly bludgeoning Anne cross-body with the purse. Anne got the blood sample, but it cost her both bruises and pride.

Expect the unexpected—this should be the phlebotomist's credo.

It made her want to start a support group for the vocationally unloved. She could picture it now: listening supportively in the company of depressed IRS agents and dentists. "Hi, I'm Anne, and people hate my job," she mumbled as she trudged through the threatening sprinkle of rain. Humor had always been her shield. When things got tough, she'd go for the cheap laughs. She was starting to feel better when the rain came down like a tidal wave.

"Aw… crap…ola." was all the disappointment she could muster before the uncontrollable laughter started. She was still splashing and waddling, laughing and crying when she noticed the music—first like the tinkle of an elaborate crystal wind chime, but getting louder with the urgency of an approaching freight train. She didn't have time to process this information before the world exploded.

Her startled scream came out in a rather embarrassing squeak when the car parked to her left had a Wile E. Coyote moment. It seemed as if an anvil had dropped from some hidden mesa high above. The car's roof crumpled and the windows closest to Anne exploded outwards. A storm of broken glass showered down from above, exploding on the ground around her, tugging at her left arm and back, stinging her right cheek.

Not an anvil! Her mind locked, hitched, locked—stuttered between knowledge and denial. The body rebounded sideways off the car and continued its impact on the sidewalk with a horrifying prolonged bursting sound. It seemed as if the impact went on and on as time lengthened, or perhaps replayed, with the onset of shock. Then the body was a lifeless rag-doll on the sidewalk before her, shattered legs twisted at impossible angles, face partially covered by one arm.

Numb, she stared for a few seconds before becoming aware that she was standing on one foot with her arms crossed above her head, hands on elbows. The arm-head-cover she got, but what was the one-leg-stand for? She would never understand her reflexes. She was a Darwinian counterexample of the first order—but then she wouldn't be reproducing anytime soon, so maybe not exactly a counterexample. "Weeded out of the gene pool", or maybe "She died that we all might have better children", would mark her tombstone someday.

She put her foot down and rushed forward with a hopeless desire to help. She knelt and actually said, "Are you okay?" Yeah, she was sure he was probably fine! A quick glance above showed her buildings with more stories of unblemished glass than she could count, ascending up into the clouds high above. "No." she mumbled, realizing this wasn't a worker fallen from a ladder or a low balcony.

She knew that she shouldn't move the body, so she sat helpless, her strained mind completely oblivious to her tablet and its emergency links. After a few more seconds, she looked about for help—nothing. The rain was her only companion on the dark street. The sound of it was static in her ears; its caress was a wet, tingling static on her skin; the sight of it was gray static in her eyes. The world was a fuzzy place getting darker and slower.

From the corner of her eye, she noticed something dark and serpentine slithering on the ground around her. She looked down and saw dark tendrils washing around her hands and knees—blood! She tore her right hand out of a puddle of bloody water and watched in horror as the falling rain did its best to rinse it clean.

Her eyes lost focus on her red-tinged hand as she noticed that, behind it, the dead man's arm had fallen aside, exposing his face. Her first impression was of a child, broken and lost. Fringed by short dark hair, his face was round and gentle. His closed eyes were small and narrowly spaced. The bridge of the nose was broad and slipped down into a small round nose. The upper lip was pronounced and looked even more so because the mouth hung slack. The chin and jaw were delicate.

Her throat constricted with pity. She didn't know this poor guy, but she could tell he'd been kind. She knew he didn't deserve to die like this. She reached out her hand to touch his shoulder, muttering inane apologies. The rain's static drone crackled all around, setting them apart from the rest of the world. They were together on the only remaining channel of a damaged television satellite floating through empty space. The blood continued to pool, continued to dissipate, she touched his cheek, her tears lost in the rain.

His eyes opened.

Unformed, powerful emotion covered her skin like a shorting electric blanket and every hair seemed to strain away from her skin. Her mouth dropped open as his closed. His eyes were incredibly blue; they held her like gentle hands, shutting out everything else, no more blood, no more rain—no more reason. This was not real.

His lips stirred. "Woohoo." he gurgled from partially collapsed lungs.

Not real. "What?" she sputtered as he struggled for breath. "It's going to be all right. Don't move." She stammered. "Help is on the…" realizing her oversight, she clawed in her pockets for her tablet.

"No. Got to tell…" he whispered, quieter than before. As his mind reasserted control over his face, the softness became less obvious. Though the innocence didn't disappear, it was surrounded by strength. Even broken, he was beautiful.

Something stirred within her. It was built on pity, formed of hope, but she wasn't sure at all what it was. Mesmerized, she leaned closer, straining to hear him above the sizzle of the rain.

"Sorry… sorry," he said so softly she craned closer to hear. His eyes never left hers. As she drew close to his face, it occurred to her that he was actually going to kiss her. Of course, this was nuts—she wasn't the kind of girl that dying folks kissed impulsively. With an effort, she turned her face from him and brought her ear close to his mouth.

"Sorry." his lip touched her ear causing the most unexpected shock. With a gasp, she realized that his left arm was over her shoulder, across her back, and holding her close with surprising strength. No thoughts came through her confusion until she felt his lips on her neck, and even then they weren't really thoughts: shock, fear of moving, distaste at being joined to someone so horribly hurt—but the weirdest and most prevalent feeling was the most embarrassing kind of excitement.

"Uhhh?" she got out before the pain blew through her. It shot from her neck inward to the center of her chest, where it seemed to ricochet around unchecked. Her throat closed, allowing no air or sound passage. Hot oily lightning filled her, deep-frying nerves, knotting every muscle.

The inner lightning pulsed, its rhythm filling every cell, blossoming and fading with her heart's beating. It slipped and pulsed like blood through her, synchronizing with the pulsing sparks that filled her vision, with the muted gong that filled her ears.

Her legs kicked out, but his arm held her tight, leaving her prostrate on top of him. The muscles around her lungs overcame the muscles around her throat and the air groaned out of her. Through the sparkling haze, she could now see her face reflected in a pool of watery blood behind his shoulder. She wondered what percentage of the blood was hers as she examined her contorted reflection. She hoped she didn't still look like this when the coroner arrived or he'd guess 'death by constipation' for sure.

The fog thickened behind her reflected image. Burning and fading, she seemed to slip away from him, from the pain, from herself. She drifted through thickening white fog until she was at last alone.

Thunderstruck and hazy, she stood in white mists, rubbing her neck absently, and wondering if Angels or Devils were next. She grinned, thinking it funny that twice in one day her carelessness had opened her to the cruel klonk of life's clutch purse.

"Hi!" a cheerful voice sounded behind her, startling her so badly she was glad her ghost didn't have a bladder. The mists seemed to quiver in response to the voice. She jumped and spun around. Where was she anyway?

Against an unbroken backdrop of brightness, he stood smiling. Not hurt, not helpless, not weak—not innocent.

He shrugged, "I did say I was sorry, right?" He gave a self-conscious chuckle with an apologetic smile and a twinkle in his eye.

And then he started talking. She saw his hands gesturing for her patience, saw the urgent look in his eyes—but mostly she saw his lips move. She could hear the buzz of his words, but she wouldn't understand. She wasn't listening because she was too busy watching the teeth behind his moving lips. They were fierce, sharp, and curved like shark's teeth. They were red with her blood.

She turned to run, but the foggy brightness went black.

Rules of Evidence

The team of two forensic techs had arrived about twenty minutes ago in a van packed with impressive looking equipment. Another uniformed patrol team had arrived while the techs were still unpacking. The forensics guys poured over the car with their equipment while Ping went over the general area of the car, scanning and scratching notes. Malloy and Rodriguez had joined the other two uniforms in broadening the search/scan to the surrounding area.

Finally, one of the techs at the car waved Ping over. As Ping approached him, the tech held up a pair of clear plastic evidence bags the size of dinner plates. "We're done with the car—touch what you like."

The tech held out the first bag. "It's been through the scanner, so it's all yours." The tech continued, "His Uni says the guy in the front was Peter Sieberg, field tests agree, but I won't have a DNA match until the judge signs off on the test." Ping took the bag and gave the contents a quick glance: the smallest piece of equipment was the card-sized flexible plastic Universal ID. The Uni was nestled against a sleek looking glasses case or flashlight and a tablet. These objects were surrounded by some simple jewelry. "Who was the passenger?" Ping asked, glancing at the other bag.

The tech handed it over, "Dr. Ivo Lutine... professor over at Rosemont."

"Professor of what?" Ping looked up from his examination of the professor's personal effects.

"Yeah, I know," the tech said leaning in slightly, "I was expecting some kind of foreign dictator or organized crime boss with a hit like this."

"What makes you think it was a hit?" Ping asked with a perfectly straight face.

"Oh, you mean like the high velocity shell through the driver's ear, or the fourteen holes and two slashes in the professor there? And I've got three things to say about those slashes..." He held up his hand and counted off on three fingers, "what...the...hell?" He waved the three extended fingers for emphasis as he continued. "From cross sections, we know the weapon's blade was at least twenty-five centimeters long, but my guess is it was probably closer to a meter. And sharp! It sliced the bones... didn't crack them—actually left them smooth. One of those hacks cut through the clavicle, the scapula, four ribs in back, five in front and bisected the heart!"

"So you think we're looking for ninja hit men?" Ping held desperately to his straight face—he thought it was still working.

"Ninja hit…" The tech broke off, exasperated, "At this point I can't rule out psychotic cartoons, imaginary friends, or little green men. Am I not impressing you with this stuff?"

Yep, the straight face had held. Ping let it go and laughed, "Sorry, it's just been a very 'impressive' day."

"Now *that* I understand." The tech turned back toward his partner.

"One more thing." Ping called after him.

"Yeah?" the tech said over his shoulder.

"What's the likely origin on the shot that hit the driver?"

"That one's hard. He was definitely hit while the car was still moving, but I can't be sure where the car was, so I can't trace the shot back—not until we finish the area scan anyway. My best guess says you've got the uniforms looking in the right area."

"Thanks." he turned away to check on the uniformed officers' progress.

Half an hour later, Ping climbed the hill and approached his car. He'd left the forensics team to finish their tedious work—now he had his own tedious work to do. His tablet was full of data to slog through. He had the raw reports from Malloy and Rodriguez, as well as the area scans. Then there was his raw report, and the data held in the tablets of the victims.

None of the bodies outside the car had a Uni or other easily recognizable equipment, though it would take the lab some time to assemble the list of their possessions from the remaining bits of metal, ceramic and plastic mixed in with all the meat.

Without a working Uni or DNA tests, the bodies would not be identifiable. He had the forensics team's incident key, which he used to program his tablet to notify him when the test results became available.

He swiped his finger over the lock plate on the driver's side door and heard the click as the lock disengaged. He pulled the door open and dropped into the seat. He closed the door and was dropped like a smooth stone into a pool of absolute silence. Outside, the nighttime city hadn't been noisy, even with the nearby hiss of highway's traffic, but the difference between that quiet and the car's insulated silence was still striking. He paused to let it soak into him. As the seconds passed, new sounds emerged from the quiet: first his regular and slowing breathing, then the calm beating of his heart. Of all the things that Ping had learned from his father, by far the most frequently used was effective meditation.

He leaned forward, reached behind him and unholstered his tablet. He extended it to full size and propped it against the steering wheel. Where to start? Sometimes there were too many questions to approach systematically. He had poked at mysteries long enough to know that it mattered where he started poking. Each line of inquiry had its own set of built-in assumptions that could color the investigation. At times like this, he liked to start purely from inspiration—let fate, chance, intuition, or God guide his first steps. If evidence (or further inspiration) led him in another direction later, it would be easier to let go of his initial assumptions since he hadn't invested heavily in them.

Eyes closed, he let his mind wander back through his experiences at the underpass, hoping something would jump out at him. He saw the Otu weeds, Malloy's strained face, the leech-flesh arm, blood and glass. He remembered scanning into the bridge wall to get holos of the shells buried inside, the plastic bags filled with the victims' possessions, almost going down when he slipped on a small patch of eviscerata near the car—not a proud moment.

Concentration broken by the memory of his brush with blood and gravity, he resolved to start with the victims' personal effects. He grabbed his tablet's stylus and brought the machine out of standby. With a few taps, he forged the data-link to the professor's tablet that still lay in the unopened evidence bag on the passenger seat. The data in its solid-state drive was encrypted of course. He'd have to request a warrant key from a judge to gain access. He quickly opened the roster of on-duty judges and winced as he saw 'Hatch, Jenna' highlighted. Jenna 'the hatchet' Hatch had an unhealthy love of her own voice, and a general intolerance for the voice of others. A call to her yielded a warrant sometimes, but without fail, it yielded a little soapbox speech on something she termed 'freedom to privacy'—like no one else understood the delicate balance between the public and private good. Sheesh.

He steeled himself for the patronizing he was about to take and touched the messaging link with his stylus. Nearly a minute passed and he became impatient. He opened the tablet's calculator and started to enter numbers with the stylus: 5 + 5, 10 + 10... after another 15 seconds, a window opened on his screen bearing the Hatchet's sleep-puffy countenance. She didn't say a word, preferring to stare at him, radiating sleepy annoyance.

He could play this game. He continued to poke away at the calculator with a gravely determined look on his face. He was working on multiplying the powers of ten now.

Fifteen more seconds passed... twenty. Ping had plenty of numbers left.

"What is it, detective?" she finally gave up.

Victory! "Oh! Hi!" Ping said with real enthusiasm. Counter-annoyance was a blast. "I didn't hear you pick up! I was just preparing a report on a particularly grim case."

She grunted.

He continued, "I've got ten to thirteen corpses and only two working tablets between the lot of them..."

"Ten to thirteen?" the judge interrupted.

"How many potatoes in a bowl of stew?" Ping asked with a conspiratorial look.

"What does that mean, detective?" Her voice was a drone encumbered with scorn.

"Lots of pieces. Not sure how many they add up to yet—forensics will be able to give a more accurate number after DNA-typing the remains. I need warrant keys for the two tablets so I can continue..."

"And you think these tablets' owners are dead? I wouldn't want to inadvertently violate his or her freedom to..."

"Definitely." he attempted to knock her from the soapbox before she got settled in.

"Are you really so sure?" she looked more annoyed. She was quicker in her next attempt. "Without evidence of death or compelling public interest, I can't authorize such an invasion of their fundamental freedom to privacy..."

there it was. "I mean, you don't even have a clear account of who's dead yet."

"Sure we do… all of them." He attached a photo of the corpse in the back seat to the outbound data stream and saw her flinch. He used his stylus to indicate the area of the corpse where the tablet was found. "It was here." He said, tapping on the image and transmitting the marker.

The judge's eyes moved to her tablet with its replica of the image and annotations, then retreated back toward the camera.

"What if it's not his tablet?" she said, voice weary.

He pretended to think about that carefully while he reinforced his outer appearance of calm helpfulness. Pretending to carefully check, as if he hadn't already, he tried multiplying a few numbers on the calculator application. "Hmm… The tablet's registry says the owner is a Dr. Ivo Lutine. The Uni found on the body was Dr. Lutine's…" dramatic pause while he multiplied some more numbers, then he put on a face of excited discovery. "Yep, the Uni's vascular scan matches the hand on the seat over there—", he touched the image again, indicating a spot on the seat maybe 40 centimeters from the rest of the body. "…it was Dr. Lutine's! And since the hand looks like it fits on the arm over here…" He cut an image of the arm and used his stylus to try to fit it together with the picture of the hand, sharing the process through the link.

"And *now* you need a warrant key." She interrupted, as satisfied as the petulant ever get.

Ping nodded. "I think time is of the essence here."

"And why is that?" she said in the attitude of infinite patience.

"We've got a cross between a mob hit, a military operation, and ritual killing," he said in the attitude of infinite helpfulness. "Two risks: these guys are crazy enough to strike again quickly, or they are professional enough to vanish into the ether. Either way, we need to move quickly."

"And the warrant key is crucial to this 'quick' movement?" She said with a thoughtful finger on her chin.

One, two, three, four, slow inhale, five, six, seven, keep smiling, eight, nine, ten. Exhale and… "Yes, absolutely crucial."

She paused again. He thought it was more an assertion of conversational control than time for her to weigh facts. Finally, she spoke. "Okay, I'll authorize one key for Mr. Lushion's tablet…"

"Two keys, Judge." he cut in ever so reasonably—he would definitely need to hit the gym for a good long while before he would be able to sleep tonight. "We've got two bodies in the same car." He attached an image of the driver's remains to the data stream. Again, her eyes flinched away from her tablet. He continued, "This was Mr. Peter Sieberg. There is the same tablet-Universal ID-vascular scan-corpse chain of identification evidence. I think it's safe to say that the tablet's owner is dead.

"I'll be the judge of that." She snapped.

Wow. It was like trying to tread water in a pool of stupid. Stupid, of course, has the consistency of hot tar. This wasn't a Labrea tar-pit kind of naturally occurring stupid either, this was a swimming pool of smoking hot stupid purposefully created to service the swimming needs of the judge's ego. Maybe he could try another tactic.

"Oh, hold on! I forgot to mention these guys—" he said in mock inspiration as he sent high-resolution images of the piles and pieces of the other bodies over the connection. "At least we don't need any warrant keys for these folks—if they had tablets, we weren't able to tell which pieces might have come from them." He continued in the attitude of someone excited by the challenges of his work: "I mean, even if we could find all the pieces and get them together, the blood and other…fluids… would be enough to mess up the electronics. Here, look at this one," he marked a nearly indistinguishable piece of smooth metal protruding from an unidentifiable piece of ravaged flesh, "what do you think that stain on the metal is? My guess is gastro-intestinal, but the forensics guy, well he was pretty sure…"

"Two warrant keys for Mr. Lootan and Mr. Sieger." She said with a drawn face and eyes that never approached her tablet's screen.

Ping sent the globally unique IDs of the two tablets over the connection, and seconds later, received the two warrant keys tuned for them. "Thanks again judge Hatch!" Ping said to the broken connection.

Union

Deep, hazy waters seemed to surround Anne and the child in her arms. At some level she knew this wasn't exactly real—probably because the cute little guy she clung to so desperately had told her no less than ten times that she was dreaming—but somehow that didn't make the situation any less tragic in her mind. The little boy was perhaps eight years old, his legs were somehow malformed and she remembered seeing him with crutches earlier. He looked up at her though cracked coke-bottle glasses with intensity and intelligence that was beyond his years and should have been beyond his ability. Despite her best efforts, he was slipping away from her.

"Let go!" he shouted again, still clinging to her waist, "You've got to wake up and get away!" His voice was urgent, but his grip on her was desperate. They hung in a dark void, clinging to each other as the depths tugged at him and the shimmering light above beckoned to her.

"You aren't listening to me!" he shouted, exasperated. But she could see the darkness below and she wasn't letting go. Somehow, if she could hold on long enough, they might both reach the surface together. If she could just hold on, she could save him—she could make a difference. The unfamiliar warmth of purpose tugged at her heart and tightened her grip.

"Neither are you!" she yelled back, already reflecting on her confusing retort.

"Right!" he laughed, "Well, I guess it's time." Then, with a smile twisted by the war between courage and fear, he let go.

"No!" she shrieked as his small body slipped from her embrace.

His fall was slower than she'd expected, as if through thick water. A few meters away, he shouted again, "Run, Anne! Run!" Despite his frail body, his voice held a deep power. It was the pressure of deep water, pressing inward, forcing her upward like a bubble.

"Don't go!" she shouted, feeling the emptiness around them both.

Lower, slower—almost out of sight, the boy noticed something below and turned to look. When he turned back to her, his face was alive with excitement. His crutches were nowhere to be seen now and he'd lost the thick glasses. He looked somehow bigger, stronger, older—more familiar. He cupped his hands and shouted to her, but she could only hear the sound of rushing water. He gestured with enthusiasm toward something in the darkness beneath him.

Then a strange inversion happened. Her perspective shifted and he was ascending as she fell upside down toward an uncertain end. The darkness he approached was now the bright morning sky; the murk that engulfed him became a bright enfolding haze. The light of the surface that Anne approached was now harsh, like a distant shiver of lightning and fire. As the boy moved further into the light, she thought she glimpsed two men in white clothes reaching out to embrace him. Then all she saw was the blackness around her as she broke through the surface and into the rain.

"Don't... go." She croaked, aloud this time, mouth full of rainwater. She lifted her head and opened her eyes onto a scene that cemented her grim memories. Reflections of her bloodshot eyes and puffy face filled her vision. Her image rippled as raindrops disturbed the dirty puddle.

Her head was the first part of her body to register with her complaints department. Behind that splitting pain was a long line of other aches and agonies jostling for their turn. They washed over and through her... wet blackness.

Her eyes opened again and were reflected back pink tinged and dark in the rain-rippled water. What was she lying on? Memory paralyzed her. Fear took her away.

"Run!" Like a carelessly encountered landmine, the force of the word blew her up and out of the blackness. Her eyes snapped open, cramping and unresponsive arms pushed her up. Terror filled her mind, stars filled her head—and he again filled her vision. Not strong him— broken him. Not deadly him—innocent him, dead him. As she levered herself onto her hands, his arm fell slack from behind her neck and landed with a wet slap on the sidewalk.

She knew he was dead. His face held none of the conviction, strength or intelligence that were so evident before.

"Run!" Her vision shimmered with the resonance of the word, her bones vibrated with it. Terror was cold black milk filling her heart, chilling her toward inaction, but she knew that inaction would be death for her, though she couldn't remember why.

She attempted to surge to her feet, but ended up going over backwards... surging to her butt instead, hands slapping heavily on the wet pavement. Desperate, she scrabbled away backwards on hands and feet.

He didn't move: legs still twisted, mouth again slack, lifeless eyes half-lidded. The rain was lighter now, but it had removed much of the blood from his skin, leaving a red-black dissolute bloom on the pavement around the corpse.

The glass that littered the ground cut into her palms, but fear wouldn't let her stop her desperate flight. At last her shaky right arm gave way and she fell on her back. Her neck flared with pain and her head connected with the pavement. Her vision narrowed as if she was looking through a short, dark tunnel. Half conscious, she blinked up into the sprinkle of falling rain.

The pain was exquisite, but one thought forced it aside: *She couldn't see him.* She knew he was dead, but she had known that once before. She imagined his eyes opening again, a wicked smile stretching over curved teeth, limbs like bags of shattered bones reaching for her. She saw innocent eyes, soft and apologetic.

"Run!" The voice seemed to come from deep beneath her, rumbling into her bones through the ground. The voice was a chorus of two speakers: young and old, sweet and hard, tender and terrible, imploring and imperative.

Before she could regain the air knocked out of her by her short fall, she was over on her stomach and pushing up. And there it was, right before her, sticking out of the cracked sidewalk like a severe steel flower. Though it was immediately clear what it was, she spent a few seconds staring as her mind refused to accept this, the evening's newest impossibility. It was a sword, buried nearly to the hilt in the sidewalk. The hilt was a marvel of ergonomic curves that seemed to beg for her hand, the crossbar was angled slightly forward; it's ends seeming to reach for the ground. The small section of exposed blade shimmered, even in the darkness of the stormy street. Even in the chaos of her fear, this implement of death spoke an odd peace to her. Staring into its elegance, she felt her heart pulled to a place of peace and discipline, from the present darkness back into a time of light, reason and learning. It occurred to her that if she could pull it from the concrete, she might be the next king of England.

Of course, the last thing she wanted to do right now was to have another strange experience. Fear reasserted itself and she pressed up from the ground. She tried to run before her legs were fully beneath her and fell painfully again; her hands, elbows, belly, then face plowing to the pavement like a foundering dirigible. Oh the humanity, she thought hazily as she mostly choked the scream of pain, which came out as a thin, pathetic sound. The rain fell on her back and splashed off the street around her as she raised herself to hands and knees and began a frantic crawl.

After another two meters of desperate hand and knee damage, she pulled her knees up under her and made a successful lurch to her feet. She stumbled forward, swinging her arms stiffly to counterbalance her shifting weight. She risked a glance behind her and saw him lying there still, dead as ever—well, more dead than before—really dead? He looked small, helpless and horribly broken, but he'd looked like that before.

She realized that she was still making the plaintive "ohho-hhh" sound that she'd started the second time she fell. She didn't try to stop it. Instead she ran, embracing its shallow comfort, letting it elongate into sobs which too soon turned into wracking gasps of physical and emotional overexertion. She had to stop. She rumbled to a halt at the near side of an intersection. Panting, she leaned against the rough stone of a building, trying to regain her breath. When she closed her eyes, his face filled her vision and waves of vertigo crashed around. Her eyes jerked open—she'd almost gone out again. Around her, phantoms of her fear filled the night air, skulking in the shadows, lingering at the edges of the light's influence.

She glanced back to the fallen man to gauge her progress: she'd gone a block.

One stinking block? She felt like she was going to have some kind of exercise-related rupture and she had only run one block; so much for her track and field aspirations. The occasional bark of hysterical laughter mixed with her panting and sobbing.

Behind her, not far from the crumpled car and the crumpled man, a door opened. Light flooded out into the street and a dark shadow fell across the sidewalk. She cut her lip on a piece of glass embedded in her palm as she pressed it over her mouth to squelch her desperate sounds. She stumbled around the corner and peered cautiously back as a well-dressed man staggered out the door.

He looked normal enough, no horns or tail or flaming eyes. His clothes made Anne think of an investment banker or some other near-north-side success story. He was maybe fifty and bald with a close-cropped fringe of metallic gray hair. He carried an umbrella in his right hand, which he deployed as he stepped from the shelter of the building. His left hand was held against his body as if he'd hurt the arm in a recent fall.

He scanned the street, looking for something—maybe he had heard the commotion outside and came to investigate. Maybe he was looking for witnesses—maybe he was looking for her. Time to go. She withdrew behind the corner and made her best speed away. She didn't see the man approach the crumpled car. She didn't see the umbrella fall to the street as the man fell to his knees beside the corpse, heedless of the rain and broken glass.

As she approached the next intersection, she looked back, terrified of pursuit. She wasn't sure, but she thought she saw a flicker of light, like a softer and more localized cousin of lightening. It came from around the corner where she had been standing. It was subtle, and on any other day she might have been able to convince herself that it was her imagination.

On any other day she wouldn't have turned and ran flat out.

Half a block later, distant but plain, she heard a piercing cry. A man screamed, long and desolate. She wondered if she had screamed when the dead man ripped into her neck. She definitely wanted to now.

Ten minutes later she approached Union Station. She became acutely aware that she was a conspicuous mess. She always felt conspicuous—ugly, fat, the clueless hairstyle—but this was different. Not only was she gone-swimming-wet, but she had several small cuts on her face and larger ones on her hands. Her pants were ripped and bloody at the knees, but that was nothing compared to the dark blood stains that went from her neck across most of her light blue sweater.

During her flight, she had considered calling the police several times. If anyone needed help, she did, but there was an unreasoning fear to deal with. Some things you just don't want to get involved with, even if you already are. To call the police would be to admit that it had happened—it would be like asking to be in on the rest of the story. She wanted out. Like always, she wanted to disappear almost as desperately as she wanted to be found.

She pushed through the revolving doors and into the station. Thankfully, there weren't many people in sight due to the pre-dawn hour. Before long, the station would be bustling with morning commuters. But for now there would be only a few security guards and the homeless trying to escape the rain.

She pushed her way through the door. Head down, she headed directly to the washroom. She still had ten minutes before her train and she was hoping to at least partially compose herself before the ride home.

"Good morning!" a hard voice said from near her left shoulder.

She had a hard time admitting this later, but she freaked all the way out—strangled yelp, arms jerking up, stumbling a few steps away, head turned away and arms flailing to keep him off of her—all the way out.

"Cool out lady! Whoa!" The unseen voice still sounded hard, but was tempered with something between pity and professionalism. His feet appeared in her peripheral vision as he stepped closer. "It's okay, but you can't stay here if you don't have a ticket."

Aw crap. She looked up from beneath her upraised arms and saw his legs, his jacket, his badge, and then finally the clean lines of his concerned face.

She swallowed hard. "Sorry... whoo... way too much coffee." She said shakily "You kinda freaked me out."

"That was kinda?" He said, somewhat relieved that he probably wouldn't have to call for backup.

"Sorry, it's been one of those nights. Fell down twice while I was running to get out of the rain." She gave him an embarrassed smile. Both deceptive and true, she was impressed with herself.

"Sure." He stared at her clothes with clear doubt.

"Really." She said, fishing for her Uni. She finally fumbled it out, and sent him her monthly train pass and ID. He checked his tablet and nodded. "Sorry to bother you then. I thought..." he paused.

"What vagrant could afford this much dessert?" She made an expansive gesture bracketing her thighs. It caught him off guard and he smiled.

"Do you need help?" He was looking at her neck, uh oh. "I've got a first aid kit in the…"

"I'm fine… just going to check out the cuts in the bathroom, then head home for a long bath and some serious sleep."

He nodded thoughtfully before pointing a stern finger at her. "Decaf."

"Yes sir." She hurried toward the bathroom.

* * *

Ping sat in the silence of his car, staring at the professor's decrypt-proof tablet, trying to make sense of this new development.

By law all electronic data had to be decryptable. Even military and governmental computers had to yield their data to an appropriately authorized warrant key. Of course, it took a federal court or an act of congress to issue a warrant key for those systems.

The encryption was nearly perfect too. Partly because the technology was nearly unbreakable, but mostly because the best defense is a good offense: attempting to crack a computer's encryption was an offense that led to jail time even for minors.

Warrant keys were issued carefully and infrequently, and oversight of the issuing judges was strict. Abuses of the warrant system were rare, and dealt with harshly. When a warrant key was issued, it was tuned to a specific computer. When the key was used, the decrypted data would be copied aside and the key would expire.

That was how it was supposed to work. A few mob accountants might have computers with non-compliant encryption, but usually not history professors. Why would a college professor risk serious jail time just to hide his data? Not usually the kind of thing you do to protect ungraded papers or pre-publication research on the Boston Tea Party.

Ping packaged a copy of Dr. Lutine's decrypt-resistant data in a secure message and sent it to the FBI for cracking. He didn't have much hope of getting the data back in less than a month, if ever. Non-standard encryption was subtle, and often reactive. Even the Feds had a less than fifty percent recovery rate.

He slipped the Doctor's tablet back into its evidence bag and reached for the driver's tablet. As he fished in the plastic evidence bag, his hand closed on the flashlight/glasses case first. He pulled it out, mildly curious. It felt comfortable in his hand, like it had been made just for him… so not a glasses case. On closer inspection, he found an activating stud in a recess near his thumb on the grip.

He pressed it, but heard only a small electronic lock rejection tone. A locked flashlight?

Ping turned it over in his hands. Other than the thumb stud and the comfortable grip, there was no further hint of its purpose. Maybe it was some kind of stun gun, but it didn't look like anything he had seen before. There were no electrodes on the end, nor any visible holes for projectiles. The business end of the assumed gun was smooth and featureless. On the other end, there was some kind of etched glyph.

He accessed the forensic scans on the item. He cut the glyph from the scan and kicked off a global search. While the search ran, he turned his attention to the internal scan of the object. There was a small amount of solid state connected to the activating stud, but no other complexity inside the object. The scanner showed the internals of the object to be solid, with no structures or mechanisms. The solid state, though unmapped as yet, wasn't enough for much more than key recognition. The preliminary forensics tag classified the object as inert-green: useless and harmless. There were no interesting mechanics, electronics, or chemicals. The scan registered the composition of the object as the same ceramic alloy used to make most firearms, with traces of tungsten and platinum.

He rummaged around in the driver's evidence bag and came away with two rings.

Each ring was made of what looked like platinum, an odd choice for a lock ring, but not unheard-of. He checked the window that held the search results for the glyph—nothing.

He opened another window and brought up the forensic team's detailed scan of the rings. He checked the composition: platinum. No surprise there. He checked for any surface marks. None bore any manufacturer's identification marks, but each bore a small replica of the glyph that adorned the bottom of the maybe-gun. The mark was scrawled lightly and less than a millimeter in diameter. They would have been too small for him to notice if he were examining the rings physically, but the scanner saw them clearly.

He slipped one of the rings on his finger, and with the end of the couldn't-be-a-stun-gun carefully pointed away, up at the roof of the car, pushed the stud—nothing but the lock-fail tone. That was expected, since the thing was basically a solid metal bar with a button.

He removed the ring and tried the other, carefully aimed the not-stunner at the roof, and pressed the stud. The results were... well, stunning.

A long blade exploded from the formerly featureless end of the device with the ringing sound of a swiftly drawn sword. The impact of the blade with the roof drove the hilt, along with his unprepared hand, down into his groin. His breath sucked in between clenched teeth. Shock ate the pain for now, but he was left with a sickening feeling in his guts that promised plenty of regret later. Pinned to the seat by the hilt of the sword, he struggled to dislodge the sword from either the roof or his... pants.

Releasing only the smallest whimper, which he liked to think of more in terms of a manly groan, his fingers searched desperately for the stud on the hilt. Through the starbursts that filled his vision, hoping that another press wouldn't double the blade's size, he pressed the stud again.

With a small shriek of metal as the blade pulled from the roof, the blade snapped back into the hilt. Relief—then pain that doubled him over. After a few moments of manly writhing—during which he slammed his forehead into the steering wheel at least three times for distraction—he was able to regain his faculties sufficiently to drop the retractable sword onto the passenger seat. He stumbled out of the car and hobbled around in a circle for a while. After a few minutes, he was able to do so without the limp. Finally, he leaned on the car's roof and tried to collect his thoughts.

Macho. If only his father could see him now. He hoped that the other officers wouldn't come up the hill looking for him. He could imagine the enjoyment that Malloy and Rodriguez would derive from his little incident. That part would definitely not go into his report.

He examined the clean, four-centimeter gash in the roof of his car. He ran his finger along the smooth edges and thought about the sharp mystery weapon that had been used to hack Dr. Lutine apart.

He opened the door, reached across to the passenger seat, and retrieved the collapsed sword. He checked the end again. It was still solid with no hint of how or from where the blade emerged. Back outside the car, he pointed both ends of it carefully away from his groin and pressed the stud again.

With the same metallic ringing, the sword shot from the hilt. Extended, the straight double-edged blade was just less than a meter long and perhaps four centimeters wide. Two secondary blades extended out and snapped back sideways to form a crossbar of about three centimeters on each side. He turned the blade and looked at it edge-on. Its thickest point was perhaps two millimeters. The edges glittered with the night's few stars.

"Where have you been all my life?" He said, wondering. Though his guts were still knotted, all was forgiven.

He held the sword comfortably in both hands, then swung it easily through the most interesting parts of the third form for mid-range weapons. Its weight was comfortable, it's mass seemed perfectly balanced. If the blade flexed at all, it wasn't evident. Perfect!

He held up the blade again and examined it, attempting to discover how it folded or disassembled to fit within the hilt. He found nothing. It was a solid, inflexible segment of elegantly forged metal.

He watched closely as he pressed the stud again. In a fraction of a second, the crossbar and blade retracted. It appeared that the blade simply slid back into the handle. Of course, this wasn't possible as the handle was perhaps one-fifth the size of the blade.

He pocketed the sword and gingerly lowered himself back into the seat. He was careful, but it still hurt. When he finished with the wincing, he picked up his tablet, which still displayed the empty internal scan of the sword. Someone had found a way around the rules of evidence established in 2032. Since then, physical evidence was not entered in court. Forensic scans were easier to present, more detailed, and harder to fake than the actual physical objects. Generally, evidence that was not deemed illegal was never confiscated, just scanned and returned. One of his responsibilities in this investigation would have been to give these objects to the victims' next of kin.

Of course, now the sword would have to go to the lock-up for illegal or dangerous evidence… eventually. He hoped he'd have time to drop this thing by his father's place before then. He wanted to know if Dad had heard of anything like this before… and he wanted to see his face when he extended the sword for the first time.

He picked up the driver's evidence bag and fished out the tablet. He used his own tablet to administer the warrant key, then copied out the data. A quick examination of the data showed that the decryption had worked. There was a sparse calendar, a few entries in the address book, two novels, and five videos. The novels were romances; filled with protagonists with long, thin fingers and creamy skin, no doubt. The movies were recent romantic comedies, with the only oldie, *Blade Runner- The Director's Cut* departing from that genre. On a whim, he pulled up the tablet's theater and checked the logs. The other movies had been recently leased and most had been watched, but *Blade Runner* had been watched about once a month since the tablet had been initially configured three years ago. He checked the file histories, which showed that the film had been in the initial transfer of data from Mr. Sieberg's previous tablet.

So it was an old and enduring favorite. The movie obsession felt like a clue. In fact, Ping would have been a lot more suspicious if he hadn't seen *Blade Runner* in the last year himself. Solid film, but only the director's cut was really worth watching more than twenty or thirty times. He had first been exposed to it in an ethics class in graduate school while training for his first career as a family counselor.

The movie takes place in a dark "future" (circa 2019... before Ping was born) where genetically engineered artificial people called Replicants are created to serve as soldiers and slaves. The story revolved around Deckard, a reluctant policeman who hunts rogue Replicants. In the movie, a ruthless band of three-year-old Replicants fought to find their creator in order to force him to give them more life than the four years written into their DNA. During the course of the investigation, Deckard falls in love with another Replicant who has been implanted with false memories and thinks she's human. The end of the director's cut was surprising in its implications.

In the class, the movie had been the basis for conversations on the nature of reality, about what happens when the assumptions on which we base our lives are ripped away. For Ping, the movie had been about alienation... about lost children. He couldn't help but feel for the Replicants. He smiled, remembering how at the time he'd wanted to help the poor doomed Replicants. Of course, it had turned out he wasn't so good at helping anyone.

"Too bad she won't live. But then again, *who does*?" echoed from his memory of the film like an accusation. Ping wondered how many other family counselors' careers had a body count. He realized just how bitter his smile had grown and did his best to pack it away—work to do. He moved on to the computer's address book.

* * *

Anne stumbled through the door and into the empty train station bathroom. She made it to one of the basins before a large wall-to-wall mirror. In the mirror, she examined the worst of her wounds... she was a mess. The cuts on her face weren't bleeding too badly, but her blue sweater was now a brown-clouded mess of rain-diluted blood. Her knees were still bleeding, and would probably bleed more when she pulled the glass out.

She dreaded looking at her neck, afraid of what she would find. She was afraid of how bad it was, but mostly she was afraid of how weird it might be. Her main barrier to investigating the wound on her throat was a surprising lack of faith in reality. She had witnessed some rather amazing things, and she knew that she should be thinking about stress and hysteria, about games her mind could have played, but she knew what she saw—okay, she had no idea what she saw, but she had *seen* it.

So, she stood, chin down, looking at the blood on the neckline of her sweater. Questions filled her mind. Was it going to be two neat holes like in the movies, or was it going to be a more realistic set of incisor-slashes? When was she going to start fading out of the mirror? Did she still have a soul, and if not would she still cry during movies? Do vampires still get to eat donuts?

Wait a minute! She grimaced and examined her canines in the mirror. No melodramatic fangs... maybe only when she was angry. "Grrrr!" She made an angry face in the mirror. "Grrrr! Rrrrrgh! Grrrrr!" She tried more diligently—nothing.

She was about to try an even louder, more embarrassing growl when she heard a flush from one of the stalls. So she wasn't alone after all... great. She fought off the impulse to flee before the flusher came out of the stall to pretend not to stare at her. Her face burned with embarrassment.

Maybe only when she was humiliated? She checked her teeth again—nothing.

Emboldened by her inability to grow fangs and her reflection's general opacity, she slowly lifted her chin, exposing a dark red... hickey? No.

Yes. A hickey? This explained why the transit cop hadn't made her get medical treatment... there was no horrible gore of injury, only the red badge of teenage affection. Sweet crap no!

Oh yes. Her hand came up to inspect it. As her fingers brushed it, a tingle crawled across her feet. That was weird. She touched the mark again and the same static electricity tingle moved across her legs, back, and then her face. It felt like a network of electric filaments extended from her little love mark throughout her body. She spent a few seconds just exploring the feeling—weird!

The skin of the hickey felt hard beneath her fingers. She bent closer to examine it in the mirror, head pulled to the left to offer her a better view. On closer inspection, it seemed more like a burn than a hickey; it was hard beneath the surface like a subcutaneous scab.

Her investigation was interrupted when an elderly woman exited the farthest stall. Sure enough, the lady did a terrible job of pretending not to stare at the fat, wet, bloody, growling chick ten centimeters from the mirror examining her sadomasochistic hickey.

After a few seconds of eyes-closed, this-is-not-happening paralysis, Anne turned on the water and pretended to wash her hands. She managed to keep her moan to a low, tight "Mmmmm" as the soap and hot water entered the gashes on her fingers and palms. She couldn't stop washing though… the point of pretending to wash your hands was to avoid drawing even more attention to yourself. Besides, this had to be good for the cuts, right?

No. The first sob caught her off guard. NO! But there was no holding back the tears. They joined the red-tinged water in the sink. In the mirror, her flushed face was contorted by grief. The sobs broke up and punctuated her moan of pain. It was unbearable and unstoppable.

She felt a light hand on her shoulder. She looked up, and saw the little old lady from the stall attached to the hand. The lady looked at her like she wanted to help, but didn't yet know how.

"It's okay sweetie," she said, "It's all going to work out."

Anne shrugged helplessly. She tried to say she was sorry, but only more unintelligible sorrow came out. Anne surrendered to the humiliation. She leaned on the sink and let her head droop. The weeping was absolute, and for a moment, all consuming.

During all this, grandma didn't move, she just stood there, hand on Anne's shoulder, squeezing occasionally. The way tonight was going, it occurred to Anne that she should probably keep an eye on the old woman's purse.

After the storm had passed, granny let go of Anne's shoulder. "You're soaked." She said, noticing Anne's smallest problem. "Let's see if we can't do something about that."

Anne actually did the abortive defense-flinch as the lady's purse came up, but the lady opened it and pulled out a small plastic pouch. "This ought to help!" She said in a voice thinned by age and softened by concern. "I've never had to wear it… I only bought it in case the weather report is wrong and I get stuck downtown without my raincoat." She held out a clear plastic bag containing a bright yellow disposable rain poncho.

"I couldn't…" Anne started.

"It's okay!" Grandma interrupted, "I've got a box of twelve at home—ordered them online. You need one twelfth of my poncho hoard much more than I need to hoard it."

Anne paused, uncertain. Grandma continued, "Don't be silly sweetie…. Go on." She said so softly it was almost a whisper. "We're all here for each other, you know." She raised one finger in mock lecture, "or at least we should be."

Anne took the poncho. The old lady gave her arm a pat, and moved toward the door.

"Thank you so much." Anne said, feeling horribly indebted.

"Don't mention it", she disappeared around the corner of the exit.

Anne was tearing the plastic wrapper off the poncho when her Uni chirped. Out of the corner of her eye she saw a thin hand disappear around the doorframe. She heard the sound of the old woman shuffling away quickly, giggling like a schoolgirl. "Get yourself a nice hot meal!"

Again with the homeless thing.

She pulled out her Uni and glanced at the transaction log. "CREDIT: $200.00 - SOURCE: <ID Blocked>".

Reflexively, Anne moved toward the exit. She had to explain that she didn't need to work for food. She had to return the money, but as she turned away from the mirror, her legs didn't do their thing and she almost fell. Could she actually be getting less coordinated? Moving from sink to sink, she slowly got more comfortable walking.

She abandoned her pursuit before she reached the doorway. At the last sink, she put on the yellow poncho. It was a large, one-size-fits-all piece of plastic, which is to say that it was a bit small on her. A little small, but a god-send! In the mirror, she looked like a big yellow ghost, but there was no blood visible except for the few small cuts on her face. She looked less desperate, maybe even less pathetic.

She would never be able to thank that sweet little old lady enough—not least of all because she would never be able to catch her.

She limped out the door, one hand on the wall for support.

Doorways and Keys

Pearly, perfect smile, diamond-hard eyes, fearsome symmetry and midnight style —the mirror showed Jin everything she loved in life—her outside. Of course, inside her soul was a lingering puff of smoke at best, hollowed out by her life's many wild rides, emptied by passion and indulgence, until only her bright, beautiful shell remained. And the hunger.

Where was Mara?

Nature abhors the vacuum, Jin thought, it was just physics… or was it chemistry? Either way, she was sure nature's carpets were atrocious—where was she going with that? She couldn't remember or really care. The point was that she was in need. The point was that here she was again, clutching the counter in another nightclub bathroom, waiting and burning with the need to feel human again, to be linked again to the family of man… to be filled and warmed by the blood of strangers and the magic of the twenty-first century.

The empty, bottomless hunger grabbed her from inside and she almost doubled over, her grip on the counter cracking one of her perfectly manicured nails. With an exercise of will, she unclenched her teeth before she broke a perfect tooth and cost herself another trip to the dentist. In desperation, she looked again to the source of her strength. And there it was: pearly, perfect smile, diamond hard eyes, fearsome symmetry and midnight style.

"Mara!" Jin shouted as the door opened behind her and the club's music and lights spilled in like a brash promise. But when she turned, she saw a stranger staring back, body covered in glitter, face covered in an enviable, unnatural smile. Harmony, Jin thought, half disgust, half desire. Jin could admit that her path was The Whole now, could admit that connectivity drugs were the only thing that could fill the hole inside her, but Harmony… she watched headline news now and again. She was wise enough to realize that tearing her own eyes out was not an acceptable speed bump on the road to bliss.

"Mara to you too." The stranger sneered, knowing Jin's pain. "You need some Harmony in your life, don't you, schaweetie?"

Jin swallowed hard to keep from drooling on herself. Not that desperate yet, she affirmed silently… not yet. Beta Tryptamine was on the menu tonight, if Mara could pull off the buy. Beta wasn't nearly as good as Harmony, but then, nobody she knew of had gone on a killing spree after taking it. "No thanks, I find it hard to clean my own vitreous humor off my fingers after a wild night out. It's even harder to get it all back into my eyes."

"Suit your…" the woman with the crazed smile raised her head in half a nod, all interest in Jin already gone. Head still elevated from the half-nod, she glided toward the nearest empty stall, rummaging in her purse. "Try to be high or gone before I link in, ok?" she said, seemingly to the air, "I'm gonna be feelin' every bit of your itch in just a few seconds, and I don't dig the pity trips." Then the giggling started and didn't stop until the stall door closed and the sound damper engaged.

She was going to dose! Not four meters away, right here, where she could really rub it in, Jin though with a rush of mania. Jin would stand and clench and burn and wait, and in seconds, that madwoman would be linked deep inside the Whole; deeper than Beta would ever go. Not that desperate yet, Jin chanted again and again.

Empty. Wilted flower, petals scattered; a promise broken.

Haiku. It may have been all the acid she'd taken during the 2060's, but every time she was jonesing for a dose, her well-used mind would just strobe out the haiku. It was annoying, but sometimes it made her feel deep… which was even more annoying.

Where was Mara? Back to the mirror for a little support. She didn't grab the counter this time, but struck her strongest pose. Her shoulder length platinum hair was accented with streaks of shiny chrome and vibrant red. Her face was youthful tight and augmented to perfection. Her inky black clothes were inlaid with holowire so she shimmered when she was out moving on the dance floor. She was perfect in every way: sensual without being crass, striking beauty enhanced with flawless evening style. Her bearing was elegance with just a hint of arrogance to heighten the mystique. Only her ice blue eyes hinted at the Hunger. Without the eyes, she could almost pretend...

Why couldn't they just legalize drugs... or at least the good ones like Beta? The worst thing about outlawed drugs was the supply. You need it—it's not around. You can't afford it—oh, then everyone's carrying. Tonight she needed, she had money, so of course, Mara's connection would fall through and Jin would be stuck trying to forget what happiness was like by drinking herself into a coma. Things used to be better before the Harms showed up and started killing their friends. Those freaks were ruining it for everyone else, even the ones they didn't kill. Now the big, bad Gov was cracking down hard. She had half a mind to kick down that stall door and kick the living crap out of that smug junkie. Of course, the other half of her mind was squarely on the side of kicking down the door and snatching her Harmony. Oh, she remembered Harmony from before all the trouble started... Jin could survive on Beta, but it was Harmony that had made her feel alive.

Her fingers shook slightly as she tried to apply the color stick to her lips for what seemed like the hundredth time, touched up her hair for the fiftieth time, repressed the urge to scream for the thousandth time.

The door opened and the music and lights washed in around Mara's sleek form. The door closed behind her and the music ended along with the wash of psychedelic lights. Mara was smiling. Smiling, sweet baby Buddha!

Jin's voice only shook slightly when she found it, "If the news is bad, lie."

"The news is not bad." Mara held up a closed fist and gestured to the stalls at the back of the room.

Feeling like lotto winners, they both bolted for the first open stall and engaged the sound damper. Mara handed over a small silver Ject with a familiar flourish. "Oh thank Shiva, destroyer of my stodgy, well-used blues!" Jin said, hands and head shaking. The dancing would be good tonight.

Rather than taking the Ject, Jin raised her chin slightly "Do me?"

Mara obliged by putting the silvery tube to Jin's neck. They smiled at each other as Mara raised her own neck and used her left hand to hold another Ject to her carotid. "Liftoff in three, two, one…" There was a hiss and a sizzle as Mara popped the Jects simultaneously.

Before Mara lowered her hands, the rush was all around them. The sensation was like a velvet fist closing around her body, pressing her inward, away from her skin. The sensation wasn't so much about the pressure as it was about losing herself in the velvety folds of the giant palm. "Thas sho good." Mara cooed from somewhere quite distant. Dissociative giggling hailed down around her in the small stall; some was hers, some was Mara's. She could tell which giggles were hers because they fluttered like hummingbirds out from her center. They passed through her mouth on the way out, tasting like cherries and butane.

Then the song started. She was singing, Mara too, in perfect synch. Jin didn't know the song, but Mara did, so Jin sang just as loud as they shared each other, linked into The Whole. They were like backup singers to the Beta, dancing and singing in the glory of the link.

"Hey." Mara said again.

"Mmmm?" Jin's eyes fluttered open.

"Lets hit the floor," Mara hooked a thumb over her shoulder, "the first five hours are the clearest burn."

Then there was a moment of crystal clarity. The world slowed and Mara expanded to fill Jin's vision. Though their lips didn't move, they were talking about something. They were sharing the moment, part of The Whole, two neurons in the same communal brain.

Under Jin's unflinching stare, Mara's pupils began to dilate, eating away at the painfully blue iris until her eyes were only black and white, until they were only black. Without moving her lips, Jin asked Mara what was up with her peepers. "Dunno" Mara replied in an equally silent manner. Black-eyed Mara seemed to be speaking from a stream of doors in Jin's mind, each opening and closing around a single word, then moving out of the way for the next door and word.

Mara's black eyes were vibrating now. Nifty. "Shall we?" Mara gestured to the stall door as the moment ended.

"This is stellar Beta, Mar." Jin said as they crossed the bathroom in a perfect syncopation of shifts and steps. The dance had already begun.

"Beta?" Mara said, laughing. "Couldn't find any Beta."

"Right!" Jin said conspiratorially, pushing the bathroom door open into the wider club.

* * *

It was early morning when the unmarked police sedan with the foil patch-tape on the roof pulled to the curb in front of the modest apartment complex just north of Rosemont College. The neighborhood looked like any college ghetto. There were small vehicles of every expense and taste filling the multilevel garages. Plants and posters filled windows. Fliers for parties, bands, and ads for used bicycles crowded the obligatory bulletin boards. Early morning joggers ran the zombie gauntlet as they slipped around the shuffling remains of those returning from a long night out.

Ping was here for Alexander Ahmed, the most promising lead from the murdered, sword-wielding driver's address book. Ping re-examined Ahmed's records from the civil database. He was twenty-two, a bit on the scrawny side, being a full centimeter shorter than Ping. The photo linked to the ID record showed a young man with an aggressive hairstyle painted like glossy chrome. His polished style and slack clothes made him look like the archetypal college sophomore living life in the party lane.

Sometimes looks are deceiving. Ahmed had won the Hawking prize for scientific innovation at eighteen for work with swarming nanomachine control systems. Less than two years later, he won the Rumbaugh semaphore for cooperative AI security heuristics. Shortly after that, he graduated with a Bachelor's of Science in Computer Science from the University of Washington.

So now, two years later, instead of claiming his place among the technical illuminati, he has chosen the road less traveled… way less traveled. He'd chosen the road of a master's degree in History at sleepy Rosemont College and a part-time job grading papers for the now extremely dead Dr. Ivo Lutine. Ping wasn't exactly sure how much History TAs made, but he was pretty sure it was a lot less than the seven-figure salary Ahmed had surely given up to take the job.

With a shrug, Ping got out of the car, patted the tape-covered hole in his roof, and headed for the building's entrance.

Cold sunlight and the smell of freshly mown lawn dominated the morning. It was a stark contrast to the grisly dark beneath the bridge he'd left only hours ago. In places like this, in the optimistic light of the morning, it was almost possible to believe that the extremities of the world's problems were bounded by lost love and pop quizzes.

The front door's security system admitted him after verifying his police ID and he strode into the sparse lobby. The only inhabitant was a bristly-haired student maybe in his early twenties. He was sitting on a couch, engrossed with his tablet.

Ping made his way carefully across the freshly mopped floor. As he passed, the guy on the couch glanced at him over the top of his expanded tablet. Perhaps he was waiting for someone he didn't know well, because he gave Ping a surreptitious, but longer-than-usual appraisal. The kid probably realized his mistake and his eyes returned to his tablet.

Ping exited the slippery lobby and entered a waiting elevator. He pushed the button for the fourteenth floor.

As the elevator doors closed, Ping's eyes settled on a red-brown smudge near the handle of a utility closet across from the elevator. The elevator's doors closed before he got more than a glimpse, but his memory and imagination combined to turn the probably innocent smudge into part of a bloody handprint.

Back on the first floor, across from the closed elevator doors, behind the door with the smudged blood, sat the freshly used mop and bucket. Though the empty bucket and utility sink were clean, the mop head was still tinged with the rust-black residue of blood. The pieces that added up to three bodies were concealed in two cleaning supply cabinets, wrapped in multiple layers of thick industrial trash bags. Beneath the cabinet, lying where it had fallen in the rush to conceal the morning's violence, was half of a military auto-pistol. Half of the barrel, the front corner of the trigger guard, and the bottom of the grip and magazine had been removed by a single, clean slash. The edges of the slash were smooth, as if an industrial laser had cut the metal and ceramic of the gun.

Before Ping's elevator had reached even the third floor, the man in the lobby pulled the phones from his ears and paused the movie he'd been watching. For a moment, his gaze lingered on the frozen image on the screen: Roy Batty, leader of the outlaw Replicants, stood in the pouring rain, a white bird folded in his hand. Blood colored his face, but a look of resigned sadness softened his eyes and an odd smile pulled at his lips.

A similar mix of mirth and melancholy passed through the man's eyes as he closed and stowed his tablet. He stood and turned to look back toward the elevator bank, his face set with grim purpose.

* * *

Jin swam like a fish through the crowded sea of humanity, lost in the lights and sound and the fury of her tainted blood. Around her, the dance floor's lights painted every surface with dazzling patterns. The music shifted and fluttered around her—everything designed to maximize her experience.

The club was impressive, but the real show was the people; it was like having a family, she assumed. Everyone she saw, she understood. It was like she had somehow passed through them, coming away with some sense of their essence. This was magic, the magic of the twenty-first century, the magic of the mind. It was like Mr. Spock said once: "there is nothing real outside our perception of reality." Spock... deep.

She slithered and danced among the other fish in the crackling electric sea, thinking happy thoughts, feeling faux compassion, simulated empathy—loving everyone she saw. The energy around her made her want to dance harder, faster. She was an expanding mushroom cloud of love, a fiery flower blooming bright, even as the outer petals fell away to ash.

Then something changed, like the shiver of a predator slipping silently into the water—the school knew, even if the individual fish could see nothing. Around her, the crowd still smiled and danced, the music still thrummed, but some of the eyes that floated around her were set a little harder, some of the smiles seemed tighter, colder. Some of them felt it too: something hungry was in here with them.

She was being watched—eyes from the darkness bored in, singling her out. The friendly, energetic music that still surrounded her seemed to acquire the character of a suspense video soundtrack. The broken, sinister tones were still hidden a few layers down, but emerging like a slowly drawn knife.

Jin felt suddenly exposed, one side of an open doorway with light coming from behind her and an impenetrable darkness across the threshold. There was no way to close the door, no way to run back into the light. Around her, darkness and laughter. "Couldn't find any Beta." Mara's voice hissed out of Jin's memory.

* * *

After a seemingly endless elevator ride spent under the severe oppression of a harpsichord and tambourine rendition of Jimmy Hendrix's *Are You Experienced*, the door opened into a dim hallway. Ping navigated the twisted and dividing hallways until he found 1413.

He took a deep breath and knocked. Within seconds he heard a click as a hand was set on the knob from inside. Strange, he thought, at six on Sunday morning, he'd expected to drag Ahmed out of bed.

He waited. Perhaps twenty seconds passed with no further action from inside. Behind the door, someone lurked, possibly with his hand still on the knob, probably staring at Ping through the peephole.

Waiting and watched, head filled with a repeating loop of harpsichord Hendrix, Ping felt the hall lengthen away from him in both directions. The door before him seemed to gather significance under his stare. Small nicks and scratches traced over its faux wood surface, the documentation of previous and inscrutable violence.

Perhaps the unreality that had governed the world beneath the overpass had reached out, through sun and the freshness of morning, to touch this place. Perhaps the lurker behind the door was a part of that violent unreality. Perhaps the rational explanations that Ping came here seeking were the unreality.

He put on a more earnest smile and knocked again.

After twenty more seconds of silence from inside, Ping pulled out his badge and held it before the peephole. "Police. I'm looking for Alexander Ahmed."

There was a muted chirp from behind the door—probably Ping's credentials being verified through the lurker's tablet—followed by more waiting, apparently followed by a decision.

The door cracked open and one eye appeared beneath a patch of glossy chrome hair. "What is it?" The kid asked with a comically bad approximation of sleepy cool, his mellow expression betrayed by furtive eyes.

"May I come in?" Ping gestured toward the door.

"You have a warrant?"

"Do I need one?" Ping arched an eyebrow dubiously.

"Uh… no." The kid looked confused by the question. "Just trying to understand the parameters of our interface."

"Parameters…?" It was Ping's turn to be confused.

The kid tried for an affable chuckle, but hit nervous laughter dead center. "Come on in."

The door opened into a dim world of efficiency and clutter. The lighting was indirect and low. A combination living room and office was separated from a small kitchen by a counter with a row of cupboards above it. There was precision in the arrangement of the sparse furniture and the few tasteful hangings on the slate colored walls.

Over this order was a seemingly recent layer of short-term debris: drink containers, instant food packages, and more drink containers. Dirty dishes clustered around the sink and littered an expensive looking computer desk. The coffee table was dominated by a decorative bowl of antique metal keys. A discarded jacket was rumpled on the couch.

"All-nighter?" Ping asked, examining the clutter.

"Sure… multi-nighter." the kid said. "It's rare and special when I have policemen or firemen over… can I interest you in some coffee or cornflakes? Sorry, I'm out of donuts."

"Cornflakes please." Ping said, "cream, no sugar."

Smiling, the kid directed him toward the couch. "Make yourself at home, detective…"

"Bannon." Ping moved the coat and sat on the couch facing the door as Alexander headed for the kitchen.

"So detective Bannon, how can I help you?" he said amid the clink of bowls.

"Do you know a Peter Sieberg?"

"Nope. He's not one of my students, is he?"

"I'm not sure. You know Dr. Lutine I assume."

"Ivo? Yeah, he's my boss. Great guy." He was rounding the counter with two bowls. "Not the kind of guy who usually brings the police to my apartment at six in the morning though." He handed Ping a bowl and sat down on the chair across the coffee table.

"What's this about?" made it around his first bite.

"I think I'm here to help you." Ping said, picking up his spoon.

"Ivo sent you?"

"Not exactly. I think you're in trouble." Ahmed stopped chewing. Ping let that hang in the air as he took his first bite. After he swallowed, he said, "You make a mean bowl of cornflakes."

"Thanks," Ahmed said around the same half chewed bite. "Police trouble?"

"I think so, but I also think that might not be the worst of your troubles."

"Meaning...?"

Ping dropped his spoon into his bowl and fished in his jacket pocket. He brought out a chromed tablet and placed it next to the bowl of old metal keys on the coffee table.

"What's that?"

"You're the computer expert, you tell me." Ping took another bite. Then another as the silence lengthened. The kid's knuckles turned white around his bowl and fear seemed to be pulling at his eyes, Ping was pretty sure he was regretting opening the door. Ping was struck by the image of being in another doorway. Ahmed was on the other side and examining him through the peephole. He had his hand on the knob, but couldn't decide if he should let Ping in. Ping left him to decide as he continued to eat, his crunching filling the deepening silence.

Ahmed put down his bowl and picked up the chromed tablet. He extended it and turned it on. He made a few pokes with the stylus. "Locked."

"Really? Can you explain that for me?"

The kid looked confused, "It's not mine. Am I supposed to be able to decrypt it or something?"

"No," Ping set down his empty bowl, "I am."

He let that sink in as he paused. "It didn't yield to a warrant key, and I can't figure how that is. I mean, you'd have to be a Rumbaugh semaphore to figure how to do something like that eh?"

Ahmed looked relieved. "Wow, so now I'm a hacker... okay." He laughed, shaking his head. "So you read my record. I left computers behind man."

Ping's eyes went to the computer desk, then back to Ahmed.

"Touché. Mostly behind then."

"And why was that? Why give up so much money and prestige? You could have had it all."

"All of what? Money? Some kind of fourteen-hour-a-day grind? That's not what life's about. Didn't your mom ever tell you that?" He dropped the tablet on the table and sat back, crossing his arms.

"Actually she did. Though she could never explain why a prodigy would suddenly throw away his gift." Ping smiled at the irony. He actually could understand why a prodigy might not follow their gift as a profession. He realized he had paused for too long, so he concluded with "Mozart composed until the day he died."

"Yeah, now *that* was a happy ending. Maybe he should have written music for fun and spent more time with his kids."

"So now you only program for fun. Is encryption hacking fun? Are you one of those guys who get a rush from toying with prison time?"

"Believe me, I don't need any more rush in my life right now. Again, what's this got to do with me? This isn't my tablet and I didn't hack it for thrills or cash. Why are we talking?"

Ping steepled his fingers and thought about how to continue. "Where were you last night?"

"Right here. I s'pose the change logs for my files could verify that, but you'd prolly think I hacked them too." His glance indicated the computer desk.

"Programming for fun?" Ping asked.

"Definitely not grading papers. Why?"

"Patience. There's some more stuff I need to ask before I can say anything… it's a cop thing." Ping smiled reassuringly. He was pretty sure the kid knew a lot more than he let on. However he was growing more certain that Ahmed didn't know anything about the scene under the bridge. He wanted to get out of inquisition mode before he dropped the bad news.

"Did you get along well with Dr. Lutine?"

"*Did* I..." the kid trailed off. Oops. "You said '*Did* I.'" His eyes seemed to glaze with imagined possibilities.

Ping raised his hands for calm. He was going to have to be more careful, "That's not..."

"Oh...my..." Alexander's eyes focused on the tablet resting on the table. "That's Ivo's tablet, isn't it... when?"

"Two this morning." Ping said. "He and his driver were killed in their car just west of the city."

"His driver?" There was an uncertain pause. "Peter Sieberg? Is that who you said before?"

"So you did know him?" Ping prompted.

"No...yes. I think I knew him, but not by that name." There was a blank stare of shock on his face, as if connections were breaking in his mind, leaving him numb.

Or perhaps the connections were forming. "How many other people did you find dead with them?" It was Ping's turn to be shocked.

"How did you...?"

"More than twenty?" The kid looked him dead in the eye.

"We're not sure, the revised count is now between eleven and fifteen... there's a lot of pieces."

"Good!" Ahmed slammed his fist on the coffee table so hard that a few of the keys fell from the bowl and clinked across the glass tabletop. Ahmed looked around the room, face belying an internal struggle. His eyes were glistening with unspent tears, but just when Ping was sure he was going to break down, he clutched the couch's arm and spoke in a decisive tone.

"I'm a dead man." Alexander's eyes locked on Ping's—a drowning man casting about for help, "Dead. And I'm not too sure that you aren't dead too. If Ivo's dead... if they're *both* dead, we're just as dead."

"I don't know—they're pretty dead." Ping said shaking his head, remembering.

Alexander nodded ominously, and there came a charged moment of silence into which an otherwise innocent sound slithered.

From outside, a key slid into the door's lock.

* * *

Jin had a mother, but she wasn't here now. No one was left to protect her. Though people surrounded her twitching body on the nightclub floor, no one could turn on lights that would dispel these shadows. There was no refuge from the dark, glistening insects that bored through her.

The swarm of jittering insects continued to pour through the door from darkness. More of her light went out and she was in another place—five years old, running into her mother's room well past midnight. She'd fled the terror of sleep, nightmares still clinging to her like her wet clothes. She knew there was an intruder in the house. Unseen, unheard—but she *knew* he was there.

But now mother's bed was empty and no covers were deep enough to hide her from this darkness.

Jin screamed like the little girl she had become again. The darkness was all around her, pressing inward. The intruder was here, stalking down the hallways of her mind, blackening everything it touched.

Her body convulsed. It screamed incoherently, clawing at its own flesh. Around it, the circle of jaded dancers widened. They knew the drill. Three bouncers built like trees arrived. The cops and ambulance had already been called. She'd become a statistic.

* * *

The dual tones of both Ping's guns unlocking sounded nearly simultaneously. They were in his hands, thrust out towards the door. He was off the couch before the door cracked open and moving sideways to keep the opening door between himself and the intruder as long as possible.

Ahmed was still on his couch. His arms had flown out to the sides in surprise at Ping's quick action, but then he'd frozen. His eyes were wide with shock, staring at Ping. Behind him, the door swung wide and light spilled in from the hallway, overwhelming the room's dim lights.

The first thing Ping saw was the visitor's lengthening shadow sliding across the floor, then a small form was silhouetted against the hall's light.

"Whooooaannt say nooooowhooh…" she saw the guns, stopped singing, stopped cold.

Ping registered female, registered her holstered gun— registered her badge. Left hand on the doorknob, right holding keys, face moving from affable to hard—she was absolutely beautiful.

Her skin was the color of cocoa. She wore no discernible makeup. Her patrol hat mostly hid her kinky close-cropped hair. She was a perfect contrast to Ahmed. Where his appeal came from style, hers seemed elemental... elegant. As he took her in for the first time, Ping was almost certain he could hear music, slow and passionate, hovering at the edges of his mind.

"Police—don't move!" Ping commanded, already feeling foolish.

"Yeah police! Who're you?"

"You know her?" Ping said without taking his eyes off of the woman.

Ahmed seemed to realize that Ping was not immediately going to shoot either of them. He looked both relieved and very surprised.

"Man, *nice* draw!" Ahmed said with the rash laughter of a man pardoned seconds before his certain execution. He glanced over his shoulder at the new arrival, "I see you've been listening to that Curve I gave you, babe. Man, you should have seen it! One second we're talking, then Pow!" He thrust his arms out, hands forming mock guns, his face a parody of gravity. "Seriously, it was like watching Roy work— only in slow motion."

Ping was now feeling completely foolish about his little Malloy/Rodriguez tribute to freakout. At least he hadn't made the terror squeak. This was yet another thing he was hoping to keep out of his report.

"Sorry." His guns came down from combat position to ready position. He took a step back toward the couches. "Mr. Ahmed here was just telling me I was a dead man when... slow motion?" Ping said, feeling stung.

"Jeez baby, you're not usually so scary," the woman in the doorway said. "You've been practicing." She said, wagging her finger at Ahmed. She closed the door and pocketed her keys.

"Slow motion?" Ping muttered, holstering his guns, "really?"

"Now why are you telling the nice detective that he's a dead man, honey... hey, why is the nice detective here?"

Ahmed faltered. The bubble of his levity burst—Ping could almost hear it. Silence settled uncomfortably between the three of them.

"What?" She demanded at last, looking at Ping.

He was completely at a loss for how to continue. This investigation kept twisting on him. Most cases involved scratching for any bit of relevant information, then building a thin tapestry of the probability of guilt for the prosecutors to work with. This case was a continuing explosion of surprises and strangeness. At least it was interesting, he thought with a mental shrug. Mostly his job was tedious.

He sat on the coffee table facing Ahmed and waved her to the couch. "Sit, please."

"I'd rather stand." She said, squaring her shoulders.

"Suit yourself, but I have a feeling this is going to take a while." Her presence here was beyond surprising. It would probably cause procedural problems, potentially involving internal affairs. Now that was a mess he didn't even want to think about. He ran his fingers through his hair.

"I don't think this can take a while." Ahmed said, remembering his former urgency. "You've got to understand, I…we can't stay here."

"You want me to take you in? This isn't usually how these things play out—it's usually my idea."

"No. I need you to trust me—at least a little more, before we really talk. Please, we don't have any time now."

"Why not? You have another girl coming?"

"Yeah, maybe I could see this fancy draw of yours." the woman said, pacing behind the couch.

Ahmed closed his eyes, took a breath. "Tell me. How did it happen?"

The woman stopped pacing.

Now it was Ping with his hand on the doorknob; Ahmed and company were outside, waiting for him to open for them. His gut said that he needed their info as badly as they needed his. He took a breath and went with his gut. "Someone knocked out the Big Brother at Houston and Miller at around 1:15 this morning. They were making sure no traffic infraction video caught them in the background as they waited or worked."

The woman approached Ahmed from behind. She put a hand on his shoulder. He put his hand over hers. Ping continued.

"Probably before two, Lutine's car was rounding the corner when a sniper's shot came through the driver's widow. He died instantly."

"The driver? You mean Lutine's *dead*?" She interrupted. The way she said "dead" made it sound like this was the most ridiculous thing she had ever heard. It also struck him as sounding somehow wrong. It seemed almost as if she was shocked that a sniper could kill him.

"No, the driver was a man named Peter Sieberg." Ping said. She looked puzzled.

Ahmed looked up at her, "Honey... I think it was Roy."

Some kind of tremor passed through her as a disproportionately large shock registered. "No." she said. She moved to her left, stumbling absently around the couch until she finally collapsed onto it next to Ahmed.

"So where's Ivo?" She asked both of them. Ahmed covered his eyes with his hand and clamped his mouth shut.

"In the back seat." Ping met her eyes. She understood.

Grief seemed to wash over her, pooling in her eyes. Her face softened with a deep, deadening sadness. But as he watched, her face tightened again with realization. Fear sharpened her eyes, raised gooseflesh on her arms. She looked around the room as if searching for lurking attackers. Her eyes settled on Ping, full of obvious distrust. Her right hand strayed casually toward the holster on her hip.

Ping resisted the impulse to move his hands closer to his own weapons. He didn't want to provoke another confrontation. These people had information he needed. That information was leading them directly into an intense and immediate fear for their lives. He needed to understand.

He continued, "When I say I have absolutely no idea what happened next, I hope you can accept that. What I do know is that the car came to a stop against a concrete wall beneath an overpass near the intersection. There something took the top of the car off—we found most of it, along with what might sum up to one or two bodies, fused to the bottom of the bridge overhead. When we got there, the area around the car was strewn with what might turn out to be between ten and thirteen more corpses. We found Lutine in the back seat. I'm sorry."

"They're dead." She seemed to be trying the words on, not liking how they fit.

"How did he die?" It was Ahmed, eyes still concealed by his hand. The voice was rough with emotion, his muscles stretched taught with internal pressure. "I've got to know."

Ping shook his head, "The less we dwell on that, the happier we'll all be."

The woman was crying now, tears but no sobs, hand still near her holster.

Ahmed removed the hand from his watery eyes and met Ping's gaze. Ping had expected tears and sorrow. He was mistaken. What he found in Ahmed's eyes was fury.

"Shot, slashed, burned… eaten?" He held Ping's eyes.

Eaten? Boy, he hoped that last part was sarcasm— probably not. "Slashed. Shot."

"No. This was hours ago!" The woman said, realization fueling new panic. "Why aren't they here yet? We've got to go now…right now." She said, expediency reigning in the fear that still colored her voice.

"If you feel it's too dangerous here, I can take you into protective custody." Ping said.

Neither liked this idea, but it was the woman who was first to speak. "Detective, believe me, there's nothing you've got that could protect us. There's nothing grunts like us can do against these people."

"Which people?"

"The kind of people who could kill Roy and Ivo." Alex said.

"This isn't a game show." Ping said, "Stop giving me answers that require more questions. I can't help you if you won't trust me."

"You don't get it!" The woman said, "You can't help us. No one can. We've got to get out of here!"

"You are going to have to do better than that. Talk to me!"

Her gun left her holster quicker than the eye could follow. The draw was textbook perfect, no telegraphing, almost silent, directly on target with little wasted motion. Ping made a mental note to compliment her on it if they both survived the next few moments.

There was only one person in the room who had a better draw. Ping's left hand intercepted her gun so softly she didn't at first register that she'd lost control of the weapon. His left hand drew her pistol across her body and off the fighting line between them while his gun left his holster. His right hand extended out over his left arm and his gun stopped, hovering before her right eye. The small 2mm hole in the barrel hung cavern-large in her vision.

"That was a pretty good draw." He said conversationally.

"You too." The woman said with only slight pause to find her voice.

"Shooting a police officer is a serious offense." Ping continued as if discussing the weather.

"Yeah, so I'd advise you not to do it." She came back right away. Her hard eyes were still dusted with tears, but they didn't flinch away from his, despite the intervening and presumably distracting gun before one eye. She was tough, which made her even more distractingly beautiful, if that were possible.

She glanced aside to Ahmed quickly, "So much for your Amp."

"Told you he had a killer draw." Ahmed said, pressing himself farther back into the couch.

Ping favored them with an amused smile, "Why'd you try to shoot me?"

"I wasn't going to shoot you… maybe just tie you up."

"I am greatly comforted."

"You don't get it!" she said, defiant in her desperation, "They should have already been here! No way are they going to take out Ivo and Roy and leave Alex alive."

"Disgruntled history students?" Ping droned out the irony.

"Listen! If we don't get out of here right now, we'll end up like Ivo."

"Then you'd better start talking. Let's start with the dreaded 'they'. Who would 'they' be?"

"No, detective," Alex said with an air of finality, "not here, not now. If three SWAT teams were here with full air support, they wouldn't be able to help us."

"I'm listening."

"No, you're not." The woman said, "We've got to go! Now!"

"This is getting us nowhere." Ahmed said, "I'll have to show him."

"Show me what?" Ping arched an eyebrow and shifted his gaze to Ahmed.

Ahmed gestured to the computer desk.

"If you let go of the gun, he can show me whatever he wants." Ping said.

The woman nodded and released her pistol, which was already under Ping's hand. He slid it into his jacket pocket. He moved his pistol back to the ready position, parallel with the ground near his ribs, not pointing it directly at either of them. He backed up a step "OK, slowly now."

Ahmed stood and went to the computer desk. Ping gestured for the woman to follow where he could keep an eye on her. At the desk, Ahmed placed his palm on the lock plate and the desktop bloomed to life with multiple 3D windows of something that looked like visualizations of abstract math or particle physics.

"History papers?"

"Research Ivo had me working on." He gave a tight smile over his shoulder as he closed the visualizations. "I really don' know what it is yet, but that's a longer story than we have time for." He opened another application and began some simple configuration. Ping jumped as beat-heavy trance music filled the air and colors began to pass over the display in syncopation with the rhythm.

"You are *not* about to play me your favorite song or something…" Ping said, surprised for the hundredth time since midnight.

That got an amused chuckle. "This will only take a few seconds, but I'm going to need to concentrate. Please try to whisper if you need to talk, and absolutely no flash photography is permitted." He cracked his knuckles and hunched toward the display.

The music was jarring at first, but then became hypnotic… Ping rather liked it. It was deeply layered and filled with complimentary beat structures. He holstered his weapon and looked at the woman inquisitively. She raised her hands and shook her head with a "don't ask me" look on her face.

"With all the gunplay, I didn't catch your name." He whispered.

"Ralonde Jackson, but everyone calls me Rae. I'd like to say 'nice to meetcha', but it ain't."

Ping nodded. "I know what you mean."

Ahmed's head bobbed with the music, eyes closed now, colors and shadows washed across him. Rae's eyes moved nervously from door to windows. Windows? They were on the fourteenth floor… what was she looking for out there? Some of the surrounding buildings were high enough to allow snipers to target the windows, but the apartment's privacy glass was on full opaque so they were invisible from outside.

"Just when you think things couldn't possibly get weirder…" Ping whispered, gesturing to Ahmed's micro-boogie. He got one soft "ha!" in response.

Still grooving with the music, Ahmed turned around. "Hey, aren't those your keys?" He pointed to the bowl of antique keys on the coffee table.

"Oh!" Ping said, moving to the coffee table. He picked up the set of keys on the top... sure enough! He didn't remember setting them down... or getting them out of his pocket for that matter. It was going to be a long day. He pocketed the old metal keys and rejoined the others at the computer desk.

"So where's this amazing evidence?"

Rae's face was unreadable. Ahmed looked nervous but determined. "We can't show you yet, detective Bannon. Time is too short and it isn't safe here... or really anywhere."

"So what was with the music then?"

"We'll have to show you later—and you've got that thing to do." He turned to Rae. "Grab some of my clothes... enough for both of us. We won't be able to stop at your place. I've got to download some stuff and get some spare equipment."

"I'll need to get out of the work clothes too." She moved back toward the bedroom.

"Yeah, but bring them, you never know when they'll come in handy."

"Hold on just a minute here..." Ping held out an uncertain hand. Somewhere here he'd lost control of the situation.

"Oh, that's right detective, don't forget Rae's gun."

"Right," Ping said, handing over the weapon. "But that's not what I meant..."

"You need to get moving, detective. Don't forget that thing, you know… it's pretty important. You're barking up the wrong tree here, the guy you're going to want to talk to is…" Ahmed put a conspiratorial hand on Ping's shoulder as Rae disappeared into the back of the apartment. "Sparky." He looked around to make sure they were alone before continuing. "He's going to be in the school library tonight at nine o'clock, fourth floor, in the psychology section. Keep that a secret." He clapped Ping on the shoulder and turned away.

"Don't leave town." Ping said with an authority he didn't feel. "We're not done here."

Ping walked to the door and fumbled for his keys. It was really detrimental to his tough cop exit that he couldn't get the door open right away.

"You only need those from the outside." Ahmed said.

Ping looked at the old metal keys he had been trying to fit into the smooth surface of the doorknob. "Yeah."

"…of your house." Ahmed finished with a solemn nod.

LIVING DEAD

And all our yesterdays have lighted fools the way to dusty death.
Out, out, brief candle!
Life's but a walking shadow;
a poor player, that struts and frets his hour upon the stage,
and then is heard no more:

–William Shakespeare, <u>Macbeth</u>

Before her, ashes.

Anne's eyes were locked on her plate, but all she could see was just how pointless her life would be. Chattering others surrounded her at the portable table. Though she loved them all to varying degrees, she couldn't raise her eyes to look at them. If she did, they might look back, might see her, might realize.

She wanted to cry, to run away, but what she wanted most was to hide. Her fork and lips still moved in the elaborate dance of dinnertime camouflage. How much longer could this last?

"Hey Anne, why so glum?" Her cousin Jamie asked from across the table.

"Mm." She said, nodding. She hated the frilly dress she wore... he'd probably noticed that first and felt compelled to start a pity conversation—Jamie was nice like that.

"This isn't you anymore," Jamie continued, undeterred. "Or it doesn't have to be."

This was not happening. The death of hope was not a moment she wanted to share, even with well-intentioned relatives. Without looking up, she said "Mn-hmn" in her most noncommittal voice. Please, she thought, let this end soon. Each utterance brought her closer to sobs, closer to the uncontrollable tears that even now burned behind her eyes.

"Anne." He said, voice deepening into the voice of a stranger. "Anne, listen to me… life is about the future. It's about what you will do *now*."

Shocked, she looked up, across the table, and into the dead man's sharp blue eyes.

"It's all up to you now… and I'm not even exaggerating when I say 'all' here." He said with a warm smile. She could find no malice in his voice or eyes, though the memory his face brought was of the blackest terror.

For an instant, the world was filled with rain.

Kind eyes and soft voice, he continued. "I see you, Anne. *You*. I know you can do this."

Rain. A hot spike of pain drove from neck to heart—she was running through white mists.

She must have blinked because now something was chasing her through impenetrable darkness. Unseen but not unheard, the wolf's howls grew louder and deeper with each occurrence. She stumbled and went down, her shriek filling the darkness.

"Wait just a minute there Anne…" a clear, playful voice from above. She looked up and saw a light dividing the blackness above as a very white man in a very white robe fluttered down from above. No kidding—he was actually fluttering with two feathery wings and a halo that must have been left over from someone's elementary school play. Sprawled out on the cracked, bloody concrete, she waited… this would definitely be worth seeing.

As he descended, she heard a choir singing some fairly strident church-type music. 'Hallelujah! Good tidings! Hey, check it out sista!'

The angel with the tinsel halo alighted on the car next to her. The car's roof crumpled as if he weighed several tons. Broken glass from the car's shattering windows danced on the ground around her.

"I bring you good tidings…" he declared with the up-raised finger of piety she'd seen on a stained glass window somewhere. He stepped lightly onto the sidewalk in front of her and cracks radiated away from his feet. The unseen choir backed him up with a resounding "Goo-ood tidings sista!" Around them, the nighttime city spread.

Then she realized it was the dead man again. "Good tidings owv geweat zhoy!" He managed to finish around his mouth full of shark's teeth.

The choir concluded with an emphatic, "Gonna eat you like a sandwich sista!" Then there was silence.

"Wi you zhdop vhat?!" He exclaimed, probing his new teeth with his index finger.

But she was back in flight, really hauling too—as opposed to the normal dream flight mode where you felt like you were running in yesterday's oatmeal and moving in geologic time. The sidewalk, then grass, and then pavement blurred beneath her feet. She was in the suburbs now, passing donut shop after ice cream store after donut shop. She was getting a bit tired…

She skidded to a halt in front of a shop with a huge poster of a plate of donuts with a scoop of ice cream where the hole should be. "Heyyyy." She said. She pushed the door open and paused only briefly to make sure no one saw her enter such a den of iniquity.

Inside, she looked back out through the window. Something had been chasing her, though she wasn't sure what anymore. She'd think more about it over a snack.

"What can I get for you?" a friendly voice from behind her. She turned to the counter, "Well my man, let's start with a little bit of…"

The dead man stood behind the counter with a plate of ice cream topped donuts like the picture in the window. He wore a bright white and red striped uniform with a small white cap. His smile seemed genuine, but nervous like a kid on his first date.

"We really need to talk Anne. Why not do it over some err… donut ice cream?" He glanced down at his tray, then back to her with a mischievous grin. "You know Anne, your mind is a deeply weird place, and coming from me that's really saying something."

Tempting. Except that she thought it more likely that he'd be the one eating. Sure enough, she looked again and noticed that the fangs were back, and the mouth was split impossibly wide. Something dark and wet crawled up from his throat and peeked at her from behind his teeth.

"I've got something to share with you." He said in a voice like a warped record.

Her scream faded as her eyes opened to reveal a strange landscape of cloth. Shaky hands pushed out and she rose painfully away from the bed. The familiar room was dim yellow, the pain was hot orange. She tried to turn her head to look about, but her neck felt like it was in a vibrating iron cast. The world shook—no, it was her— every muscle was knotted with uncontrollable cramps, her bones felt like bows bent at the ready.

She'd escaped death on the street only to die in her own bed, she thought as her tenuous control of her arms faltered, and she landed back onto her bed. She shivered and convulsed there for an unbearable, immeasurable time. She felt like her muscles would split under the strain, but she couldn't make them relax.

Was this it? You know, the big "*it*". Anne didn't believe in heaven or hell, but for the first time it occurred to her that it didn't matter at all what she believed, it only mattered what really was.

She considered the complete dearth of useful information that she had used to arrive at her beliefs on the subject. If the afterlife was an eternal hellscape filled with torture and tax preparation, it didn't matter if she believed in reincarnation or paradise. She was transfixed by dark resonant epiphany: what she believed was not a get-out-of-jail-free card for wherever she ended up when these convulsions finally ate the last life from her body.

Looking back, she guessed that she had been living dead for so long that she had just assumed that being really dead would be more of the same grindingly humiliating thing. Now though, standing on death's rickety porch, the afterlife (if there were such a thing) seemed a lot less subjective and a lot more unknown.

Sure, *now* she thought of this. *What's after this?* The question was an abyss above which she dangled. *What's next?*

It might have been minutes or hours before she slipped into oblivion.

* * *

When she moved, it hurt. If she didn't move, it just threatened to hurt. As she became more aware, this constant threat became unbearable in a Chinese water torture sort of way and she began to shift and fidget. Though this did hurt at first, it slowly became a manageable thing.

For the second time in the last day, Anne was surprised to be alive. Her second brush with death had left her feeling hopelessly alone, powerless, and just a bit hungry.

The bed beneath her was wet. The damp, tangled sheets clung to her as she moved. Her entire body tingled. Her mouth tasted like zombie brain crap. With great effort, she rolled onto her back, and from there she sat up on the bed. The room swam for a few seconds before the wave of disorientation receded.

The room beyond the bed was cluttered, small, and only partially lit by yellow light coming from an over-ornate desk lamp her stepfather had given her for her sixteenth birthday. A veneered shelf held her collection of old hardcopy books. A mismatched dresser held her clothes and was topped with an accretion of trinkets and memorabilia—

crystal figurines, perfume bottles, framed pictures of cousins.

She had mixed feelings about her home. It was comfortable and familiar and entirely hers. Sometimes when she arrived here after a hard day's work, she felt independent and secure, the queen of her small domain.

But hers was a palace of isolation, a home of slow warping separation. Sometimes as the hours ground by, she would run out to the store, any store. Sometimes she bought a toothbrush or socks, other times she simply loitered. She'd walk aimlessly through aisles of products, buying only distraction, feeling like a vagrant begging for spare attention. Her fantasy at times like these was striking up a conversation with someone met by chance. Of course she would never try... the need was too close, too dear to brook any thought of failure. She remembered once in a convenience store several months back, a man had asked her if she had tried some drink or other that he was thinking of buying. She mumbled that she hadn't, but she never saw the drink or the man, because she had looked immediately at her feet, had immediately turned away.

A sense like heat washed over her. Insight. That's what fear does—it makes you turn away from the things you really want, away from the things you need. Then it taunts you later, it tells you that you are too weak or broken to be happy, that you don't deserve it. Fear's only happy when you're not, only content when you're hungry but as still as a deer in headlights.

For as long as she remembered, she'd thought that she worshipped no God, but this was a deception. Fear was her God. She had built Him altars of emptiness and worshipped Him in temples of isolation. She'd wasted her life in his service.

Assuming this was alive, she felt like she'd been given a second chance. If she was alive, she was done with Fear and his little smelly minions.

First things first, she wobbled unsteadily toward the bathroom. She didn't want to start her new fearless life with wet pants. She looked down as she passed the mirror as always. Ok, she was *almost* done with fear and his smelly minions.

A few minutes later, she searched through the medicine cabinet, parsing through her dewy-decimal encoded library of misdiagnosed cures. Past the antidepressants, to the left of the sleep aids, behind the mood eveners…ah! Painkillers.

She exceeded the recommended dose and washed the capsules down with water cupped in her hands from the sink. Straightening with the aid of hands on the edge of the sink, she faced the music and looked into the mirror.

And immediately burst out laughing. She was a yellow plastic mountain! The shiny yellow plastic of the wrinkled poncho covered her like hair on a gorilla. The hood's elastic border puckered around her grave face and dripping chin. A black tuft of hair had staged a prison break and now protruded from under the elastic and was plastered to her forehead. She looked like an imaginary friend on some over-the-top children's program. She looked like Grimace and Big-Bird's love child.

Cautious of her stiff limbs, she struggled out of the poncho. Underneath, she was a wreck. Ripped and stained clothes, the same cuts and bruises, though they were looking better today. She angled her head to take another look at her atomic hickey, but wasn't able to locate it. Weird. She probed the area with her finger and felt only a slight hardness beneath the skin.

In videos, the mark always disappeared when the vampire turned.

Now that was just crazy thinking… if she let it continue, the next thing you know she'd be wearing wet ponchos to bed. She grimaced into the mirror, stretching her lips back over her teeth. She had an almost imperceptible flash of the dead man's curving teeth from her fever-dream, but her teeth were just as they had always been. She was too exhausted to try the growling again; besides, that worked better as a spectator sport anyway.

The windows were completely polarized, so she had no idea what time it was. A small pang of panic hit her as she realized that she probably hadn't set the alarm last night and might have overslept. She consulted her watch and breathed a sigh of relief as it told her that it was only 6 pm. She still had five hours before she had to be at work. She struggled out of her destroyed clothes and into the shower, fighting her uncooperative limbs every step of the way.

Later, in the kitchen she felt much more normal. It was amazing what a twenty-minute shower, fresh clothes, and an overdose of painkillers could do for you.

Still alive. With the oddest sense of optimism, she reached for the refrigerator door, looking for something to feed the ol' fire. She cried out in pain as her hand smashed into the closed door, fingers crumpling painfully against the handle. As always, she had just expected her hand to close on the fridge handle, but her reflexes had dropped the ball.

As she shook the soreness out of her fingers, she noticed that felt odd too. It was as if she had to think more, envisioning nearly every little movement or her body would do the wrong thing. She took a few steps in the cramped kitchen and noticed that she really had to focus to do it, and try that while chewing gum? ...forget about it.

She shuffled back to the fridge and flexed her sore fingers a few times before trying the door again. Carefully, carefully, she felt the cool metal of the handle, relaxed her fingers and they opened around it—now just a gentle squeeze and she could pull the door open. Unfortunately, just as she was getting into that final squeeze, she started to lose her balance and had to divert her attention to remain standing. Seconds passed and she had her leg muscles appropriately tensed and was ready to turn her mind back to opening the refrigerator. That was when she noticed that her hand had fallen back to her side and she'd have to start all over again. It was amazing she hadn't killed herself in the shower.

She leaned in and braced her left hand on the freezer door for support and tried the refrigerator door again with her right hand. Success! She stared at the fridge's brightly lit contents with great interest.

She was starving! She reached for the milk with her right hand, but her left arm forgot its job and collapsed, slipping down the freezer door as she fell forward. As her hand fell free, her head dented the freezer door. The shock of the impact made her forget about her legs for a second and they forgot what they were supposed to be doing too. Her knees buckled and hit the ground so hard she could swear she saw a bright flash hiding in all the pain.

Her hands didn't automatically go out to catch her, so she rolled sideways off her knees, banging her head on the cupboard, then slumping onto her side. Her reflexes were still on holiday, so her head cracked on the floor. Her legs finally realized they were supposed to be standing and kicked out, leaving her stretched out on the floor before the open refrigerator.

Yeah. Feeling much more normal, she thought, the brief optimism fading somewhat. You know, it really was amazing what an overdose of painkillers could do for you. She rubbed her head, looking up at the open refrigerator.

After a few moments of mental preparation, she made her first attempt to stand. She had never looked graceful while getting to her feet. There was usually a lot of grunting, straining and rocking. But today, it was something special.

Ten minutes later, with only a few (perhaps eight) more bruises, she stood beside the open refrigerator, clinging desperately to the counter with both hands. Sweat beaded on her face, she shivered with effort as she put all her mental energy into standing. Holding knees together, keeping her quadriceps flexed, calves tense... she'd never realized that you had to flex your butt to stand... amazing. But if her concentration lapsed, any or all of these muscles would assume it was someone else's job to make standing work. It was like herding cats through a prairie dog colony.

You never miss your body's autopilot until it's gone, she thought, feeling like a stranger in her own body. This was more than just the medication she took—heaven knew she'd taken higher doses in the past. This was serious, this was new, this was… getting worse, she thought, clawing at the air as she fell backwards again. Panic caused every muscle to go rigid. It was as if her mind had shouted, "Help! Do something!" and every muscle had responded with maximum effort. Tense to the point of cramping, her brittle body crashed to the floor like a fallen tree.

Unblinking eyes staring at the ceiling, she lay helpless for a while. Fear crushed in around her like a gaggle of vultures looking for a super-sized meal, and hot tears flowed from her eyes. She didn't have the ability to sob, so the emotion just simmered at the back of her neck, unreleased. The open refrigerator mocked her from above.

She thought it ironic that she would in all likelihood die prostrate before an open refrigerator. She wondered briefly what her obituary would look like. Well, at least Elvis had it worse.

She felt a weight above her, slowly pressing her back, out of the light. Back to somewhere below the floor, where an enfolding darkness waited. And in that darkness, she knew the dead man was still waiting. She knew because she could hear him calling her name.

Down, into the darkness: floating, falling, and then her eyes opened to reveal a familiar white mist above her. The carpet was gone and she now lay on a bed of wild, unmowed grass, the sound of wind around her. It was the sound of loneliness—air moving through the chambers of a hollow mountain.

She stood up and looked around. She was in the grassy ditch in the median of a six-lane highway by the sea. The cars blurred by; wispy impressions of color and form. The sea was troubled. White waves rolled slowly in, adding a dull roar to the howling wind. The perspective was unsettling: slow moving waves behind the unrealistic speed of cars moving at what appeared to be hundreds of kilometers per hour.

The light seemed to come from nowhere and everywhere. Though the misty sky was painfully bright, no sun was available to cast shadows. She seemed to be in the middle of a huge, cloudy fishbowl.

She had been here before. Though she couldn't remember what was next, her heart felt heavy with tragedy, stretched thin with sympathy. Something terrible had happened here, and it was about to happen again.

She squinted into the blurring cars, trying to pick out the van she knew would be here soon. Then time changed and the cars slowed to a crawl, the waves stopped moving. The howling wind dropped to a low hum, barely perceptible at the low end of her hearing. About a hundred meters away, an antique sports car changed lanes before clearing an antique minivan fully. The car clipped the minivan on the front left fender which, together with the evasive swerve the minivan had already begun, drove the minivan toward the median where Anne stood.

Actually, directly toward her, she noticed with a start.

She tried to move, but her legs were made of wood and rooted to the ground. She brought her arms up in slow motion, covering her face as the minivan barreled toward her, throwing divots of grass from locked wheels.

Then the slow motion ended and the minivan rushed her at full speed. She didn't scream as it hit her, but then she really didn't need to as her perspective shifted. When she opened her eyes, it seemed the car had picked her up like a mid-crash hitchhiker. She was now riding in the back seat behind the driver. Out of the frying pan...

The slow motion perspective was back as she looked around the interior of the doomed minivan. A middle-aged man was wrestling with the steering wheel, his graying hair tossing about as he tried to save his family. The minivan swerved, fishtailing and bouncing over the uneven turf, with each swing of the van's tail getting wider. There was a woman in the passenger seat, apparently startled out of sleep by the unfolding accident.

Anne felt a sympathetic pang in the chest as if this were her own mother. She hated to see her so scared, wanted to reach out and touch her, hold her, tell her it was going to be all right. But she knew it wouldn't be. That's why Anne was here... because it wasn't going to be all right.

The woman twisted left, reaching over her partially reclined seat, toward the child behind her. Anne followed the direction of the woman's futile grab and saw first the small metal crutches on the floor behind the passenger seat, then the child just coming out of sleep in the back seat.

Her first thought was of a little startled angel. He was maybe eight years old, but she could tell by the expression on his face that something was different. The small downward sloping eyes held a fuzzy innocence she recognized from some of the 'special' kids she had worked with in the hospital. She really hated drawing blood from the Down's Syndrome kids. Though they were usually brave, in the end they couldn't understand why the lady that talked so nicely eventually brought out the needle. This was worse.

The minivan's front left wheel slammed into something that Anne didn't see. The car jolted with an abortive deceleration, followed by the start of a twisting roll forward and left. With another shuddering slow motion crunch, the car's front bumper buried itself into the earth of the median. She looked up to see that the van was going over. The cold grip on inevitability tightened around her.

Inside the car, the slow motion was unflinching. Debris from the car's floor filled the air. Empty juice boxes and snack wrappers floated by as the driver's airbag deployed. It drove his struggling arms apart as it expanded, filling the car with smoke. The passenger's airbag deployed, catching the twisting woman in the back, snapping her head back and up. Her hand had almost reached her child, but now it flailed away as the airbag and the fury of the crash had their way with her.

Anne dove sideways, reaching for the child. She wanted to hold him, shield him from the maelstrom, from the grisly events that unfolded in the front seat, as the car's roof crushed downward as it smashed into the ground, but something stopped her cold. The child was looking directly at her with bright, blazing blue eyes. He studied her intently through thick glasses, knocked slightly askew by the crash. The ground then sky then ground passed by in the window behind him, glass and dirt floated through the air between them. His eyes didn't blink; he didn't wince with the impacts. Around them, the fury became muffled, like the slow crashing of waves heard from under the water.

"This is how it started for me." The boy said, his voice clear against the muddy cacophony of the crash. "You've seen how it ends." he said with an ironic smile. "Born of the storm, my life death's whirlwind, it was unavoidable I'd exit with its fury in my ears."

"Wha?"

"They are coming for you, Anne." he said, smile disappearing, "They are coming, and it's up to you now. It's up to you to stop them."

His steady voice was a lifeline in the dissolving sea of violence, and as she clung to it, the scene around them further dimmed. The sound of rending metal softened as they sank inward toward a peaceful emptiness.

"But what about your parents?" She said, voice small with shock.

He glanced toward the front seat and the tragedy that still unfolded there. His gaze seemed to waver as it lingered, softening slightly. "I've missed them for so long now, you wouldn't think this would still hurt."

He paused, "I was the one who was supposed to die first. They always thought the mourning tears would be theirs." Then he looked back to her, grim determination in his eyes. "But they're gone now, and if I ever see them again, it'll be in the next minute or two. We don't have much time."

DISTURBING BEHAVIOR

The metal key thudded against the smooth biometric pad of the car door's lock. Ping's even features creased in consternation. He withdrew his hand and examined the keys. He'd tried each one twice, but none seemed to fit into the lock. There was a moment of disorientation as he realized that he didn't know which key should work… it had to be one of them.

As he stood by his locked car examining his keys, he felt someone watching him. He looked around and saw a man staring at him from the entrance to Ahmed's lobby. Ping stared back, casually spinning his key ring around his index finger. It was the bristly-haired guy he'd noticed in the lobby on his way into the building. The guy from the lobby didn't look away, seemingly content to engage in a staring competition. There was something odd about his appearance, though Ping couldn't put his finger on it right away—something odd in the shape of his face, in the placement of his features. The watcher's stare seemed to deepen into a silent form of communication. There was something else in his gaze: Concern? Anger? Menace.

Whew, Creepy. The key thudded against the surface of the lock pad again and Ping realized he'd lost the impromptu staring competition. "Hmm." Ping said absently, looking at the ancient keys, then his shiny, new car. He looked back to the watcher, ready for round two... gone. He looked around... really gone. The only movement was the sway of the old trees in the light wind.

Maybe the guy had dashed back into the lobby... maybe there were other keys in his pocket. He fished in the pockets, but came away with nothing. Maybe something was wrong with the lock... he stooped to investigate. The smooth metal of the lock had a few superficial scratches from the keys, but other than that, he couldn't see anything wrong. He rubbed absently at one of the scratches on the biometric pad with the tip of his index finger and heard the accept tone.

He spent a few seconds in terrible confusion before finally shrugging and opening the door.

* * *

Unseen in the upper branches of a tall tree near the building's entrance, Dek angled for a better view. One hand gripped the tree's trunk so tightly that cracks radiated away from his fingers. The other hand moved a smaller branch out of his way as he craned his head around the trunk. Above him, his right foot hooked around the thinning trunk, holding him inverted while his left foot drew circles in the air. He balanced upside down about six meters off the ground. He loved this, but no smile showed on his smooth features. His business today was death, and he knew the six men and one woman he'd killed since midnight were just the start of a long, dark day.

He waited for the policeman to get his car open, then waited much longer for him to drive away. He could picture the poor guy inside the car, trying fruitlessly to get those ancient keys into his car's biometric ignition. Ivo's apprentice had obviously had some fun with the befuddled Detective, but that wasn't Dek's primary concern now... today his business was Ahmed.

One foot on the path to vengeance, the other drawing circles in the air, Dek waited. The swaying of the tree comforted him, distracted him from the white-hot fury that threatened to burn him away. He closed his eyes and tried to lose himself in the caress of the wind, the rustle of the branches, the sway of the tree—the subtle harmony that God loved to hide in any experience, no matter how dark or pointless He let the world get.

At last, the car with the silver patch tape on the roof drove away. He smiled with anticipation. Now that the Detective was out of the way, Ahmed would be making his move. Ahmed was the target, and Dek was going to follow him and kill until he got some answers. He unhooked his foot and balanced momentarily, still holding the trunk with his right hand; his right arm extended perpendicularly from the line of his body. He relished the sound of the trunk splintering under the strain.

Then he let go and swam down through the branches.

* * *

As Ping closed the car door, the silence was unsettling—
he had something important to do.

His tablet chirped. How was he supposed to think with
all these interruptions? He unholstered it and checked
the caller ID; it was his captain. Without extending the
tablet, he held it before him so that he could see the exposed portion of the screen and its camera could register
his face. He thumbed the connection open.

The round face of Captain Hafiz appeared. He was a
thickly built man of about fifty with dark features and
a habit of playing with his mustache as he spoke. His
grandparents had emigrated from India, which explained
his dark complexion, but he had grown up in some unknowable region of the United States that left him scarred
with an accent not unlike a pirate in a cheap video. He
had a deep, booming voice, and a flair for drama. When
he got excited, it was easy to picture him on a wooden
deck with cutlass and parrot, bellowing orders to a surly
crew.

On the screen, his face was a parody of gravity, as always.
It had taken Ping some time to get used to his gruff management style, but that was before he realized that Hafiz
was often angry but never too serious about it. He liked
to laugh just slightly more than he liked to yell.

"Bannon!" The captain shouted with the usual agitated
melodrama. He then gave Ping the stare of a man who
had laid out a clear question and now awaited a well-rea-
soned response.

After a few seconds of silence, Ping tried to move the
stalled conversation along. "Er... Captain?" Ping asked
with his waiting-for-the-punchline tone.

"Ten minutes!" The captain raised a stern finger between them, giving Ping the full angry-captain-nostril-flare experience.

"Slightly too terse." Ping observed.

"FBI! Do I have to spell it out for ya?" The captain shouted again, but Ping's trained eye picked up the sparkle in his eyes. The captain loved harsh humor... he just wasn't very good at it.

"Oh," Ping said reasonably, "I'm sorry captain, but you've reached the Chicago PD. If you want the FBI, perhaps you should hang up and try again."

"No, Bannon! Our happy friends from the FBI are eager to speak with you."

"You actually know happy, friendly people in the FBI?"

"Well, all right, they might be happier when drag your carcass into my office in ten minutes!" He tapped his finger on his desk for emphasis. "There's two very serious-lookin' schmucks loitering about wastin' the taxpayers' money."

"Very funny Captain," an urbane voice said from off-camera, "but this is rather urgent."

The Captain glanced up at the unseen speaker, giving him the 'you bother me' look Ping knew so well. Then he looked back, raising his eyebrows conspiratorially. "So Bannon, you heard the nice agent... make yourself available for our federal pals."

"On my way, chief." Ping severed the connection and buckled in. He grabbed the wheel in his left hand and started the car—or tried to. His key didn't fit, no matter how many times he flipped it over or wiggled it. After about thirty seconds, he looked inquisitively at the keys in his hand. Which one was supposed to fit? He couldn't remember.

* * *

Anne woke with the strangest feeling of calm. Not the everything's-going-to-be-okay kind of calm—but the kind where you're tougher than the tough times. Of course, this feeling faded somewhat with the onset of reality. Perhaps the first cold water thrown on her tranquility was the slick of drool on the floor near her open mouth.

She sat up. Hey! Smooth sailing! She still had some aches and pains, but she could move. She glanced back at the floor, just to make sure her dead body wasn't still lying there… nope, just the drool. Alive after all! It made her feel like she'd been dating death for years, but he just couldn't commit. She had a moment where that made her feel bad, but then she smiled and decided to attempt standing again.

She got to her feet with only a little unsteadiness. Her body's autopilot had reengaged, but she still felt uncoordinated, like her body was still in the breaking-in phase. She only stumbled once on her way back to the fridge. She closed the refrigerator with a real sense of accomplishment. "Ha!" She opened it again, closed it, opened it… held her hands out in triumph, "How you like me now, punk!" She slammed the door again and pirouetted, but had to steady herself on the counter half way through the maneuver. After only the briefest moment of dizzy uncertainty, she finished big with an accusing point at the fridge and another exuberant "Ha!"

She was still starving, though she definitely didn't trust that milk anymore. She checked her watch to see how long the fridge had been open—10:52pm. NO! She was going to be late for work two days in a row!

Wow, she shifted gears fast. A few hours ago, she thought she was dying for the third time in twenty-four hours, but now, paroled by the Reaper yet again, she could still work up a dander over being tardy to her dead-end job.

She retrieved her tablet and checked the messages. Two were from work, both wondering where she was. Oh no. She checked the date. She hadn't been out for four hours... she had been out for twenty-eight. She hoped she still had a dead-end job to return to. Well, at least she hadn't tried the milk... that could have been a curdled, vomiting disaster.

She hobbled toward the bedroom, slamming her shoulder painfully into the doorframe on her way through.

* * *

Ping stepped through the scanners and into the station.

The duty officer looked up from her work and held up a hand of greeting from behind the glass. Though Ping couldn't see it, he knew the officer was seeing his scan on the HUD projected onto the armored glass between them. Of course, she knew Ping or she would pay a lot more attention to the scans of his guns, badge, and maybe the collapsed sword in his pocket.

Ping smiled and approached the vestibule. "Audrey!"

The sergeant was perhaps fifty, with the soft physique of the desk-set. She had an open face and dark hair with a thin stripe of gray that went from forehead to the end of her ponytail. "Nice keys Bannon, where'd you get them?"

Ping looked at the ring of metal keys he had been spinning absently on his index finger. "I left them on the table."

"When? In kindergarten?"

Ping shook his head, a little confused.

She moved on. "You hear the Feds are looking for you?"

Ping nodded gravely. "I've been hearing rumors of vigorous cavity inspections."

"I've always said you shouldn't store stuff in there, it's just asking for trouble." She said, leveling her stylus at his pants.

Ping gave an amused snort and continued through the door. Upstairs, he headed for the Captain's office. As he approached the glassed-in office in the center of the floor's cubicle farm, he could see the vague forms of three people through the partially polarized glass. Time to meet the Feds.

He knocked; the Captain waved him in. His key clinked off the Captain's smooth doorknob a few times before someone opened the door from inside.

"What are you doing, detective?" the dark-suited man with his hand on the door asked. Reinitiating the keys' orbit around his index finger, Ping ignored the question and entered the captain's office.

As he entered, Ping examined the two Feds. They were both large and moved with the efficiency of athletes. The one who had opened the door looked like a cross between James Bond and an aging surfer. His sandy blonde hair was expensively cut and meticulously arranged. His smile was professional and entirely false, if you spent the time to really look. The Fed leaning against the far wall was a dark-haired, slightly more handsome version of his partner. Both men wore a look of assurance that bordered on arrogance, which was to say that they looked like Feds.

"Lieutenant Bannon!" The blonde agent said, releasing the door and moving to Ping's side by the captain's desk. "Good to finally meet you." He glanced sideways at the Captain and continued, "So this is the man who broke the Three Rings eh?"

"You probably don't want to say that too loud around here... it was a bit of a team effort." Ping said, shaking the Fed's extended hand. "And you are?"

"Garvey, FBI. This is agent Neiland." He said with an absent wave in the direction of his partner. "No need for modesty, detective. We're all professionals here—it's okay to be proud of your accomplishments."

"So, Garvey, were you buttering the Captain this bad before I arrived?"

The Captain snickered, nodding. "He said he liked my painting." The captain hooked a thumb at the oil painting of a pig in a field of daisies that hung behind his desk.

"No. Really?" Ping reexamined the horrible painting the captain's wife had given him.

"I told you he was gonna be a prick." the darker agent said, still leaning against the wall.

"Ah... and you must be Bad Cop." Ping said, holding out his hand.

It went unshaken. "You know Garvey, I already like and trust you, but Bad Cop here scares me. You know..." Ping paused, stroking his chin in a parody of deep thought, "...the weirdest part is that the two of you together make me want to cooperate fully."

"Very funny Lieutenant." Garvey said in a pleasant tone as his partner stepped away from the wall and cut in. "Perhaps you oughta' get a leash on your man Captain..."

The Captain was laughing behind a clenched fist. He made almost no sound, but he was wracked with repressed guffaws and turning just a bit red. Neiland didn't finish.

"They still don't teach irony at Quantico, do they?" Ping relaxed his posture and waited, still spinning his keys around his index finger.

There were a few missed beats as Good Cop and Bad Cop regrouped, this gave the captain time to master himself. "Our federal pals here want to assert jurisdiction over the bloodbath under the bridge. ...and hopefully want to buy my painting." The captain's laughter started again.

"You know your wife would kill you slowly." Ping said, "Hey, that was quick." It had been less than six hours since the car had been found. "How?"

"We've got sources." Bad Cop said, turning to the window and the dim maze of cubicles beyond.

"We've already downloaded your preliminary data." Good Cop said. "We just need a few moments of your time for a quick debrief."

Ping looked at the Captain for support. "Why is this a federal case? Were any of the victims mail carriers?"

It was Good Cop who responded. "It's not that simple, detective. There are aspects of this case that are quite sensitive. Though we're not at liberty to discuss all of them, I really would appreciate your cooperation. Here's what I can say: Dr. Lutine, one of your victims, was involved with something that could pose a serious risk to national security."

"So he wasn't a history professor?"

"Well, actually he was."

"Doing a scathing report on what really happened between George Washington and the cherry tree?"

"I'm afraid it's a bit more sinister than that, Detective. People have been killed."

"I had noticed that." Blank stare—these guys just weren't humor-oriented. "You mean besides under the bridge?"

"Yes. Let me assure you, whatever Lutine got, he deserved it."

"I don't think anyone deserved that." Ping said, troubled. His trip to student housing might prove a lot stickier than he imagined. If what Good Cop was saying was true, then there was at least one extremely beautiful Chicago cop on the wrong side of this. He thought he had been skirting a minefield, but now he found himself uncomfortably close to its center, and his last step had ended in an ominous click.

"What's wrong Detective?" Good cop's eyes portrayed a concerned curiosity, with hardly any glimmer of the amusement that Bad cop was emoting.

Oops, game face slipped. He couldn't hesitate without seeming evasive. Sometimes it's best just to charge in, letting the chips fall where they may.

"I've got to admit I'm a little surprised..." Ping said. "My guess was that Lutine's crowd were wearing the white hats."

"Lutine's Crowd?" Bad Cop said. The Feds glanced at each other.

...and sometimes it was better to just keep your stupid mouth shut. Well, nothing to do now but forge ahead, "I interviewed one of Lutine's History TAs this morning. He seemed like a nice enough guy." The agents' tablets came out. The debriefing had begun.

Good Cop went next. "What was his name? What makes you think he was one of 'Lutine's crowd'?" His stylus was poised above his tablet.

"His name is Alexander Ahmed. I found his contact information in Lutine's driver's tablet. I had just come from his apartment when the Captain here called. He seemed to be fairly close to Lutine, seemed like a reasonably solid citizen, if a bit quirky. Gave me cornflakes." Ping smiled.

"Corn flakes..." Good Cop said, writing. "Did he seem to know that something was up with Lutine?"

"Exactly what was up with Lutine?"

Good Cop looked up. "I'm really not at liberty to say, Detective. I thought we'd covered that already."

"Well, he seemed to know something was 'up.' But I'm trying to make sense out of the impressions I had when talking with him. I'm not sure I could say anything more useful without knowing what type of thing I was looking for." Bad Cop opened his mouth to interject, but Ping continued, holding up his hand for patience. "I'm not trying to be difficult... I'm just saying it might help if I knew the sort of thing that might have been beneath the surface. Quite frankly, the meeting left me more confused than enlightened."

"Did you record the conversation?" Bad Cop asked.

Ping shook his head. "Sorry. We were in his living room so I couldn't legally record him without permission. Plus I thought he'd be more forthcoming if he didn't feel like every word was being recorded to be used against him later."

Good Cop had his stylus resting on his chin. He was clearly thinking about Ping's request. After a pause, he began. "Detective, I need to remind you that even this limited information I'm giving you is confidential and highly sensitive."

"No you don't. I get it."

Garvey nodded, but Bad Cop looked nervous. He seemed to be restraining himself from restraining Good Cop. Serious stuff, apparently. Ping tried not to look too expectant.

"Several years ago, we became aware of a quiet movement in the country, actually around the world. They have vast resources, but keep such a low profile that they went undetected until then. They seem to operate like some more refined form of organized crime. Not as crass or overtly violent, but here and there a body will turn up, or more often, someone will just disappear." He paused, considering how to continue.

"What is their goal?" Ping asked.

"I can't comment on that." Good Cop looked apologetic. Ping wasn't sure the Feds even knew.

"This case is important because it's the most open of the murders. Certainly the most spectacular."

"Were any of the other cases... strange? Like this one?"

"I'm afraid I can't comment more than I already have on that."

Ping was silent for perhaps another thirty seconds, but no further information was forthcoming. "So, I'm looking for any connections or contacts Ahmed might have mentioned?"

They looked interested. Garvey's stylus was again at the ready.

"Sorry, he didn't mention anyone else. One thing that might be interesting to you though is that Ahmed won both the Hawking prize and Rumbaugh Semaphore before he graduated college. He's a prodigy with computers but he gave it up—or so he says—to be a history TA for Lutine."

"I don't suppose he told you why." Bad cop asked, but his smirk said that he already knew.

Ping shook his head. "Yeah, gave me the slacker life-is-not-work line, but it didn't pass my smell test."

"Anything else?"

"Yeah, he was scared when he heard that his professor had been killed. I think he knew about your conspiracy because he was sure he would be next."

Everyone looked shocked, but it was the Captain who spoke. "And where is he now?" he asked like a parent of a toddler might have asked "And whose poo is that?" After a rhetoric pause, Hafiz continued, "Why didn't you bring him in, or at least call for someone to watch his house?"

Ping was puzzled. Yeah! Why not? His finger was beginning to chafe from the furiously spinning key ring.

"Well, I'm not sure... I actually told him that's what I was going to do..." Ping thought some more, "Then he told me we couldn't protect him... I'd just come from the bridge, so I could see his point. I told him he couldn't go, so he said he had something important to show me—something convincing. Then he fires up his computer and surprise! He plays me his favorite song or something, pointed out that I'd dropped my keys... and the next thing I know, I'm getting back in the car."

"Are those the keys you dropped?" Bad Cop asked, pointing to the key ring whistling around Ping's index finger. The beginnings of a smile pulled at his lips.

Ping nodded, feeling somehow naked. He caught the spinning keys and looked at them.

Though Bad Cop was openly smiling now, Good Cop mostly succeeded at hiding his amusement, "You have an antique car, Bannon?"

"Ah... no."

"Antique house?"

"no." Ping said in a small voice.

"What's with the antique keys then?"

Ping had no idea.

Bad Cop was now wallowing in his amusement. "So, you just left our material witness who fears for his life at home? Now that's some solid police work. Did you at least give him your gun for protection?"

Ping shook his head, resisting the urge to check his holsters.

Now this was disturbing. What was wrong with him? He felt like he'd just woken in the middle of a chess match he'd been playing like checkers... checkmate, Mr. Bannon.

"So, anything else you can tell us?" Good Cop said, putting away his tablet.

Dazed, Ping thought. He couldn't mention Ahmed's girlfriend yet—she was a cop and he wanted to do more checking before involving IA. Also, Ping had trouble picturing Ahmed or her as a part of a criminal conspiracy. "No... 'oops' pretty much covers it."

"Well, I guess we're done here." Good Cop said too quickly. Bad Cop was smiling broadly and giving Ping the thumbs-up every time he could catch Ping's eye. These guys knew something. They understood his bizarre behavior. The Captain looked like he was going to make Ping walk the plank, but the two agents were ready to leave. Ready to leave because they understood this, didn't need to question him further... realized he couldn't help them anymore?

The Captain's face was tight with surprised and gathering anger. Ping battened down his hatches and prepared for the onslaught of the storm.

Bad Cop was looking from Ping to the Captain, getting ready to enjoy the show. When Good Cop stood up to leave, Bad Cop held up a finger, "What's the hurry? I'd like to see how this turns out." He flashed Ping the thumbs-up again.

Good Cop shot his partner a glance somewhere between stern and indulgent. "Thank you for your time Detective Bannon." he said with a smug grin coloring his tone. Bad Cop kept the thumbs-up going and added, "If we need more help, we'll give you a call."

Ping hated these guys. The door closed behind them.

"Crap with corn Bannon!" Captain Hafiz shouted, "What were you thinking!"

The smaller objects on the desk jumped and shivered as Hafiz repeatedly used the desktop for emphasis during his tirade.

* * *

The normal thirty-minute commute seemed to take hours. She couldn't get into any of the books or movies on her tablet, so Anne stared out the window. At times the train seemed to be moving backwards.

Downtown, she hurried through the park belt surrounding the Chicago River on her way to the hospital. She loved this part of her walk, her favorite part was the flower gardens, but this time of year there were too many bees for her liking. She had always been frightened of nature's creatures, fearing that they mostly wanted to make her a part of their food chain. 'Eaten by bees', now that was a realistic fear—just another little offering at the Fear-God's altar.

She had called from the train to let the lab know she was both alive, and going to be late. She'd given her boss the most bogus-sounding tale of illness-induced slumber. In the end, she got the usual polite acceptance. Her coworkers were always understanding about being a bit late.

Of course, in her mind, the kindness of her coworkers wasn't due to an easy-going nature or kind motivations. She imagined them pitying her. 'Oh, that poor Anne, we've got to be sensitive to her disability. She's got special needs and special challenges we need to appreciate.' She could picture their condescending faces as they discussed her obesity, '...perhaps she needs to rest more frequently when walking, or maybe the elevator in her building has a weight capacity that keeps her waiting for an empty car.'

Of course, none of this was fair. They probably were just kind, easy-going people. But Anne couldn't shake the picture of them talking about her tripping over the fat rolls on her ankles or some such... "Eeeow!"

A bee, probably on his way home after an early-evening nectar binge, flew into her forehead, its buzz interrupted by a slight tick as it bounced off of her skin. She only let out a small scream, but the flailing of her hands about her head was entirely involuntary. In the middle of her flailing, the buzzing stopped. Maybe she'd hit it?

Ninja hands, she thought, partially recovering her composure. She looked about, embarrassed. The park was mostly empty, but there were a few people close enough to stare at the jumpy fat woman.

She tried an embarrassed chuckle and shrugged her shoulders. She took a few more steps before she felt something move between the index finger and thumb of her left hand. She brought the hand up to investigate, and gave the full belly scream.

The bee was caught, it's wings pinched neatly between her fingers. It was wiggling its little pointy butt, looking for some payback. She flung her left hand away from her, trying to pitch it as far away as possible, while sweeping the air with her right hand, hoping to shoo the little hungry devil away. As she did this, she felt the most disconcerting click between the thumb and forefinger of her right hand.

She brought that hand up—now the bee was caught there, its stinger useless between the tips of her right thumb and forefinger.

More screaming, more flailing. Now her left fist closed with the bee held gently between her third and fourth fingers. Still screaming, she shook her left hand, forcing the fingers wide apart.

She looked at her left hand... nothing. Whew! When she felt something crunchy pinched between her right thumb and index finger again, she was too shocked to scream. Slowly, she brought up her right hand—sure enough, there was her little pal, waiting patiently with its wings pinched between her fingers. It wasn't wiggling, wasn't looking for payback—honestly, it looked like it was praying for death. Poor little guy.

She watched the bee intently as she slowly forced her fingers apart. It fell to the ground with a barely audible pop. It lay there for perhaps five seconds before it righted itself and began to crawl away. Fascinated, and just a little shell-shocked, Anne watched as it crawled about a meter away and then took off, staying low and heading directly away from the bee juggler.

Awww... A large weight of realization pushed aside her curiosity and confusion. She looked slowly about at the people staring at her slack-jawed. Some had risen to their feet in alarm, there was a ball of ice cream on the ground next to a little girl holding an empty cone in her hand. Ok, so that was a lot of screaming and flailing. Nothing to do now but look at her shoes and walk away. She'd had a fairly embarrassing life to this point, but the last two days had been a crescendo of humiliation.

"Don't do drugs kids." She said into the shocked silence. She hurried away; gaze locked on her shoes, hand shielding the side of her burning face.

* * *

Well, that was pleasant, Ping thought as he descended the stairs feeling about a meter tall, which was a few centimeters shorter than usual. What was in those cornflakes? In one of his more amusing moments, Captain Hafiz had postulated that it might have been distilled stupid.

Ping was sure that the Feds were now rocketing out to Rosemont College, calling ahead for backup. He wondered what they would find. Magic cornflakes or no, Ping hoped Alexander and Rae had made it away safely. Of course, he wouldn't mind running into them again—he still had issues.

"How'd the cavity inspection go, Bannon?" Audrey said as he passed the security booth.

"It was a real monkey trap." Ping managed a smirk. "Little guy just wouldn't let go of the nut long enough to get his hand out." There were some people in the world that were just fun to make laugh, Audrey was one of them, and Ping couldn't stop trying.

"You think they'd cover that in orifice inspection training." She shook her head, smiling. "Buck up little camper. You remember the reaming the Cap gave you during Three Rings?"

Ping nodded. "Now that was spectacular."

"But it ended up okay, right?"

He nodded again.

"So will this. Go out there and get back on that horse."

"No more horses for me today."

She gave him a curious look. He continued, "I'm heading to the lab... Cap ordered a mandatory drug test... 'for actions unexplainable by the usual stupidity' the order says."

He left her laughing in her bulletproof booth. Yep, always worth it.

* * *

The lab was dazzling fun.

The automatic doors swooshed open before his extended key could touch them. The keys were equally useful as he attempted to open the bathroom door, plastic sample cup in hand. After a fifteen-minute wait, he was as surprised as anyone that his results came back clean. Both blood and urine were free of drugs.

A few minutes later, Captain Hafiz called for a little more sadism. He'd received an electronic notification of the test results, so he'd called to point out that now there was absolutely no excuse. He told Ping to go home and try to sleep the stupid off. Tomorrow would supposedly entail some exciting deskwork involving parking violations.

Of course Ping knew better. His Captain liked to blow hard, but not long. Tomorrow all would be forgiven— that's just how he worked.

He checked his thumb watch: eleven in the morning. He was exhausted; he was starving. He had time for both food and sleep. The Feds and the Captain had relieved him of his current case, and he had ten hours before he was supposed to be in the Rosemont college library.

Though Ping now had enough presence of mind to realize he wasn't going there to meet 'Sparky', he had a hunch that he would be glad he went.

Of course, that might just be the cornflakes talking.

* * *

Anne hustled through the door and into the nurses' lounge. She had exactly negative thirty-five minutes to get clocked in and she had a hunch she wasn't going to make it on time.

She hurried to the small bank of half-sized lockers on the far wall, located hers near the center of the top rack, swiped her thumb across the lock pad and jerked on the handle. Two sounds registered essentially at the same time: the failure buzz of the biometric lock, and the pop of the locker opening. Then came an oddly lucid moment: Anne stood, holding the opened locker in her right hand, her left hand still holding her jacket, while three small irregular pieces of metal seemed to float lazily toward the ground.

The bits of metal hit the ground with three distinct ticks and a minimal amount of bouncing. The next five seconds passed with no further motion as Anne tried to assess what had just happened. Finally, she turned her attention to her locker. The handle was slightly bent and the door itself bowed out in the middle where the handle was attached. The metal on the inside of the door at the top and bottom where the latches had been was bent and broken—apparently the metal bits on the ground were the missing parts of the latches.

She swung the locker closed with a labored creaking sound. The hinges were bent and the door no longer closed completely. The door swung back open twice as she tried to get it to stay closed. She banged the door with her palm to try to seat it, but the door bent too far, now bowing in at the center. The door stayed closed, but the top and bottom corners protruded perhaps three centimeters.

"Aw crap!" she hissed, looking around the empty lounge.

Blushing furiously, she pried at the bottom corner of the door. Finally, her fingers found purchase and she managed to get the locker door open. Unfortunately, she also managed to break the bottom hinge and further bent the bottom of the door outward.

She dropped her coat on the floor so she could work with both hands and took a deep, not so calming, breath before continuing. She gently opened the door as far as possible so she could examine the damage to the hinges. As she did so, she noticed the contents of her locker: a king-sized Snickers bar, half a six-pack of Mega Slim Quick chocolate flavored shakes, and half of an eight pack of Diet Coke.

Aw, she thought, private stuff—secret stuff. She reached down with her left hand to grab her coat, planning to throw it over the locker's contents, but when she stooped down, she heard another pair of snaps and winced. The detached locker door hung in her right hand, it's final hinge broken.

Several more seconds passed as she reeled between denial and deep anxiety, rocking from foot to foot and tapping the broken locker door against her hip. Then she had a hopeful idea, and pinched her right forearm with her left hand.

"Ow!" she whispered as her pinch resulted in pain rather than waking.

She jumped when her tablet chirped in its holster at her hip, her eyes jerking to the doorway. Her eyes rolled toward the heavens, though she knew there was no help for her there. "What now?" she whispered. After taking a few seconds to get her breathing under control, she propped the locker door against the wall and pulled out her tablet.

"Kelley. Go."

"Anne, I need you in 1003 when it's convenient... I need a complete panel and a tumor screen." Dr. Wyler's friendly voice crackled from her tablet. "No hurry though, I'm headed downstairs for a shift in the ER. I won't get a chance to look at the results until after that's over... hey, you feeling better?"

"Doing great. Thanks." Anne said, staring into her broken locker. "I'll be there in five."

"Great. Thanks, Anne."

Anne clicked off her tablet and holstered it. After a few more seconds of anxious thought, she picked up the locker door and tried unsuccessfully to wedge it in place. She thought she had it once, but it fell off as soon as she turned away, clattering noisily on the tile floor. She tried several more times with increasing speed and frustration, only managing to further deform the door.

She gave up and leaned the bent locker door against the wall. She then tried to arrange her jacket so that it covered the contents of her locker. Finally, she threw the candy bar and the Slim Quick shakes in the trashcan and hurried out of the lounge.

There was silence for several seconds in the empty lounge, but then the door opened again and Anne rushed back in, even more flustered. She tried adjusting the coat to better cover her remaining stash, but eventually she threw the Diet Coke in the trashcan and hustled back out the door.

AMPLIFICATION

Ping left his car in visitor parking and walked the three blocks to the library. Night had fallen and the evening was cool. The air was fresh and the world seemed clean and full of promise. The full moon lent a silver sheen to the cobblestone walkway and the surrounding grass. He walked forward clearing his mind, making room for inspiration. A strange anticipation filled him, a quickening of the heart not unlike the anxiety before a first date. He should have brought flowers, he thought as he hurried down the path.

Logic told him that he was about to spend a few hours waiting in a college library. It told him that he would leave disappointed—it told him he should use his time there with self-help books. Of course, logic told him that he was nuts. Ahmed had probably enjoyed the irony of sending him to the psychology section of the library. But in his heart he knew that something would happen. He'd always been the cockeyed optimist, but like all optimists, he had a high tolerance for disappointment.

He entered the library's bright foyer. It was Sunday night so the place was fairly busy with those cramming for Monday tests or completing projects due in the morning. There were perhaps fifteen students in varying stages of desperation, each moving with frenetic pace in the circle of hell reserved for procrastinators. Ping smiled; some things never changed.

He moved through the jumpy, disheveled crowd. He passed the elevator bank and found a less-used stairwell in the corner of the building. He checked his watch again: eight-thirty. He wanted to make sure that he was the first to arrive, just in case he wasn't on a snipe hunt.

He moved up the stairs two at a time. The second and third floors were fairly crowded as they contained the bulk of the library's research stations and presentation rooms. He arrived at the glass door to the fourth floor. The color-coded guide on the door indicated that this floor contained tutoring resources for the Math, History, Psychology, and English Departments.

Ping paused to switch his tablet into private mode, disconnecting from the building's network. He then set it to continuous scan, hoping to pick up clues or record evidence that wouldn't be instantly available to his Federal friends over the net. He then collapsed the tablet and placed it in his jacket pocket so that his hands could be free in case of surprises. He stepped forward, the door swooshed open and he walked into a large common area.

A few students were scattered across the low maze of cubicles and desks, working alone at research stations built for two. Ping guessed the tutors were off-duty at this time of night on the weekend. In the center of the common area were four empty cubicles labeled with the names of the Departments with a tutoring presence on the floor. Around the edges of the room were about eight presentation rooms; seven of them were empty.

The windows of the occupied presentation room were polarized and the door was shut. As he walked across the room, Ping stopped next to one of the students, a wiry black girl of about thirty with close-cropped hair like Alexander's cop girlfriend. She wore ill-fitting slacker apparel, and there was a stuffed backpack near her feet on the floor. "S'cuse me. Did you see who who's in the presentation room?" Ping asked with his most unconcerned voice.

She looked up from her terminal with an amused expression. "Depends whose askin'."

Ping fished for his badge. "This is official bu…"

"Whoa, quick-draw!" She said playfully.

Ping stopped with his hand on his badge—her voice sounded familiar. He stared into her face, his brows knit with the scrutiny. Behind the acne-scarred complexion, ignoring the slight asymmetries of her face, he could just make out Rae. She must have noticed his eyes widen in surprise because she laughed. He stared slack jawed for a blink—she was almost completely unrecognizable. The beauty that had before been so evident now could only be glimpsed in the sparkle of her eyes, in the subtle arc of her smile. He managed to get his mouth closed finally. "What, no fake glasses and rubber nose?"

She nodded, smiling. "I know. It's pretty disorienting at first."

"What is?"

"Come on, we can't talk here. Your Fed pals have already been here—they tossed Alex's cube about an hour ago."

"Ah! My good pals! You talk to them long? Charming bunch."

Smiling, she collected her belongings into the already stuffed bag and stood. "Didn't talk to them at all. C'mon."

Ping followed her back out the door and into the stairwell. They ascended to the eighth floor, an archive reserved for storing historical books and paintings. Of course everything there had been scanned and was available in the library's online archives, but there were still some books and other items that were kept in hard copy for aesthetic or historical reasons.

Undisturbed darkness pooled behind the door's glass, turning the door into an obsidian mirror. As Rae moved forward, approaching her reflection in the dark glass, the door opened and darkness fled before the flicker of automatic lights. They were the first people on the floor.

The lights illuminated a wide central access aisle with a cluster of information kiosks surrounded by aisles of compressed shelving. The shelves were on tracks that allowed them to move to create aisles between them at the touch of panels on each end.

"It's kinda' funny," Rae said as the moved down the wide central isle, "This is the only place in the library you can find real books."

Like many library archives, this one was outfitted in the style of libraries of ages past. Ping surmised that the intricately patterned carpet, believable but veneered paneling and faux wood shelving was an attempt to achieve an atmosphere of knowledge steeped in the mystique of age.

Rae didn't stop until they reached the wall on the far side of the room. They stood in the box canyon made by the wall in front of them and the compressed shelving on both sides. Ping glanced around, "I'm assuming we're not lost."

Rae gave him a smile that was a window into the beauty she'd radiated this morning. "You'd be wrong about that detective." She raised her eyebrows and touched the access key on the end of the last row of shelves on their right. With a low hum, the six stacked shelves shifted away from the wall, leaving an aisle between the wall and the first movable shelf. "If we're not lost, no one is." The soft clunk as the shelves halted seemed to punctuate her words.

The new aisle before them was perhaps six meters long and less than a meter wide. At the other end, Ping could see another narrow access aisle running parallel to the central aisle. Across the access aisle was another stack of compressed shelves.

They entered the aisle with Rae in the lead. Halfway down, she stopped before a steel door in the wall on their left. She stood aside and gestured for Ping to enter.

Ping's key clinked off the featureless metal knob. He heard a mostly suppressed laugh from over his shoulder and turned to find Rae with a hand clasped over her mouth; laughter sparkled in her eyes.

"Sorry—just couldn't resist." She gave him a playful punch in the shoulder, opened the door, and strode into the darkness beyond, still smiling. After a second spent staring into the blackness, he followed.

The door closed behind him, leaving them in absolute darkness. He heard Rae fumbling for the switch at his left, then a faint chirp from somewhere off to his right. A rumble came through the wall, followed by a muted impact like the closing of a heavy gate. The shelves outside had again moved to cover the door. He was trapped... and fairly uncomfortable as a few seconds passed in darkness. Better safe than sorry...

The light came on, catching Ping in mid-draw. Rae turned from the light switch to face him and her eyes went to the half-drawn weapon. He slid the gun back into its holster with a shrug.

"I think he's getting slower, Rae."

Ping turned around. Ahmed sat against the wall at Ping's right with his expanded tablet on his lap. Ping's thoughts flitted between curiosity, amusement, his keys, and revenge.

The room was small, perhaps four meters on a side. The only light was from a still-flickering fluorescent utility tube in the middle of the ceiling. The dim light was insufficient to dispel the shadows that lingered in the corners of the room. The room was cluttered with cleaning equipment and spare desks and chairs. The walls were adorned only with electrical conduits and a large junction box. After surveying the room, his gaze came to a rest on Ahmed.

Ahmed looked to Ping for some kind of response. After a few seconds of Ping's most inscrutable stare he became nervous and busied his hands by twirling his tablet's stylus absently around his fingers. "You've got questions." He said at last.

Without terminating the stare-down, Ping held up the ring of keys, dangling them in the air between them.

"A necessary distraction." Alex said.

Ping tilted his head fractionally, gaze still locked on Alex.

Ahmed held up his hands. "Look, we couldn't talk before for a lot of reasons. You seemed like a pretty solid guy, you were also massively confused... this meant you would be getting pulled from the case any minute—one way or another, depending on how much you discovered."

Ping raised his eyebrows, surprised.

Ahmed continued. "How did I know you already got pulled? Honestly it's because you're still breathing. Where to start... Look, I was serious about us being in danger. If they thought you were a threat, you wouldn't be here now. The Obscuring was for your own protection as well as ours, the keys were to make you look stupid, to convince them I'd Cast you good... but I admit that part was pretty funny, heh... Sparky was to bring you here."

"You know, even I didn't understand that, babe." Rae said from over Ping's shoulder.

"Bring me here? Why?" Ping said, not lowering the keys.

"We need help. We're in trouble." Ping continued to stare, so Alex continued, "Plus you had a great draw... you even beat Rae, which is pretty impressive."

They both smiled at Ping nervously. He gave the keys a jingle.

"Ah! Gotcha!" Ahmed stopped twirling his stylus and made a few decisive clicks on the surface of the tablet. Thin music filled the air. "Just a few seconds here... I've still got the training wheels on with this stuff..." the music grew in intensity and complexity. In less than half a minute, Ahmed's eyes had lost focus on the tablet on his lap. His head swayed slightly, his shoulders moving in small circles with the beat.

Ping was having a real problem staying angry with these people. As he watched Ahmed bug out with the music he couldn't completely suppress his grin.

Then something shifted.

Ping stumbled slightly and Rae put a hand on his shoulder to steady him. He'd broken through the surface from the murky depths of confusion and up into forgotten clarity. The air in the dank little room tasted sweet. As he looked back over the day since he had left these two this morning, it seemed as if he had been sleepwalking. Now he saw things more clearly—of course he still had no idea what he was seeing more clearly... but it was clearer.

"What...?" He said mostly to himself.

"Welcome to the real world, Neo." Ahmed said, switching off the music.

"Huh?"

"Never mind. Look, that cloud of fog that just lifted was an Obscuring. I Cast you so that those keys from my coffee table would occupy a significant portion of your unconscious mind, disrupting your focus and making you susceptible to manipulation. That part was mostly for show... I coulda' Obscured you without the keys, but then they might not have caught on as quickly. They might have tortured you to death before they realized they didn't have to. Besides, it gave you something to do with your hands eh?"

Maybe he could stay angry with this guy after all. Ping was willing to give it the old college try. "Cast me?" Ping said, focusing on the anger management.

"Oh, here we go..." Ahmed ran his fingers through his hair.

"Cast me? Like in a play?"

"Nope. Like in a spell."

"Uh-huh, sure."

"Well, it's not exactly magic like chicken blood and pentagrams, but..."

"Ah, so now you're a wee Leprechaun eh? When'd I get a peep at yer wee pot o' gold?"

Ahmed looked frustrated. Not to worry though, he probably had a spell or potion to fix that.

"Explain the keys then." Ahmed folded his arms.

"Drugged my cornflakes. Some kind of mind control device attached to your computer." He knew it wasn't true, but he had to say something.

"Explain this." Rae said from behind him.

He turned around and barely held his mouth closed. She was beautiful again. Every line and curve was in its ultimate proportion and position. The most amazing part was that if he tried hard, he could still see the acne scars, could still see every asymmetry as it had appeared when he'd seen her on the fourth floor. But now her imperfections were the capstone in her beauty. This wasn't makeup or a hologram, she didn't look different—he was looking at her differently. There was a confidence in her eyes that was intoxicating.

He was speechless. As he watched, she put her hands behind her neck and unclasped a small black-on-silver cameo necklace. As her hands came down with the necklace, subtle changes appeared in her countenance. Proportions didn't change, but grew somehow less in-gratiating to his eye. Imperfections unknitted themselves from the lattice of her beauty, drawing and distracting his eye. Her visual symphony devolved into a trio of tin whistles.

"Was that cornflakes?" she said with a smile that brought back the memory of her beauty. With a shock, Ping real-ized she was still beautiful; bright eyes and a quick smile illuminated the beauty of a warrior's spirit. After she re-alized that Ping was skipping his turn in the conversa-tional flow, she held out the cameo. "Ok, let's play 'Find the Hoax.'"

Ping took the necklace and examined it closely. The cameo looked familiar... it took him a few seconds to realize that the ebony silhouetted profile on the silvery background was Rae's. He looked up at her. "Turn to the left." She obliged, smiling. Yep.

"He gave you this?" His eyes shifted to Ahmed briefly. She nodded. "And you don't have a problem with that?"

She knew what he was talking about. "Boy did I!" she laughed.

"She said it was like buying her plastic surgery for our anniversary." Ahmed said. "I was lucky she wasn't wearing her gun."

"But eventually I understood."

"Understood what?" Ping asked.

"That it doesn't change how I see her." Ahmed paused for emphasis. "It just makes everyone see the Rae that I do."

Back to speechless. That was probably the sweetest thing he had ever heard. It had to be a line. "And you buy that?"

"You haven't seen him try to lie yet. It's pathetic." There was a mischievous twinkle in her eye, "Go ahead. Ask him if he has a teddy bear."

"Hey now!" Alex blurted out too quickly, blushing.

Ping turned the cameo over in his hands. The chain and back of the cameo were silver. He noticed a small etching on the back. A chill went through him as he bent closer... it looked like the same kind of mark that was on the pommel of Sieberg's retractable sword. He fished in his jacket pocket and came away with the collapsed sword. He flipped it over and examined the mark on the bottom, looking from it to the necklace and back. The marks were similar, but not the same.

"What's that?" Ahmed asked, looking at the sword.

"I was hoping you could tell me." He handed it to Ahmed. Ahmed turned it over in his hands. "This is Ivo's glyph, but I'm not sure what it's for... give me a second to Cast a Scan and maybe I can tell you."

"I think I can help you out with that one." Ping took the lock ring from his pocket and put it on. He held out his hand for the sword.

"Call me Alex, please." Ahmed handed it back.

"Ready?" Ping said. After a second's pause to allow curiosity to build, he thumbed the activating stud. As before, the sword rang from the hilt. In the small room, the metallic ring seemed to continue for a few seconds before finally fading away.

Seconds passed in silence. Finally, Rae spoke. "Honey, I know what I want for our next anniversary."

* * *

"Lab's here!" Anne said as she entered the ER.

She was feeling much better—almost good. The call to maintenance hadn't been as painful as she feared, but then she'd only told them that she thought something might be wrong with her locker door. She had a feeling she wasn't done answering questions about it yet.

Anne followed the screams to where Dr. Wyler waited.

"Just a sec," the doctor said while two orderlies and an EMT attempted to hold a Harm still enough for him to administer a sedative without breaking the needle.

Though she was already cuffed and strapped to the table, the Harm was fighting so hard that it took the orderlies another twenty seconds before they could fully immobilize her arm.

"His eyes open in their bathroom is the key!" the woman shrieked as she fought against her restraints and the four men, her expensive shoes kicking and her red-silver-white streaked hair drenched with sweat. Like most Harms Anne saw, this one was dressed for a hot night out; her expensive-looking black shimmering outfit was torn and stained with blood.

Finally, Wyler made his move and the needle went in. The Harm screamed incoherently. The needle came out and everyone stepped back. The Harm jerked and flailed in her restraints as the powerful sedative went largely unheeded through her veins. "You... won't be laughing on his swing. Only the mirror, the outside... only left." She moaned through gritted teeth, her muscles taut against the restraints.

"Well Anne, she's all yours!" Wyler said brightly.

"Oily bugs through the doorway!" The Harm shrieked from behind him.

"Thanks," Anne said. "Nice needle work, Doc."

The doctor put a hand on his chest and gave a quarter bow. "From you... high praise. And how's my favorite vampire?"

"Can't complain," she lied.

"You get a haircut?"

She shook her head as she inserted a flexible needle into the barrel. The doctor shrugged and glanced back to the Harm, who was now making more peaceful incoherent sounds. "I'm gonna need a CBC and a Harm screen. Surprised?"

Anne grimaced. "Nope."

"Enjoy!" He gave her a playful smack on the shoulder as he went past.

Anne took a deep breath and stepped toward the Harm, who was now wiggling her head and gurgling. This was the worst part of her job. Sure it was dangerous, these guys were nutty strong and violent, but the worst part was the anticipation. You never knew what was going to happen. So far Anne had gotten away with two ripped jackets, lots of spit, and one blood splattering from a biker who had bitten the tip of his own tongue off. She was lucky. There was an RN in Vegas that had a finger bitten off just last week.

About five meters away, another Harm was screaming bloody murder as Wyler vied for position with his needle.

* * *

"I really want to chop something with this!" Rae's excited voice came from behind Ping, where she was swinging the sword around quickly but somewhat inexpertly.

They both turned to her, amused. "Ain't she great?" Ahmed whispered.

"I have no official comment, Mr. Ahmed."

"Alex, please."

Ping smiled and nodded.

"Ivo called it 'Neural Clarity', but I think 'Amp' is more descriptive."

"So, you put two kinds of whammy into the cameo. She puts it on and the rest of the free world sees your woman in a new light and she gets quicker too?"

"Quicker, more agile, more coordinated—sharper. It's a Cast that refines the clarity her mind's interface of her motor nervous system. Forging it into the silver was a real bear to pull off."

"So, if I put on her necklace, I get cuter and deadlier?"

"Nope. It's tailored for her. You put it on and you start to look weird from the perception Cast... I mean vomiting weird. Then you get dizzy from the ill-fitting Amp... vomiting dizzy."

Ping shook his head. "So you Spellified the keys? But how, they were across the room..."

"Nah, I Cast *you*. You've gotta understand, there are Casts and Forges. I Cast you, but I Forged the cameo. A Cast is like a spell. A Forge embeds a Cast into the fabric or nature of an object."

"Ah!" Ping said, laying on his best Irish accent. "So ya spend all day a'castin' fer rainbows, but ya Forge yer little lucky charms do ya?"

Rae snickered. "You do a mean Irish."

"You haven't seen my mean Irish yet."

Alex's tablet chirped for the second time in the past two minutes. "What's that? You getting messaged from other nerds in the wizards-only chat room?"

Alex was looking at his tablet. His stylus was spinning around his fingers again. "Nope... I've got a camera cluster mounted above the study area outside.

Got it alarmed to notify me when any of the doors open. In the past couple of minutes we've had two visitors."

"Innocent looking, book loving visitors, right babe?" Rae stopped swinging the sword.

"Well, now that you mention it, they're both thirtyish, in top physical shape, and though they came in separately, they seem to shop the same Ninja Gap for clothes." Alex shook his head. "They're searching the aisles, but neither is looking at the shelves. I think we might be in trouble."

The tablet chirped again. There was a moment of silence.

"Well?" Ping said at last.

"Another one." Alex said, closing his eyes and angling his head away with a theatrical wince, "Same approximate description, but meaner looking and slightly more female."

"Well, at least we're trapped." Ping said, looking about the room.

"Yes dear, we'll always have trapped." Rae put her hand on Alex's shoulder and gave it an encouraging squeeze, followed by a slightly less charitable shake. "Good job picking a secret rendezvous with no back door, honey!" She gave him a warm smile and a solid punch in the shoulder.

"Ow!" Alex rubbed his shoulder, but he smiled at her as if he'd only felt the encouraging squeeze. "There's not much to do now but wait and hope they aren't absolutely certain we're on this floor."

"Hope they just go away? This is our best plan… swell." Rae said, handing the sword to Ping and reaching under her jacket to check her concealed pistol.

Ping retracted the blade and shrugged his shoulders. "Hey, it might be nothing. Here, let me have a look." He moved around behind Alex and peered at the camera feed on his tablet. "Uh oh."

"What?" Rae and Alex said in unison.

"These people obviously got low scores at ominous suppression school. If you try hard, you can almost hear the suspense music."

Rae had moved into position over Alex's other shoulder. They both nodded.

The tablet chirped again as the elevator door opened. A man who looked like an aging surfer-turned-banker stepped in.

"Oh boy," Ping said without enthusiasm, "it's Good Cop."

"You know him?" Alex asked.

Ping nodded. "Yeah… his name's Garvey. He and his partner gave me the reaming about your keys."

"Uh oh." Rae said, shaking her head and looking at Alex. "This guy and his fraternal clone tossed your cube downstairs while I was waiting for the Detective here. He was packing."

"Yeah, he should be, he's FBI." Ping said.

"No… *packing*." Her eyes shifted to Alex, full of meaning.

Alex turned his head to Ping. "She means he posts to the wizards-only chat room."

"You mean someone put the hex on him like you did to me?" Ping asked.

Rae shook her head. "No. I saw him use it when they were searching Alex's cubicle... probably Cast Vision to see if Alex left anything hot behind. He's in the club."

"Hot?"

"Forged... like Rae's necklace." Alex answered.

"So maybe the Feds have a special Lovecraft squad or something. These guys interrogated me when I was still fiddling with your keys." Ping paused to punch Alex in the shoulder, "They know something's up with Lutine and folks like him."

"Ow." Alex said, rubbing his shoulder again, "Yeah, the Gov's got Savants... like your grade school had federal agents. Governments come and go, but the Clans go back forever."

"Clans?"

Alex held up his hands, then after a slight pause, continued. "This is big trouble... There's a lot of stuff I don't know yet, but you've got to believe me here: we don't want to stay and chat. If these are the guys that interrogated you, then I think they're on the side of the people who killed Roy and Ivo."

"Now that's a cheery thought!" Rae hissed, fingering her cameo. "These guys managed to take down either of them alone and asleep, I'd be scared, but both..." She trailed off, shaking her head.

"So you're saying that Lutine and Sieberg were like Yoda and his more powerful twin?"

"They were more like Yoda and his love child. They acted like father and son. Course they weren't," Rae said, "didn't look a thing alike."

Alex shook his head. "Lutine was more like Gandalf than Yoda, but Roy... he was scary. Don't get me wrong, he looked like he wouldn't hurt a fly and whoa, if you ever saw him with a baby in the room you'd think he was a more intense version of a favorite grandma. But your image of him changes the first time you catch him playing."

Ping looked troubled. "Playing? You saying 'torturing animals' or something?"

Alex gave a nervous laugh. "No. When it came to animals he was more the compulsive petter... Rae, you remember the time Roy had the puppy at Ivo's office?"

She laughed. "Who could forget... he had that little rat on his head for a while."

"Anyway, that's not what I was talking about. Once I came early for practice on the roof of the Grant building. Roy was showing off for Ivo... it was the weirdest thing. Ivo was laughing, Roy was capering around doing some pretty amazing gymnastics—flips and stuff. They hadn't seen me yet, so I stood in the doorway and watched. The tricks got more intense—but with a sense of humor. One I remember was a multiple flip that ended in a landing on his head and shoulders with his arms out to the sides. He just stopped with his legs going straight up, kinda twitching—I almost yelled, I thought he was dead. But Ivo just laughs harder, and in a second, Roy's up again and smiling."

"Then some birds go overhead and boom! Roy's gone and a second later he comes back down with a pigeon nicely folded in one hand. I checked the place he landed later and there were cracks in the ceramic of the roof."

"You're saying he flies." Ping said, unimpressed. "Like Superman."

"I'm saying he jumped at least four meters up with enough precision to catch a bird in mid-flight without harming it. I'm saying he landed like an Olympic gymnast... not just nailed the landing, but did it with a flourish... then he gets all melodramatic and says something about crying in the rain, waving the bird around for emphasis. Ivo was amused, but it creeped me out."

"All these moments will be lost in time. Like tears in rain." Ping quoted, a connection forming in his head.

It was nice to see someone else shocked for a change. "How...?" Alex asked.

"It's from *Blade Runner*."

They both stared at Ping, confused.

"The video... really old movie. I found a well-watched copy of it when I decrypted Sieberg... Roy's tablet. Now I think I get his nickname too. The guy who said that line in the movie was named Roy..."

"Huh?" Rae said.

"I don't have time to explain *everything* to you people."

"Yeah," Alex said, lost in thought, "He'd been badgering me since forever to watch it with him... I'd always intended to, but..."

Another chirp came from Alex's tablet. They looked down in unison. The stairwell door had opened again and another man and woman in dark clothes entered. They were holding hands.

Ping, Rae and Alex suppressed laughter with varying degrees of success.

The hand-holders were both looking around the room in an awful approximation of casual. Their hands were clutched, but both were clearly uncomfortable with it. They never looked at each other, and when they moved they were both so decisive they were yanking one another about. It was comically bad cover.

"Lets just hope they're this bad at searching." Ping whispered.

They all had a grand, if quiet, laugh. They were all going to die.

On the screen, one of the casually dressed agents approached Good Cop. Alex turned up the volume on his tablet so they could hear.

"Sweep's complete. No sign of them. You sure they came to eight?"

"Quite." Good Cop said, giving a theatrical sigh, "We're going to have to get a little less subtle then... bring them in."

* * *

Anne pulled over a stool and sat at the Harm's left elbow. The listless Harm's head lolled away from Anne, drooling fiercely, no doubt. Anne breathed a sigh of relief.

Sometimes the sedatives didn't work at all. Maybe she'd be extremely lucky and the Harm would wake up when Anne was long gone. The needle went in without a flinch. Anne popped the vac tube into the barrel and watched it fill. When it was full, she popped it out and attached the second one. Almost there.

Whispered as if in her ear, she heard dry laughter, "Look for us, find you won't."

Anne jumped. She looked around, searching for the speaker. The ward was full of other patients, but none were close enough, or creepy enough, to be the whisperer. She leaned across the Harm's slack body and looked down at her drooling face... nope.

Great, now she was hearing things too. Nearby, the screaming continued... the current subject was elves, for which the other Harm obviously had some ill feelings. The clamor intensified as the other Harm worked one hand out of his restraints. There were now two EMTs and two orderlies trying to get him subdued enough for Wyler's needle.

"So anxious!" The dry voice croaked from nowhere, full of menace. "Does it so long for our embrace? Can its fragile heart feel the coming?"

"Who's there?" Anne whispered, looking around, not wanting to attract attention.

"As if it hears, what does it feel?" Amusement crackled like dead leaves through the words, but the most disturbing part was the guttural sound that followed... like a deep growl, but with a touch of machinery. It was not the kind of sound any mouth could make.

Anne's every hair rose away from her skin, straining outward with fear. Ok, now she was really wishing she hadn't said anything… well, it's never too late to start. She set her unseeing eyes on her work.

The vial was full of inky blood. She removed the needle from the Harm's lifeless arm and began to fumble the full vac tube out of the barrel. 'Time to go, time to go, time to go' spun through her fear-fogged mind—a mantra, a syntactic snake eating its own tail. It was one thing to try to stop worshiping the God of Fear, but quite another to ignore him when he puts in a personal appearance.

Anne stopped with the vial of blood between her fingers, staring at it intently. It felt like she was holding a bag of bugs… though she could still feel the smooth texture of the vial's glass between her fingers, there was another feeling too… like small, ephemeral ants were crawling over the vial… spreading out over her fingers and hand. She stifled her scream and fought the urge to throw the vial across the room.

But then she saw it. Shimmering from inside the vial, like static on a damaged television, blue white chaotic energy seemed to pulse and vibrate from the blood. Even through the vial's glass, it was burning her hand. Anne realized that she could see the vial the same as always… no static, no bugs, but it was as if she had another sense, or an overactive imagination, that seemed to embellish the vial with the added lightshow. "What?" she whispered absently.

"It does! Smells its fear! It… *Hears!*" The last word dropped about five octaves, seeming to rumble through the ground. She looked around again... didn't anyone else hear this? It didn't look like it.

Trembling, she clinked the tube against the receptacle in her tray several times before she got it stowed. Time to go, time to go, time to go.

Anne had a hand on her tray, lifting it as she pushed her stool back. Then she stopped dead, still sitting on the stool. On the table in front of her, the Harm's head was slowly turning in her direction. Anne wanted to run away screaming, but a terrible curiosity gripped her. The Harm's face was almost in view now, her profile was covered with her platinum and red hair, but as her head continued to turn, the damp hair began to fall from the face... a few strands... a few more.

Silence washed through the ER as the other Harm's screaming cut off. She hoped Wyler had succeeded with his needle, but couldn't force herself to turn away and see.

The Harm's head continued to twist until she was looking directly at Anne and her face was at last visible. Wrong. The eyes were wrong; the mouth was wrong.

The eyes were bulging with a dark amusement that danced like a shadowy bloodshot flame. Like most Harms, her pupils crowded out her irises, but this seemed even less natural, if that were possible. The black of her pupils seemed to be crowding the white out of her eyes, too.

The mouth was pulled into a tight rictus, lips stretched back over clenched teeth, like someone expending all their energy showing the world just how happy they really were. Her top lip split, spilling blood onto her teeth. Veins and tendons stood out on her neck and arms as she struggled against the restraints. In a flash, Anne realized the most disturbing difference in the Harm. It wasn't the eyes, not the smile, not the blue static her imagination painted into the Harm's dead, black eyes. It was control— no screams, no thrashing—the Harm's chaotic insanity had seemingly been replaced with a distilled evil kind of insanity.

There came a sound like the bursting of a watermelon and one of the Harm's shoulders slumped, dislocated. Still, her damaged arm continued to strain at her bonds. Her eyes locked with Anne's, her smile still gathering intensity.

Anne was powerless. She was held fixed by the intense eyes. The strangest sense of déjà vu crept in around her tingling mind... oh yeah, she'd been here before, seen this same video the last time she'd walked home from work. Time to GO!

Anne surged to her feet, sending the stool flying. The edges of the Harm's right eye darkened red-black as a blood vessel burst. New screaming was now coming from the location of the other Harm, but it wasn't him screaming. It was Wyler's terror that rang out loudest among a new cacophony of urgent shouts and crashes. With a large effort, Anne broke eye contact with whatever this Harm was becoming and looked across the room, toward the screams.

The other Harm was a large black man with the most clueless hairstyle Anne had ever seen outside of a mirror. He was behind the doctor with an arm around his neck. Somehow he'd gotten out of the restraints—one of the EMTs was down, holding his face. The other was clearly dead with an unidentifiable piece of metal protruding from the side of her neck.

"Ninjas should not do drugs", Anne said into the ether of unreality that again surrounded her.

Two orderlies were poised a short distance away. They had their stunners out, but were holding their fire, not wanting to hurt the doctor, not wanting to provoke the Harm. The Harm's glare was fixed on Anne with the same lip-splitting grimace. The same distinctive obsidian mirth danced in his eyes.

This was not normal Harm behavior! They were violent, they were psychotic, but they did not work together, they did not have a plan or a purpose. Sure, Harms seemed evil, but these guys looked like the devil's butler on payday.

Like a preoccupied moviegoer might take a bite of popcorn, the Harm bent down and bit a chunk out of Wyler's ear without breaking his stare at Anne. Screams were everywhere. The ambulatory and uncowed were scrambling for the exits. Two beds away from the melee, a mother tried to cover her unconscious and bandaged daughter with her body. This was a bad night to visit your local ER.

Wyler's eyes were straining at their sockets, casting about wildly for help, solace—anything. His hands were clawing ineffectively at the arm around his neck. She could clearly distinguish his scream from the rest of the cacophony.

The ruse worked. Both orderlies fired, one hit the doctor in the side, knocking him thankfully insensate. The other shot hit the Harm full in the face. He staggered back. Wyler began to slip out of his loosening grip. Both orderlies rushed forward, one fired again, but the shot went wide.

Anne noticed three things essentially at once:

First: Things were moving in that surreal dream-state slow motion that trauma survivors often describe.

Second: The Harm wasn't as stunned as he appeared— she could tell from the horrible grin that a direct hit from a stunner should have made impossible. She could actually see his eyes darting between the approaching orderlies, little evil wheels turning in his head. Things were about to get much, much worse. Blood ran down Wyler's slack face, staining his shirt, the Harm's grip was tightening again around his neck. Anne knew Wyler's wife, had played with his new baby in the break room just last week. The Harm wasn't done with him.

And third: (and most disturbing of all) Anne noticed that she was now lumbering toward the Harm, feeling like a slightly heavier version of an enraged rhino. A new feeling coursed through her, warm and smooth. She was going to help.

Well, she was going to die trying to help anyway—'A' for effort.

She charged toward inevitable death feeling free.

* * *

"*Less* subtle?" Rae said, astounded. "How could they possibly be *less* subtle?"

"They've probably got uniforms they're going to go put on." Ping said.

"Maybe that was a signal to start a musical number?" Alex said, struggling to keep his voice quiet.

Outside, Good Cop lifted a hand and shouted, "Game's over! Scanners!"

The five in the room reached for their bags. Two brought out portable scanners, while the other three brought out compact 2mm automatic weapons. They began the search pattern anew, scanning through racks and walls.

Rae spoke first. "Ok. That is slightly less subtle."

Ping didn't yet see a way out. He pulled out his tablet and switched it out of private mode. He left the recorder running. Nobody was going to believe this.

"What'cha doin?" Rae asked.

"Calling for help."

"Yeah. Good luck." Alex said without enthusiasm.

Ping opened a connection through the emergency ports at dispatch, or tried to. The tablet was out of private mode, but it had not yet connected to the Library's network.

"No luck eh?" Alex was shaking his head. "The first thing they did was yank down the net here. I checked when I first realized we were trapped."

"How're you maintaining connectivity with the camera out there?" Rae asked.

"I love it when you talk technical." Alex smiled, "Old school direct connection. Guy at the spy store told me it was better not to connect to some appliances through the net... guess he was right. I'm direct wired to the archive's bookshelf controls through the box there, too." He hooked a thumb over his shoulder at the junction box on the wall.

"I'm really trying to resist saying, 'we need to get out of here', guys." Rae said.

Alex was flipping his stylus again. "I've got the beginnings of a plan. You shoot as well as you draw Detective?"

* * *

Terror, sympathy, fury; the emotions chased each other through Anne's mind. Black, white, red; their heat and color cycled through her, burning her, filling her— waking her.

She approached the Harm and Wyler in a crystal clear slow motion. As she ran, the emotions cycled faster, blurring together until they were only perceptible as a single and unfamiliar emotion. With an almost audible click, she realized that this new feeling was the passion of determination. This was what it was to have a purpose, what it was to be alive. Hmm... so that's what it felt like. Nice to find out so close to the end of her life, but better late than never.

The two orderlies rushed in. The Harm's face smoked from the stunner blast. Wyler flew headfirst into one onrushing orderly. Their heads connected with a sound Anne would hopefully forget soon. Blood filled the Harm's grimace. He turned to the other charging orderly. The orderly faltered, losing the commitment of his attack; the Harm didn't hesitate.

Anne's mind recoiled from the last orderly's fate, not least of all because she was probably about to share it. But her heart beat hotter, her blood flowed wilder; she was either shouting or screaming, but she was doing it so slowly she couldn't tell which. It seemed like she had begun her mad charge minutes ago, but she had only crossed perhaps six meters, and she still had another three to go. This wasn't just the adrenaline slowdown she had earlier thought. Maybe this was her new vampire nature, she thought with an internal shrug—if so, she was definitely going to feast on this Harm's corpse when this was over.

Two meters to go. Running had definitely changed for her. It seemed that her skeleton was moving faster than her flesh, as if she were an Olympic swimmer attempting to race through a pool of her own private jello. Normally, running was about keeping her weight from dragging her to the ground like an over-eager high school wrestler on steroids, but now she was running with efficiency and even grace. Weird, she thought as she vaulted over a wheeled gurney and the tough-looking leather-clad biker-type-guy trying to crawl beneath it.

One meter to go. The Harm had his arms up in front of him like an odd cross between a professional boxer and Frankenstein's monster. He waited for her in blood and cruelty with his demon's smile. Were all the Harms in the ward tonight just misdiagnosed satanic possessions?

As the Harm filled her vision, she wished she didn't have so much time to think about what she was doing. But then, to her great dismay, she got her wish.

Into the oddly muted speedscape through which she ran, the sound of her scream sped and expanded. Everything accelerated and her arms tangled with the Harm's in a blur of movement and jarring pain. Terror quenched her fury as her vision narrowed and she grew numb to her actions.

Her teeth rattled under the impact of the Harm's first savage blow. She was not going to live to regret this.

* * *

Garvey looked around the library archive. He hated these undercover operations. Though his suit looked good on him, he didn't like wearing it. He didn't like having to play nice with the cops, but mostly he hated having to restrain his natural impulses. At least now the time for restraint was over, at least now it was the time for action. Yep, he had an all day pass for the circus and he was giddy with thoughts of the play to come.

The Grunts were moving though the moveable racks of books, scanning methodically for their prey. He heard the door open and turned back to the entrance. His partner walked through the stairwell entrance with six more grunts behind him. The grunts had their automatic weapons and scanners out.

"Let's fan out!" Nieland shouted at the grunts as he moved to Garvey. "This won't take long."

Garvey nodded. "What's the rush?" They shared a wicked smile.

The lights went out.

It was dark as a tomb for an instant, then the emergency lights above the stairwell engaged, lighting the exit, but not much more. There wasn't even enough light for shadows.

"Find the breakers for this level, Smith!" Garvey shouted.

"Net's down sir!" the shout came back, "Can't access the schematics."

"Then scan for the wires... follow them!" Garvey shouted, then he lowered his voice, "Grunts." he said with derision.

"Yep." Neiland muttered, "you've gotta tell them every little thing." Then he shouted, "Skip your torches! Get your seers on!"

As Garvey fumbled his seers out of his jacket pocket, the room filled with the sound of electric motors and slow mechanical movement. He slipped the stylish glasses on, configured them for zero light operation, and the world turned into a clear, green-tinted approximation of daylight.

Someone had activated all of the densepack library shelving. All the racks of books were sliding on their runners in a seemingly random pattern, closing and opening isles between them as they moved along their tracks. Since they'd dropped the library's net earlier, either Ahmed was using the Loom, or he'd hacked into the shelves' wiring directly. Garvey was sure it was a wire hack because the only Cast he was using would have alerted him to any abnormal activity in the Underworld. If Lutine's apprentice so much as tried a pattern stretch, Garvey would be able to pinpoint his location.

The moving shelves were slowing down the search, making traversal between the main aisles slower, but that was all. Like turning out the lights, this was only a distraction. If Lutine's apprentice were going to try something, it would be now.

Standing in the archive's central hallway, Garvey opened his mind and dove into the Underworld, where his Cast stretched out, searching. If the apprentice tried anything, Garvey would be ready for him.

"Stay sharp!" Neiland shouted, "They're probably going to make a break for it!"

* * *

Weapons drawn, Ping and Rae moved out into the inky blackness of the aisle. Ping went right; Rae went left. They couldn't see a thing since the agents weren't using their flashlights and the exit beacons didn't come close to reaching the back of the cavernous archive. They were blind, but if you could believe Garvey about the seers, his men were not. Ping's sunglasses had a night-vision mode, but he'd left them in the glove box of his car. Alex's camera cluster had a zero light mode, so he could still see from within the utility room, but Ping and Rae had to take it on faith that they weren't currently in the sights of one of the agents. Ping wondered if they were trying to capture him or would just shoot on sight. Either way these palookas were likely to shoot first and ask questions never... they were just that subtle.

There was a corner here that Ping was hoping not to turn. What if these guys really were federal agents? What if Garvey and company were wearing the white hats? What if pigs *could* fly? He didn't yet know exactly what was going on, or who the players were. He didn't want to shoot anyone, but he wanted to be shot even less, and he had the distinct impression these guys didn't bring handcuffs.

His left elbow brushed along the shelf to keep him oriented, both his guns were held close but ready before him as he slipped through the darkness. Before him, a gray patch of darkness resolved from the absolute black. He had reached the end of the aisle, but didn't dare poke his head around it toward the dim light for fear that it would get shot off by the unseen gunmen. He closed his eyes and waited for Alex's big move. Thirteen vs. three, three pistols vs. at least eleven automatic weapons plus whatever Good Cop and Bad Cop were carrying.

* * *

Inside the utility room, Alex watched Rae and Ping get into position on the ends of the aisle. He wondered when the bad guys would notice that the shelf they leaned against was the only one in the archive that wasn't on the move. Given enough time...

He watched the movements of the agents outside, looking for the best opportunity. One of the scanning teams approached Rae's position, but fortunately they were scanning the exterior wall that ran perpendicular to her aisle. There were another two teams in the central aisle close to the Detective.

He touched the activating button with his stylus. Now or never. As the screen went white, he moved the monitor window into the background.

Now that they were off balance, it was time to prepare for phase two.

* * *

In a jittering flash, the lights blazed back to life. Ping and Rae opened their eyes fractionally and got to work. Rae's gun hummed out of standby as she pivoted around and braced her arms against the shelf. Her targets were taken off guard as their seers went white with the flood of light. In a second the seers would adjust to the bright vapor lights, but by then it wouldn't do these two any good. The first shot went behind the ear of the one with the gun. The next two went into the chest and throat of the one with the scanner.

She bolted across the aisle and slid on her butt between two shelves on the other side of the walkway. She rolled over into a prone shooting stance and the moving shelves bumped into her sides and moved away.

There was an oily tendril winding through her guts that she could not ignore. She'd just killed two people. Her mind kept trying to drag her focus to the possibility that they had families—children. She made a small involuntary sound as her heart rebelled at where her will had taken her. In her five years on the force, some of it spent in Chicago's worst neighborhoods, she had never needed to fire her weapon outside the training range.

She gritted her teeth and forced herself back into the moment. Harsh reality was that if she was very lucky, those two were only the first of many. Fury rolled through her, there had been plenty of times when people had tried to kill her, but this was the first time she'd been forced to kill someone else. She used the fury to crowd the guilt off of her mind's stage.

Her ragged scream ripped out of her, seeming to pulse though her clenched hands as she fired through a row of shelves, hitting a partially hidden gunman in the knee, then in the head as he fell. Now was the time for ruthlessness, for death. Later she could curl into a ball of doubt and self-loathing—if she was lucky.

If she killed enough to live.

* * *

Squinting in the new light, Ping rounded the corner. He braced his right arm against the shelves and steadied it with his left arm, the pistol in his left hand pointing cross-body. He rounded another corner as he shot the agent with the scanner first. Logic would have told him this was the wrong order, but he wasn't thinking. Times like this were made only for reflexes. Some people in the martial arts community insisted that fighting was like chess. Of course, if the round timer in chess were set to fifteen milliseconds, chess wouldn't really be chess either. Ping believed what his parents had taught him: fighting was reflexes, resolve and geometry.

The woman with the gun was the next to fall. Behind them, Good Cop and Bad Cop were struggling to get their seers off. He hit Bad Cop in the shoulder before Good

Cop tackled him out of the way. Ping managed to hit Good Cop in the calf as they fell into an aisle and the shelving closed around them.

Behind them, Ping saw four more agents. As their guns came up, Ping snapped off three ineffective shots then retreated back around the corner.

Automatic gunfire erupted from everywhere. The air about him filled with dust and fragments of books, shelves, and wall. Keeping low, he scrambled back toward the center of the aisle, away from the storm.

"Now would be a good time, Alex!"

* * *

Alex touched the I-Candy icon on the screen. The screen's contents melted away, a reflection blurring then fading in a disturbed pool. All resolved to blackness, then a play list appeared. He made a selection and hit the start button. The air around him seemed to fill with a resonant Gregorian chant.

He tried to relax, but the tension wouldn't go... nothing like a little mortal peril to really frazzle the nerves. "Calm down baby, you can calm down, hey?" He muttered as the chant broke out into polyphony. The choir sang in harmony, each part of the harmony pulling the mind toward its distinctive melody. As he had been trained, he wrapped his mind around the music, letting it expand.

Training wheels. Ivo liked to call this "Pattern Stretching". If he lived long enough, he'd learn to Cast without it someday.

The active compensation built into the phones in his ears canceled out maybe ninety percent of the gunfire, but it was still a distraction. He increased the volume as the beat started. First it was a simple drone punctuating the chant. Then the synths moved in and the chant became the filigree around the outside of a deepening musical pattern.

On the screen electric milk moved in deeply layered fractals. The patterns shifted in syncopation with the complex lattice of the music. He pushed his mind into the patterns. In his mind's eye, he saw the patterns stretching off the sides of the screen, extending in a sphere around him, finally joining behind his head. He floated inside a continuum of blending sound and light, stretching outward into the synaesthetic patterns. Soft, lemon-flavored electricity crawled over his skin in time with the joining patterns of sound, light, and thought. He let his eyes lose focus as he focused on a component of the beat that hid layers down. He let it expand until it was the primary sound he heard, felt, tasted.

There was a tingle of final anticipation and then he fell. Inward. Downward. Behind his eyes, below his feet, inside his bones, the complexities of the Underworld unfurled and he exploded out into its light. Ivo liked to call this place the world's utility crawlspace. Here, the plumbing and wiring of the "real world" could be seen—could be manipulated.

And so, washed of the things of the world above, he approached the Loom. Far away it seemed the music changed, but this was a caress on a sleeper's face, unfelt in the dream. He had work to do.

Ivo had been teaching him a Cast that he called "Brownian Dissonance"—with Ivo it had always been about the polysyllabic. The point of the Cast was to overwhelm an electronic device with a randomly distributed series of dissonant pseudomagnetic fields.

He started with the template for that Cast, attempting to change the amplitudes of the vibrations, tuning them to harmonize with metal. He then accessed the template for a Cast that affected ferric pliancy, which was the first Cast Ivo had taught him—the spoon-bender. He took these two simple Casts and began to knit them together, combining their purposes. It seemed to take forever to get the patterns integrated. Fortunately, here in the Loom, time was stretched thin. Here, seconds could stretch on for what seemed like minutes.

He didn't want to think about the odds of a novice successfully contriving an ad-hoc Cast like this. It was dangerous and probably wouldn't work, but it was the best he could do.

Passion and focus—Ivo said these were the keys to all interaction with the Loom. Alex had focus in spades. It was what made him so good with computers. Of course, you didn't really need passion to create fractal security algorithms.

To this point, Alex's greatest work had been the Forge of Rae's cameo. Even Ivo had been impressed. It had taken him forever, but when Rae was involved, Alex found he had more passion than for any of Ivo's assignments. Rae's life depended on his work now. All of their lives did. The trick was to turn fear into passion, rather than paralysis.

He put just a little power through the conjoined weave. He then quickly found the frays and misflows and quickly reincorporated the problem sections.

This was not going to work.

He remembered long ago Ivo saying that it was easier to destroy than to create—this was his only hope. This Cast was more like a drunkard brandishing a chair than building a fine piece of weaponry. Forging Rae's cameo had taken about four months to get right, but today he had only seconds.

Quickly, he Cast the weave of Vision and saw through the eyes of the Loom just how desperate things had become out in the archive. Rae and the Detective had made a decent accounting for themselves, but he could see they didn't have long to live. One of the assassins whipped around the end of the row of shelves where the Detective was crouching. Not yet!

In the pristine speed of the Loom, Alex saw the Detective move in the glassy smooth slow motion of action movies. Ping changed the geometry of his crouch, shifting his weapons ever so slightly. The assassin's finger was still tightening on the trigger of his assault weapon when three bullets from the Detective's twin guns tore through his chest.

Shifting his view quickly to Rae, he saw the strained look on her face as she fired from a prone position between two shelves. He saw the tears on her hard face, determination and sorrow behind the bright, furious eyes. This was killing her.

Passion. Looking at Rae it seemed to flow into him, leaving him both more alive and more uncertain. This was the moment of truth. He threw off the Vision and composed the pattern of Collection. Power began to accumulate around him, drawn to the substance of his will. Soon he was straining to maintain the pattern of his Cast through the pressure of the building energy. He needed dangerous levels of power to make this work over a large enough area.

Ivo had told him that with time and practice he would be able to channel much more power. Once he had seen Ivo in a Cast with enough raw power to kill Alex many times over. But then Ivo was quite a few centuries now without the training wheels. Ivo could Cast dry, though he liked to work with Reggae music in the background. Alex had tried to get to the Loom with Bob Marley once... he didn't see how it helped Ivo. To each his own.

The pressure grew until he felt he would unhinge with it—bone and thought splintering, dispersing into welcoming oblivion. He was at the heart of a whirlwind, but the wind was whirling into him—tearing through him, blinding his mind. His will faltered and his crude Weave began to dissolve. Now or never.

He let the power explode into his clunky weave. The Cast crystallized and blazed before him as it expanded out into the world above. He reeled for an instant in the hollow silence of the departed storm—had he actually pulled it off? Had it fizzled out? For a few ticks of the atomic clock, he was too overwhelmed to care.

Unseen, somewhere in the Overworld, his new Cast shattered. Alex's first indication was a shift in the currents of the Underworld—the receding sea before the tsunami.

Then the backlash came. It crashed over and through him, an avalanche of light.

Blackness.

* * *

Ping hit the end of the shelves at a dead run. He crossed the narrow aisle between the stacks of shelves in a wild leap. As he landed on the other side between two closing shelves, he caught a foot on one and went down hard. The fall probably saved his life. He hit the floor awkwardly between the shelves, bruising his shoulder, losing one gun and his wind. He was immediately showered with debris from a barrage that tore through the shelves at chest level. As the shelves moved away again, he blinked and wiped the debris from his face.

A few aisles closer to the exit, he could hear Rae returning fire, a few plinks in the midst of the hailstorm of enemy fire. "Move Rae!" He shouted. "Keep moving..."

A black silhouette appeared in the space between the shelves behind him, weapon at the ready. Someone must have pursued him down the aisle as he fled. His remaining weapon was already twisting toward the attacker, but there was no way he could win this race.

His gun was perhaps twenty degrees off-target when a tidal wave seemed to turn the world inside out. His vision blurred and wavered in the wake of the muted fury. The dying harmonics of an unheard or unremembered explosion rattled the air, lingered in his head. The lights stuttered out, and most blew. Flickering near-darkness returned and silence covered the room.

Unbelievably, the gunman at the end of the shelves hadn't sawed him in half yet. Ping's own weapon came on-target. He pulled the trigger.

Nothing. His ears felt dull, like they were filled with water. His vision still shivered slightly. All the gunfire had stopped; the loudest sound he could hear was his heart, and the rasp of his labored breath.

The gunman was making sharp gestures with his weapon as he repeatedly pulled the trigger with great emphasis. He attempted to clear the bolt while Ping found a more effective use for his own pistol. His thrown needle gun hit the gunman squarely on the forehead with a crack that came as a dull thunk through Ping's watery ears. The gunman dropped like a bag of hammers without even the volition to clutch at his damaged face.

Alex, Ping thought, now he owed the little centimeter-shorter runt his life. He wondered if he'd been able to take out all the weapons in the room.

He could barely see through the dust and jittery shadows. Somewhere a few lights still flickered sporadically. He found his other pistol within arms reach, but dropped it into his holster without trying the trigger. It was subtly warped, barrel curving perhaps three millimeters to the left. Ozone tinged the air as a few of the shelves' motors labored against warped gears, tracks, and casters. A low electric hum moaned about him as he struggled to his feet.

Alex's work must have either stunned him or affected his inner ear because he couldn't immediately stand without holding on to the now immobile shelves. The dizziness subsided to a manageable level after a few seconds.

He made his way unsteadily to the end of the aisle and poked his head around the bullet-pocked end cap. In the walkway between the stacks of shelves were two corpses at about four meters. Farther back was another corpse, and three visible gunmen. One had been coming down the aisle when Alex had opened his little present. He was now on all fours, retching into an expanding pool of bile. Farther away another gunman stumbled out from between two shelves. Ping rounded the end of the shelves and entered the aisle where Rae was now swaying on hands and knees. The gun still clutched in one hand supported part of her weight with the barrel pressed into the floor.

There was a low, wrenching moan and a rumble through the floor as the building settled around it's newly warped infrastructure. "Geez Alex!" Rae whispered.

"Uh-huh." Ping said from inside his personal haze. "Let's go..."

He grabbed Rae under her shoulders and helped her to her feet. She staggered and put a hand on the shelves for support.

"It passes quickly." Ping lied. "Come on."

* * *

"We should've brought more Grunts." Neiland said through clenched teeth.

"That would have helped." Garvey said as he tried to staunch the blood flowing from Neiland's destroyed shoulder. "Of course, *you* still would've managed to get shot. What's this, the fourth time you've been shot since we met?"

"Third. I believe that's a hole in your leg, too."

"Bullet hog. Mine's just a scratch. Keep pressure here." Garvey pressed Neiland's left hand on his wounded shoulder. "I don't have time to try to heal this... gotta deal with Lutine's lackey before he does any more damage.

"Hurry back, you know I can't work a healing yet... That Jamming was sure a surprise." Neiland said, smiling through the field anesthetic his medkit had administered before the Jamming turned it into a paperweight. "Not bad for a newbie."

Garvey drew his pistol and nodded as he examined the warped metal. "Never seen a Jam that left metal warped." He shrugged, "We've still got a few surprises left too. Be right back."

He stood shakily, favoring his wounded left leg, and shouted. "Check your weapons! We're going medieval! Cover the door!"

He closed his eyes and accessed the Loom. From the templates available, he chose the weave of Grappling—it wasn't the most effective weapon, but it would likely be the most satisfying.

* * *

Ping and Rae stumbled back into the greater darkness of the utility room. "Alex! Alex baby?" Rae hissed into the deep silence, but there was no reply. They both fumbled toward where Alex had been sitting. Ping heard Rae stumble and go down hard in the dark. "Found him." She said from below. "Help me get him up."

They managed to get Alex's slack form up between them and together they dragged him out the door. They turned left and moved as quickly as possible down the aisle of shelving, across the side passage, and into the aisle of shelves where Rae and Ping had spent the final seconds of the gunfight. When they hit the wall at the edge of the room, they turned right, toward the exits. As they moved, Alex began to stir. First mumbling, then he began to take a few weak steps as they dragged him between them. "Shhh, honey, it's gonna be okay, but you've gotta keep it quiet." Rae whispered in his ear.

Three rows of shelves were stacked up against the wall with the exits. They approached the last open aisle between the shelves and Rae darted her head around the corner to survey the scene by the exit. She shook her head and they took a few steps back. "Six by the door... all with what look like hunting knives now." she whispered.

"Hooboy." Ping said dryly. "How are you with knives?"

"Two words: 'sicked out', I could never use one in anger." She shuddered. "But that's okay, I don't have one... you think I could bluff them with the pistol?"

Ping shook his head. "You can tell by the knives that they know what's up... I don't think you're gonna fool them."

"Maybe I could shame them into letting us by?"

"I've still got Roy's sword..."

She looked horrified. "You could really...?"

"I know what you mean." He gave her a tight grin. The idea of using an edged weapon was pretty grim, and anyone who thought differently hadn't given the matter much thought. Getting stuck with one was even more unappealing. "We do need to move though. Feds or no, I have a feeling their reinforcements are coming before ours."

"We've got reinforcements?" She raised her eyebrows.

"Er... no. Not unless you and Alex mobilized your local wizard's club."

"Yeah, we called them all." She shook her head. "But we're already both here... and I'm only an honorary member."

"Stay with Alex. There's a small chance I'll be back." Ping reached into his jacket pocket and put a hand on the collapsed sword.

"Stranger things have happened." She said as they sat Alex on the floor and leaned him against the wall.

"No kidding." Ping stood and turned toward his grim work.

"So, who here needs the orthopedic enema?" Ping shouted as he stepped from between the shelves. He channeled his fear into an art he liked to call "game face maintenance". Sometimes to look good is to feel good.

The five men and one woman spread out around the doorway to the stairs, raising their blades. Most were wearing that evil gonna-get-to-cut-someone grin considered socially acceptable in pre-murder situations. Ping had always been bad at bravado. But then he was pretty good at what would come next.

There was a moment of disorientation as he flipped through the air like a rag doll heaved into the air. He colliding with the... uh... ceiling. Yep... below him was the floor… that hard thing against his back was the ceiling. A cloud of dust from the destroyed acoustic tiles surrounded him. He'd slammed through the suspended ceiling and was now pinned against one of the building's ventilation ducts. Dazed, he looked around… none of the knife-wielders had been affected by the sudden reversal of gravity.

"Whoa… guess I get the enema." He mumbled, shaking his head.

"Detective Bannon!" Good Cop said, limping out of the now immobile shelving on the other side of the central aisle, "I must say I'm a little surprised to see you're playing such a *key* role in our investigation."

Ping groaned at the pun and the unseen force that was now using him to crumple the ventilation shaft above him.

"You'll never get away with this, Garvey!" Ping wheezed with his most melodramatic voice, expending all his energy to shake a fist weakly before him for emphasis.

They both had a good laugh, though Ping's terminated in a series of coughs.

"You never cease to amuse Detective. I think I'll kill you in a minute. But till then…" Good Cop wiggled his finger theatrically.

Ping fell the nearly four meters to the floor, landing with all the grace of a dead fish dropped at the market.

"Nice landing!" Garvey laughed, clearly enjoying his work.

Eyes closed against the starbursts that filled his vision, Ping wondered what the connection was between evil and laughter. If he had to do it over, this would have been the subject of his dissertation. "I thought… you were supposed to be… the good cop." Ping choked out, spitting blood from lips twisted between a smile and a wince.

"Oh I believe you'll find that I'm rather bad." Garvey said, grinning and nodding with the admission, "Especially with someone who was so rude to my suit." He gestured to the bullet hole in his leg.

Ping wheezed and ached. His right knee was broken from the fall. After a few seconds he could breathe; after a few more he got his aching arms beneath him and pushed up enough to see Good Cop. "And I… suppose… this means you've got a wee pot o' magic gold somewhere too." He gasped.

"Shhhhh!" Garvey hissed, raising his finger to his lips.

The floor, ceiling, floor, blurred before Ping's eyes, followed by a painful impact with a fresh piece of the ceiling. His breath went out in a groan. "Ow."

"Indeed!" Garvey was so pleased with himself Ping thought he was going to give himself a little medal. His laughter seemed only a little forced.

"So…" Ping choked out "This is when you… lay out your entire nefarious plot, right?"

More laughing. "No, detective! This is when I squash you like the bug you are, then I think I'll pull the woman's arms off… then maybe I'll lay out my 'nefarious plot' for Mr. Ahmed… probably during the torture, I think. I don't think he'll be capable of really appreciating it afterward."

Ping was almost sure he heard Rae say "Ahhh… crap." from back in the shelves, but he might have imagined it. Either way, it made him smile.

The pressure on his chest and legs intensified. The ceiling wasn't giving. Breathing became impossible, but he wasn't going to asphyxiate. Nope, this was to be a bug-squashing. Garvey's face was a mask of sadistic triumph. He was taking it slow, relishing.

Now this was exactly like family counseling, Ping thought—helplessly watching as the wrong thing happened—a conductor on life's train wreck. Ping preferred the more satisfying job of the policeman: wading through misery that you knew wasn't your fault, looking for justice.

He felt a rib crack, then snap. Purple starbursts filled his vision and an electric static filled his ears. Before his mind's eye, he saw the familiar face of a young girl, innocence amplifying the accusation in her eyes. Fury burned hot around the pain, but it was an embracing fury, welcoming the pain.

FIRE

FACES OF THE DRAGON

The exploding glass caught everyone off guard. The thick tempered glass of the library archive door had kept the minimal sounds of quick, brutal death outside, so the grunts had no warning when the corpse parted the door's unbreakable glass like a curtain of plastic beads. Deep in the folds of the Loom, Garvey arguably should have seen it coming, but like so many times before, he'd become immersed in the thrill of the moment. He'd been looking forward to killing the little Asian detective since he'd seen him this morning.

The detective's limp body fell from the ceiling as Garvey's focus shifted to the shattered door. "It's Bower!" one of the Grunts shouted, looking at the corpse that had come to a rest perhaps three meters inside the doorway. They'd left Bower guarding the door into the archive, but he'd obviously blown it. The Grunts took up defensive positions around the jagged opening, bracing themselves for an assault.

Beneath the small, inward-facing floods of the emergency lights around the exit sign, the dark breach framed with the remains of the shattered door took on some of the essence of a dragon's cave; it's consuming darkness seeming to shroud only deeper and more terrifying black. There was a slight stir in the shadows, then an unimposing man with short bristly hair stepped through the destroyed door and paused beneath the exit sign. His attitude was casual, his stride easy. "Hi!" He said into the stunned silence. The voice was friendly, amused.

He gave a quick nod of acknowledgement to the assembled killers. "Anyone know where the cooking section is? I'm halfway through a cake when I realize I can't remember if I need to whip or stir the batter. I tell ya, spoon or mixer... it's these details that make all the difference."

With a shout, one of the Grunts charged, twin knives flashing. The newcomer didn't flinch, didn't move at all until the tip of the first knife was half a centimeter from his throat. Then there was a blur of motion; sharp sounds that came too quick to count, and the Grunt's body hit the floor so hard that the impact could be felt through the shoes of the remaining killers.

The newcomer stood casually, seemingly in the same position as before the attack, the lines of his face softening from terrible rage back into a mask of reason and curiosity. He held up a hand, palm out.

"Look, by now you folks realize you're in deep trouble, so it's time to decide. We can do this the easy way or the hard way." He said reasonably, "This is actually my third killing spree today, and I'm way over my homicide limit for the week, so I'm going to give you folks a gracious deal: you put down your wee little knives—you walk away peaceably right now, and I'll kill you." His smile broadened, mirth and menace mingling like fuel and air awaiting the smallest spark.

"*And* you'll kill us?" one of the Grunts said.

"Hmm," the newcomer said with a smirk, "apparently you've seen through my little ruse." He sighed with mild disappointment, "Abandon all hope."

Beautiful weapon, Ping thought through the sparkle-haze of the blood slowly returning to his brain. Sprawled on the ground, neck craned to stare at the newcomer; he was reminded of an exhibit at an air-show he'd attended when he was thirteen. He had been impressed with the terrible beauty of a gun node on the nose of a short-attack craft. Its every line was symmetry and efficiency. Its many rotating barrels and the surrounding fairing had the sleek fearsome look of a shark's mouth, but the overall impression was of beauty strengthened by purpose. This guy radiated the same aesthetic—terrible, irresistible beauty. For some reason, he'd seemed less impressive in Ahmed's lobby this morning.

An ephemeral flicker disturbed the floating dust between Good Cop and the bristly-haired killing machine, but then things happened faster than anyone else could see.

Dek had almost missed the action again. A sharp pang of regret crystallized in the firestorm of his rage. For the second time today, he'd been there to face Alex's hunters, but when it had really counted, he'd been too late.

In a time continuum where hummingbirds would float motionless on cushions of thick, downy air, his sword came out. It's ringing was a low resonant hum of shifting harmonics in the heavy air. Dek's clothes stretched and tugged backward with the first eddies of force from the blonde Savant's Grappling. His torso began to rock with the slow dissonant violence of the kinetic Cast. But his legs were already compensating, holding him upright, allowing the force to drive him back. His feet slid across the floor, glass crunched, and the blade hummed through a short, direct arc. The blade was fully extended when it tore through the Cast around him. The blade lit with the tracings of the Loom as its Forged steel sheered through the blonde guy's weave and the Loom's raw power burst from the destroyed Cast like oil from a severed wellhead.

At his speed, the explosion sounded like a wave slowly crashing on a rocky shore. Dek struck again, cleaving downward as he leapt forward. The results were less spectacular—a final spurt of emptying power, but he liked to be thorough.

Though he probably wasn't yet aware of it, the amateur Savant was already swimming in a backlash of power that blew back from his shattered Cast. He'd left the ground and entered a contorted backstroke. Dek left him for the moment and turned his attention to the Savant's henchmen.

Payback wasn't sweet, but it was coming.

A nearly imperceptible contortion shivered through the world as the bristly haired guy from Alex's lobby struck the air before him in a blur of implied motion. The sword that came from nowhere lit with lines of power as it passed through the seemingly empty air.

The world was still a bit fuzzy around the edges from his brush with Garvey's magic flyswatter. Ping was still considering the possibility that this was a postmortem hallucination when the last body fell amid the newcomer's blade tornado and he stood alone in the archive's entrance.

Ping made another connection as the sound that Rodriguez described as a flag in high wind died and the newcomer stopped in the midst of the destruction he'd wrought. His still-ringing sword was traced with fading lines of power and edged with blood. Eddies of dusty air still swept around him as his clothes again succumbed to the downward pull of gravity, settling over his now motionless form. An instant later, sparks flew as the blade retracted.

Ping must have blinked because the newcomer was now standing over him, staring down intently. "If it makes a difference, I'm not going to stand between you and your cooking." Ping wheezed.

The guy's face softened into a smile. It was an amazing transformation... his face and eyes were expressive—pure. In the span of a single tick of the clock, he was transformed from cold fury to warm compassion with no hint of pretense at either extreme.

"Why did you kill them?" Ping asked between waves of pain from knee and chest.

The newcomer's eyes flicked to the corpses by the door and back. "They didn't take my cooking seriously."

"No," Ping paused as the last bit of numbness left his broken knee and he almost passed out from the pain. "Why did you kill Roy and Lutine?"

The newcomer looked troubled, hurt, then angry again... uh oh, this was it! Ping reflexively brought up an arm to ward off what would come next.

But it didn't come.

"I didn't." The newcomer said, voice thick. "I was too late."

Ping lowered his arm and again regarded the newcomer. The shark's face was desolate, but just when Ping was convinced he would break down into tears, his face hardened again. "But I think we're about to find out who did, and why." His damp eyes shifted to a point behind Ping.

"Excuse me." He said politely, stepping over Ping, toward Good Cop.

"No problem." Ping got out before the world gave a final shiver and went black.

Getting farther from the light, Ping heard Rae shout from far away. "Roy! You're alive! I knew it!"

"Nope." Came the reply from almost as far away. "My brother's dead."

Garvey moaned, a weak and utterly hopeless sound. He'd also heard the accusation in the newcomer's voice.

* * *

The pain was intense. There was no sheltering fog of shock, no refuge of unconsciousness to separate Anne from the screaming of her flesh. Her head hurt from the fist she'd taken, but by far the worst pain was from her arms and hands. The Harm seemed to be grinding them to giblets. She'd been trying to scream for what seemed like an eternity of pugilistic hell, but her voice was just starting to catch on.

She saw a few stars, but not much else. Her eyes were still squeezed shut. A part of her wanted this guy to kill her and get it over with. But beneath the familiar fatalism was something unfamiliar, something new—her will. Through the pain, behind the closed eyes, under battered flesh, something kept her pushing forward, struggling into the storm. Wyler was somewhere on the floor just behind her and this Harm was not going to get another crack at him.

She remembered what death felt like before: the fallen man tearing into her, the near-death convulsions of that night, the sinking paralysis of the next day. She remembered those helpless times at what she'd thought was the end of her wasted life. She didn't remember much of the physical pain, or really any of the fear of death. What she remembered clearly was burning remorse for a life unopened; its gift still sitting beneath the evergreen and ornaments, its brightly colored wrapping paper still intact.

She remembered the pain of looking back over a life so utterly wasted, squandered on fear and self-pity, its wonders and failures unexplored. She'd spent her days clinging to the fence between life and death, afraid of both.

She still stood between life and death, but now she was different. With life cowering behind her and death's ruthless henchman before her, she had finally picked a side in the struggle. Sure, her old God Fear was lurking in the corners of her mind, yammering. But now the sound of his voice evoked only a hot fury. If somehow she lived through this, after the reconstructive surgery and months of physical therapy, she was going to track the Fear God down and beat him with her crutches until he begged for mercy.

Pain exploded up from her right elbow again and she heard and felt the crunch of breaking bone. Her eyes popped open from the shock, and she saw feet flying by... she didn't remember going down, but wasn't all that surprised. At least not until she realized she was still standing and the Harm's feet were upside down before her and flying from right to left. Pain and another sickening crunch came from her left knee and the flying feet changed trajectory, swinging loosely toward her as the Harm's upper body whirled away from the impact with her knee.

Clarity. The world almost stopped under the weight of Anne's epiphany. The Harm was clearly dead, its little evil plans unexplored. Its arms and legs swung without volition as it spun away from the beast that had killed it—the beast that was now looking in disbelief at her own bloody hands and wondering how she could live with this.

"We see you! *See! You!*" The dry leaves voice hissed from the air around her, but it was blowing away now, fading into whispers and crinkling, then gone.

Her eyes went to the other Harm. She was still strapped into the gurney where Anne had drawn her blood. The restraints had held, but she had not. Her rigid body was contorted in death, the horrible rictus frozen on her darkening face, blood flowed from her eyes and nose.

Murderer. The word bloomed in her mind, driving all other thoughts aside. She could feel the weight of the big, confusing universe pressing in on her, could feel a patented Anne Kelley anxiety attack looming. The room was silent. All eyes were on her, mouths gaped, pressure mounted.

But then she was saved. Wyler groaned. His face was still slack, but his eyes were riveted on her and filled with at least three kinds of shock.

She bent quickly and picked him up. He felt like a feather. She put him on a gurney and applied a sterile pad from a nearby triage kit to his bleeding ear. He didn't flinch. Time for bedside manner...

"This probably feels worse than it actually is." She said conversationally. "Why, I heard of a man in Seattle who had his whole head bit off and he's fine now."

"Wpfr." Wyler said.

"You're going to be okay. The stun you took should wear off in a few minutes."

"Wmph." He gave what might have been a twitch or a nod.

"See?" she said, giving him what she hoped was an encouraging smile, "you're already starting to bounce back."

Using some adhesive film, she anchored the sterile pad to Wyler's damaged ear and started to move on to the next victim, but she felt a weak hand on her wrist. She looked back and saw that Wyler had grabbed her. "Wow." he said finally, lips pulling into a warm smile, his eyes damp with thanks and relief, "Wow!"

She smiled and blushed. He released her wrist and she placed his arm back on the gurney. His smile broadened, her blush deepened until finally she turned away. As she moved on to the fallen EMT, she keyed the emergency code on her collapsed tablet. She assumed someone else had already done the same, but it never hurt to be sure.

"...no way! Supergirl's thinner... and blonde." a young girl's voice came from outside Anne's field of vision. She turned and saw a boy and girl of about six years old, clutched in their frightened mother's arms. The mother stared at Anne with a sort of bemused horror along with everyone else, but the boy replied. "Well, she's not Spiderman, that's a boy!"

"Maybe it's the Incrangible Hulk?" The girl offered reasonably, but the boy made a few clicks on his tablet and presented it to the girl. "Nope, green. See?" He said decisively. Mom made no moves, thought no thoughts.

"Maybe she's a new one?" The girl said, turning to look at Anne again.

"A new one." the boy said, awe in his voice. They both stared and nodded.

"Hmm," Anne said, nodding, "a new one."

INSIGHT

Ping woke with a start and a massive headache. His dreams were getting weirder, that was for sure.

The room was unfamiliar. The lighting was indirect, coming from a recessed border where the walls and ceiling met. The ceiling was an odd cross between stucco and textured brown finger-painting. With a little effort, he pushed himself up on his elbows and looked around. The walls were a lustrous dark wood, unadorned by hangings. The lines of the furniture were efficient. The overall look was that of well-funded eccentricity.

His chest hurt, or more accurately, stung. He now remembered ribs breaking as he was ground into the library archive ceiling by a sadistic wizard who might have worked for the FBI. No wonder his dreams were weirder now.

He fingered his ribs, but the pain wasn't as intense as it should have been if the bones were broken, or even cracked. It felt more like needles had been inserted into the bone, but it didn't hurt more or less as he moved or pressed on them. Maybe they hadn't broken after all? Maybe he'd been sleeping for six weeks. He swung his feet off the edge of the bed. More aches, but none as serious as he expected. The worst was his right knee, which had the same localized sting as his ribs.

Someone had undressed him, which made him just a bit uncomfortable. At least they hadn't robbed him of his underwear. It was times like this he was glad he was in top shape... and didn't prefer furry leather Daffy Duck lingerie. It was one thing to be stripped naked by strangers while unconscious, but quite another to think of them poking his belly or laughing at his most private fashion sense. At least his vanity hadn't been irreparably harmed by Good Cop's little tantrum.

His shoes were by the nightstand at the side of the bed, along with the rest of his possessions. Warped pistols, warped badge, Uni, warped tablet—warped ring of old metal keys. He picked up the keys, "You again." he said with a small shake of his head. He dropped the keys back onto the nightstand.

The remnants of his clothes were neatly folded on the floor by his shoes. The scuffs and bloodstains on his shoes took a back seat to the wholesale destruction of his suit. The shirt, jacket, and pants had been slashed into several large pieces with a very sharp instrument. It was as if some capricious adolescent had hacked them in pieces and then, snickering at his prank, folded them neatly for Ping to discover later.

He stood, stretched, and made for the closet. There he found a wealth of clothes. Most were black or earth toned. He selected a pair of dark baggy pants made of a tough organic fiber, a black T-shirt, and a dark brown loose-fitting jacket. The clothes were slightly big, but he wasn't swimming in them. Apparently, the owner was only slightly less runty than Ping, further proof that it was indeed a small world after all.

He returned to the bed and dressed. He slung the now-empty holsters under the jacket and tried the tablet—useless. He filled his holsters with the pistol-paperweights and useless tablet. His badge and Uni went into pockets in his pants and jacket.

At the door, he paused. He put a hand on it and eased his ear against the rich wood. From the other side he heard the distinctive sound of absolutely nothing. He felt the same giddy optimism he'd felt as he had approached the library. Of course, he thought, that had worked out well. But his was not an optimism to be ruled by the memory of bad experiences or any other form of wisdom.

This was Wonderland. Though it was a dangerous and completely daft world he had blundered into, he found comfort in its distractions. He didn't fear the death that seemed to hover around every corner—harsh experience had taught him that death was unavoidable even back in the real world. Here, bereft of familiar surroundings and comfortable routines, his mind was occupied with mystery, with the riddle of survival. He felt that in stepping through the looking glass he had left some of the worst parts of himself behind. He felt free. Of course this, like most feelings, was utter nonsense.

He shrugged and opened the door.

Across the hallway, he saw his reflection in a waist-to-ceiling mirror. He looked ragged. The well-worn clothes didn't detract from his trauma-survivor look, but his eyes still had the same sparkle, his lips were in the half twist of implied mirth that he preferred to wear. Life was a cruel joke, but he was good at laughing.

He stepped into the hallway and looked around. To his left, the hallway ended in a door about four meters down. To his right were a few doors on either side of a longer hallway that ended in an open archway into a larger room.

Ping turned right and headed toward the archway. As he approached, he heard snatches of conversation. There were definitely more than two speakers, but none sounded familiar until he was almost to the archway.

"...saying Deckard was a Replicant? I didn't get that at all." Rae said.

A slightly familiar voice replied, "That was the point of the 'Too bad she won't live, *but then again, who does?*" line.

"Then there's the origami unicorn… like his dream." Alex said.

Ping rounded the corner. He knew what they were talking about. "I hope this isn't a private film festival."

The three looked up from their positions on a pair of couches before a large wall-screen frozen on the *Blade Runner* credits, not the dorky cloudscape of the original ending, but the dark background of the director's cut. In the corner of the screen was a bright green PAUSE.

The bristly-haired guy with the shark-gun look studied Ping for a moment. He glanced sideways to Alex, who sat on the other couch with Rae.

"Have a seat, Detective." Rae said, "We thought you'd never wake up."

"How long have I been out?" Ping said, moving toward an empty chair. "And where exactly are we? ... and who took my clothes off? ...that just makes me feel creepy."

The shark raised his hand, smiling. "I'm used to making people feel creepy."

"Figures... that was my favorite suit."

"Sorry 'bout the alterations," Alex said, "but I had to do some work on you."

Ping gave him a dubious look, thoughts returning to keys.

Alex elaborated, "Four broken ribs, shattered patella in your right knee—man, that was messy, the kneecap was in three pieces and a lot of splinters—hairline fracture of your left tibia, right radius... bit of internal bleeding."

"Don't forget the pre-arthritic spurs on three of his knuckles." Rae said.

Alex shrugged with mock arrogance, "Well, as long as I was in there..." He stretched his arms, cracked his knuckles. "Hey, by the way, did you know you've got a lot of healed microfractures in your hands, arms and lower legs?"

"Our detective is a pugilist, Mr. Ahmed." The Unnamed said.

"Actually, I'm a Capricorn." Ping replied with a shrug.

The Unnamed spoke again. "You're lucky that Alex isn't as bad with the Loom as he thinks."

"I'm lucky you forgot your recipe." Ping ran his hand through his hair. "A loom? You're saying he wove me a bandage or a potholder or something?"

"Not *a* loom—*The* Loom." Alex said as if that should mean something to Ping.

"*The* Loom." Ping gave a knowing nod constructed from the fabric of sarcasm.

Rae spoke. "As to when and where you are, it's been about thirty hours since the library. We're at Roy's house on Lake Geneva."

Ping stared down at his clothes, feeling creepy again.

Guessing his thoughts, the shark spoke again, "Don't worry Detective, you are welcome to them... he'd have given them to you if he still could."

"So what is 'The Loom'?" Ping asked.

Alex got melodramatic: "No one can be... *told* what the Matrix is..." his eyes darted about, looking for laughs and knowing winks, presumably. What he got was a grin from the shark and blank stares from Ping and Rae.

Frustrated at being the only one inside his inside joke, he continued. "It's like what you keep calling my pot of gold... the engine of 'magic', but it's just a tool like pliers or a quantum microscope. Well, not really a tool so much as a key abstraction that allows your mind to work with otherwise incomprehensible forces..."

"Thanks for clearing that up." Ping interrupted.

Rae nodded, "Yep, that was pretty bad, babe." She turned to Ping, "You should see him trying to tutor history... I'm telling you, there's no way Lutine hired him for his teaching skills." She gave Alex's knee a squeeze and finished. "Now, you know I love you, but you couldn't explain dinnertime."

"It's the time when dinner is eaten." Alex muttered, looking a bit self-conscious.

Rae turned to Ping, "It's his pot of gold."

"Gotcha." Ping nodded.

The shark smiled, his eyes darting back and forth between the speakers, his face a window into almost childlike amusement. At times like this it was almost possible to forget the blood and shattering blades as five knife-wielding killers met their end in less than two seconds. It was almost possible to forget the look on his face as he stepped toward poor, evil Good Cop. Almost.

The shark's clear eyes settled on Ping. The amusement didn't depart, but his gaze seemed to focus—to bore into him in an offhand way. It took only an instant for Ping to shift from examining the shark, to feeling like a frog on a high school lab table.

Ping blinked. "I didn't get your name, mister...?

"Call me Dek."

Another connection. "Of course. Do all of the... whatever you guys are... get their handles from *Blade Runner*?"

"Nope, just Roy and me. It was our game. Even Ivo's other children thought we were a bit daft. You know the movie?"

Ping nodded, "So there are other...?"

"Replicants?" Dek nodded. "Most in the trade call us 'Torpedoes', but Ivo never called us anything like that. He thought of us as his children"

"You're saying that you and Roy are brothers? Android brothers?" Ping asked with much less irony than he'd intended. All eyes turned to Dek.

There was a pause as Dek considered, then finally, "There are a lot of labels that could describe us. I think 'Lost boys' is a lot more accurate, but you have to give Roy some latitude in the naming... he really loved that movie." Dek's lips twisted into a bitter smile. "We could both identify with being apart from humanity, different, disconnected."

"So, you're saying that Lutine was like Tinkerbelle Tyrell," Ping said, "All fairy dust and genetic engineering?"

"Well, that's not incredibly inaccurate. Before he found us, we were both orphans, completely alone, quite unwanted. He definitely changed us, but I don't understand the Loom well enough to say how much genetic engineering went on, if any."

He paused, so Ping asked, "So Lutine adopted you both?"

"Nope. He sort of collected Roy. You've got to understand that back then if an orphan with birth defects just disappeared, anyone who noticed would be mostly relieved."

"Back when?" Ping asked.

"1676 for Roy—in St. Petersburg." There was a moment of silence for temporal improbability.

"Peter Sieberg?" Ping grinned, remembering Roy's alias, "I can see why he wanted to pick his own name."

Dek's eyes sparkled with pleasant memory. "When I was a kid, Ivo used to call him Peter, I think it was his real name. If he had a last name, Roy couldn't remember it."

"You said birth defects." Rae said.

"Trisomy 21. Down's Syndrome. Roy and me both."

There was a subtle mental disorientation as understanding settled on the three of them. "What did he *do* to you?" Rae asked.

"Gave us balance. Clarified our minds, reworked our bodies—aligned us with the Loom. I can feel it you know, sizzling always around and through my thoughts. I can't use it consciously like Alex or Ivo, but it's always there, burning."

Ping fell silent, thinking. The conversational disjunction seemed to be shared by Rae and Alex, who were lost in their own thoughts.

At last, Dek broke the silence. "Ivo made me in 1989. He plucked me out of an orphanage for kids with disabilities after my parents died in a car crash. He made me for another Savant named Issak Kaspari."

"Kaspari?" Alex recognized the name.

"Who's Kaspari?" Ping asked.

"He's one of Ivo's friends. Major Savant from the east coast. I've met him twice, when he came to see Ivo. Very… self-contained guy. During both meetings, I think he said a total of six words. The last time was just a few days ago."

Dek nodded, "That's why I'm in town. My father got an urgent call from Ivo a few days back. The next thing I know, we're rushing to Chicago. Then Ivo and Roy…" he trailed off, face hardening.

"Father?" Ping asked.

"Sounds better than 'Master', doesn't it?" Dek gave a wry smile that quickly warmed, "...also more accurate. Issak has always been good to me. He raised me since I was about eight. He and Ivo are my fathers, Roy was my brother."

"What was the emergency?"

"No idea. Issak was very closed about it... even more than usual. But I could tell he was really bothered, maybe even scared... which says a lot."

"Why?"

"Because Savants, especially the old ones like Ivo and Issak, don't scare easy."

"Do I want to know how old they are?"

"Don't we all? I know that Issak was pretty definite that there had never been a King Arthur, but that's about it."

Ping sat back, too many questions. His mind felt numb with the implications, too many to map out, to understand. "I need to check in at the station..."

"I don't think that's a good idea." Alex said quickly. Both he and Rae were shaking their heads.

"Remember the library." Alex said. "If anyone finds out where we are, it's all over... those guys have eyes and ears everywhere."

"Who? Who has eyes and ears everywhere?"

"Our friends from the library." Dek said.

Ping had an unbidden vision of the five knife-wielding killers' last moments. Eyes and ears and lots of blood everywhere. He winced "And just who are 'they'?"

Alex and Rae exchanged glances, then looked to Dek for help.

"We don't know." The shark said at last. "It's not like the clans brand themselves with easily recognizable tattoos."

"Did Good Cop provide any enlightenment?" Ping said.

"He did a lot of screaming..." Rae trailed off, her expression darkening with memory.

Dek looked uncomfortable, angry—then finally sorrowful, "He was not cooperative, and far too dangerous to leave alive."

Ping had an irrational flash of pity for the sadistic Fed—it must have been terrible for him. Terrible that he didn't get to finish squashing him and Rae before torturing Alex to death. And now his 'nefarious plan' would go forever unexplained. He'd have to lay a wreath at Mussolini's tomb for Agent Garvey someday.

With a mental shrug, he moved on. "So, do we have any idea why 'they' killed Lutine?"

There was a pause. All heads shook.

"How did you get to the crime scene under the bridge so quickly? I'm assuming it was you the officers took a shot at." Ping asked Dek.

He nodded. "I was talking to Roy when it happened."

TEARS IN RAIN

Dr. Ivo Lutine sits in the near quiet of the car. It's only near quiet because Roy is chattering excitedly. Kaspari doesn't come to Chicago often enough, so Roy's got a channel open with his brother, trying to make some free time together work.

Ivo had asked Roy to damp the car so he could have some silence in the back seat, but that's not part of Roy's plans. He'd engaged the noise damper, obedient little guy, but dialed it down so that Ivo can still make out the conversation.

In spite of the weighty matters that need to occupy his mind, Ivo smiles as he listens to his son work. Nearly every sentence in his conversation with his brother contains some manipulation, subtle and not, aimed at Ivo. Because Ivo loves him, because there's clearly some time this evening, because they never get to Chicago anymore, because family is important, and Roy doesn't need sleep and they've fought plenty of demons before and Ivo is just being paranoid... perhaps his brother could meet them at their hotel, yeah he'd try to float that by Ivo later... of course Ivo would be reasonable enough to allow that... on and on.

"Roy, perhaps the damper isn't fully engaged." Ivo shouts into the noise-canceling field between him and the front seat. Roy pretends not to hear, though they both know that he could hear even if the field was at maximum and Ivo whispered. "Roy!"

"You say something dad?" Roy's shout comes through the damper at the level of a quiet conversation. After a few more seconds with his hand cupped dramatically at his ear, Roy switches off the damper and repeats, "You say something?"

"I asked if perhaps the damper isn't at full power."

"I just turned it off so I could hear you."

Exasperating. For what seems like the twelfth time today, Ivo tries to marshal enough energy to get angry with his son. No use. He ends up laughing. "All right, if Issak is crazy enough to let him go, you guys can hang out at my house tonight."

"You hear that? Movie night!"

Oh no, not *that* again. "Maybe you should go to Issak's penthouse?"

Those two and a movie could mean only one thing. Ivo would end up stuck between his sons, watching Roy Batty crush the head of his creator, a mad genetic engineer type named Tyrell. During the uncomfortably long scene, his two sons would steal partially concealed glances at him and each other, it would be a big menace-off, replete with sneers and winking until one, then both of them started laughing like the loveable buffoons they were.

The things we do for love.

"No *Blade Runner!*" Ivo decrees, gesturing emphatically.

"You hear that, Bro'? Dad says it's *Blade Runner* night!" Roy laughs, steering the car left and reaching for the damper, mission accomplished.

The end of the world—you'd think it would crowd everything else out of his mind, yet here he sits, mind lingering on his wonderful, frustrating sons. Ok, he's glad they could spend some time together tonight. Together, they will save the world somehow, but Ivo is only concerned with saving it for them. What's a world for without those you love?

Ivo uses the remote to kick up the music in the back seat—just in case Roy's got any more plans. The Ganja rock resumes with an unfamiliar and jarring crash. Glass and some type of dark powder fill the air. There is an instant of Disneyland-abstract uncertainty, followed by the steely reassertion of his disciplined mind. He dives sideways toward the floor. He also dives inward and feels the lightning filigree of the Loom stretch up from the Underworld, branch out through his clothes, and out into the Overworld.

The two-shot salvo has left gossamer ripples of power in its wake. The Shield that should have protected them was dissolved by the chaos the bullets carried. Cracks extend from the bullets down through the Underworld, through the Loom. No Cast could have stopped them. Ivo recognizes this chaos, knows things are about to get much worse.

Tracing the bullet trails back, he finds that a round has missed his head by less than three centimeters. There's something else that he knows, something he can't think about because now is the time for action, not for...

He moves his Vision away from the slowly rolling car, back along the path of the bullets until... *there!* In a tuft of Otu on the side of the hill next to the road are two shooters with military sniper rifles. Not for long.

The two fly through the air, their rifles wrapping around their necks, not too tight though—he wants them to feel what comes next. Up three meters then down as hard as Ivo can will. The bodies yield far more than the pavement, which craters under the impact.

There are three groups of four each moving in from different directions. No flesh puppets yet, but they'd be coming soon. Shells tear into the roof from above, but they never make it through the cloth on the inside of the car. They ricochet away from Ivo's hastily constructed Shield. There is a larger, two-part impact on the roof as two assailants drop from the bridge above. The fabric of the Shield sizzles and parts as a Forged blade slices through the roof. Ivo quickly compensates and redirects the Shield's power flow before the Cast can unravel.

That's not powder, Ivo realizes as the deep red aerosol begins to settle wetly on his face and clothes. Don't think, don't think. Act. It's not too late. He's used the Loom to mend many serious injuries in the past, and his heart is singing with a desperate love. The Loom's power seems to swell and crystallize around him—clearer, more pure in response to the purity of his need to help his wounded son.

The roof explodes away from the car under currents of power welling through Ivo's darkening mind. Though the blade-wielders are quick enough to leap out of the way,

Ivo holds them in place until the roof of the car reaches the bottom of the bridge. They join with the bottom of the bridge above him in a continuum of fusing blood, bone and metal. There is a low groan from the superstructure. Dust falls from the length of the bridge.

The disturbance in the currents of the Underworld gives Ivo enough warning to divert the onslaught of the first Savant. Ivo recognizes her weave-work. Her craft is the sloppy work they teach in Asado. Her Casts are as elegant and subtle as a stone axe.

Before he can counterattack, he has to draw the machine pistol a few degrees to the right. The man holding the weapon, if you can call him that, stands perhaps three meters away. His twisted face seems to be made of black, oily leather. Black, oily leather now shifting from fierce to frightened, touching surprise lightly on the journey. He perhaps senses what's next.

Ivo pushes outward and down, grinding, grating the low-order demon across the pavement. Before the end of the first meter, he's leaving a dark wet mark. At about meter five the scream terminates, the chipped bones stop at ten meters.

The Savant's next assault is already in progress. Time compresses, the speed of the Loom begins to depart as she attempts to force Ivo back into the Overworld. Ivo bores into her Cast and travels back toward her, hidden in the outward flow of her power. He arrives at her interface to the Loom. Unnoticed, he inserts a graft of his own weaving into the template she is activating.

With an interrupted scream, she explodes outward, splattering the creatures around her. Startled by the unexpected shower, they scatter. An instant later, they scatter again, bisected by lines of force wielded by their intended target.

Strengthening the weave of Vision, he pushes his perception outward, looking for what he knows must come. There! At the edges of his Vision, the disturbances in the flow of the Underworld's power indicate about fifteen of the puppets converging on him. He can't see them because of the interference they cause, but he knows what he would see all too well. Fifteen this time. Their master is getting stronger.

The shells tear into the concrete wall behind him, his blood seems to rush inward, collecting in his abdomen. When he looks down, he sees the hole. Shock has been all used up, so all Ivo is left with is a hole in the stomach. No emotional implications, no feelings of fear, outrage, or violated frustration. Hope keeps him moving. It's not too late.

The shooter ends in a pile at the base of the wall on the other side of the underpass, a spent dot under the red dripping exclamation point of his demise.

The blood stops flowing onto Ivo's shirt. No time to fix the damage, but maybe a little direct pressure will buy him enough time to get Roy out of here before...

No.

His eyes move to the front seat; the dam bursts—no father should outlive his son.

There amid the blood and shattered bone lie the remains of his bright boy's stolen potential.

His hand still grips the twisted steering wheel now embedded in the safety glass of the windshield. He must have ripped it off in a spasm as he died; his strength, speed, lightning mind, sense of humor, hellish persistence—all useless now.

Ivo slips back into the Overworld, lost in a tornado of what might be grief or guilt. Blood again flows from the ragged hole in his gut. He doesn't care. He is thinking of the small hand on his face as he worked the light into Roy's mind so long ago, the trusting smile that is no longer attached to that hand.

He doesn't have the few minutes it would take for him to care about the world again. He has the heart to fight for family, for survival, but not revenge. Before he can again care about the black wave that he knows is washing over the world—long before he reacquires the desire to fight, or even survive, the army of the Outsider is upon him.

* * *

Dek is downtown at Ivo's lab when Roy's side of the conversation ends in gunfire and the clock starts. Five seconds to broaden the communication link, and access Roy's tablet. Two more seconds to use its GPS client to determine Roy's location.

Dek doesn't stop to call Issak, who has stepped out of the room for a few moments. He doesn't stop to get a car, doesn't think to button up his shirt or grab his coat. He hops off the examination table, grabs his sword and goes straight out the seventh floor window. He lands in a shower of broken glass on the elevated train track that straddles the street below. Fifteen seconds.

He drops to the ground and sprints from street to street, sometimes from car to car, leaving a wake of agitated late night partygoers, irate cabbies, and damaged property. At five minutes and about eight kilometers, the sword comes out, it's ringing lost in the rush of the air he speeds through. Despair fills his eyes long before he arrives at the bridge, long before his tears are proved necessary.

Like always, he feels the Savant's work before he sees him. His heart fills with hope as he approaches the destruction. Of course they survived.

No. Not Ivo. He sees the Savant near the bridge, perhaps one third of the way into a cleanup operation. Though he's still two hundred meters out, Dek can tell by the stiffening of her stance that she has sensed his approach. There is work to be done, so his despair moves into the shadows as his work smile comes out to play.

He feels the Savant's Cast. It seems to coalesce around him, swooping in to inflict whatever havoc she's cooked up. His sword flashes through two arcs too quickly for even the Savant to see. The Cast explodes into background energy as Dek explodes through its remnants and into sword range. He needs answers, but he knows what's happened here on a visceral level. It is still efficiency that drives his movements, but it is rage that burns through him, threatening to leave him ashes. The Savant falls quickly and in several places; seconds later, the three grunts guarding the Savant share her fate.

Then, for a moment he is absolutely still, not breathing except to sample the air. He listens to the thousand small sounds of the night. He had felt this Savant like the tingle-chill of static electricity, but now he feels nothing and he knows. He knows now he is alone in every sense of the word.

Ivo's car is stopped against the wall beneath a highway. Its roof is missing, it is surrounded by destruction like only Savants can cause. Ivo lived through the initial assault. Perhaps they got away. But Dek *knows*. He doesn't know how or why… maybe the world just seems smaller now.

He scans the area, but sees no movement. He moves toward the car.

Dek creeps forward, needing but not wanting to see. As he nears the car, Roy's shoulder appears first. Even the irrational hope fades. Nothing comes to replace it—not grief, not rage… only emptiness.

"Like tears in rain." He hears himself say, placing his hand on his brother's. The hand is still knotted around the steering wheel. Dek slides his hand back along his brother's arm, coming to rest on his elbow, squeezing gently. He tries to say something, maybe 'goodbye', but only the first half of a whimper escapes his lips.

Emotion is still inaccessible for him, but a scream is tearing through his mind, so loud he can't hear it. Deaf, dumb, and feeling nothing, he moves to the back seat. He can't accept what he finds there. He stumbles around the car to the passenger side, feeling weak, dreaming. In his deafened mind, there is only the hollow sound of despair—wind through an empty mountain, reverberant with feeling.

Into his numbness, a single, small sound intrudes—the rush of the air around a falling object directly above him. In his grief, he waits perhaps fifteen milliseconds longer than he would normally, but he's got plenty of time.

Without looking up, his sword clashes three times with the blade of the man dropping from the bridge above. From the speed, accuracy, and the way the attacking blade was redirected multiple times during each strike, Dek knows he faces another Torpedo.

Behind him, the Torpedo lands lightly and attacks five more times. Dek parries based only on the sound of the blade and the feel of it through his own blade when they meet. The still unseen torpedo takes a few steps back, and shouts "You killed my master!" with great passion and clear frustration.

Dek waits a few more seconds, still staring into the back seat of Ivo's car, but no further attacks come. "Master eh?" Dek says finally, still not looking up. "What are you, a dog?"

With a fierce shout, the unseen torpedo attacks again and again, quicker than any human could have seen, but Dek parries every blow, though this time he had to turn half away from the car to do it.

When the attack, and the frustrated screaming after it stops, Dek again speaks slowly. "So, I killed your master, did I?" He finally releases his last look at Ivo, turning his head slowly to face his assailant, pausing briefly to assess him. To Dek, he looks like a B-movie martial artist— stylish, baggy clothes, hard face, trendily cut blonde hair that was highlighted at some upscale salon. His flashily-crafted sword is actually glowing with a cold blue fire… amateur. "Is that supposed to make us even?"

The Torpedo shifts his stance slightly, adjusts the position of his blade to look more aggressive, but he says nothing.

"Except it doesn't." Dek says, fury clipping the words. His face ticks and his body shakes with the inner pressure, but the only overt show Dek allows is the wicked smile crossing his face, "Sure, I killed your master, but you killed my Father—and there isn't enough blood in the world for a down payment on that."

Dek's sword rises between them, his intentions clear in his hard stare. "Well, you take what you can get, I guess."

The Torpedo understands at last what he should have been expecting since his ill-conceived attack began. He takes another step back, but it isn't far enough, not by an interstellar distance. Dek's blade tears through him four times before he pauses to destroy the Torpedo's blade with a massive blow. The sword Issak made for him so long ago cuts straight and true, severing the other man's blade at the base. Dek flicks his wrist and the backstroke removes the other man's head.

Not enough blood in the universe, Dek's hot, shivering mind compresses around the thought. His scream tears out into the night, again and again, until he has no more breath and is again empty. He stumbles backward until he is stopped by the overpass wall. He leans against it, then slides down until he is sitting with the wall at his back. His sword lies impotent on the ground at his side. He feels nothing; time passes. The world around him begins to flicker.

Strobes of blue and red shift the shadows on the ground around him. He has no idea how long he has been sitting, but the police are here.

* * *

The confused child sits, suspended upside down, still strapped into his seat. His head hurts, but not as much as his broken leg. What did he do wrong? His eyes sting with sticky unfamiliar tears. The inside of the destroyed minivan is tinged red and blurry. His thick glasses are gone and his face is wet.

Below him, he sees one bent crutch lying on the roof. The roof is bent worse than the crutch. His parents are sleeping in the front, but though he screams, they don't wake. He hopes they aren't angry with him.

Clouds of dust and smoke blow through the air; wind makes a hollow monster sound as it blows through one broken window and out the other.

He doesn't have any more air for screaming, so he hangs alone in the dust with the wind monster all around him, gasping and fading.

What did he do wrong?

BETWEEN ROOMS

At times like these, Issak Kaspari liked to picture himself as a mad scientist, surrounded by arcane machinery. He wished he could put the final twiddle on knobs, make sure that electricity arced appropriately between scenic anode and mysterious cathode—perhaps throw a large rusty switch or two.

It had always bothered him that from the outside it looked like he was having a particularly boring yoga session. Inside though, between his ears, or down in the Underworld, his current weave shimmered on the Loom, putting even the most impressive Frankenstein soundstage to shame.

Here, in the deepest subbasement of his New York estate, the earth helped channel the energies he accumulated. The earth's darkness surrounded the firestorm of his work. If this worked, this would be a quantum leap for his craft. If it worked, he would be able to see the very fabric of the Loom, the fabric of all creation.

Boring yoga indeed.

He rechecked his rechecks, retuned his retuning.

* * *

Anne sat in the nurses' lounge under the watchful gaze of two uniformed officers and the accusing stare of her destroyed locker. The officers had asked Anne every question in the book twice, but no one had told her what she was supposed to *do* now.

She was afraid. More than fear though, she felt completely uncertain. No one had yet acted like they were going to imminently arrest her, so what? You just killed— *very* killed—someone, and then what? You go home? You go to prison? They give you a medal and an honorary police doughnut? You go to witness protection? If anyone knew, they weren't telling her.

She sat in a plastic chair, watching the officers pace around her, waiting in terror for one of them to ask her about the destroyed locker with the king-sized jacket in it—her name was even on the bent locker door leaning against the wall—but time dragged by and no one else seemed to notice.

The cops were polite, but she repeatedly caught them staring at her. This, she understood—she didn't know what to think of herself either. The Detectives had been in to interview her several times. She'd done a lot of crying, had said "I don't know" a lot, but she couldn't bring herself to mention the fallen… behickeyer. That would only be an invitation to more questions she couldn't answer, and perhaps increase her chances of ending up in a padded cell. She had mentioned the dry leaves voice, but had downplayed it when she realized that she was the only one who heard it. Maybe just someone panicking as the melee began… right.

Anne had no sooner managed to convince herself that she was done answering questions when the Feds arrived. The lounge door opened to reveal a man and woman, both in dark, well-cut suits. Both had the air of confidence and easy authority of the actors on her third-favorite show, *FBI Files*. This was definitely going down on her permanent record. She rested her face in her hands, wondering how much longer until someone brought out a desk lamp and the questioning started in earnest.

The woman, obviously the leader, waved the uniformed cops out of the room. She had an open, efficient-looking face that could be called pretty by the charitable. "Miss Kelley?"

Anne nodded.

"May I call you Bethany?" She asked, pulling up a chair.

"Call me Anne, I go by my middle name." She said without looking up.

The woman settled into the chair across from Anne while her partner leaned on the counter by the mini sink behind her. "I'm agent Hawthorne, this is agent Mendez." Mendez nodded, completing the introductions. "The officers downstairs told us some... interesting things." She raised an eyebrow, examining Anne.

Anne nodded, face still in her hands.

"I know this must be difficult for you. I'll try to be brief, but there are some questions I need to ask." She gave Anne a smile that was half support, half apology. Anne straightened in her chair, pulled her hair back, put her palms together with her index fingers to her lips, nodded again.

"Ok, first question: What was that downstairs?" Hawthorne exclaimed casually, shaking her head. "I mean, wow! I watched the surveillance logs... I've never seen anything remotely like that! I thought that doctor was a gonner, then pow! You blur across the room like Supergirl and backhoe a whole mound of karate on that Harm. You actually had him upside down in the air..." she paused, hands still gesticulating in the air, seemingly looking for words big enough to contain her wonder, "How?" she finally asked with a bemused smile and a small shake of her head.

"Spinach."

"Indeed," Hawthorne paused, examining Anne, "But we both know there's more."

Yep. Wasn't that the truth? Anne sat in uncertain silence.

"This wasn't the first strange thing that happened to you, is it?" Her gaze and her smile didn't waver.

"I just want to go home." Anne said, desperately trying to keep her eyes away from her destroyed locker.

"We'll get you there, Anne. But first you've got to come clean. First you've got to trust us."

"I trust you to throw me in a rubber room." Anne said, partially committing herself.

"You think we could? I never got high marks in hand-to-hand combat, and Mendez..." She spared her partner a glance over her shoulder, "I've seen him shoot... you've got nothing to worry about." Hawthorne said, voice dropping to a conspiratorial whisper.

Mendez shook his head sadly. "You put one hole in the shooting range roof and nobody forgets."

"See? We work for the Keystone division at the Bureau. I'm afraid we're only a danger to ourselves." She gave her head a resigned shake then looked at Anne with a small, steady smile.

If this was a ruse to get Anne to lower her guard, it was working. She was so weary that it would be a relief to set all deception aside, come all the way clean. Of course, talking doesn't always lighten your burden; this she'd learned when addressing the dry-leaves voice in the ER.

"How did you sleep the last couple of nights?" Hawthorne asked.

Wha? What did she know? There's no way she could know about her nights of a thousand near death experiences. Anne felt exposed and guilty, but stayed silent.

"They say you missed work yesterday."

"Ah!" Anne said in far too obvious relief. "Right! I was way sick."

"You seem… better." Mendez said. Something seemed to catch his attention and he pushed off the counter and approached the table where Anne and Hawthorne sat. He stopped short of the table, looking at something on the floor on the other side. Hawthorne turned to look at her partner, a small, confused smile on her lips.

"Someone's wasting food." he said.

"Wow." Hawthorne said in the 'why are you talking?' voice, "Really?"

Mendez bent down and after some rustling in the trashcan, stood back up with half a six-pack of Mega Slim Quick in his hands. "I love these things." he said.

For Anne, this was a far more terrifying moment than the attack of the demonic Harms in the ER. Her hands covered her burning face as she focused on not hyperventilating.

"You'll have to excuse my partner," Hawthorne said as her partner broke a Slim Quick shake from the six-pack and put it in the chiller on the counter. "He's a bit uncouth when it comes to free food." Her voice was friendly, but both Feds were now staring at the gargantuan coat in Anne's destroyed locker.

The chiller beeped and Mendez removed the frosty can. "Anyone want some? There's plenty to go around." he said, popping the can open.

Ignoring her partner, Hawthorne made a few taps on her tablet, extended it to full size, and slid it across the table beneath Anne's sheltered face. Anne held her breath and moved her fingers so she could see. On the largest open window was a picture of a horribly overweight woman, gone-swimming wet, with cuts on her face and hands, and a large gash on her knee. Blood covered the woman's clothes. She looked miserable and very scared. She also looked like she'd never had a date... was it that obvious?

Anne's heart sank. Caught. Anne was pretty sure they'd already nailed her for destruction of property and conspiracy to hide poor dietary choices, but what if they connected her to the body of the fallen man? Of course they'd think she'd killed him. They don't even give double homicide convicts dessert in prison... she was screwed.

After allowing enough time for Anne to confess to anything she desired, Hawthorne continued, "This wasn't your first fight, was it Anne?"

Revising her odds away from witness protection in favor of prison, Anne had no immediate comment. Her vision narrowed; she wondered if she was going to faint.

Realizing that Anne wasn't going to speak, Hawthorne dropped another bomb. "This is from the Eye on a beat officer at Union Station. You remember him? The strangest part doesn't show up without a little enhancement though..."

She used her tablet to zoom in, leaving only Anne's neck filling the window. There was the deep red hickey with small dark tendrils extending away from it under the skin. "What was that mark Anne? You don't have it now."

Anne's hand went to her neck. These guys were definitely not Keystone Cops. She felt empty, desolate, exposed— not unlike a sea cucumber after its big panic move.

"I think a Vampire made out with me." she said.

* * *

Dek stared at Ping earnestly. "I insist."

He was not taking 'no' for an answer. Of course, Ping didn't want him to. Still, he hesitated.

"The Samurai believed that the blade was the vessel of a warrior's soul. I don't give this lightly." Dek's face softened, "I expect you to honor his memory with its use."

Ping closed his hand around the hilt. He bowed his head in acceptance.

"It'll tear apart anything the Loom can build. Very handy for dealing with guys like our pal Garvey—if you're quick enough to use it."

His eyes shifted to the doorway leading deeper into the house. "Take care of them." Somewhere in there, Alex and Rae were still sleeping. "They're like adopted second cousins once removed, but they're about all that's left of my family." His tone belied tears, but after an instant, his smile returned. "We'll all probably be dead by tomorrow anyway." He gave Ping a too-hard smack on the shoulder and walked out the door into the dim evening sunlight. Charming.

Descending the steps, Dek paused; he looked back over his shoulder. "Whether I find Issak or not, tell Alex to start looking for me in a few days. Remember, the locator won't work if I'm dead." He smiled brightly. "Oh yeah, look under Roy's bed. 2-0-1-9-pound. Got that?"

"Got what?" Ping said, but Dek was gone.

* * *

Issak Kaspari floated in cold blackness. Was he dead? He hoped not, because this sucked. Then an explosion: blinding light and intense pain that drove him inward. The strobe ended, and he cringed again in the darkness. This better not be death.

Though he tried to steel himself, the next burst caught him by surprise, left his shredded nerves echoing with the experience. The next several bursts of light came faster, each following the last with increasing frequency until he was in a shimmering brightness, then a steady white light.

As the light became the norm, he began to acclimate. By the time the light was flickering, he could think again, by the time the darkness had completely departed, he could think in polysyllabic words.

Alone in an unbroken field of light, Issak began to remember. Had it worked? Could he get back? This better not be death… if so, there were billions of the devout who were in for the Big Letdown.

Not dead. The Loom was still accessible here, though it was more like remote control. He felt the immense power of the cast that had driven him here. He was at the tip of the spear that he had thrust outside the known universe, down through the Underworld, and into… what?

His thoughts were disrupted by a dry voice that seemed to come from everywhere. "Bix osu, bin shuga prada."

At first they were just sounds—deep, resonant sounds. But then he realized this was the old language. "Little alone creature, I need I play" was his best guess at translation. The old language—the implications were staggering.

"Who are you?" Issak thought he asked. Though upon further reflection it was more likely that he'd asked 'what were those'. He needed to clear his head. It had been centuries since he'd used this tongue, and then only to keep Roy in the dark about the birthday party he and Ivo were planning.

"You speak. Think you? Power you have?" The voice crashed over him like a ping-pong avalanche. Issak was pretty sure his translation was getting better.

"I'm a traveler." Issak might have said. No, he'd just said 'I wiggle'. Close enough.

"I am Outsider." The thing said over about five seconds, seeming to relish most of the syllables, holding them on its tongue until they were fully spent. "Your power is no salvation." It purred like a building-sized panther on quite a lot of Valium. Was it louder? Closer?

Issak didn't like the sound of that. Pressure built around him. It increased as if he were sinking into deep water. Something was pressing in on him. The pressure became pain.

"I come in peace. I come seeking knowledge. Where is this place?" Issak hoped this was a misunderstanding that could be resolved with a little diplomacy.

Dry laughter surrounded him, sinister and slow. "My exile has ended." The power in the words grated across Issak's soul, scraping across the surface, looking for purchase. This thing seemed to be pushing in on him from everywhere, trying to get inside.

"Where you are is me." The dry voice boomed. "Where I go is you. You are the door between the rooms." The words jittered through his flesh, stabbing inward like dull butter knives.

Nice. Time to go.

* * *

"Anne, if you don't let us in, we can't help you." Hawthorne's voice didn't hold a hint of frustration. She was good at this.

"The body you found on Franklin yesterday—I was there." No turning back now.

There was a moment of barely perceptible confusion in Hawthorne's eyes. "Please continue."

"I was coming home from work, when this man falls out of the sky in a shower of broken glass. First I thought he was dead, but then he's apologizing... grabbing me. Then there's this pain..." she realized she was touching her neck, "The kind without a bottom, you know?"

Hawthorne's face was intent but unreadable.

"I lose consciousness, and when I come to, he's really dead. That's why I look like I do in the picture... cuts from the glass on the ground, his blood all over me. And the nuclear hickey."

There was a pause, so Anne continued, "Vampire, right?" Her forced laugh seemed well... forced.

Mendez was shaking his head. The good-joke smile caught on his face was held back only by a force of will from blossoming into the full belly laugh he was feeling.

Hawthorne remained unreadable. "You're... serious," she said, trying to decide.

"Who was he?"

"Who?"

"The fallen man. The guy you guys found on the street."

The agent prodded her tablet several times, examined, prodded some more. Finally she looked up. "Anne, we didn't find any crushed body on Franklin... or anywhere else."

"Broken glass? Destroyed car? Any window washers report a missing window?"

More tapping with her stylus, then "No."

Maybe she needed the rubber room after all. "But there *are* two dead Harms and lots of destruction downstairs, right?"

More clicking, then a look of surprise. "No."

Mendez's amusement subsided, replaced by concern. He pushed away from the counter and approached Hawthorne from behind. He leaned over her shoulder, trying to verify her results, Slim Quick shake still in his hand.

"All electronic records... camera logs, police reports... they can't all be gone," she said, clearly confused. "Even my preliminary notes are missing."

"No. There's no way..." Mendez started.

There was a loud crash as the door burst open and slammed against the wall. Three men in suits burst in, guns drawn.

* * *

Ping opened the door and crossed back into the bedroom. The bed was still rumpled, his clothes still in pieces by the nightstand. It was the same yet different. Now this place held a quiet significance, the peace of the tomb of the revered dead. Now it was a piece of a larger monument to a fallen giant. If you believed Dek, and Ping did, then this room's last occupant had been born before Ping's great great grandparents... and had lived until two days ago. Now the dead giant's sword rested in Ping's jacket pocket.

It seemed somehow quieter, though he was sure it had been perfectly quiet before.

Ping approached the bed. He knelt and looked beneath. Like a hotel bed, the frame went from the bottom of the mattress directly to the floor, not allowing anything to be slid beneath. He rose and followed the edge of the bed around to the other side. There he knelt again. This time he was rewarded by a recessed handle and a keypad built into the base of the bed.

He entered the code Dek had given him and was rewarded by a lock accept tone. There was a muted thunk as a fairly substantial lock disengaged. Ping pulled the handle.

A meter-wide drawer slid out. The top was clear armor glass. Through the glass, Ping could make out several boxes, and formed receptacles for four weapons. Three of the receptacles were filled.

The empty space was obviously for the collapsed sword in Ping's pocket. There were two pistols and a compact fletcher. He lifted the glass and reached for the pistols. Light, functional—not the same make as his ruined pistols, but they would do. He found four fifty-round magazines of two-millimeter ammunition. He slid one into each pistol, and spent a few moments transferring the weapons' locks to his lock rings. He heard the ready-tone, then stowed the pistols in his holsters. He left his warped guns in the drawer. The extra clips went in his jacket pockets.

Next, he examined the fletcher. The weapon was perhaps half a meter long with a pistol grip in back and another collapsible handle under the barrel. It fired 10mm shells containing twenty-five 1mm fletchettes. There was a thumb switch on the pistol grip near the trigger that selected the firing dispersion. At low dispersion, they would hit within a 10cm diameter at five meters, at high dispersion, they would hit within a one-meter diameter at the same range.

He found a two-shoulder harness for the weapon. He mounted one clip of ammo in the weapon, and put two more in the harness. He set the weapon and harness on the bed and examined the other contents of the drawer.

The first box was a miniature fireproof safe, which was odd because the drawer was itself a fireproof safe. He hesitated before opening it; he wasn't sure if Dek had intended him to grab the weapons and leave Roy's privacy otherwise intact. He weighed this concern against the chance that anything else here might help keep them alive.

The lid lifted to reveal memorabilia. Ping lifted a small pewter cross. It was crudely constructed... it looked old.

Ivo looks across the yard of the St. Petersburg Home of the Innocents. The wind cuts through his heavy wool cloak and the coat beneath. The smell of the city is held somewhat at bay by the frigid air. Around him, children in inadequate coats play. He will assuage his guilt by sending coats and blankets here later. What he intends will be divine or monstrous, but only time will tell.

He wouldn't need to be here if power didn't corrupt—if he weren't so desperate.

Apart from the others, one boy sits. His pudgy fingers toy with a small amulet of some kind. Curious, Ivo moves closer. His shadow falls across the boy of perhaps eight. He looks up with small, innocent eyes.

Monstrous, Ivo thinks, approximating a friendly smile, "What's your name, child?"

"ooooh!" the boy says, removing the cross, smiling with an intensity that seems to use every muscle in his round face. "Mmmmh!" His small hand stretches up. Ivo takes the crude pewter cross; stares into it for a moment.

The boy stares up at him: proud, smiling, cheeks red from the cold. Monstrous.

God help me, he thinks, smiling down at the boy now entirely enveloped in his shadow.

Ping fingered the broken metal where a loop once held the cross to a chain. Part of the loop remained, a half circle, terminating in two rough ends. Looking at the cross, he felt an inexplicable connection to the dead immortal.

He returned the cross to the box. There were several plastic rings that looked like gumball machine prizes, quite a few pictures, and a plastic-encased picture of a young man in aggressive looking clothes with confused-looking hair.

Ping picked up the picture. As he did so, he realized it wasn't just a picture. It was some kind of case, flat and about the size of his hand. After several gentle prods, the case opened to reveal a plastic disc clipped into the right side. In black letters across the refractive surface of the disk "Vanilla Ice" was written. Ping had no idea what this might imply. There was a short message handwritten in loose script on the inside of the cover:

> *Roy,*
> *For Pete's sake, please*
> *'drop this zero and get with the hero'*

—Happy birthday '99,
Dek
PS: No! Word to your freaking mother!
Clearly outside the joke, Ping closed the plastic case and
returned it to the box in the drawer.

Ivo is across the street with Kaspari, up in the thirtieth-
floor presidential suite of the hotel. They have concluded
the second day of some kind of Savant confab with six of
the other old ones. They'll probably be here for the rest
of the week, so Dek and Roy have slipped out to get food;
fuel for tonight's movie-fest. On the menu is the obligatory
'Blade Runner', but tonight they are leavening the experi-
ence with 'The Matrix' and 'Cool as Ice', a movie that al-
ways makes them laugh until they hurt. At least now Roy's
stopped shaving lines in his eyebrows and haircut—that
was hard to live with.

Dek endures Roy's Vanilla Ice fixation with calm determi-
nation. He's desperately hoping that this is a phase, and
not a long-time tradition. For now, he laughs a lot, both
with and at Roy. You'd think the centuries would make him
more outwardly mature, frumpy even. Not Roy. Dek hopes
he will take life as casually when he's Roy's age.

They enter the 24-hour convenience store and begin to
load up with bizarre snacks. They are perhaps fifty percent
loaded when a group of loud kids enter. They are big, ath-
letic types, larger and older than Dek. Dek thinks they are
probably in college, but he's not sure. It seems to Dek that
the kids are play-acting for each other. Each is trying to
outdo the others with their badness, or bravery, or stupid-
ity or whatever they call their willful rudeness. Behind the

counter, the clerk looks nervous. The air seems to thicken with the potential for violence.

Of course, at sixteen and full of power, Dek is feeling somewhat excited by this. He steps toward the rude college kids, intending to ask them to cool out... and just see where that leads him. He hasn't gone a step when he feels a firm hand on his shoulder.

"That wouldn't be fair, huh bro?" Roy is smiling down at him, love in his expression, as always. He's always the frustrating voice of reason. Except when it comes to music and eyebrow fashion.

"What?" Dek asks, knowing perfectly well that Roy has guessed his intentions. He smiles sheepishly when Roy's only answer is a knowing and persistent stare.

"Circus peanuts." Roy points. Why does he have such an intense love affair with the ridiculous?

"...the Retard." One of the loud kids finishes, looking right at Dek with his bad-boy grin.

Dek can't really say he's sensitive to the insult. You have to look hard now to see the telltales of his birth defects. Brightness, purpose, clarity... these are the substance of his life now. Still, he'd like to step forward... just to see where this could go.

"Dek..." Roy halts him with a look. After a few seconds of silence, he continues, "At times like these, I like to think... 'what would Vanilla Ice do?' It helps to guide me."

"He'd brandish a weapon and get sued!" Dek hisses in an exasperated whisper.

"Yep... and look how happy that made him." Roy said in his best Ward Cleaver voice. "See? Does the 'Nilla not hold the key to all true wisdom?"

"You are my Yoda." Dek shakes his head in defeat.

"Don't you forget it little bro!" Roy claps him on the back and steers him toward the circus peanuts.

They are insulted three more times before they leave the store loaded with snacks, feeling better than when they arrived.

It was one of the best movie nights yet.

Ping shuffled through pictures, letters, ticket stubs, post-cards from odd locales—the small keepsakes of four centuries of life. There was a black and white picture of a woman with big hair. On the lower right corner, someone had written in black ink: "You're just the cutest lil' guy, but take it easy on the java. Sweet dreams --Patsy Cline."

Ping knew Patsy: beautiful voice, impeccable timing. He was now only dimly aware of his initial purpose of looking for survival-related items. Now, he was lost in a quirky nostalgia for the life of this stranger.

He flipped through perhaps five more pictures, stopping finally on one of Roy, holding a little pudgy boy on his knee. The boy had the telltales of Downs Syndrome in his face, but it was his open-mouthed smile and the pleasure it implied that drew Ping's eye. They were both smiling, Roy was pointing to the camera and glancing down at the little angel on his lap. Then he realized that it was Dek on Roy's lap, and a sweet ache passed through him. Then the sweetness passed, leaving only sorrow in its wake. Dek had lost everyone. Everyone except his adopted father, Kaspari.

Of course, he might have lost Kaspari too. They would hopefully know soon... whenever Dek got back.

He had gone to find him, rescue him possibly.

"Good luck, my friend." Ping said softly, closing the safe.

* * *

After the initial jump, Hawthorne didn't move; she knew the intruders had the drop on them. Mendez, lacking somewhat her finesse, or perhaps having a more pessimistic view on the intruders' intentions, went for his gun. Immobile, fascinated, Anne watched. He was fast! In one fluid movement, he dropped his Mega Slim Quick shake and drew his gun. The gun left its holster and extended toward the men at the door; his finger was already squeezing the trigger when the half empty shake can hit the floor.

Not fast enough. The intruders clarified their intentions somewhat by drilling Mendez twice. Ironically, Mendez's shot went wild, striking the ceiling, but Anne didn't think the guys at the Bureau were going to tease him about it. The two high velocity needles put him down hard, coloring the wall behind him red.

Hawthorne kept her passive game plan intact, but there was now fear available for view in her eyes, if not in the set of her face. At this opportune moment, Anne's ex-deity, Fear, put in a final plea for her renewed oblations—half price paralysis, bonus regret.

Anne wasn't buying. She realized that she had a game plan too, or at least the new bee-juggling part of her did. She was moving. She came out of the chair, twisting away from the door, grabbing the back of her chair, swinging it like a thirty year old high school freshman swings a poodle-skirted co-ed in a sock hop movie. With a start, she realizes that both her legs are in the air. She's twisting, spinning with the chair through a 360-degree orbit, the ballerina she had desperately wanted to be as an awkward third-grader.

Her left foot reaches out for the floor and she lands, more panther now than ballerina. The chair leaves her hands as her right leg comes down before her. One of the invaders leaves the ground with a sickening chair-body crack. Bet he didn't think he'd be killed by a plastic chair when he woke up this morning, Anne thinks, already moving forward. She doesn't run directly toward the invaders, but at an angle that requires them to swing their weapons a few more degrees to track her. The dead man and chair still fly through the air, now heading earthward. Anne reaches the wall in mid stride, leaning away as her extended foot connects with the wall about a half-meter up. Anne pushes gently, but the wall still cracks. Her other leg comes up, and she runs along the wall, feet tearing into the sheet rock with each stride, finally finding purchase in the studs behind. She adjusts her gait to catch the recurring pattern of studs behind the shattering sheet rock. She doesn't have much time here, as her momentum into the wall is almost spent.

But she doesn't need much time—she's already above her prey. Trailing a plume of gypsum dust, closer to the ceiling than the floor, she realizes just how much trouble these poor killers are in. Their guns track her, firing, adding damage to the drywall, but no one can touch the bee juggler.

And then she's on them. Her assault comes from a thirty-degree elevation as she leaps off the wall above the door-frame. Her arms tangle with the first invader as she flies over him in a somersault. She lands on her feet, throwing him through a too-tight arc that is punctuated by three distinct cracks as the bones in arm, shoulder, and neck give before her torsion. The rag-doll hits the floor in what sounds like three separate impacts.

The last invader is still tracking toward her, firing. He's about five degrees off target when her left hand wraps around his gun. She jerks the gun down and outward and the finger in the trigger guard breaks twice. The gun fires one last time as the finger breaks, tearing a divot out of the floor. Her right hand is tracking along the killer's wounded and recoiling arm. The impact is a knife hand that slides over his raising shoulder and hits where his jaw and neck meet. She feels the horrifying crunch through the hardness of her hand, and then he's in a heap at her feet.

What is wrong with me, Anne thought amid the corpses, trying hard to feel bad. Hawthorne stared at her in abject astonishment—unhidden, unqualified. Anne looked at the three bodies on the floor around her with much the same expression.

"What…" Hawthorne stopped, eyes flitting from woman to corpses to the broken footprints up the destroyed wall.

"Told'ya, Spinach." Anne said inside the cloud of falling gypsum, completely lost. Hawthorne moved her head back a few centimeters; it might have been part of a nod, or perhaps just partial recoil from the strange woman who stood before her, unmasked.

The stunned silence was broken by a confident male voice from the hallway. "By now, those of you left alive are probably wondering what..." he broke off as he sauntered around the corner and saw his three men on the floor.

"I bet you are." Anne said through a sudden flash of fury. She favored the new arrival with a wicked grin because it seemed the appropriate thing to do. She wondered in passing if her new teeth had popped out yet. She probed with her tongue—nope.

He was athletic, a little less than two meters tall, black hair—crazy handsome. He wore an expensive dark suit and a quickly dissipating smile. Perhaps his most distinguishing feature was the stat-cast he wore under his suit from neck to wrist. It wasn't too bulky, though it could be perceived beneath the jacket if you were looking for it. The cast was most noticeable because it held his left arm fully extended downward and his neck completely straight. It gave him an aura of Frankenstein's monster, which Anne found amusing. She wondered when the wolf-man would put in an appearance.

"You've got some 'splaining to do." Anne leveled a finger at him, utterly failing to get the grin off her face. She hoped she was scaring him, because she was terrifying herself.

His initial answer was an ill-conceived dash back out the door. She caught him by his immobilized arm and throat. She spun him back into the room and tapped him against the wall for emphasis. The sheet rock cracked and partially deformed under the impact.

"Wait!" Hawthorne said behind her, "We need information." She came out of her chair, but then turned partially toward her fallen partner.

Anne had the strangest feeling. First it seemed that static electricity moved around and through her. Then the tingle became the gossamer tugging of water on a swimmer submerged in a river that had just changed course.

Things began to slow again as her combat awareness revved up. The ethereal current continued to intensify. She knew this feeling implied danger, but she didn't know why. Her skin crawled with caffeinated electric eels. Her clothes began to move. The man in her grasp was smiling now—eyes more than glazed. Perhaps it was a trick of light or perception, but a fire seemed to blaze there now, a cold fire composed of deep patterns of white and electric blue. Pressure built, phantom wind tossed her hair, rustled her clothes, a sound like a slow crashing wave filled her ears, then the unseen force ripped her off the floor.

Backwards through the air—upside down, then not—surrounded by sound and fury—impact. A cloud of misty white gypsum dust surrounded her from the damaged wall she was now pinned against. Across the room, she saw the hard face and burning eyes of the cast-man. Behind her, the wall shuddered and she was pressed a few more centimeters into it. It seemed to Anne that she was under the surface of a raging river, pinned to the wall by its barely-visible currents. The currents seemed to focus through the cast-man, burning in his eyes, bending to his will.

Hawthorne went for her pistol. She was quick, but not as quick as Mendez—not as quick as the cast-man, either. As her gun cleared her shoulder holster, his hand twitched toward her, fingers flicking. Another torrent of power leapt through him and Hawthorne's pistol jerked back and cracked painfully against her temple, dragging her arm with it. Anne could see her strain to pull the pistol away, strain to move her head out of the way, but, like Anne, she was caught.

Though Anne wouldn't have guessed it were possible, the cast-man's grin became more disturbing. He began to speak to Hawthorne.

"Sssssssssssaaaaaaaayyy gggggggooooodd..."

No! She was quick enough. She had time. She struggled against the river of fury that was pushing her through the wall. No use, she couldn't get any leverage against it, couldn't...

Through the wall! She began to use the force of the river to help her attack the wall behind her. Her foot drove through to the next room, her elbow shattered one of the synthetic wood studs. Ouch. Her other foot drove through and her body began to slip through the hole in the wall, feet first.

This was too slow. She would never get through the wall and around to the door before the cast-man had pulled the trigger on Hawthorne's gun. She hoped he was going for a complex sentence, but he didn't look like the wordy type. Then she could no longer see either of them as she turned her full attention to the wall that was now passing her waist.

"ddddbbbbbbyyyyyee."

The sound of the shot struck Anne like a blow. She fought harder; denial replacing the fragile hope the shot had killed. The second then third shot reached her in close succession. The river that was now aiding her through the wall abruptly stopped. Caught off-guard and mind on other things, she teetered forward. Her hands went out to keep her head from hitting the floor. She wondered who was in the room next door, wondered what they thought of the two hefty legs protruding up into their room at waist level. She was glad she wasn't wearing a skirt.

Obviously the cast-man had discovered her little ploy and was compensating. Now she was going to have to compensate too, of course she didn't yet know how. Being stuck upside down and wedged in a wall wasn't the best starting point for any plan. She pushed with her arms, pedaled her feet, but didn't make much progress. This would be funny if she wasn't about to die.

"Gggggooooooooooddddddddbye!" Mendez said as the slow motion of her combat fugue came to an end.

She pressed up on the floor and craned her neck to get a look. Hawthorne held her gun at full extension, pointing it as far from her head as possible. She gasped desperately, left hand on her face. Mendez was on the floor, propped on one elbow, still holding his gun toward the remains of the cast-man, not satisfied that he was dead. He fired into the corpse twice more... yep, not satisfied at all. Then he slumped onto his back, the gun hitting the floor as his arm relaxed. He sighed heavily.

"When will they learn that... evil bravado never pays?" He croaked.

Hawthorne snapped somewhat to her senses and rushed to her fallen partner. She knelt beside him, examining the two ragged holes in his torso. "Well, at least we're in a hospital." She gave him a reassuring grin.

"Maybe after you get the doctors you could give me a little help?" Anne said, still upside down. With no leverage, she was hopelessly stuck in the wall. One of the broken studs shifted and she slid down through the crumbling sheet rock, wedging tighter.

* * *

Rae was through being strong. There's only a certain amount of bravado and denial that anyone is capable of, and she was far past her limit. She sat in Roy's living room, holding her man, looking through the panoramic windows, across the choppy lake, and into a gathering storm. She trembled, bones seeming to knock together. She'd like to be able to pretend that this was any other Saturday night, that they were just relaxing after a day whose biggest frustrations had been boredom or work... perhaps after one of Alex's failed dinners.

Instead, she was transported back to another killing time. In the same near-fetal position, holding her mother, desolate with tears. At thirteen, she'd been old enough to understand that "Daddy's gone away for awhile," meant something more sinister than vacation. At least then she didn't know the killer. Today it would be other children's time to weep. Though they couldn't know her, they too would wish her dead.

Alex was being strong for her… holding her, closer when the shaking took her for a while. He waited patiently for her to be ready to talk. Early this morning, after they had all stumbled off to bed, Alex had come to check on her. She'd been unable to hide her tears, so he had held her then, and they had broken one of the major rules of their relationship.

Over a year ago, when she grudgingly admitted they were more than friends, they had set major and minor rules. Even now, in her misery, it brought a smile to think of it.

The minor rules were mostly tongue-in-cheek, one of Rae's was 'no rubbing my head', Alex's big one was 'no consequences for anything I say while I'm working'. The minor rules were often violated out of forgetfulness or playful mischief, but the major rules were serious. The major rules basically boiled down to three:

1. No lies, big or small. If the truth hurts, fine.
2. No hanging out in the bedroom, which was actually just a forerunner to rule 3
3. No sex.

Number one was Rae's, but two and three came from Alex. She didn't understand at first, but as time wore on and she realized he was serious, she began to believe that he might have bigger plans for her. Of course, after she found out about the Loom, she thought those plans might involve virgin sacrifice, but finally it became clear that Alex's big plan was for them to have a chance for a respectable life together with no regrets—it also seemed less likely that Alex was just in gay denial.

Her teary smile broadened even as the sobs wracked her. She held him tighter. She still wanted to punch him sometimes, but she loved him in an encompassing, visceral way. Even now she was more comfortable just being near him.

After they had been together for six months, she had to call Alex on rule number one. This led to a quandary for Alex, a decision, and Rae's introduction to Wonderland. He came clean with the simpler facts about the Underworld, and the strange metaphorical Loom "down there" that was accessible to people like Alex and Ivo. At first she didn't believe him, but there's only so much cup levitation, spoon bending, and hypnotic suggestion you can take before you get at least a little curious. All doubt had been dispelled when Alex had taken her to see Ivo. He'd shown her things that simply have no other explanation. Once he'd Cast some kind of doohickey on her that allowed her to see him working the Loom. It was the strangest combination of glass blowing and silicon etching, with just a little ironmongery and textile manufacture thrown in. It had looked like a factory, a foundry, and a little like an electric butterfly. But to say these things was to ignore the other senses: the feel of electric serpents through the flesh, the taste of carbonation, the smell of... something—blue maybe?

Alex wouldn't say what it was that made him and Ivo different, at least not more than he wasn't born that way. It was a gift given by Ivo based on Ivo's estimation of his natural talents—whatever that meant.

This morning they had broken number two on the big rules list. Alex had held her until they both fell into a troubled sleep. They'd woken in the evening, all rumpled clothes, itchy shoes, stupid grins and morning breath, but the world seemed somehow more right. Looking into his sleep-squinty eyes, laughing at his morning hair, she felt almost human again. At times like that, it was even possible to forget that you're a multiple murderer.

Sure, it was self-defense. Yeah, they were trying to kill her, Alex, and their little plucky detective. They probably liked to kick puppies and spit in fish tanks. But these thoughts were logical constructs, and mostly irrelevant in the battle for her broken heart. She had done the work of death and there was no turning back. Though her mind would fit, she could not wrap her heart around it all. Therefore tears, therefore despair.

Who was she? Could she kill and just go on living?

Images of her crimes pushed their way back onto her mind's stage. She was too tired to fight them back into the wings, so the images of blood and ruined flesh passed before her again. She saw the surprised look on their faces as her bullets stole away their lives. She wanted to sleep, wanted to just give up for a while.

Alex waited patiently to talk; arm around her, acceptance in his eyes. Whoever she was, that was okay with him.

* * *

Josh from Physical Therapy pulled on her right arm. He was a handsome Nordic type with shiny blonde shoulder length hair. Hawthorne pulled on her left arm. Behind Anne, in the women's bathroom, a nurse and an orderly were trying to force her legs up enough to unwedge her from the wall.

Anne was laughing like a moron. Fortunately it was an infectious moronic laugh, aided by a repressed fear and a general sense of uncertainty. At least she didn't have to do it alone.

Mendez had been whisked away to the ER. A needle had torn through his gut, another through his upper right chest. The police had arrived shortly after the conflict. They were now doing preliminary reports on the four corpses on the other side of the room.

Back over at the Anne-hole, the four people laughed, pushed and pulled. Finally, they unwedged her from the wall and slid her forward to the point where she could get a little leverage with her hands. She pulled herself forward, then stood up, brushing sheet-rock and splinters from her tattered clothes.

The laughter petered out into uncomfortable silence. Attention turned inexorably to the police across the room and their grisly work. No one knew what to do next. On the other side of the room, the four befuddled officers documented the scene around the corpses. One looked in obvious confusion at the half-arch of foot-sized gashes in the wall that terminated near the top of the doorframe. His stylus tapped uncertainly on his tablet.

The lights flickered. They were only out for perhaps a second, but the instant of darkness left everyone disproportionately concerned—things like that don't happen in hospitals. It's funny how you take light for granted until the darkness explodes around you. The brief, lightless pause left an almost physical sense of foreboding behind.

Anne touched Hawthorne's arm. "So, how's about we get out of here before more mystery men show up?" She whispered.

"There will be more questions..." Hawthorne led Anne away from Josh and the two others staring through the Anne-hole in the wall.

"Thanks guys!" Anne said, holding her hand up as they moved away. All three were shaking their heads. "No prob, Anne." Josh said. "You get stuck in any more walls, don't hesitate to call."

They'd already done the badge exchange, so the officers just nodded as Hawthorne approached with Anne in tow. "Who were they?" Hawthorne asked.

The ranking officer, an age-rounded man of about fifty, responded. "The one your partner shot is an FBI agent named Neiland, according to the badge and Uni on him. Problem is that he doesn't appear in their database. Might have been undercover, I guess..."

"...but then why carry his badge?" Hawthorne asked.

"Good question. We're trying to find a human in his chain of command at the Bureau for confirmation, though that could take some time." He hesitated. "Then there's the other possibility..."

"That he was impersonating an agent? Pretty serious." She looked thoughtful.

"Not nearly as serous as shooting one." The Officer's open face and clear eyes contained no humor. They both nodded, thinking imponderable thoughts.

The officer broke the silence, "The other three are also carrying federal badges, same story. You know any of them?"

Hawthorne shook her head slowly. Her grip tightened on Anne's elbow. "Was he in possession of anything weird? Strange machines, that kind of thing."

"Nope. Badge, gun, Uni, tablet, stat cast on his left shoulder."

"What happened to the shoulder?"

"Prelim scans indicate gunshot wound, fairly recent but well healed. The shot shattered most of the bones in there. 'Nother interesting thing: This wasn't the first time he's been shot. Scans picked up four other wounds, all old... and none too minor either."

"We'll be across the hall, let me know if there are any new developments." She said, leading Anne toward the door.

The door opened into a hallway cordoned off by the police. There were two more officers here. Instead of heading for the room across the hall, they turned right toward the elevators. Hawthorne pushed the down call button and they waited uneasily until the elevator arrived. Inside the elevator, Anne started to speak, but Hawthorne silenced her with a gesture. Hawthorne pressed the button for the fifth floor... trauma OR. On the way down, Hawthorne accessed the hospital's records to determine Mendez's location.

They got off the elevator and went down the hall to OR-3's observation room. They moved quickly up the flight of stairs and through the door into darkness. Anne switched on the lights. Hawthorne approached the observation window.

Below, two doctors leaned over the surgical console on the casket-sized surgical bed. Mendez wasn't visible inside the hermetically sealed operating bed. The surgeons' hands were in the control ports. Inside the bed, nano-probes performed the delicate weaving that could mend bones, stitch veins and capillaries—macro to microsurgery. At Mendez's feet, a tech monitored the patient and operating equipment so the doctors could focus on the surgery.

Hawthorne used her tablet to access the operating theater's schedule for a progress report. The damage was serious, but no longer life threatening. The ETA for the room to become available was less than ninety minutes. This implied that it would be around an hour before Mendez came off the table and another few hours of observation before he could be transported to another hospital.

Hawthorne accessed a communication window on her tablet, opened a link and waited. A pretty woman of about thirty-five with dark Latin features appeared. Her professional demeanor quickly softened. "Sarah! You better not be making lame excuses for Kyle again."

"Elena…"

"You're his partner, not his mother, you know… If he's gonna be late, then put the workaholic on the screen so he can take his medicine like a man."

Hawthorne's face remained grave. "I'd say 'don't worry', but then you'd get the wrong idea entirely. But pretend I did, because everything's gonna be okay."

On the screen, the woman's elfish face hardened with concern. "What?"

"I need you to come to Mercy Memorial right away…"

"No!" Denial, not refusal.

"Listen to me! I need you to come *hard*, you understand? I need you to call Derry, call Todd. Get here right away, come *hard*—you hearing me?"

"Yes. Come to the hospital, bring the calling circle and the utility belt, I'm taking it we're not punching in?" Though a small quaver could be heard, it affected a voice of controlled efficiency.

"Nope. We're off in the weeds on this one... way off. This is like nothing I've seen before... nothing. Don't trust anyone, not even badges. Kyle's down."

"Down?" The emotional edge moved toward the center of her voice, unwinding it somewhat.

"But not out... hurry. We're not going to be able to move for about an hour. Be here by then. We'll need a wagon and as much hardware as you can pack." Hawthorne broke the connection. She could feel the clock ticking.

* * *

Ping arrived in the doorway to the living room, fletcher in hand. Through the large windows, the last of the evening sun was shrouded in dark, crimson-tinged clouds. A storm was coming, and it looked like it was going to be a big one.

Rae and Alex were on the couch, their backs to him. He hoped he wasn't interrupting anything. They weren't speaking, so he strode forward into the room.

A few steps in, he heard a sob coming from the couch. Oops. He stopped and began to slink backwards, but it was too late.

"What'cha got, Detective?" Alex asked over his shoulder. Rae sat up straight, wiping quickly at her eyes.

"Useful gadgets." Ping replied, resuming his forward course. He circled the couch and laid the fletcher and harness on the coffee table before them. Rae looked terrible, shaken. Her eyes fixed on the gun.

"Dek pointed me to Roy's weapons. This one's for you, Rae." She didn't look up from the weapon.

Alex changed the subject, "Do you think he's going to make it?"

Ping gave the brave face, "If anyone can find Kaspari in time, it's him."

Alex filled the silence with, "What's next for us?"

Ping looked at Alex. "I thought you'd have a better answer for that than me."

"Yeah, that's what I want to hear." Alex snorted, "I'm a history TA."

Ping's turn to snort, "Yeah. Exactly." He paused. "First, we need to get out of here."

Rae looked up. "Why?"

"These hunters, whoever they are, knew Roy and Lutine well enough to set a fairly elaborate trap for them; knew enough about Alex or you to track you to the library archive."

"You're saying they know where Roy lived." Alex said.

"Not only that, they can probably locate Kaspari as well, and whether Dek reaches him in time or not, they might not be able to come back here."

"If we leave, how will we hook up with Dek and Kaspari?" Rae asked.

"No problem." Alex said, "Last night Dek had me insert a locator into him."

Ping winced. "Do I want to know where you inserted it?"

Alex laughed, "It's not a physical thing. It's a Cast like putting your thumb in a book so you can find your place again later."

Ping's wince intensified. "Nope, I definitely do *not* want to know where you put your thumb."

DEMONS

"So, you're asking me to believe you don't know any more than that?" Hawthorne asked, incredulous.

"I've told you everything I know." Anne said truthfully. It had only taken about five minutes, including exasperated pauses and questions. Anne had quite a few weird experiences to relate, but no reasons for any of it.

"I guess a vampire did make out with you..." Hawthorne said, mostly to herself.

"Of course, I haven't had any blood lust yet, though, come to think of it, I haven't eaten since before... and your partner did drink my Slim Quick shake..." Anne trailed off, fixing Hawthorne with a curious expression.

"Don't you even think about it!" Hawthorne took half a step back in the small observation room, raising a warning finger between them.

"Y'know, I am quite hungry, or should I say 'thirsty'..." but Anne could only hold the sinister stare for another second or two before the smile entered her eyes, and then pulled at the corners of her lips. After a few more seconds Hawthorne smiled too.

"Seriously," Anne said, "I saw some vending machines in the hall outside. Unless you want me feasting on your corpse, perhaps I should try some snacks and a can of juice."

"I'm not letting you out of my sight..." Hawthorne started, finger again upraised; but then she noticed that the door was swinging shut and the sound of wind was already fading like a mirage. She might have seen a mischievous smile on Anne's face, but she couldn't be sure. "Wait!" She yelled in the small empty room. Then she wrestled out her pistol and ran to the door.

She pushed through the door and stopped short just centimeters from Anne's smiling face. She almost kept her surprised cry under wraps. Her left hand flew to her mouth as if to stop the startled bleat. She was still recovering her composure when Anne said "You really want to get between a woman like me and the snack machines?"

Hawthorne was still off balance from the shock. She shook her head feebly. Surprisingly, the startled fear resolved into bemused affection, rather than the fury she had expected. She had to admit that she liked this horribly powerful woman of dubious impulse control. She just hoped she didn't end up as a midnight snack.

"I'll buy." Hawthorne said, fishing for her Uni.

* * *

The man in the Hawaiian shirt entered the deserted lobby of the hospital. He carried an athletic bag, and walked with a slight limp. He was perhaps forty-five, heavy, but not overweight. He was tall, but not scraping the door-frames. He looked pleasant, but uncomfortable.

The lobby's only other occupant was a uniformed hospital guard behind the reception desk. "Sir, our ER is closed. We can get you a shuttle to DePaul if you need non-urgent treatment..."

"Nah." The visitor drawled, "I'm here to visit one of yer inmates." He favored the guard with a bright smile and continued toward the other end of the lobby. "Ya know, you've got a bunch of vagrants out there." He said, glancing back toward the door to the ambulance run.

The guard moved from behind the desk and intercepted the visitor a few meters from the inner door. "Sir! Visiting hours are temporarily..."

"All right, sonny. I admit it... I'm here for some of that elective surgery." He slapped his butt and winced. "I just don't want it hollered all about the building, okay buddy?"

"Uhhhh... oh..." the guard stumbled for a few beats but then finally regrouped. He moved between the visitor and the door again as the visitor tried to step past. "Sir, the Feds have the building locked down... there's some kind of investigation underway..."

He never hit the floor. The man in the loud shirt grabbed the guard before the stunner rendered him unconscious. Now without his limp, the big man dragged the insensate guard back to the chair behind the desk. He sat the unconscious guard in the chair, knocking a potted plant from the desk as he arranged the guard in an approximation of sleep.

As he replaced the plant on the desk, two women slipped in through the outer doors. The first was Elena Mendez, her dark hair now pulled back into a ponytail. The other was fair-skinned with glossy red hair. Both had the same determined look and efficient manner. As the women passed the scanners, the Hawaiian-shirted man used the security console to approve the many weapons beneath their light jackets and in their dufflebags.

"Subtle. As always, Derry." The redhead said as they approached.

"The word you're looking for is 'effective.'" The big man said, using his foot to sweep dirt from the upended plant beneath the desk.

* * *

Anne was mowing through the second pack of vending machine donuts. They were bland and far too healthy to truly be called donuts, but this was a hospital, not a den of culinary iniquity. She was starving, but she still had issues with anything vegetable-infused being called a donut. Nothing says yummy like a broccoli-infused, protein-enriched, amino-balanced, chocolate-spice-flavored, piece of baked heaven from Sara Lee.

With a mental shudder that ended in a shrug, she reached for another. "Well, at least I'm not restricted entirely to blood!" She enthused around the food. "You don't know how relieved this makes me!"

Hawthorne took a sip of her protein smoothie and nodded. "Me too."

* * *

The whispercraft touched down on the roof of the hospital. It disgorged its compliment of five hard men and two harder women. As the last boot hit the roof, the craft took off, moving into a holding pattern above.

Three of the men were wearing suits and carrying Federal badges, which was to say they were in disguise. Two other men and one of the women wore dark, durable street clothes. The final woman wore an elegant suit the color of dark chocolate. Her skin and lustrous black hair belied her roots. She'd been born in sunny Goa, on the Indian coast, but now Shiva called no place home. For four hundred years now, her only home was Asado.

On her fingers were eight delicate rings of platinum and rubies. Around her neck was a dark leather choker. Her thick, straight hair was pulled back, fastened at the nape of her neck with more platinum and rubies. She strode ahead of the rest toward the roof access, arrogance in her face and stride.

Those in the guise of Federal agents had only light armament, but the comfortably dressed had brought all the tools of their trade. Shiva wore no weapons, but then she needed none.

At the elevator bank on the twenty-fourth floor they stopped. A few minutes later, they had hacked into the security system and located their prey in the observation room for OR-3.

Shiva's eyes lost focus for a moment and the lights flickered, then flickered again briefly. She smiled and her eyes fluttered open. "Ok, the wireless trunks are down, but I'll need to get to the basement to cut the hard wires." Another glance, and the elevator door before her opened, revealing the dark shaft.

"Vega, take your men and keep the cops out of the way." she said to the leader of the undercover Grunts. She stepped casually into the empty air of the elevator shaft, then hovering, she turned back to face the hard-eyed leader of the heavy weapons team. "Signal me when you've released our allies from the security ward."

The woman with the assault gun nodded, lips stretching slightly. "The gloves are off?"

"Don't kill its precious key, but you can shoot anything else that moves as many times as you'd like."

The woman didn't nod, but her grin and the sparkle in her cold eyes told Shiva that she understood.

The elevator doors closed and Shiva began her quick descent through the dim shaft.

*   *   *

The car with the metal patch tape on the roof was in the garage. A few pieces were gone. Ping examined the power plant beneath the hood but he couldn't see the difference. Alex had assured him that Dek had "done the deed" back at the library, meaning he'd disabled the 'jack system that provided satellite tracking for the car. He was going to arrest that guy later... tampering with the anti-theft system of a police vehicle was a serious offense. You get knocked out for a couple of days and the rule of law goes on holiday.

The hatchback was open. Rae and Alex were loading the back with clothes and equipment brought from Alex's apartment and borrowed from Roy's house.

"How we doing?" He asked, closing the hood.

Rae dropped another box in the back. "Alex is bringing up the rear now. You have to hit the bathroom—now's a good time. I'm not stopping later."

"And what makes you think you're driving my fine police wheels?"

Rae made a few quick jerks on a pantomime steering wheel and hooked a thumb at herself, "Amped. Remember? We might need to do some fancy driving, right?"

Ping pointed his finger at her, "Delusional." he corrected.

Alex came through the door with a large, padded instrument pack.

"Magic or science?" Ping asked, glancing at Alex's load.

"You mean there's a difference?" He gave the rhetorical pause before continuing, "Some stuff I brought from home... spare tablets, some security equipment, most completely legal."

"Most?"

"Arrest me later."

"Deal. So no phoenix feathers or eye of newt?"

"You really need to get your perceptions roughly aligned with the universe, Detective Bannon."

"Uh-huh. Ping, remember? Generally you call the cops you go on the run with by their first names... We ready?" No one's head shook.

"Lets go then... Shotgun!" Rae opened the passenger door, but stopped before getting in. Alex seemed lost in thought. "You are coming, right baby?"

He was staring a little to the right of Ping's ear. Ping turned to follow Alex's gaze, but he was only rewarded with the sight of a rather boring tool cabinet.

Alex's lips moved only slightly, "Rae, take this," he held out his pack, "In the back. Hurry." his voice was wistful, like one lost in reverie, perhaps contemplating the merits of a favorite childhood pet.

Rae was expecting a joke. There was amusement in her face; then realization froze her smile, sent chills down her spine. "What is it?" She asked. She didn't really want to know.

"Remember the library?" he droned, still obviously distracted by something neither Ping nor Rae could see. "This is going to be much worse."

"What are you... get his bag Rae!" Ping interrupted himself as realization dawned, "Close the hatch!"

Rae went for the bag, Ping turned, leapt over the front corner of the car, and ran for the driver's door. Relieved of the bag, Alex stumbled toward the back seat like a very distracted blind man. The hatch slammed and Rae ran back around the rear corner of the car. She stopped to help buckle Alex into the back, then dropped into the passenger seat.

"Don't move yet, Ping." Alex said with the attitude of one talking while holding his breath. He held one finger up for patience. "But get ready to move."

Ping ran his finger over the raised ignition pad on the steering yoke and twisted it into the enabled position. He heard the lock-accept tone that meant the car was ready to go. He used the controls on the wheel to shift into reverse, then waited with his foot hovering over the accelerator. "Who are these people?"

"Some aren't this time." Alex said, voice flat.

Both Ping and Rae turned their heads toward the back seat, but Alex didn't elaborate.

"Aren't people?" Rae asked. Ping shrugged.

A muffled explosion and the sound of a collapsing door came to them through the door to the house. A waterfall of shattering glass sounded behind the door. There was the sound of clomping boots and silenced gunfire. Maybe the neighbors wouldn't hear, but the sound of shots were clear to them in the garage.

Ping and Rae turned again to stare into Alex's blank expression, but finding no clues there, slowly turned to face each other. Rae adjusted her grip on the fletcher.

"Swell." Ping said. Rae gave a short laugh, shaking her head.

"Don't worry bout the door—I'll need you to gun it... ready, Ping? And..." Alex wiggled his raised finger slightly.

Ping's foot hovered, Alex's finger wiggled, Rae's eyes moved between them, then Alex dropped his finger, "NOW!"

Ping jammed the accelerator to the floor. All four of the car's solid polymer tires squeaked as the individual electric motors driving them compensated for the loss of traction. Each squeal shimmered in and out as the traction computers walked the line between maximum torque and the available friction between tire and pavement.

The car rocketed backward, shuddering slightly as it blew through the garage door. The door gave no significant resistance to the car's juggernaut force, causing only a small hiccup in the car's reverse acceleration and a short, if spectacular, crash. Ping wondered in passing what kind of cheap door the builder had used.

Almost immediately after clearing the door—its debris still hanging in the air around the car—there were two more impacts in quick succession. The car bounced as something substantial went under the left rear tire. An assault gun bounced end over end on the driveway as the car cleared the garage.

Ping had been unconscious when they arrived here, so the driveway and palatial yard were unfamiliar. He did his best to negotiate the dark driveway's curves as the car sped backwards. To make matters worse, the driveway wound between thick trees, allowing him only a view of the next corner with no idea what lay beyond. As if this were not enough excitement, long ragged bursts of automatic gunfire erupted from several broken windows along the front of the house, tearing through the trees, filling the air with splinters, but strangely sparing the car.

Not wanting to look a gift rifle in the muzzle, Ping accepted the luck and left his foot firmly on the floor as the car wildly accelerated though the winding, wood-lined track. They clipped a guidepost, then a small tree, but Ping wasn't slowing down. He feared foliage far less than firearms.

As the garage door disintegrated into splinters and dust around the car, Rae held on for dear life and clenched her teeth to keep from screaming. She let out only the smallest bleat as they mowed over two armed men directly outside the destroyed door.

Beside her, Ping was twisted to look through the rear window. His arm was over the seat, elbow bent, looking like any sixteen-year-old kid during the parallel parking portion of his first driving test. Her right hand whitened around the handle above her window. Her left hand whitened around the short barrel of the Fletcher. She and the car jerked from side to side under Ping's reverse navigation. Her stomach gave a spasm as gunfire erupted followed quickly by their glancing impact with a small tree. The car continued backwards. The air filled with wood chips and the whistle-crack of high velocity shells.

Grudgingly, she released the handle above the window, and grabbed the pistol grip of the fletcher. She relied on her seat belt and the force her legs were applying to the floor to hold her in place. The way Ping was driving, there was no way she was going to stick hand or weapon out the window, but she wanted to be ready when the opportunity presented itself. Until then, she tried to make herself as small a target as possible, slouching down in her seat, pressing her right elbow against the door to steady herself, and keep the fletcher pointed away from Ping.

Here she was again, just waiting for the chance to kill someone. Determination drove away doubt, desperation kept guilt at bay. Could she really just suspend morality like this? Fair-weather moralist, rainy-day sociopath.

Bright headlights flared in the night behind them, forcing Ping's eyes into slits, leaving two round purple shadows floating through his vision. "Hold on!" He shouted as he cranked the wheel hard to the left. With another squeal, the car rocketed from the driveway and into the foliage.

Alex existed in the wider world of the Loom, receiving only a small percentage of his sensory inputs from his physical body, which was now being tossed and jostled limp in the back seat of the car leaving the driveway for the forest. His seatbelt kept him from serious injury through the tambourine-stable drive—he'd have to thank Rae later for buckling him in. Heaven knew he wouldn't have remembered to do it himself. A sudden flash of heat surrounded him in the abstract realm of the Underworld as he thought about Rae. It was almost time for her, for them. He hoped they both lived long enough.

Bullets approached the car from the three killers braced in and around the car blocking the driveway. The bullets left the muzzles of the rifles in rapid succession, only a few meters apart, stretching out across the distance, reaching for Alex and the others. They tore through the air, spinning for stability, leaving trails of turbulence and radiant sound. Some of the shells were slowed and deflected by intervening trees; Alex deflected the rest.

The hot, spinning shells sieved through the bands of force he'd wrapped in expanding patterns about the car; their paths becoming eccentric arcs, vectors changing as the skeins of Alex's weaving altered the relevant physics of the space through which they flew. They thudded into the ground, curved off through the trees, flew up into the air—every direction but toward the car.

Unbelievably, Alex's hasty weave was holding. Unbelievable because he had never Cast this type of weave before. Sure, he knew how to do it now, but he hadn't a few moments ago. Weaving the Cast had been much more like inspiration than the usual hard-fought solution that usually took him hours, weeks, or months. Something was different now, either in the Loom or in him.

When the Savant with the attackers had attempted to apply Sleep to the inhabitants of Roy's house, somehow it had awoken Alex to the Underworld, drawing him to the Loom with no pattern stretching. Ivo would be proud. Would be—if these monsters hadn't killed him.

He stretched out his Vision, encompassing Roy's large wooded front yard. In addition to the maybe fifteen commandos in the house and the three by the car, there were two snipers in gray microvans a block away from Roy's gate. Thorough little killers, Alex thought. Then he noticed the things moving impossibly fast through the trees to intercept them. Better warn Ping.

Ping cranked the wheel to the left and jammed the brakes with his right foot as his left deactivated the Traction Control system. The wheels locked as the car tore across the leaf-covered clearing, bumping across the irregular terrain, nose sliding around. He jammed the accelerator as the car slid into a semblance of 'forward'. The last part of the hundred-eighty degree spin was facilitated by his TC-suppressed all wheel throttle up. Geysers of dirt exploded from all wheels, adding force to the spin of the car. Finally, he released the TC suppressor and the wheels slowed to the breaking point of their traction on the loose earth.

The car accelerated forward, dodging the first tree on the other side of the twenty-meter clearing. In the rear-view mirror, Ping could make out Alex's ten thousand meter stare. Next to him, Rae stared at Ping—obviously impressed. He smiled, arching an eyebrow at her while swerving around some rock landscaping.

"I coulda' done that." she mumbled.

The resonant hum of the car's four motors stuttered. The car began to slow.

The Savant with the attackers was somewhere back by the house. Alex couldn't feel exactly from where, but the Savant was trying to reach out and touch them. But working with the Loom becomes more difficult the farther away you get from your target, and fortunately they were driving directly away.

The Savant was pretty good. Though he—definitely a man, tall, dark suit, standing by a wall—couldn't pull off any extravagant Casts at this distance. Still, he managed to set up a weak damping-field around the car's motors. The electromagnetic fields were weakening somewhat and the motors were losing efficiency.

Alex had the advantage of distance because the target of his counter-Cast was the car around him. He unwound the patterns of force even as the distant Savant struggled to maintain them. This was a battle he could win.

Numbness lanced out from the unwinding fibers of the other Savant's Cast. Alex struggled against the sharp, icy energy that he had mistakenly engaged. He'd misconstrued the intent of the Cast. It was a Trojan horse... too weak to kill the car, but subtle enough to hide the real danger. When Alex had carelessly immersed himself in the hostile weave, he'd become vulnerable.

He tried to extract himself, but it was like trying to bathe without water, removing each speck of dirt individually. Hundreds of dark, ethereal spiders swarmed over him, stealing away the speed and power of the Loom. His consciousness seemed to narrow, the light faded from around him.

Touché, he thought in the final shimmer of light.

The motor sputtered again, but then the powerful drone evened. They were approaching the fence along the front of the property. Ping held the accelerator down. "Hold on!" His eyes flashed to the rear view where Alex lolled in his harness, apparently unconscious.

Something that had way too many teeth landed on the hood of the car, slamming its head into the windshield. Spider web cracks radiated away from the impact point and one or two of the thing's teeth flew away from the face-glass collision. Ping let out a shout that he'd like to think sounded like "yow!" but memory informed him it sounded more like an introverted librarian screaming her guts out in a horror movie.

Ping swerved right, attempting to dislodge the wolf-man or whatever had so wronged his windshield. However, the claw-studded knobby black things at the end of its oily arms had found purchase in the crack between the hood and the windshield. Its eyes burned with what Ping sincerely hoped was reflected light. It howled, showing curving teeth and a gray worm-like tongue.

He briefly considered braking, but didn't think he'd get enough traction out of the soft soil to dislodge the beast. It released the hood with its left hand, cocked the fist back and swung it forward, shattering the cracked windshield.

Twin explosions tripped over each other, blowing more glass out of the car as Rae added her opinion to the discussion. The two shots blew out most of the windshield and showered the hood with its rough diamonds. The departing fletchettes made a much less pretty impression on the oily man-thing. It's ink-black skin parted, arm deconstructing near the shoulder, face yielding... don't want to look at that!

Then it was gone, head over claws into the rushing night air.

Ping squinted into the wind rushing through the shattered windshield. "What was that?" he shouted, glancing toward Rae.

"Don't ask me!" Rae shook her head, trying to hold the fletcher at the ready through the shuddering violence of the car's journey across Roy's yard. "Just 'cause I did more shootin' than screaming don't mean I know what's goin' on!"

Ping laughed, "Hang on!"

The car slammed into the antique cedar plank fence at the side of the yard, halfway between two posts. The fence must have indeed been antique because it disintegrated on impact. The night air filled with flying wood. Ping and Rae pulled their heads down, but no flying planks entered the car. The impact jolted through the car, rattling teeth and dislodging chips of safety glass from their clothes.

The car leaped onto the pavement. It fishtailed as it turned right, away from the street that fronted Roy's property. A contrail of fallen leaves, splinters, and dirt settled behind the accelerating car.

Behind them, at the corner of the block, a woman with a sniper rifle burst from the back of a gray microvan where she had been in position to kill anything exiting through the front gate. Turning to the side-street, she leveled the weapon at the retreating car, but her hastily fired shots missed their mark and the fleeing car made a sliding turn left onto another side street.

Swearing, she lowered the weapon and pitched it into the rear of the microvan. She slammed the hatch and sprinted to the driver's door. Inside, she pulled the microvan away from the curb and down the side street after her prey. She activated the commlink in her ear, and informed the other hunters of their target's unexpected escape.

Seconds later, the others joined the pursuit.

* * *

Talia hated her job. She made her way carefully through the beds, checking for trouble. As she moved, she made extra sure not to give any of the patients a chance to grab at her. Her job was monotonous, but boredom wasn't even really boredom if it was surrounded by the constant threat of messy death.

Until this year, the security ward at the hospital had been a sweet assignment. There was time for reading while nominally watching over injured drunks and people hurt running from the police for misdemeanors. The clientele back then was mostly unconscious or disabled. Occasionally, they'd even get a high profile criminal that her kids would love to hear about.

Now though, it was Harms, Harms, and more Harms. It had gotten so bad that the hospital now had a medium security ward for criminals not currently under the influence of Harmony. Of course, Talia didn't have the seniority to get on that duty regularly. Others got to read novels and sip coffee while keeping one eye on the bad and broken. Talia got the terror and the body armor.

Yep, body armor… and not the cool kind, either. Not the kind that stops bullets and looks snappy so your kids brag about it at school. No, the armor she wore was a plastic low-friction slicker and gloves to help her stay ungrabbed and unbitten by her charges.

She was almost done with this job. She was starting to take the tension home to her kids. This was *not* okay. If it were a choice between putting food on the table and snapping at the kids for every little thing, then they'd go hungry. She'd been trying for months now to transfer to more bearable work, but it was getting to the point where she was going to have to quit. Yep, tonight after work she would dig through the classifieds… but she was always so tired at night after she got the girls down for bed. Ever since Jack died, she was the only source of income for herself and the girls. She needed a job, but perhaps she didn't need this particular one.

Silence.

No mumbling, gurgling, screaming, moaning or thrashing... it was one of those times. "Hey Jeff! Mothership's hovering again!"

"What's the time?" He called back from the desk.

"Four thirty-eight in the wee hours!" She said, checking her watch. For weeks now, she and Jeff had been trying to find a pattern or any other cause for these strange syncopated pauses. So far, they hadn't figured anything out. The pauses seemed to occur randomly, not governed by a fixed period or any environmental factors. They came several times a day now, and could last from ten seconds to ten minutes. The doctors didn't have any helpful input either.

She made her way carefully but quickly back to the desk, where Jeff was waiting with a tired but amused grin. "Don't let it get to you. You should be thankful for the break."

"It's creepy, that's what it is."

"Yeah, it is that." He shook his head. "Hey, I pulled low security tomorrow... care if I gloat a bit?"

She fixed him with a murderous look.

Then the lights went out and the world went black. Though the darkness couldn't have lasted more than two seconds, it took only half of that time for Talia's mind to fill with thoughts of the supernatural. The lights flickered back to life and she was left looking into Jeff's surprised face.

"What was that?" he asked, looking around.

She shrugged. She really hated her job.

* * *

Chase exited the security office. At thirty, he couldn't say he'd exactly lived his dreams. His dream of being an astronaut died at twelve when he'd first encountered calculus. He'd been nimble then, and had shifted focus quickly to policeman. Of course, he had never really pursued that much past his first failed academy entrance exam. The part-time security job he'd taken in the interim had settled into his routine and he'd just breezed through nearly a decade without ever fully waking.

When he thought about it, it distressed him—so he didn't think about it. He still had time to do what he really wanted... whatever that was. For now, his days were filled with sleep and his nights were full of the sparkling excitement that was hospital security on the graveyard shift.

Tonight had been especially weird... though come to think of it, he couldn't remember why—some kind of weird fight in the ER maybe. Though the details were hazy now, the memory of the mega-hot Fed he'd just left in the security office was not. His mind returned again to the way her red hair caught the light, the perfect way she filled out her suit. Maybe his long-term goals should involve the FBI.

He was still dreaming of the glamorous world of the Bureau when he felt it... something was wrong. The lobby was silent. He stood, hand still on the door, keeping it from swinging closed behind him. Something...

On the surface, everything seemed normal: Clint was dozing at the security desk like he'd seen from the security office. The light was bright and hospital-harsh, no creepy shadows or menacing rotwielers were visible, but something was, well... off.

Did the light seem too harsh? Subtle shifts or flickers seemed to affect the light at the edges of his vision, though he wasn't entirely sure this wasn't the lingering effects of last night's festivities. Was it the blackness outside the door? Maybe it was that this place was empty... the Feds had closed the hospital down because of the trouble earlier—not the hot feds, but the... um... harder-to-remember Feds from... before. Had there been a first set of agents tonight? Now that he thought more about it, he wasn't sure

Hand on the stunner holstered at his hip, Chase reluctantly let the door close behind him, feeling somehow committed to the new, ambiguously scary scene. He moved toward Clint's sleeping form. This would be the second time he'd found Clint dozing this month, but there was something in his posture that bothered Chase. Clint's head was on the desk, resting on his right arm. Beside him on the desk was a medium-sized plant from the gift shop. His face was turned away from Chase, but his left arm had slipped off the desk and hung limp toward the floor like a divining rod over a buried reservoir—right there, buddy. Clint's feet were too far back, like he'd been dragged here and placed in the chair.

Near Clint's feet, dark potting soil had been spilled. Chase's eyes returned to the potted plant. He hadn't noticed before, but the plant was bent slightly with several of its stems broken as if it had been knocked to the floor, then righted and placed back on the desk.

It occurred to him that he hadn't seen the plant knocked off the desk since the policewoman had left it earlier. It then occurred to him that he probably should have been doing less reading and more monitoring in the security office.

He moved to the desk. "Clint?" He reached out, but jerked back as darkness surrounded him for the second time tonight. The lights flickered on-off-on again, chasing the darkness and the echoes of his startled cry away. About forty minutes back, the lights in the security room had failed for perhaps a second, but then everything had returned to normal. He'd never seen a power interruption in the hospital, and now two in one night. He had the odd intuition of being stalked and very alone. He wanted to head back to the security office and see if perhaps that red-head Fed was feeling nervous and maybe even a little snuggly.

Clint hadn't moved.

He put a hand on Clint's shoulder, gave him a gentle shake. That was all it took to upset Clint's precarious balance. Clint's right arm slipped off the desk, his head lolled left and knocked against the top of the desk. He slid to the floor in a heap.

Chase jumped, barely avoided a scream, got it together... exhaled. He bent down, put a hand on Clint's clammy neck... Pulse, that's good. Breathing, too... cool, no mouth-to-mouth necessary.

He sighed with relief and went into action. He stood and hit the alarm on the security desk... nothing. Sure, it was a silent alarm, so he knew not to expect klaxons or whistles, but something was missing. It took him a second to realize what... his tablet hadn't alarmed him. He should have received a level one security page instructing him to go to the lobby.

He checked his tablet's power indicator—fine. He opened the screen enough to check the diagnostics: active, connected to the hospital's access points, but nothing else. Diagnostic pings sent across the net failed to return from points farther than the tier-one routers.

"What the..." this was just wrong. Once when he was a child, an earthquake took down eighty percent of the networks in the L.A. basin, but none of the hospitals had lost their networks entirely. Hospital, police, and some governmental networks were so hard, so massively redundant, that he'd never heard of a complete outage.

This outage was intentional, and whoever had done it was resourceful and probably crazy. You drop a hospital's net and a lot of sick people could die.

Great. Well, at least the building was filled with cops and Feds... and security guards. Glancing down at Clint's unconscious form, he didn't feel much comforted.

Then he noticed the security monitors on the desk before him and felt even less comfortable. Of the three monitors, only the one that gave him a view directly outside the doors was active. He guessed it was probably an older generation that was hardwired, and therefore not susceptible to a network outage. On the small screen, he could see a crowd of perhaps ten people had gathered by the ambulance parking perhaps ten meters outside the door. He leaned in, trying to make out what they were doing, but they just seemed to be standing perfectly still, looking at the outside of the hospital door. He glanced up at the inside of the door, but the dim and flickering lights outside in the ambulance run worked together with the gray-tinted glass to keep the door reflecting the inside of the lobby, with only the vaguest hint of anything behind it.

Chase used the control pad to zoom the cheap camera in as far as possible. The camera reached its maximum zoom with perhaps three of the people on the screen. The shadows weren't being kind to them, their faces looked too angular, and there seemed to be blood spattered on their clothes, but then Chase understood: they were wearing masks; cheap circus clown masks. There was no other explanation for the identical toothy grin that dominated each face. Perhaps they were terrorists waiting for some cue to storm the building, now that the net was down.

The camera began to flicker. Chase thought it was just interference—whatever was affecting the lights—but then he saw all three of the people on the monitor turn in perfect unison toward the entry ramp. An emergency vehicle of some kind was coming down the ramp… Chase hoped it was more cops. He looked up again at the reflective door that was now flickering with the lights from the ambulance that had just pulled up.

He looked back to the monitor, but the clown-masked terrorists were gone. He started to zoom the camera back, but before it showed him anything, startled shouts, then ragged screams came through the door from the ambulance run.

"Holy…" Chase looked up at the entrance again, trying to make out shapes in the bursts of alternating red and white light. Then he looked down at the very, *very* small stunner clenched in his hand... this didn't look like it would be a good night for him. The screams cut off, leaving behind a silence that somehow seemed worse. A small buzz sounded from the security console. His finger was still on the zoom out key and the console was informing him that the camera had reached its widest angle. He glanced back down at the monitor, which now held an image of most of the area outside the door.

He got a series of impressions in about two seconds: motion, the ambulance's open doors, two bodies on the ground next to them, a crowd around the bodies, blood... eating? And then he wasn't looking anymore—he was running back toward the hallway where he'd entered the lobby. He'd seen the 2054 remake of *Night of the Living Dead*, and he got the point.

He had run maybe five steps back toward the inner door when he remembered Clint. He skidded to a halt and ran back to the security desk. It was surprisingly hard to lift a completely insensate human; it was like lifting a bag of bowling balls. Somehow he finally got Clint over his shoulder.

He ran as fast as his heavy load allowed. He hit the interior doors without slowing or putting out a hand. He just barreled through, using Clint's butt as a battering ram.

Chase heard the automatic doors leading to the ambulance run sliding open as the hallway doors swung closed behind him. He wasn't sure, but he thought he heard giggling coming from behind him.

* * *

The last forty minutes in the security ward had passed with only the usual tension. There had been no further power interruptions, the Harms had gone back to their usual sobbing, moaning, screaming routine. It was about two hours until Talia's shift ended and she could head home to get the kids ready for school.

Jeff sat across the desk, reading a book and smiling from time to time. Talia was doing a crossword on her tablet when silence settled again over the room.

"Here we go again." Talia said, looking up briefly.

Jeff looked up from his book, smiling. "Wow. Two in one hour."

His smile faded somewhat as his eyes focused on the scene over Talia's shoulder. After a few seconds, his brow furrowed. "Hey…"

She turned to follow his gaze, but before she saw, she heard. Unintelligible speech welled up behind her like a snowball rolling downhill, picking up mass. The mumble started with only one voice, but by the time she turned to face the source, all ten Harms had joined in the sound. It wasn't words, or at least none she knew, but all ten mouths were making the same sounds at the same time. All of them had raised their heads and were staring at the startled guards. The sound stopped and there was silence again.

"Ok, that's new." Talia said.

"And creepy." Jeff finished, staring back at the Harms.

Their expressions were blank, but as Talia and Jeff stared, the Harms began to smile. They spoke again, this time in perfect unison, but there was no meaning attached to the sounds, though it seemed to have a pattern to it. After another pause, they repeated the sounds, but they were clearer this time. The third time, the words were only slightly slurred.

"All around you." They said. "All around you now. Do you feel The Coming?"

What blood the sights and sounds didn't drain from them, the implication froze solid.

Darkness filled the room, descending like a plague over the grinning, chanting Harms. "All around you now." The chorus of restrained Harms repeated in the blackness.

The Lights flickered back on then off-on again. She realized that the double shot of darkness had only lasted about two seconds, but she felt like a half-drowned sailor treading water between tsunamis of darkness.

Both she and Jeff were on their feet now, looking wildly around. "Stay with us—play." The Harms all said in perfect unison, arms and legs straining at their restraints. Were the Harm's faces changing? Their teeth seemed to grow more malevolent, their skin stretched tighter across their distorting faces.

Jeff bolted for the door. "Wait!" Talia shouted, grabbing unsuccessfully for his arm as he rushed by. Neither she nor Jeff carried any weapons for fear that they could be used against them. Talia reached for the only weapon she had. "We've got a major incident underway!" She shouted into the transceiver on her wrist, but static was her only reply. "Security! You copy?" More static.

Maybe Jeff had the right idea after all. She turned toward the door, but gunfire erupted at the airlock. It was a short burst of automatic fire that brought with it the sound of shattering glass and the unmistakable crash of a body hitting the floor. When she reached the airlock, she darted her head around the corner. Jeff was on the floor. Blood pooled around him, spattered on the walls and broken glass. He wasn't moving. Two men and one woman in dark casual clothes were moving through the shattered glass of the airlock doors. All three sported military assault guns.

She dodged back around the corner, but not fast enough. A needle from a three round burst caught her in the shoulder, knocking her off her feet, spinning her partway over. She landed on her back in what seemed to be a featherbed of shock, clutching at her shattered shoulder.

Dark laughter surrounded her. "All around you now," the chorus said.

She moaned; part shock, part desperation. Who would take care of her children now? She didn't think her sister would make a good mom, and her parents were getting old. Orphans. The word filled her with equal parts sorrow and fury.

She looked around, looking for anything she could use as a weapon. There was no place to hide, no place or ability to run. If someone handed her an automatic weapon now, she wouldn't be able to use it.

The woman came through the inner airlock door, tracking across the room with her weapon. Her aim moved across whatever the Harms were becoming and settled on Talia.

"Please…" Talia moaned, but there was no mercy in the hard lines of the woman's face, and no one here to save her. She never heard the shots.

Then she was in a bright place of familiar, beautiful music with Jack's arms around her. He was telling her that he'd missed her terribly and not to worry about the kids. He didn't really need to say it though; she'd already heard it in the music and in her heart.

Saved after all, she thought, clinging tighter to the man she'd lost and found.

* * *

Anne looked over Hawthorne's shoulder into the operating theater below. She'd worked here for six years now, had forged the intravenous connections between thousands of patients and their operating beds, yet she had no idea how the operation below was progressing. The surgeons worked efficiently, the tech monitoring the patient seemed hypnotized by the instruments before him. The time ticked by.

"You ever feel like the bull's-eye?" Anne said.

"Hm?" Hawthorne said, still staring down into the OR, only partially emerging from other thoughts.

"In your FBI life, you know… ever feel like there's a bunch of strangers out there who want you dead? Like everyone you meet is looking at you out of the corner of their eye, sizing you up? Like you're the target of a really lethal joke that everyone else is in on?"

Hawthorne examined Anne over her shoulder. "If it makes you feel any better, I don't get this joke either."

"So, you've never been the target of a vast conspiracy? Never been on the run from seemingly everyone?"

"Not 'til now." She gave a wry grin that, given a few seconds, spread into an expression of genuine humor. "...but I can't dodge bullets and run up walls."

"Neither could I before today."

"You take the good with the bad." Hawthorne shrugged and turned back to the window.

"You think I should invest in a cape?" Anne said after a moment's silence.

"Not without tights."

"I meant more Dracula than Superman." She thought for a few seconds, "Cowl, mask, or should just I go naked like Superman?"

"You don't wear glasses."

"I could start."

Hawthorne abandoned her vigil over the operation below and turned to face Anne, "You think you could fly if you tried?"

"The guy who gave me the atomic hickey sure couldn't." Her face darkened as an unexpected funk interrupted their conversational repartee.

"What?" Hawthorne said, concerned.

"He warned me."

"Who?"

"He said that they were coming, said it was up to me now."

"Who?"

"He didn't say who... just that 'they' were coming."

"Yeah," Hawthorne said, actively managing her frustration now, "but *who* said that?"

"Oh... right. I'm not sure. A little Down's Syndrome kid in the middle of a car crash."

Hawthorne blinked. She shook her head as if to clear it. Questions weren't getting her anywhere, so she tried silence. She stared at Anne expectantly.

Anne got the message, "Right... While the fallen guy was abusing my neck, the pain knocked me clean out, and I start having this dream... parts of it were as weird as my normal dreams, but other parts..."

Hawthorne nodded. After a pause, Anne continued, "Other parts were vivid, frightening... sad. In these parts, the fallen guy was always trying to get me with these huge shark's teeth..." Anne paused, shaking her head. "No, that's not fair. He was trying to talk to me, but he kept sprouting these teeth... every time it happened he'd get exasperated and I'd book on out of there."

Hawthorne bit back the questions, rode the pause out.

"I was scared like I'd never been before. Shocked... scared stupid. I thought I was dead, thought he was trying the find-me-eat-my-soul kind of thing. 'Nother weird thing: I didn't remember any of it when I woke up on top of him."

Hawthorne couldn't resist, "You're just remembering this *now?*"

Anne shook her head, "No, I re-dreamed it in bits since then. I can't wait to see what's on the all-weird dream channel tonight."

"Re-dreamed." Hawthorne said, dubious.

"Since then, I keep dreaming parts of that first dream, but I remember it kinda like déjà vu. I'm eating thanksgiving dinner at the kids' table, he's sitting where my cousin should be. I'm running through darkness and he's a descending angel. I'm in a... food store, he's the server, always acting friendly, followed by a spooky tooth-head transformation and then I'm running for my life again through another hokey scene."

"You said something about a kid with Down's Syndrome in a car crash..." Hawthorne prompted, nearly ready to slap Anne a few times and see how badly she'd be killed for it.

"Yeah, and that isn't even the weirdest part of the dream." Anne smiled, trying to keep the mood lighter than she felt. "That was the saddest part though, and by far the most vivid. I'm almost certain it really happened, but not to me."

Anne noticed Hawthorne's confusion and paused, regrouped. She told her the story of the minivan wreck as concisely as she could.

"So what did he tell you?" Hawthorne asked when Anne had finished.

"That 'they' were coming, that it was up to me... that he hoped to see his parents again soon." She thought for a moment, "I think he did."

"Did what?"

Her voice thickened uncomfortably, "See them again. I think I caught a glimpse of them as I was waking, as he was dying."

"What? The kid died in your dream?"

"No... yes. I think the little kid was the guy who attacked me. I think being the kid was just his way of making me sit still long enough to listen to him. I think he was with me when his body died... I think I saw his parents come to get him."

"So you're saying he jacked into your mind." Hawthorne said, not hiding the skepticism.

"Yeah, that's ridiculous... vampires definitely can't do that." Anne came back.

Hawthorne snorted, "Touché." Behind her business face, the implications were sinking in around the confusion... life after death? Who was this guy? She didn't buy the vampire story, but she had a feeling the truth was going to be deeply weird.

Hawthorne stood quiet for a moment. "Did he say anything else?"

"I think so, something about cracks in a room, ghosts slipping through... betrayal. Something about how I had to find some people, let them know that I'm the key... that's all I remember."

"You're the key?"

Anne shrugged, "Whatever that means."

"Ghosts?"

"Yep."

"That's all?"

"Uh-huh."

"So you basically forgot the most important part." Hawthorne shook her head.

"Check. Maybe I should try to take a nap… it might come back to me."

* * *

"Wake up, baby!" Rae shouted through the rush of the wind.

Desperation colored her voice. She strained against the seat belt, shaking Alex's leg as he slumped in the back seat. She twisted back around, released her seat belt and scrambled between the seats. The car only swerved slightly as she bumped and jostled the driver on her journey to the back seat.

The car rocketed through the sparse suburban residential neighborhood at over twice the speed limit. It swerved again slightly as Ping felt in the glove box for his sunglasses. He pulled them from the case with one hand and put them on. Outside, night and artificial day interleaved as they tore through the wash of street lamps. Ping adjusted the glasses for night vision, and the world outside clarified and tinted yellow. The glasses also provided a windbreak that allowed him to stop squinting into the wind blasting through the shattered windshield.

In the back seat, Rae was patting Alex down, looking for bullet wounds. Ping spared a few glances at them through the mirror. He didn't see any blood. Rae checked his pulse. "He's alive, but the pulse is weak! I can't find any wounds!" she shouted, worry and relief mixing in her voice. "Wake up!" she yelled. She smacked him lightly on the cheek, kissed him on the lips—smacked him harder.

"Doctor!" Ping yelled through the wind, "Perhaps you should get a second opinion before you continue that treatment!"

She hugged Alex so hard Ping thought she might break him. "What's wrong with him? What did they do?" The worry in her voice was deepening, skittering along the edge of panic.

"I'm sure he's fine, probably just blew a magical fuse like at the libr..."

A car shuddered to a halt in the intersection less than fifty meters ahead. Automatic weapons fire erupted from the back seat.

"Down!" Ping yelled, ducking his head. He stood on the accelerator and steered for the center of the car ahead.

He heard more automatic gunfire, but didn't hear or feel the thing it usually implied; no shells hit the car, shredding through plastic and metal, tearing through flesh. Either these guys were shooting blanks or they were the worst shots in the universe. It was like having a firing squad of evil B-movie henchmen. Cool. It was nice to have incompetent types try to kill him for a change.

They bore down on the car with reckless speed. As they got within twenty meters, the driver of the other car tried to accelerate out of the way. He must have figured that Ping was either dead or crazy. Either way, he probably figured that Ping wasn't going to try to avoid a solid collision at well over a hundred kilometers per hour.

Just as he thought it might be too late, Ping gave the wheel a controlled jerk and the car did it's best to accommodate his wishes. All four wheels turned, all four motors compensated as needed to maximize traction, and the suspension actively leaned the car into the turn.

Still, it wasn't enough. There was a violent pop as the front left corner of their car connected with the other car's left rear fender just behind the rear wheel. The impact shook through them, wrenched them forward for the briefest instant, bones seeming to flex from an instant of sharp deceleration, but then they were past the other car.

In his mirror, Ping could see the other car spinning end over end—a body that flew from a popped door was ejected vertically about three meters before tumbling down, limbs flailing.

"Wha...?" Ping wondered aloud, looking at the kinetic havoc in their wake. Fragments of metal and glass joined plumes of erupting dirt and grass as the car made its third impact with the ground, crossing the sidewalk and tearing through a beautifully tended front yard. The ejected body disappeared into the chaos. Ping's eyes moved from the mirror to the deformed corner of their car. The bumper hadn't been able to absorb all of the impact, so the frame of the car had bent slightly. The corner panel and hood were slightly crumpled. The car pulled a little to the left.

Well, that wasn't exactly what he was expecting from all the *Blood on the Highway* videos he'd been forced to endure in driving courses at the academy. In the mirror he saw the car behind them bounce through the lower branches of a tree, then finally skid to a halt across a driveway on what was left of its roof. It looked like a cargo tractor had hit it head-on at supersonic speed. He looked forward to his own car's damage. It looked like he'd had a parallel parking mishap.

Cool. It was nice to crash into incompetent cars for a change. Ping's chuckle was more confusion than humor.

"Uh... *what* just happened?" Rae asked, still staring back into the storm of dirt and smoke that surrounded the wreckage "I think I blinked and missed the rest of the crash."

"Ask your boyfriend. I don't think a bullet has hit us since we left Roy's garage... you think he put some mojo on our wheels?"

"Yep, strange and mysterious are the ways of my Alex... WAKE UP!" She smacked his cheek again so hard that Ping heard the report above the rushing wind.

Their first indication of gunfire was shattered glass filling the car as bullets blew through the rear window. Metal twanged as bullets plucked it, the right rear wheel seized when its motor took two direct hits. Ping wrestled with the steering wheel as the seized rear wheel skidded along the road. The car pulled hard to the right. He compensated by steering left and accelerating.

"Looks like we're on our own!" Rae shouted, releasing Alex from his harness and pushing him to the floor.

Behind them, a sedan, a light SUV, and a microvan sped toward their slowing car.

"I told you to stop hitting him!" Ping yelled, trying to keep the car going generally forward.

"Yeah, like this is my fault! You definitely blew our mojo destroyin' that car back there! Uhg!" she made a sound like Ping's mom made when she thought she was doing everyone's work, "Be right back!" Rae opened the door behind Ping and leaned out. She gripped the frame of the door with her left knee inside the car, her right knee outside, and her left elbow on the roof. She used her left arm to steady the fletcher as she dialed minimum dispersion and snapped off three quick blasts at the lead car behind them.

A quick glance in his mirror showed Ping that she was a fair shot. The driver's window shattered. Holes appeared in both the driver's-side doors. The gunman leaning out the rear window was surrounded by a halo of dark human aerosol. His gun jumped and popped end over end across the pavement and he slid, limp, back into the car. The dead man's gun finally impacted on the swerving microvan's bumper.

The driver's head bounced off her wheel, filling the night with the abbreviated bleat of her horn. Her head recoiled from the impact and she slumped right, pulling the decelerating vehicle into a right turn that the SUV behind her barely avoided. The driverless car jumped the curb, crossed a well-manicured front lawn and slammed into an ancient maple tree.

"Rae!" Ping yelled as the right front motor burned out, throwing the car into a sharp right swerve. This was enough to break the grip Rae had on the car, her open door swung wide and she exited the car backwards without a sound. Ping fought in vain for control of his crippled car.

Rae flew backwards through the cool air, clutching her fletcher like a severed lifeline. She brought her knees up hard, accelerating her reverse somersault, watching the starry sky swing by. As the ground filled her vision, she threw her arms and legs wide, slowing her spin, reaching out with her feet. The impact was harsh, but she allowed her legs to crumple. Her body again curled into a ball as she spread the impact across her legs, back, then shoulders. As she went over again, her bent knees slammed into the pavement and the shock of the impact unwound her. Her breath blew out of her as the ground slammed into her back.

Starbursts. Pretty. Ouch.

She was still holding the fletcher. Now that's determination, she thought somewhat blearily. The screeching of tires filled the air, but around that sound, a million imaginary insects seemed to be chattering, harmonizing with the pretty light show in her head.

Her eyes snapped open when the car's screeching terminated in a jarring crash. She was up far faster than she could have been a year ago—thanks Alex. ...Alex! Fletcher in hand, aching body protesting, she sprinted toward the three cars from behind.

Their car had passed her and swerved onto the sidewalk on the other side of the road. The SUV had crashed into the passenger side. The microvan was about five meters behind their car. The driver covered the wrecked car with an automatic weapon braced against her open door.

She could make out the sound of someone yelling angrily from the direction of Ping's wrecked car, then two shots rang out in rapid succession. A shock wave of panic crashed through her. She poured on the speed. Twenty meters to go.

Ping's head slammed into the window's safety glass. The glass turned partially opaque as micro-fractures spread away from the impact. He felt like his head had just struck the biggest gong at the Shaolin Temple, its reverberant ring lingered in his ears.

Turgid cloth filled his vision, fouled his every movement—trapped! He had a claustrophobic moment, already the sole inhabitant of the toe-tagged Ping Bannon memorial body bag. He struggled against the restraining cloth, and choked on some kind of burning chemical that filled the air. Coughing hurt his head, which had taken entirely too much damage in the past few days.

Suddenly there was a diffuse hiss and the restraining cloth relented. With tingling arms, he fought to clear it from his face. He was free! Then he understood: though the impact with the SUV wasn't *Blood on the Highway* bad, it did manage to slam him into the side window and deploy the car's airbags.

Then another realization hit him... he'd just been T-boned by a team of professional killers. Right! Time to move!

The spider webbed glass of his window exploded inward. He was showered with glass shards the size of pebbles, then with rifle butt. Stars exploded around him while he got cozy with a little more head trauma. The universe compressed for an instant to the few electric centimeters on the side of his head where the pain blossomed like a small mushroom cloud. His vision flashed, then went dim.

...but not dark. He forced himself to stay slumped toward the passenger seat, where the impact had driven him. With all his fluttery, barely conscious will, he forced his hands to remain limp, to not fly to the side of his head to cover or probe his damaged noggin. In his imagination, his brain was leaking from the side of his head, demanding a hand to apply firm pressure to keep things together. Nope... request denied... possum cloak engaged.

The back door opened and the car rocked down slightly as one of the killers leaned in. He prodded Alex's immobile form with the barrel of his weapon, prodded again harder. Alex didn't make a sound. The car rocked up again as the intruder retreated out the door. The handle on Ping's door was jerked, jerked again, but the car's frame had bent enough to jam the door.

There was cursing, then yanking, then more cursing with simultaneous yanking. Ping didn't smile, though it took great effort. So, this poor misguided killer had an extra-homicidal character flaw—foul language. Ping took an odd satisfaction from listening to him fail his verbal IQ test. About four words were used in various permutations to express frustration and derision—Ping translated as best as he could: "Sexually active illegitimate son, Deity may punish! Deity punished door, crap! Sexually active... crap..." The guy pounded on the door with the butt of his weapon twice in frustration, then gave the door a kick.

"Crap!" More pulling. The door sprung open at last, but the killer had left a shin in the way, which led to yet another passionate permutation of the four-word, sixteen-letter vocabulary. Ping hoped that last part meant 'mom's having sex', but he didn't think so. Eww.

Ping was always amused when he ran across what his great-grandma had called a potty mouth, though he had no idea what a 'potty' was. This really wasn't too often in the modern world. Even in the filthy circles of his old hell as a vice cop, he'd only run across a handful of people who regularly swore. There just weren't that many people left in the well-educated world who were willing to sound this dissociatively stupid, no matter how black their hearts or how dirty their hands.

It was going to be a shame to kill this guy. It would be like killing one of the last buffaloes, the last wild turkey, the loneliest dodo...

The barrel of the killer's weapon slammed into Ping's left shoulder, twisting him to the right until he was stopped by his seatbelt, face toward the passenger seat with his back to the endangered species.

"I know you're *sexually* awake!" The killer shouted. If only he knew how wrong he was—Ping was going to have to kill this guy before he blew his cover by laughing. "Wake up and sexually die, cop!"

The double explosion vibrated Ping's barrel-bruised left shoulder and put a compound hole through the back of Roy's nice jacket. When he'd been driven sideways, his right hand had crossed his chest, coming to rest on the grip of the pistol holstered, pointing backwards, under his left arm. His finger slid into the trigger guard, lock tone muffled by the surrounding holster, clothes and flesh, and further covered by the poorly assembled profanity. The two shots were followed by the thud of a job well done on the ground outside the door.

He turned back toward the door. He unholstered the weapon and covered the empty doorway where the swearing, rifle-clubbing, barrel-prodder had once stood. Ping clumsily piled out of the car, coming to a rest crouching with his back against the doorjamb.

Before him was a corpse with matching holes in throat and chest and an assault gun still clutched in one outflung hand. Ping grabbed the weapon, briefly inspected it: 3mm full auto compact assault gun with 72 rounds remaining, according to the display above the trigger guard... locked.

Rigor mortis hadn't set in, but Ping's efforts to wrest the lock ring off the dead killer's finger were vain. With his left hand, he pulled the tip of the ringed finger. With his right, he pressed the barrel of his pistol against the base of the finger, winced...

"NO!" Rae yelled as a delayed third shot came from the car. Hope drained out through the exclamation, leaving her burnt hollow. That shot sounded like an execution.

The woman covering the car behind the microvan's door whirled about, rifle tracking toward Rae—just in time to meet two volleys of dispersing fletchettes from Rae's weapon. The woman with the rifle bounced off the door behind her before landing in a heap amid the shards of glass from the shattered window.

Rae didn't stop. She raced to the microvan with the speed of Amped desperation. She leaped onto its protruding rear fender, then onto the roof. As she appeared over the top of the microvan, the driver of the SUV opened fire. The snapping hiss of a burst of maybe five rounds filled the air around her. She altered her trajectory to the right with a hard push of her left foot on the roof of the van. As she left the airspace above the microvan, she returned fire, hitting her target in the legs. Correcting as she sailed through the air, her second shot hit him in the head and torso as he doubled over.

Then she was on the ground. She touched down effortlessly, feet melding with the ground, continuing her sprint around the back of the SUV. As she ran, she pumped a string of shots into the SUV's tinted windows. She couldn't see inside until the shattering glass fell away, revealing shredded upholstery, but no more attackers. If there had been anyone inside, they were now on the floor, dead or otherwise. She didn't stop to check. Her goal was the crumpled unmarked police car before her now.

Explosions erupted behind Ping, on the other side of the car. A long string of heavy-sounding gunshots followed by the tinkle of glass, but he was showered with no glass, punctured by no bullets. Still, he was sure this was the end.

Ping slid the sticky lock ring onto his right middle finger, still gritting his teeth, applying mental restraining pressure on his dinner. Hazy purple straw seemed to crinkle about his head, filling his ears and peripheral vision, scratching across his scalp. He reached out to retrieve the assault gun from the ground at his side, but had to stop with his bloody hand leaning on top of it as the straw washed over his face—going out!

No I'm not, he thought through the numbing straw's crinkling oblivion. He had to kill several more people, find Rae, and get her and Alex out of here before he could spare time for sleep or death.

Will power was exerted and his tingling hand dragged the gun back across the ground. After a moment of intense concentration the world stopped breaking against his head like monsoon waves, and the electric straw receded to a faint crackle in his ears. He put his hand around the assault gun's pistol grip. The lock-accept tone made him shudder. At the edge of consciousness with his stolen weapon held in slippery hands, he wondered what life would have been like if he'd stayed in family counseling. Though there was humor in thinking of sitting in a circle of chairs with some dysfunctional family or other—expressing feelings, listening actively—he didn't find it funny. He'd killed more people as a cop, but not more good people. Now he tried to save people from killers, not try to save killers from losing their families.

He was about to die, behind him Alex would die, way behind him somewhere on the road, Rae either had or would die. At least now he was trying to save them, at least now he'd get to die with them.

Before him stood the familiar form of a seven-year-old girl, her hand raised as if holding an invisible mother's hand. The specter's black hair, once meticulously straightened, was in frizzy disarray. Her furtive smile had been lost long ago. The lack of light in her brown eyes was an accusation. Her clothes were twisted about her body as if frozen in sleep. Dirt covered her like a rumpled blanket, thrown off only partially upon waking. Her throat was cut from ear to ear.

He was going to die, and that was probably for the best—long overdue. Yet he will not fail and die. He could have done that long ago. Tonight, he will die trying to help. He struggled with his unresponsive right arm, and managed to get the assault gun up across his lap. He grabbed the forward grip in his left hand. The flames that erupted from the side of his battered head would ascend toward heaven, his muscles would rebel, his vision would cloud—yet his teeth will clench, his muscles *will* move. He's not done yet.

The car against his back shifted in tandem with the bang of leaping footfalls on the hood, then roof. He tried to jerk his newly unlocked gun up to cover this new threat coming from above and behind him, but couldn't pull off anything more than token resistance to gravity. His hands and the gun in them stayed on his lap.

A spinning blur above him made him reach for his holstered pistol with his left hand, but the draw and pass out neurons in his head had been cross connected. His left hand came to rest on his chest and the fog rolled in as booted feet landed in front of him.

A weapon was thrust toward him. He looked up at the cave-large muzzle directed at his face, mind divided between frustration and relief. He wondered if his mom was right about heaven and hell, wondered which would be his reward—then he saw the angel with her finger on the trigger.

"Hi, Rae." He slurred, instantly uncomfortable with the amount of misery escaping through his short utterance. "Was that a… flip I just saw?" He sobbed uncontrollably once, twice, and then the world resolved to a black halo around her shining face.

Then the blackness was absolute. He could only assume she hadn't shot him.

* * *

Below, the principal surgeon stepped away from the table. Hawthorne breathed a sigh of relief and checked her watch.

"So, what's the plan chief?" Anne asked. Below, the OR doors opened, admitting a man of about thirty with shoulder length hair and a deep, smooth tan. "If Jeremy's here, things are pretty much wrapped up."

"Jeremy?"

"Yeah," Anne said, "The guy down there with the great hair and the crass tan of science. He's another phlebotomist… he's here to unhook your partner from the operating bed. Look, he's actually checking himself out!" Below, the newcomer posed surreptitiously before a polished cabinet, making what Anne had come to regard as one of his 'handsome faces'—this one was emoting "catch you later, babe".

"The operation is over. Though you might expect to hear it in here with me, the fat lady is in fact singing."

Hawthorne turned her head and arched an eyebrow, regarding Anne critically. "You don't have to do that."

"What?" Anne asked.

"Fat jokes." Hawthorne replied.

"Oh yes I do."

Hawthorne shrugged, "Ok, then at least try to make them funny. Now 'crass tan of science'—that was hilarious." She turned back to the window and to the subject. "We wait for now."

Below, the secondary surgeon stepped back, stretching her arms. Though they couldn't hear, she was flirting with Jeremy.

"Wait for what?" Anne asked.

"For who." Hawthorne corrected.

After a few seconds, it became clear that Hawthorne wasn't going to elaborate.

The lights flickered—flickered again. Down in the OR, conversations paused and people looked up—a nod to previous eras when a flying predator might have flown in front of the sun.

"I've got a really bad feeling about this." Anne said, looking about, feeling something both new and familiar hovering at the edges of her consciousness. With an almost audible click, she placed the feeling... it was the feeling she'd had, holding the Harm's blood sample between her fingers—the same feeling of chaotic bugs jittering restlessly—looking for food.

After three more minutes, the creepy bug feeling persisted, but they were almost ready to leave: Mendez, looking like a mummy in isolation film, was transferred to an open monitor bed and connected to its systems. The principal surgeon and the tech worked on the post-op report, Jeremy and the secondary arranged a date for drinks tomorrow.

"Catch you later" Jeremy's handsome face emoted. He winked and completed his turn to go.

The doors of the OR opened inward.

A group of ten people lurch and stumble in, filling the OR's only exit.

At first their giggling daze and dishevel mark the new arrivals as the survivors of a flower-painted microbus accident. There is blood spattered among them to support this impression, but not all of their clothes follow the theme you'd expect for the passengers of such a groovy conveyance. True, most are dressed for a hip night out, but the circles of cool in which they move are obviously varied. Some wear the electric-traced black of the dated Psycho-Goth fad, while others wear the scanty leather and plastic fare of clubs with more explicit themes, a few even wear the sleek business casual of more mature pickup joints. One wears only rumpled pajama bottoms, his bare and bleeding feet leaving red-brown footprints behind him.

Most still wear the remains of broken or cut plastic restraints on wrists and ankles, the kind used to secure patients in the high security ward of the hospital. Most are still wearing the hospital patient ID wristbands. But the most obvious similarities between the new arrivals are the dark mottled skin, the black vacant eyes, the humorless grins that seem to stretch from ear to ear—the teeth reconfigured for the work of the carnivore.

Looking down on the new arrivals, Anne's mind returns to the Harm she'd killed in the ER… she saw his face as he leaned casually in to take a bite from Dr. Wyler's ear.

There is a breathless moment—the inhale before the scream—when all eyes lock on the doorway and its surreal visitors.

"I assume we're not waiting for these guys." Anne says with a smirk.

The doctors and technicians take a collective step back from the door. On the gurney, Mendez slumbers through the terror congealing around him, wrapped in protective plastic film and insulating layers of sleep. To Anne's eye, he looks uncomfortably like a burrito on the counter of any Latin-themed restaurant. And the customers have arrived.

But they aren't looking for burrito… the entire demonic group is staring up at the mirrored glass behind which Anne and Hawthorne stand.

"Oh my God." Hawthorne hadn't struck Anne as overly religious, but that definitely sounded like a prayer.

Splinters fly into the small observation room and a booted foot follows the door inward briefly. BOOM! The rest of the invader shoulders the door out of the way, her weapon tracking toward Hawthorne and Anne as they stand by the observation window across the small room. Behind the hard looking woman with the poor door etiquette, Anne can make out two more figures with assault guns on the small landing outside the door.

If that had been a prayer, Anne didn't think that this was the answer the Fed had hoped for.

Hawthorne's gun is coming out. Already clear of the holster, it is extending toward the new threat at the door. 'Fool her once...' Anne thinks, remembering Hawthorne's passivity the last time someone with dubious intentions had the drop on her. She isn't as fast as Mendez, but even if she were, she wouldn't make it before the already-firing assault gun finds her.

Anne is moving.

With unreasonable speed and confidence, Anne lunges toward Hawthorne and the strong-looking window behind her. Anne's left arm goes around Hawthorne's back and her right hand sweeps up Hawthorne's right hand in mid-draw. Anne's finger slides over Hawthorne's into the pistol's trigger guard. She hears the pistol's unlock tone and realizes that she does in fact have a plan. Anne presses the gun away from the invaders at the doorway and toward the observation window.

Anne squeezes gently, conscious of Hawthorne's delicate bones, the gun fires a stream of five shots, crossing the observation window, blowing through, leaving behind a lattice of semi-opaque shards held together by safety film.

Still holding the increasingly confused Fed in a waltz-like death grip, Anne leaves the ground, now completely committed to her nutty plan. She leaps past the now-squeaking Fed, ducking her head and shoulders into a sideways roll that leaves her flying toward the damaged window backwards and parallel to the floor. Squeak now a scream, Hawthorne is waltz-wrenched off her feet and toward the window after Anne. Shells tear through the air around them, snapping into the wall on the far side of the room.

Pressure builds against Anne's back until the sound of crunching glass comes from behind, then around her. They pass through the window in a storm of glass and into the air perhaps six meters above the OR floor.

Then the world is floating glass and Hawthorne's expanding scream. Squinting against the cloud of glass, Anne cranes her neck right, looking for the ground. Unsuccessful, she looks back over Hawthorne's shoulder. There it is—maybe five meters down now and coming up fast.

Anne releases Hawthorne's gun-hand, and grabs her shoulder. Using it as a lever, she juggles Hawthorne, trying to move her into position above her, so she can catch her when they land. Hand over hand, Anne manhandles Hawthorne into position. Looking briefly at Hawthorne's terror-rigid face as it spins by, Anne realizes that if they both live through this somehow, Hawthorne will probably feel honor-bound to kill her for this.

Impact found Anne's feet wide for support, her knees bending to absorb the shock. The glass showered down around them as Anne caught Hawthorne's spinning and panic-rigid form. Anne tried to spread Hawthorne's deceleration over as great a distance as possible, but she was pretty sure it still hurt.

Then the fury was over and the world was at an odd equilibrium for a second or two. Anne stood near the center of the OR with Hawthorne in her arms like the cheesy cover of a gay romance novel.

"Sorry 'bout that!" Anne said, giddy triumph running through her.

Chilled bloodless, Hawthorne emerged from the panic-blurred experience in a quick succession of degrees. Degree one: A shock like being hit by a speeding Nerf cargo transport. Degree two: The sound of rushing air had transformed into the click-tinkle of showering glass. She was pretty sure her body had stopped spinning, though her inner ear told her differently. Degree three: She remembered standing in the observation booth and being attacked, then whirling, spinning hell, then here. Degree four: The realization that this was only a *near*-death experience so far. Degree five: The realization that she would have to kill Anne Kelley for this.

The breath she had not screamed out had been knocked from her by the impact, so she was left with her mouth open and eyes squeezed shut against the storm of falling glass. Every muscle was taut with anticipated demise. Though there wasn't any air left for it, her lungs squeezed anyway, needing just a little more scream.

She managed to disengage the lock on her throat, and the air jerked and hitched into her burning lungs. "If..." gasp, "you ask me...", wheeze, "if I'm okay..." She gestured with the weapon trembling in her right hand. "Pow."

Slow, evil chuckling filled the air around them.

* * *

In the janitor's closet among disinfectants and other implements of order and cleanliness, two men hid in complete darkness. One breathed in long, regular cycles; the other was investing a significant portion of his willpower into keeping his labored breath from drawing unwanted attention from the other side of the door.

Chase would be able to handle this a lot better if it weren't for the laughter. Outside the closet door, *things* shuffled by. No talking, no crashes of destructive fury, no melodramatic moaning or growling; just an occasional ripple of introspective laughter that had to be categorized as 'mischievous evil'. (i.e. that evil which has just a little extra time for play)

Chase shivered, thinking about what playtime might be like for such creatures. In his minds eye, he saw their misshapen faces on the security cam in the lobby. Their eyes dead, their faces pits from which all humanity had been strip-mined. They exuded the attitude and overall fresh look of hell's supermodels. He remembered his brief glimpse of the bodies and blood on the ground outside the ambulance and had to force his mind to stop trying to reconstruct that scene.

He clenched the stunner tighter in his damp palm. If that door opened, he didn't know whether he would use it on whatever came through the door, or on himself.

Outside, another chuckle sent chills jerking through his nervous system.

Until the End of the World

So close your eyes
For that's a lovely way to be
Aware of things your heart alone
Was meant to see
The fundamental loneliness goes
Whenever two can dream a dream together

– Wave
A tale best told by Frank Sinatra

Like a dungeon beneath a grand and polished palace, the gym lurked in the second and third sub-basements beneath the shining steel and glass of the immense Grant building. The first sub-basement held *Fleck's*, a stylish Euro-club, complete with bars both smart and less so. It was mainly frequented by singles looking for a connection; many would use the club to unwind after their workouts, looking to showcase newly stressed glutes and biceps. It was a popular club, not least of all because, unlike gyms of previous times, it was exceptionally hard to meet people while working out… at least in the less geeky sense of the word.

In the bottom level of the club were the VirtuaTrainers, and in these trainers, there were two travelers sitting by a fire, talking easily and getting closer—metaphorically speaking anyway.

It was five minutes to the reboot and the two travelers rested after a particularly difficult engagement. They sat around a small fire in the dark emptiness of a ruined subterranean city, casually talking while they waited for their friends. Smack busied himself polishing the last of the blood from the etched runes of his enchanted blade, while Angel used a spell to reinforce the enchantments on her battered armor.

Not far outside the reach of the fire's light were the corpses of their most recent enemies. Nearer to the fire were three man-sized bundles, neatly wrapped in white silk. Their party had been culled by death from its initial five to only he and she. Since they were both sure that there is always life after death, there is no mourning or remorse as they watched over their fallen companions.

Over the past few months, they have drawn closer, their friendship deepening in ways that made them both comfortable and not. But then it's not always about comfort. Sometimes it's about discovery, perhaps even about hope. Sometimes it's about taking chances, and tonight Smack was ready to take one.

They kept the conversation light. No talk of the meaning of life, ethics, or politics—they were discussing Angel's day job.

"Brain surgery?" Smack laughed.

Angel shook her head, reveling in the story, "Yeah, but that ain't the funny part. It's the look in his bleary eyes. He's got this look like 'beat that cop!' It's like he's challengin' us to prove he don't just have a little piece of his brain missing."

"Ah, so he's immune to sobriety tests because he's disabled. I hope you weren't insensitive enough to insist."

"I'm afraid we were. He never took the test though. As he stepped out of the car, he tripped on the curb and fell flat."

"Not good!" Smack sheathes his blade. "So, did he?"

Angel lowered her flask. "Did he what?"

"Have brain surgery?"

"Nope, though I wouldn't rule out brain damage of some kind. My guess is his parents were cousins… though I'm not sure that qualifies as brain damage." She offered him the flask, but he waved it away with his own. "Anyway, he's completely insensate on the sidewalk and never so much as twitches a finger until the next morning in his cell. He woke up all hangover-cranky and wondering where he was."

Their laughter halted when an echoing scrape reached them from outside the light of their fire. Smack is gone in a flash. Ignoring the soreness in his muscles from their last battle, he plunged like a shark into shadow and danger. His bright sword was lost in the ruins outside the circle of firelight. Angel remained by the fire, staring into its depths—bait again.

With a hand beneath her cloak, she moved her fingers through the arcs that activated the spell of Sight. The spell flickered in her eyes, and the three intruders appeared before her mind's eye. They were approaching slowly, probably hoping to catch them off-guard.

She smiled, evil plans forming. With another hidden gesture, she made the pattern for Farspeak and whispered into the fire. "It's them. I think they're trying to get the drop on us. Lets have a bit of fun, babe."

Perhaps twenty meters away, crouching in the blackness, Angel's spell put her whispered words in Smack's ear. He was distracted by her use of the familiar term. It had to be unhealthy to feel this way about someone you've never really seen. 'Forbidden passion' sounded a lot less geeky than the reality of his feelings.

"Gotcha... babe." He whispered into the mystic channel between them. They both smiled.

"Ready, honeymuffin?" She said playfully.

"When you are, sugarbumps."

"They're to your right... poofakins. You take Lo Pan, I'll get the others."

"Poofakins?" he whispered, "That's just wrong. In position now, snugglebunny." He whispered, gripping his sword with both hands. On the other side of a partially fallen wall, he heard a boot scuff on the broken stone of the walkway.

He bent his knees, coiling before the strike. Then he was sailing through the air, pulling his head back and his knees up. He loved this part.

Angel traced a subtle pattern with her hands and the fire rushed out to engulf her, tickling harmlessly across her skin. The torrent of flame swept her up and carried her toward the intruders. Swimming in the fire geyser, she streaked through the darkness, shadows radiating away from the brightness of her star. Flames leapt from her outstretched hands, striking two of the startled Avatars dead center. One managed to deflect the fireball with a large metal shield, but he was still rocked back, staggering from the impact. The third intruder's staff moved toward Angel, energies building along its length.

From above, Smack tumbled out of the darkness, blade flashing. The blade struck the staff between the Avatar's hands, cutting it in half with a blinding flash of released energy. Smack followed the down stroke into a crouch, and then jumped into a spinning roundhouse kick that hit the reeling wizard in the jaw; Lo Pan landed on his back, dazed.

The staggering shield-bearer recovered his footing, and with his patented 'Mighty Shout', swung his heavy axe at Smack. There was a ringing clash as Smack's blade intercepted the axe. The clash of weapons had a definite victor as the axe's head split in half, severed by Smack's humming blade. The sheared part of the axe head spun through the air, catching Smack on the forehead with its flat edge. With the same type of luck that doesn't kill people in freak car crashes, but only leaves them maimed, Smack hit the ground unconscious, but not dead.

"Did'ja see that?" Rygar shouted, brandishing his axe handle in victory. Everyone who saw was laughing. Angel halted her assault to see what all the laughing was about, and joined in when the others explained. Though unconscious, Smack was laughing too, poking fun at his own performance.

"Serves you right!" Lo Pan waved his broken staff at Smack's unconscious form. "This was my best reserve weapon!"

"Sorry about your spawnfodder, David" Smack couldn't stop laughing long enough to really achieve the sarcasm he intended.

"Spawnfodder!? Now this really pisses me off to no end! Two thousand platinum! That's what you owe me!"

"Yeah, an' you owe me four thousand for guarding your stinking corpse… but don't worry, I take credit."

The broken staff bounced off Smack's unconscious form.

"Hey now, old man!" Smack yelled from the land of the unconscious. "Don't be kicking your old pal when he's down!"

"I'll show you kicking…" Smack's fallen body received a few playful kicks before his eyes fluttered open.

"You are so dead again." Smack grogged out through his newly functional mouth.

Lo Pan leapt away as the rest of the group turned to watch the show. He made a dash for his decomposing corpse, and quickly relieved it of his dragon pole. "Now we'll see who does the dying!" He shouted with more than a hint of melodrama. He held the staff aloft, then slammed it down between his feet. A sound like thunder's louder brother threw everyone off their feet and collapsed a few dilapidated buildings around them. When they looked again, Lo Pan stood at one end of a long crevice that had opened in the ground.

"Yeah. 'By the power of Grayskull!' We know the drill." Smack said, clamboring to his feet.

"That's right, baby! And don't you forget it, either." Lo Pan said, turning back to his corpse, "...now, no more fooling around. The reboot's coming up fast!"

Reminded of the impending deadline, the three formerly dead Avatars scrambled to recover their equipment from their silk-wrapped previous incarnations. They stowed the gear they arrived with in their packs. Later, they would store the reserve equipment in the lockers at the inn near the spawn point, so they could retrieve it quickly the next time they died.

They were mostly done when an even tone filled the air and a cool voice spoke in every ear. "Scheduled outage in thirty seconds. Save-point in twenty-eight seconds."

"Man, my workout ain't half over either." Rygar complained as he buckled the last of his armor in place.

"You did get to do the big corpse-sprint back from town." Smack said.

"Workout my butt!" Angel laughed, "Rygar, everyone knows you're a cutout."

"Your butt?" Lo Pan asked, giving the object of discussion a glance. "What's that supposed to mean?"

A gossamer list of their current possessions appeared in the air near each Avatar.

"I was about done anyway." Angel verified her list and sat down to await the end of this world.

Smack looked through his semitransparent list at Angel, pretending to check his inventory before the save-point. Here she was tall with smooth ebony skin and snow-white shoulder-length hair. What will he see when he sees her with his own eyes? He could have looked at her

ID photo when he'd hacked the server's database. He'd only harvested her name and the name of her gym. He wanted the rest to be a surprise.

He was still looking at her when the world ended.

Shivering sparks, static he feels and tastes—blackness.

The first thing he became aware of was the feeling of the water surrounding him. His strained and twitching arms and legs were held immobile by the resist-net that went into lockdown when their server went down. His eyes were open, but they might as well have been closed. The darkness was absolute.

He heard the lock release tone and closed his eyes. After a moment of increasing light coming red through his closed eyelids, he tried to open his eyes. The low light still seemed too bright, but with a little blinking, it soon became bearable.

The resist-net disengaged with a clunk, followed by a muted hydraulic hiss. Slow currents in the water caressed his skin. In the increasing blue light, he saw the resist-net clamshell move back from his body, freeing his sore limbs. He'd never been able to shake the image of the resist-net as a huge gray mouth. Its inner surface looked like a large plastic tongue, studded with taste bud sensors and servos.

After a long and quite painful initial stretch, he disengaged the connectors that linked his helmet with the gym's network and spent the next minute reeling in the vertigo of the disconnect. Finally, he floated up half a meter, pushed the lid of the tank open, and struggled from his workout and out into the real world.

He stood shakily on the heated metal grate near the tank, dripping wet and dizzy. He took his helmet off, staggering slightly as the sense-tape separated from its place on the back of his neck. He stowed the helmet on a shelf and grabbed a towel from the rack above the shelf.

Two tanks away, she was emerging. She was short, but not compared to him; her skin was the rich color of cocoa. Her body was muscular on a thin frame. She leaned against the tank and pulled her helmet off. Her eyes were closed as she collected herself. Her acne scars added a weathered character to her face; her ample lips seemed still to smile. Maybe she's thinking about him?

Angel.

So, that's what she looks like. Beautiful. Now for the hard part—easy conversation.

He moved to the stretching benches and began the painful work of insuring he retained his current range of motion after the intense workout. Essentially, the VR experience was candy coating around a full-body workout. He didn't understand how people used to work out before VR Gyms... people like him probably didn't.

He was into his second circuit of leg stretches when she sat down on the bench two meters to his right. She wasn't looking at him, but of course he was used to that. Even though he had played his way to perfect physical fitness, he still wasn't the kind of guy girls stole glances at.

What was he doing? Fear made a final plea to control his actions, but foolishness won out in the end. "You at the Pain Foundry, too?" He tested the conversational waters, feeling stupid before he'd gotten out the first syllable.

She glanced at him, then quickly away. "Yeah. How'd you…?"

"You got out with me… I figured it was the scheduled maintenance."

Her eyes darted back to him then back away. "Yeah. Though I don't usually admit I go in for that wands and dragons stuff."

"Your secret's safe with me." He said with a nod. "You play there often?"

"I choose to exercise my Fifth Amendment rights." She smiled an unexpectedly dazzling smile, then glanced quickly at him again. "Why do you play at a server all the way in Washington State?"

He laughed. "I just moved from there… haven't met any friends on the local servers yet. You?"

"Oh, I have some good friends there." She smiled.

"Alexander Ahmed." He held out his hand.

"Rae Jackson." She took his hand, gave it a quick shake. She looked at him a little bit longer before looking away.

"Hey, maybe I've seen you online. What's your handle?" He asked, knowing the answer.

* * *

You can't deny
Don't try to fight the rising sea
Don't fight the moon, the stars above
Don't fight me
The fundamental loneliness goes
Whenever two can dream a dream together

- Wave

A tale best told by Frank Sinatra

"I'm not sure I'm ready to get married," she said, looking at him like he'd just dropped his pants in public, "I mean, I've only known you three months."

"Eight months." Alex corrected.

"I've only known what you look like for three months." Rae said with a smirk.

"Oh, it's all about physical beauty with you now?" He shook his head, "So superficial." He said in airy condescension.

"I've only known your name for three months."

"You've known Smack for eight months," he said reasonably, "and that's who you'd be taking to the altar. Besides, think of the wedding gifts."

"You are such a geek." She said trying for a look of shocked indignation.

"You might get that Black Cloak of Aragoth you've been hoping for…"

She laughed, "This is sinking to a new low…"

"So the answer is 'yes'? Ah! You've made me the happiest Avatar in all of Gorgo!" He said, laying on the irony.

"Keep it down!" she hissed through clenched teeth, giving him the fiery eye of death. She covered her face with her hands and shook her head despondently. "This is not happening."

"You can invite all your cop friends…"

"NO!" Her head snapped up, terror filling her eyes.

He shook his head in mock condemnation, "You are so easy to provoke… are you sure you're a good cop?"

"I don't even know if you're gay yet."

"You're not saying if we sleep together you'll know I'm not gay, are you?"

"…so the answer is 'yes'?" she said with enthusiasm.

His eyes smiled; his head shook, "I think you have a problem with commitment."

"I'm not the one who wants to get digitally hitched."

"Exactly."

"Hey, is this some kind of geek dating ritual? You know—like the dork version of going steady or something?"

"Always the nerd anthropologist." He said, reaching across the table, past the greasy food, around the protein-infused soda. He placed his hand over hers and looked directly into her eyes. "You know, I've felt steady from the beginning."

She smiled, perhaps even blushed a little. There was an uncomfortable pause as something heavier than the normal banter passed between them.

It didn't take long for her to break eye contact. "Net stalker." She jabbed an accusing finger at him while picking up a fry with the other hand.

"High priestess of the order of Xandock." He jabbed back, just a little louder.

"Shhhh! Man, you're embarrassing!" She looked around praying no one had heard.

"This man giving you trouble, officer?" The rather stealthy waitress at the end of their booth said. Rae jumped, then froze with her eyes closed and her lips tight.

"Nothing a little police brutality wouldn't correct." Rae said in a measured tone.

"She won't marry me." Alex said.

Rae's eyes opened, giving him the look of impending death.

After a moment spent in appraisal, the waitress gave Alex a short nod. "Yeah, I get that."

"You are really endangering your tip." Alex wagged a finger at her.

"We all know who wears the tip in this family. You need any dessert?" the waitress asked, turning to Rae.

"I tipped yesterday!" Alex tapped his finger on the table.

"Yeah... A dollar—I look like a gumball machine to you?" the waitress asked, arching her eyebrows.

"A dollar fifty." Alex said, looking guilty.

"You used a fractional dollar?" Rae was horrified. "Only tax software considers pennies... oh, I forgot... you are tax software... I'm dating tax software."

"So we *are* dating!" Alex made the male triumph gesture with his fist clenched and elbow cocked, "Yes!"

"Never marry a poor tipper, honey." The waitress said, walking away.

Three weeks later, Smack and Angel were married in a big ceremony in a castle near the Cliffs of Echoes. Even some Avatars from rival clans came. Proving that even virtual gift registries do work, Angel received the Black Cloak of Aragoth from a very thoughtful immortal.

Alex got her a wedding ring that allowed her to levitate.

Unfortunately, she lost them both a week later in an unfortunate eaten-by-dragon incident.

* * *

"It's not a lie!" He was angry, and that realization had an odd effect on her—she couldn't remember ever seeing him mad before. His anger had a crystallizing effect on her rage, like an ice pack applied to her broken heart. Well, at least now they're beyond the glib banter, even if it's only at the end.

She'd known it at some level—knew that she'd only be burned by love... would ever be its refugee. She didn't need him to tell her she wasn't pretty; that was something she'd always known.

The scale of her rage was an uncomfortable indicator of just how much she'd let her guard down. Well, she wasn't going to make that mistake again.

The cameo lay on the floor where she'd thrown it.

Oh no, here come the tears, she thought bitterly. Her eyes blurred, and her lips began to twist... what's next?

Uncontrolled sobs. Dammit. She turned to the door, intending flight, just needing to get out. His hand clamped around her elbow, stopping her. "NO!" He yelled.

She was walking a tightrope between rage and sorrow, and she was going to fall. She couldn't look at him.

"I love you!" he shouted, shaking her arm slightly.

She snorted, hope reasserting itself in the most infuriating way. But she knew that couldn't be true. "It's over." Her gaze fell on the fallen cameo, ashamed of how much she wished what she saw...

His tight grip on her arm stopped her second retreat. "This the part where I knock you out?" she said though clenched teeth without turning back.

"Do what you have to do... I'm not letting go."

"Why not?" she shouted, whirling about on him. She had to give him credit for only flinching slightly—he really wasn't the physical type. "You can give your Stepford Action Barbie necklace to someone who would hit you a lot less for it."

"It's not about me."

"Really." Her eyes rose to meet his. "So it's someone else who you want to see me like I was pretty..." her voice faltered on 'pretty'.

His expression softened with empathy. This wasn't what she wanted—pity. This was the bottom of the deepest well in hell. The muscles of her right arm tensed... yep she was actually going to hit him.

"It's for someone else." He said, looking directly into her eyes.

Her arm didn't relax, but it didn't slam into his head either. She paused briefly, off balance.

"It's for you."

That got him a bitter bark of laughter, and she was still reserving judgment on the punch. "You're so full of sweet."

"Rae… listen to me… trust me for just a sec here." He said, looking earnest. Maybe he actually believed the crap he was shoveling here. "I just wanted you to see yourself the way I do… I wanted you to believe."

"By giving me a mask? A mask!" Her voice caught, her fist unwound; she sobbed. "I thought maybe you…"

"It's not a mask."

"It's a paper bag." She moaned.

"It's you, Rae."

"*That* isn't me!" her eyes moved to the cameo on the floor.

"No, Rae." He put a hand on her face—she flinched away. "This is, Rae…" He put his hand on her shoulder, "This is you… That's all the necklace shows you… what I see every day. It shows you who I see, *how* I see."

"Hooray. And with your little gift, I can be your dream girl." There was hope in her voice, hiding behind the fear and rage. The hope burned, by far the weakest and most dangerous of the emotions. She wished it would just die. Yet here she stood, listening with one ear and a reluctant heart.

"Rae, please. Please just give me sixty seconds. For all the goofy things we've been through together, for our friendship, for yourself… just sixty seconds."

She didn't answer, but she didn't move.

"I ate eggplant for you." He said like the final statement in a brilliant oratory, and gave her just a hint of that crooked smile she loved so much it hurt. He took a step backwards, waiting for her to bolt, hands up between them. When he was convinced she wasn't going to flee immediately, he scooped up the necklace and returned to her.

"Look." He pointed to the wall mirror where this fight began. It was still cracked from the impact of her fist.

She made no move at first, but then turned slowly. She was a wreck, looking teary and weak. The crystalline cracks were a net cast over her reflection.

He was behind her. "Thirty seconds more. Please."

He put his hands on her shoulders, trying to make eye contact through the mirror. He reached around her throat. His hands met then separated again, trailing a silver chain between them. "Look." He said.

She forced her eyes to meet her own in the mirror.

"Watch for the change." Slowly he brought the necklace to her throat. The cool metal on the back of the cameo touched the skin at her collarbone, and a subtle twist seemed to tug at her vision. In the mirror, she shifted from herself into something truly impressive.

"Paper bag…" she mumbled.

"Paper bags cover you." He said, fastening the clasp. "This uncovers you. Tell me, what's different now?"

"I'm beautiful."

"No, I mean specifically. What's specifically different?"

She looked hard at her nose, which was no longer too wide. "My nose." She looked at her eyes that were no longer beady. "My eyes… everything."

"Really? Are you sure?"

"Don't play with me."

"I'm not. Not at all." He unclasped the necklace. "Now watch your nose closely… don't take your eyes off of it…"

He removed the necklace, but the dimensions of her nose didn't change. "How?" She said, almost forgetting that he was there. She now looked like she always did, but her nose hadn't changed from when she was perfect. In fact, it almost looked good.

"Now look at your eyes."

She obliged, almost more curious than afraid now. He put the necklace back on; her eyes didn't change… yet they were beautiful.

"Now you see what I do. It doesn't change how you look." He paused for effect, "…*it changes how you see*. It makes you see yourself like I see you."

Something shifted in the universe; unseen shackles loosened, threatened to fall. "Who'da thunk…" She said, hot with emotion, yet lighter somehow. She put a hand on the glass, palm forward, fingers spread, feeling the sharp lines of the cracks. Through this cracked window, she saw herself for the first time. Through the tears, she smiled.

His reflection smiled back. "At last, we see the same thing."

"Why?"

His right hand slid from her right shoulder across her throat, coming to rest on her left shoulder. His left hand moved across her waist, completing the embrace. She felt his warmth behind her, his breath on her ear. "Selfishness." His reflected smile broadened.

He was baiting her. He must feel pretty confident that she was done with that face-smashing impulse. Her stare shifted from her reflection to his in the mirror. She waited.

When it became obvious she wasn't going to ask again, he continued, "I needed you to believe I could love you. When your dad looked at you, what do you think he saw?" He gestured toward the cracked glass. "He saw beauty, just like I do. The weird part is that you saw something else. Baby, you're beautiful... you're just stupid too."

"You... love me." The sarcasm wouldn't work, though she tried, it sounded as forced as a warped drawbridge with rusty hinges.

"Now listen, you stubborn woman..." he whispered, "I love you. I might screw up, might even hurt you sometimes, but I'm never going to stop loving you."

Though her cheeks burned, she didn't look away.

"Not till the end of the world."

She's never seen him completely serious before. "You proposing something?" She said with a twinkle in her damp eyes.

His flinch was barely perceptible, "Ah! Some kind of proposal, you say? Those kinds of questions..." he made a show of scratching his neck uncomfortably, "Well, they take a long time to ask properly..."

"Sure." She interrupted, shaking her head and rolling her eyes with theatrical disappointment. She was more than willing to get back to a more comfortable level of flip banter, "Someday you're gonna grow up, Ahmed—maybe I'll still be around..."

"…but I think I've been asking for some time now." He said with such deadpan delivery she didn't at first realize he was kidding… and then she realized he wasn't. He was staring directly into her frightened eyes, steady as ever, but slightly less dorky, maybe.

Her mouth moved, trying to find some sarcasm, but willing to settle on irony if that was all that was within easy reach… no luck. Her lips stopped, and they were both left staring at themselves in the mirror and watching fear and hope fight it out in a desperate jello wrestling match in her face.

"'Buh da?' is not an answer, Rae."

"Sudden." she said, for lack of something better.

"Sudden? I think I've been asking since the first time I told you 'no.'"

Shock. Time passed, things changed. Now she still stared into cracked glass, full of fear and purpose. Things were different now, but her hand still pressed against cracked glass, palm out, fingers spread. "Not till the end of the world…" She whispered, crying still, but now, her tears were bitter.

Behind her ephemeral reflection, inside the car, Alex lay like a discarded rag doll. She was afraid to open the door, afraid to discover the worst, but she had to move. Now it was all up to her. To her left, Ping sat unconscious, slumped against the open front door of the car, dead or dying; blood matted his hair, stained his jacket from neck to shoulder to chest. Her eyes returned to Alex, she removed her hand from the glass. Her reflected eyes hardened, her jaw set, and her reflection slid away as she opened the door.

Lost and Found

Dek stood on the edge of a bridge above the five southbound lanes of highway 12, perhaps fifty kilometers south of Roy's house on Lake Geneva. He still needed to get farther away before he dared call Kaspari. Dek knew his call would be traced and his position fixed by the resourceful hunters still on their trail, and he didn't want to give them any reason to disturb Alex and the others before they got underway.

Twisting around, his eyes scanned over the approaching traffic. There! His eyes settled on a two-module cargo transport approaching the bridge from the north. An instant after it disappeared beneath the bridge, he jumped. His jump was nearly parallel with the street below because he needed to bridge the speed differential between himself and the transport.

He flew through the air, dropping slightly as gravity exerted its slow acceleration on him. The truck appeared below him, the low rumble of its engine emerging from the rush of the slipstream. As he fell, he reached out with hands and feet, spreading his impact over as wide an area as possible to avoid waking the driver. Dek was reasonably sure the driver was asleep because the transport traveled in a guide lane and it was well after sundown.

The cool exterior of the transport slid beneath his hands. He'd hit the truck a bit slow, but he had plenty of time to find handholds in the slow motion world of his own speed. He hadn't been out hitching for decades and he'd forgotten how fun it was. Roy used to take him out hitching all the time. If Ivo had known what his kids were up to, he would have felt obligated to get a bit stern. That's why they always told him they were going out to a movie or some other half-truth.

Here, a barnacle attached to the speeding transport, Dek smiled at the memories of loved ones and simpler times. Then he stopped smiling when he remembered why he was here, why he was doing this. He was here because his world had been destroyed. He was here because those loved ones were gone and times would never be simple like that again.

The lust for power was something Dek would never understand. This lust seemed to only bring destruction and misery to those who acquired it. It was an over-full grail that sloshed destruction on pursuer and bystander alike.

The pursuit of power had brought many enemies to Ivo's door. Entire clans had focused their considerable resources on Ivo's exploitation or destruction, and yet he had never dealt them more damage than required for defense. But now, heaven help him, Dek was going to make sure those who had destroyed his family got every bit of the destruction they deserved. He wanted it more than anything else. He wanted it more than he wanted to breathe, more than he wanted to live. These people took something precious from the world, but never again. Those monsters would not live to ruin more lives, bring more misery, to leave anyone else this desolate. As Roy would say, "They were going to join Mr. Lem Li in the hell of being cut to pieces."

The transport pulled into the exit lane for highway 176, so Dek changed cars a few times, ending up in the back of a pickup truck continuing south towards Rosemont. As he sailed between the speeding vehicles, he couldn't help but enjoy himself. He knew Roy and Dad would want him to be happy—though Dad wouldn't want him to be happy Hitching.

He smiled, and for a moment he was wrapped in the warmth of their memory. They were a quirky lot; strength and peccadilloes meshing like cogs in an odd gearbox. Each of them was unique, but they all fit together to make something beautiful—a family.

His tears slipped from him, taken away by the wind. He wanted to scoop the sorrow out, replace it with hate. He was afraid that this sadness would make him weak when the time came for action. It was too much; it would make him falter. But in spite of his best efforts, the sadness deepened until it was a physical feeling, like slow fire in his chest.

He looked about, half expecting to have a Kenobi moment, receiving a little glowing visit from his dead family. Of course, he was still alone with the speeding traffic. But he couldn't shake the impression of his dead family appearing to him in glowing Jedi robes. He could almost see the scene play out in his head—they would show up, affecting faux gravity, then Roy would blow the mood by telling Dek to 'use The Force', or some such nonsense. They'd laugh like idiots while Ivo waited, affecting the patience of the pious dead, until his kids sobered up enough for him to deliver whatever Really Important Message he'd come from beyond the grave to deliver. Dek could almost see them, could almost feel their arms in the wind about him. He laughed and cried, speeding at almost 200 kph down highway 12.

Forgive. The thought entered his mind like a breeze, warm and scented of summer.

And then the moment passed and he was alone in the battering slipstream. A sweet pain remained; daring him to push it away, but his rage was gone, or at least far enough away that he'd have to reach out to touch it. It no longer smothered him. His suspicion was that the next few days would bring a lot more murder, but he'd do it because it had to be done—not out of weakness, not out of rage. He was free.

He jumped and was again lost in the rushing wind. There was a change in the quality of the ambient sound as the bridge passed beneath him with a whoosh. He flew perhaps half a meter in front of a cargo transport that was crossing the bridge. He had time to spare a wave for a startled trucker, and then the bridge was gone from beneath him and he landed on another cargo transport.

Free.

* * *

Rae lay curled around Alex's comatose form in the middle of yet another geek exhibit. They lay in the top bunk of youth-sized bunk beds in the small, dim room that had been their sanctuary for the last two days.

At times like these—and there had been many times like these since she'd started dating Alex—it helped her to picture herself as the Jane Goodall of nerds. She lived among the little monkeys, observing, even participating in, their strange introverted rituals, yet fundamentally not nerdy herself. Nope, she was a strong, black woman, she was a tough cop on one of the city's toughest beats—she had plenty of street cred.

If she played online games while she worked out, that was because she liked to work out and was bored. If she was in love with a computer geek, it was because he was sexy in his own dorky way, because he was wise and infuriating. If she cried when she lost her online wedding ring when that Morgoth Dragon ate her, well…

From the lower bunk, a polite but urgent voice counseled her to "seek medical attention" for the hundredth time today.

Around them on the walls were holos of Pachinko Molasses and several other Anime characters she didn't recognize; all big eyes, improbable hair, and comic relief animal sidekicks with names like Yabbachu. On the top of a nearby dresser were intricately painted figurines of all the major characters from J.R.R. Tolkien's *Lord of the Rings* trilogy.

The room, until recently occupied by Ari and Mir Olafsen, ages 7 and 9, seemed the archetypal dwelling of suburban preteens. However, Rae couldn't shake the feeling that this was a geek spawning ground. This was an unkind thought, especially since the children's father was currently risking his life to shelter them. But she couldn't keep the thought at bay, or the warm smile that it brought with it. Someday she would admit that she was a geek lover... not out loud so Alex could gloat, but inside... maybe... someday.

Soon after her arrival here, the boys' father had admitted that his sons' full names were Aragorn and Faramir. Shooey.

There it was again—that stupid smile.

"Seek medical attention." The synthetic-tinged voice repeated from below. She looked at the clock radio mounted to the wall near her head: 12:30 AM.

She was tired, but couldn't sleep. She had the worst kind of cabin fever: the kind where a vast conspiracy of killers was looking for the cabin, and everyone dear to her was hanging out on death's rickety porch, sipping lemonade with the reaper.

Lying there in her fear and desperation, the smile broadened as she thought more on the boys' father: Barbarian by night, VP of marketing by day. In cyberspace, he was a burly barbarian with a wicked axe and a penchant for destruction. Out here in meatspace though, he was a family man with two sons and a sweet, round wife. He was fairly round himself, since he used a cutout to play from home instead of in a gym's VirtuaTrainer like she and Alex preferred.

He was possessed of an infectious smile and a red, round nose. Beardless with graying hair, he looked like Santa's son asserting his individuality. Yet within him beat the heart of a lion. Sure, online Rygar knew no fear, but there was no reason for fear there. Out here in the real world, though, when Rae had shown up on his doorstep with two vegetables in a shot-up microvan, Jerry Olafsen had taken them in. Though technically she'd never met him before, he'd turned out to be a true friend.

She'd located Jerry through the account information that Alex had hacked from their favorite game server way back when he was scheming for a date with her. Alex still had contact info for almost everyone in their online clan stored in his address book. Jerry was the only one within a three state radius. It was odd to think how much she owed to that little cache of illegally obtained info. Back then it had led Alex to her. Now it had led them all to shelter.

She really hadn't been thinking much when she came here. She only knew she couldn't use her Uni for fear of being tracked. This ruled out everything from refueling the car to buying food. Going to the hospital for Alex and Ping was out too. She couldn't shelter with friends because the hunters would search there first.

Desperate, she had finally delved into the loosely connected realm of geekdom for help. She'd been pleasantly surprised to find such warm welcome in the home of an online acquaintance.

"Seek medical attention."

In a weird way, she had relished unfolding their predicament to Rygar... er, Jerry. She had enjoyed seeing his skepticism melt into giddy interest, then leap over doubt's precipice into awe. At first, she'd been tempted to try some far less improbable lies, but then she came to her senses and realized she didn't need or want to lie. She'd seen gooseflesh as he came to believe, though her proof had been somewhat meager at first. It had basically boiled down to badges, wounded companions, and a story so improbable that no liar would even try it. Of course, her trump cards had been her cameo and Ping's sword. Also, she suspected that Ry... Jerry had wanted to believe so hard he could probably see the face of the fantastic in a bowl of properly stirred oatmeal.

When she gave him the whole story he had sent his wife and kids out of harm's way to visit his wife's aunt. He'd stayed behind to 'keep up appearances' at work, and because he said he hoped to be helpful. She had a sneaking suspicion he just wanted to see some action, just so that he could write it in his journal or something. She'd tried to explain to him that it's just a bit harder to share exciting stories when dead, but he wouldn't hear any of it.

What to do next? This was the question that had dogged her for two days of lying low. Her early plan called for Ping and Alex to wake up on their own, but now she was being forced to consider plan B... whatever that was.

"Hey Rae, seek medical attention."

Motionless before, now she lay frozen. The voice had sounded as synthetic as ever. After a few disbelieving seconds, she rolled over, leaned her head over the side of the bed and looked down at Ping. Comatose as ever, the medkit still attached to his head.

She considered pinching herself to make sure she hadn't dozed off. Nope... this was awake. She could smell Alex's rank two-days-without-eating breath, she could feel the bed, the covers.

She waited through the remaining seconds of the one-minute interval.

"Seek medical attention." The voice droned. Time to investigate.

She disentangled herself from Alex and the blanket. As she did so, she had a comfortable sense of precognition: together in their small, cozy home. They were old and gray, waking up late on Sunday morning, maybe expecting a visit from the grandkids. They would unravel themselves from their own blanket and smile like idiots.

She spared a moment to look at his sleeping face. She wondered how he would look old. She hoped she was going to find out.

One quick movement later, she crouched on the floor before Ping's bunk, a vision in silver-black cameo and sensible underwear.

Ping lay before her, swaddled in a Pachinko Molasses blanket. He just looked so cute. The child's bunk bed was probably the only kind of bed that would look too small for him. Like Alex, she and Rygar had stripped him and suited him up with the iron diaper and armband. She smiled again, remembering the unsavory scene of hooking them up with the bedpans and the IV feeders. Rygar had borne the brunt of the iron diaper part, thank the merciful heavens.

Ping's head was mostly hidden by the medkit. She'd retrieved it from the trunk of his destroyed car before they left the crash site. After she'd strapped it to his wounded head, it had stopped the bleeding and fused his cracked skull. Ever since then, it nagged her every sixty seconds to get more serious treatment for him. Being a police medkit, it was impossible to disable the urgent care warning, so she had endured it for two days. It wasn't that she didn't believe its advice… she just couldn't see a way to get into a hospital without ending up dead.

Though she could see how the hunters had found them at Roy's, she still wondered how they'd been found at the library. Magic? Tech? Alex would have an opinion if he were around to ask. Which brought up another question that had been wracking her brain for these last days: what was wrong with Alex?

Ping's wounds were serious, but at least the medkit could tell something was wrong. That knowledge was somehow comforting. At least comforting compared to Alex's wounds, whatever they were. There wasn't a mark on him, but he just wouldn't wake up. Jerry had purchased a high-end medkit when he had bought the diapers and IVs. It had pronounced Alex healthy, but slightly anemic. As her dad used to say, "On a scale from one to ten, it was unhelpful". Good ol' dad—he was beyond her reach, too.

The world started to close around her again. The walls seemed to bow inward with the weight of a hostile world. Here she sat helpless as Alex lay comatose… a probable victim of a ravenous magic rabbit that had popped out of his hat to eat his brain.

"Seek medical attention, babe."

Her head snapped up. She was sure she'd heard it that time. However, sixty anxious seconds later, the same canned announcement she'd been listening to for days returned.

She checked the medkit. It had plenty of power left, and all the diagnostics came up green. But then there probably wasn't a diagnostic for demonic possession.

Ping still registered in serious condition with some form of medical mumbo-jumbo wrong with him. She checked the medkit for directions to the nearest medical facility. Mercy Memorial. Downtown?

There had to be a hospital closer than Mercy... that was a good fifty kilometers away on the near north side of the city. A feeling of significance washed over her. Alex had found a way to communicate with her... it was the only thing that made sense.

Two minutes later, she burst into the study to find Jerry's limp form in a recliner, dead to this world. From time to time, an arm or leg would twitch as some motor neural stimulus made it through the cutout. It was a sad, geeky sight. The only way she could rationalize Immersive Gaming was as a workout vehicle in a Gym.

She moved quickly to his side. She was giddy with possibilities, happy to have a course of action, no matter how vague and dangerous. She ignored all etiquette and ripped the cutout sense-tape from the back of his neck.

He made a sound halfway between squeal and quack. Every muscle jerked as the cutout suddenly stopped working and his brain was caught in mid shout to his online muscles. Well, he actually made two sounds... the second was somewhat more flatulent.

Rae laughed as Rygar again became Jerry. "Wha?" He said, clearly disoriented.

"Sorry Jerr," she couldn't stop laughing, "we've got to go… hey, you didn't just mess your pants didja?"

"Not sure… where we going?"

"Not 'we' we… me and the vegetables."

"They're awake?" He said, clearly more relieved than angry. He was such a good sport.

"No, but I think Alex just managed to send me a message through Ping's medkit."

He looked more confused, rubbed his eyes. "Let me guess: he told you to seek medical attention?"

"Actually, yeah."

He shook his head. "You are a strange woman, Rae. I'm coming too."

"No way. We're probably gonna die… Laura wouldn't bake me any more of that bread if I got you killed too."

"Hey, I bake the bread around here… and you sure look happy about it." He said, levering the recliner into the upright position.

"About bread?"

"Going off to your death".

"He sent me a message." she smiled, triumphant.

"Seek medical attention?" he said, standing, stretching, emoting sedate skepticism.

She hugged him. "Thanks Jerry, you saved me… saved us all."

"…for a much better death to which you will now go?"

She paused. "Yeah." She gave him an earnest nod and a bright smile.

"How can I help?"

* * *

The stolen and dejacked microvan was loaded with their equipment. Jerry had helped her dress Ping and Alex. He'd helped her load them into the back seat. Her fletcher and the assault gun Ping had picked up were with Ping's guns and sword in a duffle on the passenger seat. Next to the duffle was a potted plant stolen from Jerry's den. While Rae changed into her work clothes, Jerry had wrapped the pot in red foil and ribbons, he'd even written a card that said "Get well soon, fictitious yet strangely believable relative." Next to the plant was a loaf of homemade bread—that was a snack, not more cover.

Jerry crouched at the driver's window. "Is there anything I can do?"

"You mean anything *else*." She put a hand on his arm as it rested on the window frame. "Thank you."

He smiled uncomfortably. "You sure you won't let me come?"

"Painful death is poor thanks, Jerr." She gave his arm a squeeze.

He nodded. "Should I go to the press if you don't make it."

"If we die, forget us. It's the only non-suicide option."

He looked thoughtful for a few seconds. "If you make it…"

"We'll be back." She finished, punching him in the shoulder. "Alex still hasn't met you or the family."

He nodded, "Yeah. Don't be strangers. I'll want to hear everything."

"Count on it."

"Seek medical attention." The medkit counseled from the back seat.

"Seek medical attention." Jerry said, holding his hand up in solemn farewell.

"Seek medical attention!" Rae enthused, her fist in the air. Still smiling, she backed out of the garage, conscious of just how fast the warm lights of the garage were lost in the enfolding darkness.

* * *

Dek sat at one of his favorite sushi bars five blocks from Ivo's office in Rosemont.

Today the food he ordered was only cover. He sat at the back in a booth, rather than at the bar like usual. Asuko was on duty tonight, so he enjoyed some light conversation before she had to move on to other customers.

Alone in the dim booth, he pulled his tablet from his jacket and turned it over in his fingers. Before he could get down to the business of finding Ivo and Roy's killers, he had to find his second adopted father. Of course, this was assuming that Issak was still alive.

It was also assuming he could convince Kaspari to fight. Issak was a great guy, but he was just a bit lacking in the passion department. Ivo and Issak were like brothers—they'd known each other for centuries. Still, Dek had a shadow of fear that Issak would think more about flight than fight. It wasn't that Issak's heart was cold, but it seemed to Dek that it was just old and, well... somewhat pragmatic. Issak's mind was deep and subtle, and perhaps it ruled his heart a little more than Dek would like.

Dek loved him, warts and all... and right now, he was all Dek had left.

Here goes. He spent a few hundred milliseconds reconsidering the sketchy details of his plan: Check his messages, maybe call Kaspari—see what pans out. Sketchy.

With the planning out of the way, he righted the tablet in his hands and switched it on. Immediately after he passed the security locks, he was presented with new messages. There were three: two video feeds and a text message, all from Issak. The receive date marked the first video at ten minutes after he had fled from Ivo's downtown Lab. Dek tapped the message.

Kaspari's even features filled the tablet's screen. He was bald, with a tight fringe of iron-gray hair. His face looked stern as always, like the world's most patient wolf. Of course now that Dek had known him for decades, he realized that beneath the harsh façade was an atom-organizing discipline and focus. Roy had called him the RomuBorg once casually. Issak had a good laugh about it... he definitely had a sense of humor, though it largely focused on the ironic, like now:

"I like the decorating you did in the exam room. Much more airy." His face didn't crease with a hint of humor. His eyes didn't sparkle. His dry delivery was the envy of snooty butlers the world over. "Since I didn't see a stain below the window, I'm assuming that you will return my call, no?" He broke the connection.

Issak had the most exquisite accent; subtle, precise, completely untraceable to any origin language or region that Dek could discover. Though intriguing, it was barely perceptible, even for Dek. He had asked Issak about it, but had never received an explanation more satisfying than, "I've lived in many places."

The second message had been sent about twenty minutes later. He played it. The face that filled the screen was controlled as ever, but subtly different—strained, perhaps. He was terse: "Call me. Carefully. Soon."

He opened the text message. Also terse: "No call. Come. Where we first met."

Gotcha.

Before he switched off his tablet, he linked it to his Uni and paid his bill. After an unsuccessful moment of impulse suppression, he left a five hundred thousand dollar tip. Under cover of the table, he snapped the tablet in half. Going underground.

He stacked the two pieces of the tablet in his concealed hands, and broke them again. He pulled the optical storage from the piece that had been the upper left quadrant of the ruined tablet, and crushed it to powder between his fingers.

He left the untouched food on the table and got up from the booth. He took two steps toward the door before halting in mid-stride. He returned to the table and scooped up two spring rolls. Underground food usually stinks.

He paused again outside the restaurant's door. He stayed just long enough to hear the excited scream from inside. To live is to fly, he thought, remembering the line from an old song. He was gone before Asuko bolted out the door looking for him.

* * *

The stolen microvan passed Mercy Memorial Hospital for the third time. Rae looked right and left, but didn't slow. It was a mid-sized building, maybe thirty floors, on the near north side of the city. Its stone was dark brown, its windows the deep gray of privacy glass, its overall impression was that of a twenty-first century castle. It seemed quiet, but for the moment, she was content to circle the block, attempting to wear a matching moat around the neo-baroque structure.

At a little before 2 AM, the only light was from the city itself. The light from below the sparse clouds gave the sky the color of a child's dream of the deep sea. Behind her, the mantra continued on one-minute intervals. "Seek medical attention."

"Stop naggin'!" When she'd left Jerry's, the idea of taking action was a relief—exciting even. Now, in orbit around the hospital, the end of her waiting seemed less to beckon and more to loom before her.

Finally, on her fourth circuit around the block, she turned right and headed down into the building's underground parking structure. Descending from night into artificial daylight, she guided the gray microvan to a halt in a small dead spot between two security cameras near the hospital's ambulance run. She gently unloaded the comatose bodies onto the sidewalk. After a few seconds spent resisting the mighty pull of common sense, her will won out over her fear and she closed the sliding door and got back into the driver's seat. A sob caught in her throat when she saw them lying abandoned in the rearview mirror, but then she rounded the corner and drove down through the levels of the parking garage. Though spaces were available on the second level down, she took the microvan all the way to the eighth, and lowest, level.

After winding through the whole level to find the most isolated spot, she settled on a parking space between two supports where a dim light left a few shadows.

She was about to see how much time her crazy plan would buy them.

She rummaged through the padded case Alex had brought from his apartment. After a few moments of tech archaeology, she located the item she sought. She removed the badge from her uniform and placed it on the interface pad of the item Alex had called the Hacktronic 3000. It was a little invention he'd been perfecting since his senior year in high school. It had been through many revisions, including four major rebuilds, but the machine's purpose had remained unchanged: to facilitate security mayhem.

Basically, it was a ROM rewriter.

Rae smiled at the memory of the first time Alex had introduced her to his little project. They had been together romantically for perhaps two months. Rae hadn't yet been told that she didn't live in the real world, so she was still shockable by illegal technology. She had been feigning interest in Alex's hobbies, so he had shown her his pride and joy. She hoped she could remember how to work it.

The HT3K (Alex's idea of a pet name, at least he'd stopped calling her 'girlfriend 1.0') rewrote the read-only Assisi chips like the ones in Unis and almost any other security system's hard keys. Alex might well be the only person in the world with the ability to do something so fundamentally dangerous to civilized society. With this machine and a few pieces of information, you could wire yourself to look like anyone digitally.

With her work tablet, she pulled up a local copy of an arrest report from three weeks ago. It had been a brawl at a downtown club that had been finally contained after eight officers had been called to the scene. From the report, she harvested the badge ID of Jeanette Woods, one of the two other female officers on the scene, and the only one of Rae's ethnicity. She transferred the number to the HT3K, and after a few false starts, wrote that number into the "unwritable" Assisi chip in her badge.

Of course, she had no idea if it would work, and no way to test it without exposing herself to a query. This was probably not going to work. Even if it did, macro security daemons would eventually notice the same key in use at two locations.

She used the HT3K to re-tag her tablet and Uni to seem like they were Jeanette's.

She attached the badge to her chest, grabbed the duffel and Jerry's plant, and stepped from the microvan.

* * *

"That was fast! You guys have them stacked up in the back of the ambulance?" Lynda's stylus was poised above her tablet.

"Two males, one with field-treated head wounds, the other comatose with no physical indications." the taller of the EMTs said, not looking up from his monitoring equipment.

"Just really sleepy, huh?" Lynda gave him a look of laconic amusement.

He nodded, "I think this medkit's been on for a while…"

Lynda interrupted, her stylus already moving. "I need their Uni keys."

"No ID."

"Why is this never easy?"

"Because it's life, not video."

Lynda summoned the triage doctor for a DNA ID authorization. "They stable?"

"They'll make it to the OR, but I don't have any prognosis."

"What happened?"

"No idea. We found them in the parking garage."

Lynda's stylus paused. "In *our* garage?"

The EMT nodded.

"You open a police incident yet?"

Both EMTs shook their heads. The shorter one hooked a thumb over his shoulder, toward the door. "We just stumbled over them a few seconds ago… just outside."

The doors from an internal hallway on the right of the ER reception opened. A uniformed patrol officer entered carrying a duffle bag over her shoulder and a potted plant that screamed 'hospital gift shop'. The alarm went off as she stepped through the scanner just inside the door, but everyone could clearly see the pistol on her hip.

Behind the security desk, Clint cleared the alarm and waved the woman through.

She nodded to the triage nurse and the EMTs. "Can anyone point me to the maternity ward?"

"Whoa. Speak of the devil!" the shorter EMT whispered.

"You on duty?" Lynda asked.

"I'm always on duty," the officer responded, "what's up?"

"These two were abandoned in the parking garage..."

The officer looked skeptical, "They look a little old for child abandonment... besides they look like they might work here." She smiled at the EMTs.

The EMTs exchanged glances. "I think she meant these guys." One said, gesturing to their unconscious charges.

The officer nodded. She set the plant down on the security desk and pulled out her tablet. "I'll open the incident... how long before visiting hours are over?"

"For our pals in blue? Never." Clint said with a smile.

"Well, okay then, lets get started!"

Lynda nodded, gesturing to the corner of the desk. The door to the ER opened, admitting a thin, kind-faced man in his forties. He wore the loose garb and requisite white coat of an ER doctor. "You rang, Lynda?"

"Yeah, I need authorization to do a medical ID on two John Doe types."

"Describe the scene when you found them…" The officer said to the EMTs, stylus poised over her tablet.

"Officer…" Lynda consulted her tablet, "…Woods will be handling the police report."

"Swell." The doctor turned to the two patients. After a few moments of rudimentary tests, he used his tablet to authorize the DNA ID. He sent the patient with the head wound to OR-1, and the sleeper to imaging for a deep scan.

The officer was finished getting info from the EMTs and was waiting patiently. "I'll need your incident key for the report, Doctor…"

"Wyler." He said as he transferred the hospital's incident key to the officer's tablet. "Anything else you need from me, Officer Woods?"

"What's up with them?" she said in an offhand manner that struck him as somewhat contrived. Maybe she was new on the job, nervous.

"The one with the head trauma is pretty straightforward… multiple blows to the head, concussion, some fractures patched by the kit on his head. We should have him out of surgery within an hour. Only weird thing was that the medkit's logs show that it's been on him for about two days. Now, the other one is deeply strange. My portable couldn't find anything wrong with him, but the IV in his arm's been there for two days too… Maybe the deep scanners or the neural mappers can pick up some clues. I'm having the scans forwarded to neurography for analysis. Hopefully we'll know more soon."

The officer looked thoughtful. "They were found in the ambulance run outside the ER. Any other weird stuff happen here recently?"

"Heavens yes!" The doctor chuckled. "We're Harm central around here. It doesn't get much weirder than that. You see someone try to eat their own fingers and pretty much everything else is boring as cold oatmeal."

The officer gave her head a knowing shake. "Yeah… when will that fad die out?"

"Not soon enough." The doctor said. "I long for the return of Heroin."

"Yeah… I'm going to poke around the scene where…" The officer was interrupted by a woman's disoriented shriek from outside.

The doctor gestured toward the entrance. "And here's tonight's first Harm, no doubt. Care to stick around for the show?"

"There aren't enough donuts in the world… Thanks doctor."

The officer moved toward the interior doors, then turned back. "Where's your security post? I'll need to see the logs from the place where the victims were found."

"Straight ahead. Follow the signs… you can't miss it." The doctor turned away as the exterior doors burst open. Two EMTs wheeled in a gurney with a screaming woman strapped to it. Her platinum and red-tipped hair was disheveled, soaked in sweat. Her fancy black, holo-traced party clothes were ripped from her struggle against the restraints.

Rae rounded the corner and pushed the call button outside the hospital's security post. After a few seconds, the buzzer sounded and she pushed into the small room.

"What can I do for you officer?" The room's only occupant was a lanky surfer type. He sat before a panoramic display, reading a publication about really fast looking cars on his tablet. The display before him held multiple open windows, which monitored the entry points and key areas of the hospital. The room was dark; the smell of stale coffee colored the air.

"I need access to a security feed. Need to do some research on two John Does found in the ambulance run."

"Sure thing!" The guy leaned forward and made the necessary checks of Rae's credentials. Satisfied that she was in fact Jeanette Woods, faithful minion of the CPD, he authorized her for the access. Rae's tablet chirped as the interface opened to the hospital's security systems.

"Just camera logs?"

She nodded, "Yeah, thanks."

"No prob. They were actually found off camera, so I don't know how much this will help."

"Yeah. Maybe I'll find a clue or something." She gave him a wink.

"So, how's life in the big leagues?"

"Big leagues?"

"I've been thinking 'bout giving the academy a try for a while now."

"You should… it's a great job. Not like the videos though."

"What's the best part?"

"Pulling cats out of trees."

"I thought the fire department took care of that."

"Helping old ladies across the street?" She gave him a smile.

"You get to help old ladies a lot here… maybe we should switch."

"Too many Harms here. I couldn't stand all the action."

He beamed, sitting perhaps a little straighter in his chair. "Yeah, it's a rough and tumble job. Hospital security, it's not for everyone."

Behind him, on the wall, the doctor stalked the Harm on the gurney, waiting for the right moment to make his move with his syringe.

"Keep an eye on that." Rae gestured toward the screen and turned to go.

Minutes later, Rae found a private corner at the end of the hall where Alex had been taken. There was a small, uninhabited waiting area with vending machines and a few chairs. She sat with her back to the wall and used her tablet to open the interface to the security system. The surfer had given her access to the entire hospital's surveillance system. Cool.

She opened a window into Alex's room first. He had already been through the scanner, and now was on a gurney in a holding room awaiting the imaging specialist's recommendations. He was the only patient in the room.

Next, she opened a window into OR-1 where Ping was undergoing surgery. She couldn't tell how things were going. The camera showed two surgeons with their hands inside ports in a coffin-sized box. At the foot of the box, a tech monitored their progress. The soundtrack didn't help much either. When they weren't talking golf, they spoke largely in the mumbo dialect of jumbo. Sometimes Rae had trouble knowing which jargon was medical and which was golf... she understood neither.

She opened windows for each entrance to the building, looking for the arrival of more killers like those at the library. She opened another window showing the roof, just in case.

All settled in. She scanned her monitor windows with an intensity she believed the surfer would have found both impressive and mystifying. Of course, her life and that of her friends depended on her vigilance. She considered opening a commlink to the surfer to ask for the authorization to monitor the hospital's alert notifications. She decided against it; mostly not wanting to arouse any suspicion.

After perhaps five minutes, she noticed that something was wrong.

Uniformed police officers began to arrive at a disturbing rate, eight within the next ten minutes, including two plainclothes detectives. "Uh, oh." She muttered, scanning the camera portals on her tablet.

As the eleventh officer arrived, she rose to the surface of her panic long enough to open portals to all the cameras in the elevator cars. There were no officers in any of the cars. Of course, she'd have to check the camera logs to find who may have already used the elevators, but she knew that nobody had gotten off at her floor since the elevator bank was in sight to her right.

She was still scanning the elevator logs when an orderly arrived to move Alex.

Grudgingly, she suspended her tablet and went to investigate.

When she arrived at the door of the holding room, the orderly was already on the way out with Alex's gurney.

"This guy going to surgery?" Rae asked, raising a hand in greeting.

"Nope. Doctor says move him to a semiprivate. They had to send his scans to an expert in Delhi... could take a while before we hear back."

Rae tried not to show any relief, which wasn't too hard, since she was still pretty worried about the cops on the first floor.

"What's up on the first floor?" The orderly asked, looking conspiratorial.

"What'cha mean?"

"Oh, I thought you were with the badges downstairs. Heard there was some kinda ruckus down there."

Ruckus? She and the vegetables didn't qualify as a ruckus, so she hoped he was right. Rae shook her head, shrugged her shoulders. She felt downright suspicious. Time to go. "I've got to get a statement when he wakes up... where're you taking him?"

"Seventeen thirty-eight."

She nodded, "Thanks." She strode away. Time to find another private corner... maybe a closet. As she walked, she opened her tablet. Nothing exciting was happening at the level one exits, but Ping was gone.

Not waiting to find a quiet place to work, she pulled up the camera logs for OR-1 and cued through them as she walked.

"Seek medical attention, my butt!" she grumbled as she walked and worked. She had no idea what that meant, other than it was derisive—she'd heard her grandma say it once when she was six. It made her laugh. After she'd heard it said, she'd been insufferable. She had repeated it with anything she didn't like. "Clean my room? My butt!" "Bedtime? My butt!" "Stop saying 'my butt'? My butt!" Her dad had been patient, but her mom had been less patient with grandma.

There! As she scanned backward through the OR-1 logs, Ping was wheeled backward through the doors by an orderly. Then, as the reversed playback continued, he moved back into position, the orderly left backwards, and the surgeons and tech returned to surround him. She breathed a sigh of relief.

She stopped briefly in the waiting area. Without sitting down, she pulled up the logs for the camera outside the fifth floor elevator bank. She scanned back until she found Ping and the orderly getting off elevator three backwards. She closed that window and accessed the logs for the camera in elevator three. Continuing this pattern, she found that Ping had been transferred to a post-operative recovery room on the seventh floor. The live feed from his room showed that he was not yet conscious, though that annoying medkit had been replaced with a white bandage bound around his head. She wondered briefly if he was bald under there. She hoped so.

Scared but smiling, Rae moved to the elevator bank.

On her tablet, she closed all the monitor windows except the five elevators, Ping's and Alex's rooms, and the elevator bank on the seventh floor. After insuring that the elevators weren't packed with cops, she pressed the call button.

A few minutes later a car arrived bearing a mother in her thirties and a five-year-old girl whose blonde hair was pulled up into a single vertical ponytail that only children and mental patients can wear well. The mother was looking pensive; the little girl was carrying a festively-beribboned plant from the gift shop. Like all five-year-olds on a mission, the little girl looked giddy with excitement. Rae returned her smile.

Two minutes later, Rae entered Ping's room. The room was dim, with lights only bright enough to keep her from bumping into the furniture. He was an inky shadow in the bed. Putting her back to the room's camera, she pulled up a chair and sat beside the bed. As her eyes adjusted to the gloom, she noticed that he was stirring.

"Detective?" Rae shook his shoulder lightly, "Ping?"

He moaned, shifted.

She knew it would probably be an hour or so before he was allowed visitors, and probably a few more before they would allow him to move about, but this was kind of an emergency. She shook just a little more aggressively. "Ping, wake up!" she hissed.

"Don't start slappin' me." He said.

"Well I ain't kissin' you, that's for sure." The relief was an uncomfortable weight in her voice. She was no longer alone.

"Where are we?"

"Hospital. Downtown."

He tensed. "Either you're kidding, or I don't remember the situation correctly."

"Hey, you're the one whose been nagging me for two days to 'seek medical attention.'"

"Two days!" He tried to sit up—failed.

With a groan, he lay back on his pillow. "I feel like I've been clubbed on the head with a rifle butt."

"Ah, at least your memory hasn't failed."

"Rae, why are we in a hospital… why aren't we dead… is it over?"

Rae ticked her answers off on three fingers. "Alex sent me a message. Dumb luck maybe? Nope."

"Where's Alex?" Ping asked after a few seconds of processing time.

"He never woke up from that nap he took while we were driving on Roy's lawn."

"Not in two days? But he sent you a message. From where?"

"Good question." She took a few minutes and told him the basics of what had happened.

"Sounds like we're in trouble," Ping concluded, "still."

"Hey, at least you got a nap."

"You bring my sword?"

"*Your* sword?" Rae raised her eyebrows.

"Dek gave it to me. Made it sound like a holy charge. I had the most disturbing dream about it. Help me up."

Rae patted the duffle on her back. "Got your Excalibur right here babe, brought clothes and all the toys." She put an arm around his shoulders and pulled him into the sitting position. After a few more seconds, they worked together to get his legs over the edge of the bed.

Ping sat in a swoon, rocking from side to side. "I need a wheelchair. Where's Alex?"

"Ten floors up, in a semiprivate. You gonna be okay while I get your chair?"

Ping thought he might have nodded. He must have, because Rae let go. He didn't fall, though he had to clutch the bed with both hands to prevent it.

After a moment of swaying nausea and blurred vision, she returned with a wheelchair in tow.

"So, before this is over, how many more times do you think I'm going to be beaten unconscious?"

"About once every two days." She gave him what he perceived as a blurry smile, "...more, if you can regain consciousness quicker."

Even the small snort hurt his head. "Ow. I think I was only awake for two hours between my last two comas."

"You think that's a scary prospect? Try this: You think you're bald under those bandages?"

His elbows were on the armrests of the chair and his palms were pressed to his head to stop the agony the laughter cost him.

"Personally, I'm betting on the Ernie-Bert tuft."

"Stop. You're killing me." He groaned, laughing weakly.

"Don't try to stop me, you don't know how long the line was."

"Stop!" He managed from under the pain of the laughter.

They wheeled down the hall toward the elevators.

* * *

Dek sat like a medieval lord surveying his fiefdom from the ramparts of his baroque brown stone castle.

He crouched on the ornate Façade that adorned the hospital's roof, soaking in the beauty of the surrounding city. This was one of his favorite view spots, though he was sure no Chicago tourist brochures listed it. Perched like a gargoyle on the neo-baroque stone of the hospital, surrounded by the skyscrapers that jutted up on all sides, night filled with the city lights that lit up the clouds above—moments like these could stretch out into hours of wondering appreciation… if he had the time. It had only been hours since he'd left Alex and company in Lake Geneva, but he could feel the clock ticking.

Below him, vehicles of every type coursed around the buildings like electric blood moving through the body of the nighttime city. Tonight was going to be something special. If only he had time to stay. There was a storm brewing... a big one. The air was already lush with the fragrance of the first sporadic showers. Wind drove rivers of clouds across the lowering sky. Soon the clouds would brush the tips of the buildings. Perhaps there would be lightening. He loved stormy weather.

Reluctantly, he stood. He took a final look at the surrounding spectacle. He breathed deep, then leaned out and dropped headfirst over the edge.

The hospital's dark gray windows slipped by slowly. Again, he spread his arms, feeling this was the preferred configuration for the in-flight Superman. He raised his arms above his head, caught a ledge three floors from the top of the building. As he fell past, he applied pressure, bending his elbows as his momentum drove him into a somersault. Halfway through the roll, as the lights of the city spun through his field of vision, he reversed his grip on the ledge— gripping with his fingers where before he had pushed with his palms. Head tucked, his back slammed into the stone wall. He rolled down the wall the length of his spine, until his feet fell flat on the wall with his legs crouched. He let go of the ledge and his momentum carried him into a tight crouch with his feet against the wall. At about ten degrees elevation, he jumped with all his strength. Behind him, the brown stone cracked as he rocketed nearly horizontally away from the wall.

The sound of rushing air filled his ears. Below him, the bright street slipped by as he threw himself into a mid-air roll. He added a full twist because he had the time, and because it was fun. Still more time, so he did the flip in layout position, limbs outstretched, fingers scything the chill night air, back straight, head moving from side to side, drinking in the show as the city swung around him.

The parking structure across the four-lane street approached before gravity had time to pluck him from flight. He hit the top level perhaps five meters from the edge, landing on his feet, but then rolling twice to absorb some of his horizontal momentum. He came up from the second roll, did a half twist and planted his feet. He leaned forward and crouched slightly as he skidded backwards across the floor for two meters before coming to a stop, arms outstretched, head lowered. He loved city travel.

After a motionless second spent savoring the action passed, he dropped his arms and turned around.

…and almost slammed into a horrified family of three. The parents were perhaps thirty, and stared in slack-jawed wonder at Dek's big show. They were still too amazed to be frightened, but if he hung around long enough, he knew that's where they'd be going. Between them, a girl of perhaps three slept in a stroller. Perhaps they were returning to their car after a day of sightseeing in the city. Dek had a feeling he'd just been the big finale.

"Hi!" He said brightly, feeling both embarrassed and terribly cool. He touched his forehead in salute and then burned it on out of there. To the shocked parents, he seemed to simply disappear in a rush of artificial breeze.

He still had quite a few blocks to go before he reached his destination.

* * *

Thankfully, they weren't alone on the elevator. This kept Rae quiet long enough for Ping to think.

He assessed their situation, which was pretty desperate. He knew they had only a few hours at most before the macro daemons flagged Rae's hacked Uni. Once that happened, the police would be here within minutes. They had to get out of the hospital right now.

And then there was Alex. The hospital seemed his only chance after two days in a coma, but to leave him here would be to give him to their hunters. Ping remembered Good Cop's talk of torturing Alex to death before Good Cop's own grisly death in the library archive had spoiled his plans. It was clear that Alex was the one "they" were primarily gunning for. He knew that Rae would never leave Alex here.

Ping knew he wouldn't leave Alex here either, so he was at a loss for what to do next. He relaxed in his chair and cleared his mind. If he ever needed inspiration, it was now.

Nothing came to him except for memories of dark coma dreams from the last two days—dreams filled with Alex's blood and Rae's screams.

* * *

The room was bright with the glare of artificial sunshine. Bright music from a pair of harmonizing classical guitars and the crisp smell of rain on fallen leaves filled the air.

Rae knew from some IQ Channel show seen in the distant past that coma patients were kept in artificially stimulating environments. The light would shift from deepest night to equatorial noon; the music would shift in type and volume and sometimes lapse into silence; the scent in the air would rotate from pleasant to foul, from strong to faint. The idea was to try to engage the patent's senses and entice them back to the real world.

The bright lights, jovial music and fresh smell depressed her terribly. Somehow, all the pleasant sensations confirmed her tragedy—made it more real somehow. Alex wasn't coming back.

She faced one of the inky windows, trying unsuccessfully to keep her tears from the wounded detective. He was trying unsuccessfully to pretend he didn't notice. She studied her reflection as it mingled with the shifting lights of the city behind the black glass. She raised her right hand, put her palm on the glass, fingers spread. The reflection's lip quivered, its face streaked with desperate tears.

Ping was in his wheelchair, feeling somewhat stronger, but not wanting to risk a fall; he still didn't feel confident in his equilibrium. He felt even less certain about his plan. He stopped turning the collapsed sword over in his hands.

He leaned over Alex's comatose form and put a hand on Alex's chest. He felt the regular breathing, closed his eyes, pondered black thoughts. Sometimes you have to do things…

"You know what I studied in school?" Ping said, surprised that he'd spoken.

Rae shook her head, still facing the window.

What was he doing? "Family counseling."

Rae shook her head. "Share how that makes you feel, detective."

Ping's laugh was more release than humor. "Yep, I wanted to help people. I really thought I could make a difference." He put a hand on the monitor panel next to Alex's bed. He lifted the plastic guard and hit the panic button beneath. The alarm was silent here in the room, but he knew the floor nurses and the on-duty doctor would be joining them in a hurry.

"You said 'thought'. What changed your mind?" Rae asked, voice thick. She seemed grateful for the conversation's distraction.

"I had this family... they came to the clinic I was interning at while I finished my dissertation. They'd been having trouble: abuse, drugs—the whole enchilada. I got assigned to them from the pool because I'd requested the tough ones. I was going to write my dissertation about motivating dead-enders to try, about the benefits of keeping the family together at all costs." The words were just tumbling out now.

"You're not kidding." Rae realized. "You know, I think you'd be good at it, come to think of it..."

"You'd be wrong." Ping winced, swallowing hard. "The father was an insurance exec, the mother was the substance abuser, the child abuser; emotional and physical. The daughter was eight, but she had this look—like she was ancient—wise like the Buddha. She had a quick draw sense of humor, but the smile was a lot slower out of the holster. It was worth it when you saw it, though.

"The daughter?" Rae said.

Ear to ear. Dead eyes accusing. She was before him now whenever he blinked. His hand closed around the sword. "Yeah." His voice caught. "Yeah, the daughter. We were making real progress I thought. They had all committed to see the process through. They were happy the last time I saw them… going for ice cream after they left. I had this warm feeling inside—I was doing something valuable." He was speeding up now… he could hear the commotion at the end of the hall.

"Nobody knows what went wrong. On the night before our next session, they found the husband shot in the bathroom, the daughter they found in the kitchen, throat cut ear to ear. The mother ate the gun in the garage; her bag was on the passenger seat all packed for her big get-away trip… guess she changed her mind."

The business end of the collapsed sword pressed against Alex's chest. Running footsteps outside; Rae turned around. Her eyes went first to the door, fear and misery in her expression. But then she noticed Ping and Alex. She saw the sword. Her hand went out toward them, imploring. "NO!" She screamed.

"It was my fault." Ping pressed the activating stud; the blade rang out through blood, bone, and mattress, finally burying its tip in the floor below..

* * *

"Look at this dad!" Roy shouted, prodding the corpse with the end of his blade.

"Just a sec." Ivo said as the corpse of the last Savant from Asado's little hit team disintegrated in the lattice of his

Cast. Attempted murder is always a drag, especially when it's your murder that's attempted, but cleaning up afterward was always a distasteful task.

Ivo took a few more seconds to touch up the hasty mend he'd put on his broken femur then hobbled over to where Roy was standing. The battle had been much tougher than he'd expected. Some kind of chaosing energy had actually pushed him out of the Loom in the middle of the battle. It was like nothing he'd seen before. If it wasn't for Roy, he'd have been killed right then.

"Am I not cleaning these fast enough for you master Peter?"

"Roy, Dad… It's Roy, comprende?"

You'd think he'd pick 'Ace' or 'Spike' if he was going to pick his own name. But what could Ivo expect from someone who loved circus peanuts so much?

"Sorry Peter," Ivo smiled, "I'm sure I'll remember next time. What've you got?"

"Look at this…" Roy drove his blade through the chest of the dead creature. Sparks leapt from the wound, crept along the length of the blade. "Someone's forged these things… it's in their flesh."

Ivo looked at the chaotic energy bleeding out of the wound for a long time. It was a struggle for him even to maintain his view into the Underworld this near to the body's chaos. Was this Asado's secret weapon—some new kind of Forged demon?

"That's not a Forge." He said, not bothering to hide the concern in his voice. "It's something else. Primitive. Powerful."

* * *

Dek looked through the new glass and into the examination room. Here was where it had all started for him, the beginning of the beginning, the beginning of the end. Here, about eighty years ago, Ivo wove new life into him—here he had been born again. Upstairs, in the penthouse, he had met Issak Kaspari for the first time. It was here, three days ago, that he had heard Roy's last words and smashed through this very window.

Symmetry.

The new glass exploded inward around his fist. He stepped into the small room. His coat still hung on the hook on the door. He retrieved it, put it on. He paused to indulge vanity, checking his look in the mirror on the wall by the exam table. The long coat made him look like Harrison Ford. Right on!

He stepped to the door and moved silently from the room. He moved through the darkened hallways to the elevator bank. Inside the elevator, he hit the emergency stop, but not before putting the tip of his sword through the two camera nodes inside.

He really didn't know what kind of reception to expect here. Wasn't sure whether Issak would be alive or dead, held prisoner, or waiting with the cavalry. For all he knew Issak had gotten bored and left. In any case, Dek wasn't taking any chances. He opened the maintenance hatch in the top of the elevator and slipped through it. Above him, the four corners of the elevator shaft seemed to converge in the distance.

He grabbed the cable, intending to climb to the penthouse. Grease squished between his fingers. "Eww!" he whispered, looking around for something to clean his hand. He looked at his newly recovered coat, his shirt, but in the end decided on the wall of the shaft.

Plan B. He jumped to the narrow ledge one floor up. He repeated this procedure, jumping upward from ledge to ledge, spiraling from wall to wall and floor to floor as he jumped up the concentric ledges like a spiral staircase.

Fresh and warmed by the light exercise, he arrived at the eighty-second floor. He balanced with one foot on the service ladder, the other on a junction box, and leaned into the doors. He wedged his fingers into the crack between them and slid them open. He emerged from the shaft's darkness into the low ambient light that Issak preferred when he stayed here. He took a deep breath to sample the air. He could smell food prepared not long ago and a hint of the cologne that Issak wore. But also something else... sharp and corrupt, like copper filings sprinkled on rotting meat. Nice.

Collapsed sword in hand, he crept deeper into the penthouse. He moved down the hallway toward the kitchen, where light spilled out of the doorway. From the kitchen, he could make out the soft, hesitant notes of a piano—Schubert. Yep, Issak was definitely here, and understandably troubled.

For such an excessively disciplined man, Issak sure had a weakness for the most sentimental of sissy music. Dek found this one of the most touching details of his adopted father. Ok, perhaps the only really touching detail. Dek loved Issak; he was bright and energetic—kind even, but he would come off as chilly even at a convention of Nazi math professors.

Whenever Issak was really feeling down, he pulled out the Schubert and lost himself in the intimate, perhaps even schmaltzy music. Dek's heart extended toward his father. Just like him, Issak had lost almost everything.

A warm smile emerged on Dek's face. Listening to the faint piano tinkling, he leaned on the wall, remembering happier times. For Christmas in 2004, Dek had given Issak the complete Barry Manilow boxed set. Issak was not amused. But from time to time, Dek would hear it at night, coming from Issak's room.

This was Issak: Hard on the outside, squishy and warm on the inside. Kinda like monkey crap.

"What are you laughing about, Dek?"

"You, of course, you old softie."

The music died, "If you're done lurking, please come in."

Dek rounded the corner into the kitchen, smile still on his lips. Issak was sitting at the small kitchen table, a tumbler of scotch half empty on the table near the half-empty bottle. Before him on the table were a few volumes of Ivo's scrapbook. The non-sealed part of Ivo's thirty-something volumes of picture-adorned history was a fun read, but if this was the sealed part, there wasn't anything Issak would be able to do to keep Dek away. He'd use the sword if he had to.

"I've been expecting you," Issak beleaguered the obvious.

"That's not…"

"Nope. I still haven't found his sealed books."

"Too bad. I hear he's got a nude painting in there of you from the 1600's."

"That's a lie." Warm humor escaped through the cracks the scotch had made in Issak's composure. Dek noticed the plastic seal for the scotch lay on the table near the bottle; he'd never seen Issak drunk before.

Issak seemed to realize that he'd lost his ironclad composure like most people might realize their fly was open. He seemed to clamp down on the emotion, but as he did so, Dek saw self-loathing in his face. Misery.

"Don't worry," Dek said, "Hey, we're together now. We're gonna work this out. I was afraid I'd be too late."

"Too late..." Issak mused, face darkening.

"What's all this about? Why did we drop everything and come to Chicago?"

Issak raised his tumbler. "The end of the world."

"Yeah, we couldn't have seen that from New York." Dek rolled his eyes and slipped into the chair across from Issak.

"I'm sherious." Issak slurred. He gave Dek a melodramatic wink. What was that for? It was probably just the alcohol winking. In more than eighty years, he'd never seen Issak wink.

Dek gave Issak his full attention, and perhaps a full minute to realize it was still his turn to talk.

"Not long before we came to Chicago, Ivo was attacked by three Savants and perhaps twelve grunts from Asado."

"Yeah, I remember Roy telling me about that. Asado has never been that major of a threat. Their kung fu is not strong."

Issak smiled... the scotch again. "Nope, but they had a major advantage. It was a lot closer than Roy probably let on." He paused for effect, and to refill his cup. "A new alliance."

"Not with Ciarac again..."

"Ciarac is gone."

"Gone, meaning..."

"All of them, Savants, grunts, government moles, families, friends, the producers of their favorite television shows... gone."

"Like 'on vacation' gone?"

"Like 'haven't found all the pieces yet' gone." Issak didn't look up.

"Last I heard they had fifteen Savants, maybe seventy grunts and a handful of demons..."

"Now you've heard more."

"How long ago?"

"When isn't the question... what you want to ask is *why*."

"You really parcel out the info in small chunks when you're drinking, Issak."

"New alliances." Issak said as if providing the clue that linked it all together.

Dek waited again, got bored. "See? Come on, spill the beans."

Isaac closed his eyes, then blew out a long breath. "Berlioz, Gamma, Valenza, Nikko… gone."

That was a lot of beans. It had been so long since Dek had been afraid that he wasn't sure this was it. Cold static fled in waves across his skin. He seemed to shift slightly away from the world. Six clans couldn't be gone, that was over a hundred Savants, maybe thousands of grunts, and three or four Replicants like Dek and Roy. This was not possible. If this was indeed the end of the world, it had gotten off to a great start. Dek did the quick math. Almost a quarter of the clans were gone. How could he not have known? Ivo and Roy were only a small part of a larger catastrophe.

"All of it…" Issak gestured expansively with his glass, "All my fault."

The chill continued to build around Dek. His vision blurred. Fear maybe, but this was something more. This was the working of the Loom. "Issak… what?"

Dek heard rustling from the other rooms of the house. He struggled to move but failed.

* * *

"I can't say how much I think you're right on this one, chief!" Roy shouted brightly from the other room. Heightened senses—he'd leave them out next time he remade someone. Ivo reinforced the room's sound damper with a little spice from the Loom, finally achieving real privacy.

He was about to apologize for the interruption when he heard Dek's voice through the commlink. "Yeah, me too!

You guys are definitely on the right…" His voice was cut off as Issak waived a hand, reinforcing his own damper.

Though their conversation had been grave only a few moments ago, they now regarded each other with airy consternation. Issak shook his head, a grin spreading across his face. Issak rubbed his temples, covering his eyes with his hand. "Replicants." He said. They both laughed.

"Connectivity drugs?" Issak brought the conversation back on track.

"Harmony," Ivo replied, "according to the amount in their blood, each of the things had used it no more than eight hours before the attack."

"Demon junkies?" Issak asked, traces of his smile lingering at the corners of his mouth.

"Not demons." Ivo said, "Humans. I think the Harmony's an enabler—a catalyst."

Issak didn't respond. He gave Ivo his full attention.

"There are cracks in the fabric of reality still running through their flesh, down through the Underworld, out to… to somewhere else. The flesh has been changed, but not by the Loom… by whatever outside power is forcing its way into our world. Issak, it's getting stronger."

Issak immediately suspected. Cracks through the Underworld, leading somewhere else. He'd been somewhere else recently, met something sinister there. He didn't believe in coincidence. His mind returned to the feeling of the Outsider pressing in on him, trying to get under his skin, trying to get behind his eyes. He imagined what might have happened to him if the doors to his mind had been wedged open with connectivity drugs.

"Maybe we do need to come to Chicago." Issak said.

* * *

Issak's voice dropped to a whisper. He leaned forward. "I broke it Dek. And now it's here. It's going to flood the earth and no one can touch it..."

Kaspari was looking at his hands resting on the table. "It might be weeks or months, but this is the end of the world we know."

As Issak spoke, Dek's limbs seemed to move away from him, as if he were stepping back away from his body along some fourth dimensional axis. Yep, this was fear. Not for his life, not of whatever was happening to him now—it was fear of a final loss. His parents, Ivo, Roy, and now Kaspari—it was fear of having nothing left.

"What have you done, Issak?" Despair was a black sea on which he floated. But curling through the depths of fear, like a dark serpent felt rather than seen, was a terrible rage. It didn't have to be this way. If they'd all stuck together, they could have solved this.

Issak raised his voice again, as if speaking to the lurkers shuffling about the house. "Do you feel it leaving?" He said like a drunken villain in a melodrama. "I'm extracting your alignment, your tether to the Loom. The gift Ivo gave you."

Dek was almost sure Issak's next act would be the patented Evil Sneer preferred by black-clad villains and those named 'Snively' the world over.

"It needs it to complete its transition to this world," he said with another theatrical wink.

"Your mamma." Dek's grin was the cold twist of a man with nothing to lose.

Issak laughed. Not an evil cackle, but not the generous reward for a joke well told, either.

Though Dek's hearing was diminished by whatever Issak was doing to him, he could still hear the shuffling that was coming slowly down the hallway behind Issak.

"There's someone you need to meet." Issak said: evil grin and sad eyes. The shuffling was all around them now. The darkness in the hall behind Issak seemed to open into a distant and much lower world; a world where bats and wolves competed for the affections of their dark masters. Sheesh.

Shapes coalesced from the darkness, first as outlines of men and women, then dark eyes, sharp and moving in unison, then faces and limbs disfigured by new and more lethal purpose.

"Metal band roadies? This is your new crew? Not impressed." Dek said. The fear was gone. The sorrow was covered. The rage was gonna come out and play.

He could move his hands somewhat, his feet below the ankle, and his head and neck. He put on a big show of struggling against whatever force Issak was using to hold him. The small movements he made were sluggish, perhaps as slow as he had moved before Ivo had breathed the power into him. Still, he had work to do before the end. "You killed Ivo... killed Roy." Dek bored a hole into Issak with his stare.

"I" All nine of the things at both entrances to the kitchen said in unison, "Killed them." Issak still sat across the table, eyes lowered. He opened his mouth, but then shut it again.

Dek looked around at the all-chant chorus. "You guys do rounds, too?"

"Ivo discovered them... what they were doing. After Gamma went down, after Asado made their play to kill Ivo." Issak paused for another swallow from his glass. "Some of the things that attacked Ivo actually fouled his interface with the Loom. Later, he found out why."

"After digging Roy's sword out of them, right?"

Issak nodded. "That's when he found the cracks." another swallow, "Through the disfigured corpses were ragged cracks into the underworld, through the Loom itself. My cracks."

Behind Issak, the lurkers shifted their heads in unison, rolled their eyes. Dek laughed, "If you're done talking about your crack, I think your new pals would like to get to the killing me part."

After an evil stare that lasted a few seconds, Issak continued. "Their goal tonight is not murder, but larceny. Tonight they need what now hovers around you... they need what you're now ready to give... you see? You are the key."

"To the executive washroom?"

"To the world... to the Loom." Issak said with a more agitated wink—what was up with that? Dek didn't really care, "Just a little blood linkage to forge the connection and it's theirs to use."

One of the disfigured crowd stepped forward, humorless smile stretched taut. Nice teeth.

Issak was still talking. Blah blah ghosts from below, yadda yadda cover the world. He really could bang out the verbiage sometimes. Dek was listening now as always. He'd parse through the info later with perfect recall, assuming he lived. If he didn't live, he really didn't care what Issak's plans and motivations were.

Dek was looking down at the table. Teak wood. Unusual in this day and age, but then the table didn't come from this day and age. Roy had built it long ago. He'd given it to Ivo, but not before he'd worked perfection into every centimeter. At first glance, the table seemed simple, utilitarian. But upon closer inspection it was full of subtle beauty—the lines were carved freeform so there were no straight edges anywhere. Gentle curves drew the eye around the edges. The sparse, but intricate carvings enticed the eye to linger. The table suited Roy, suited Ivo.

Tears filled his eyes. This grief could only be distracted by massive quantities of violence. Of course, it could only be conquered through forgiveness. He felt that as certainly as he felt the power leaching out of him, as sure as he felt disgust as Issak dragged his tumbler across Roy and Ivo's table—would it kill him to use a coaster? The demon was rounding the table as Issak blabbered on like he had all the time in the brink-of-destruction world. What was it with overconfidence and the evil? He used to be so careful.

"… save them, but I can save you now…" Issak was saying.

The flash that came next surprised everyone. No one noticed the lock tone or the ringing blade—the snap of the hammer drowned by the roar of the gun—but the demons that surrounded the table staggered as the shockwave burst outward from Issak's destroyed hand. Dek was surprised that the disruption his blade had caused in Issak's Cast should affect them. They must be more sensitive than they appeared... you really can't judge even demonic books by their covers.

Of course, no one was more surprised than Issak, as he gaped down at the tip of the Forged blade that protruded from the back of his left hand as it rested on the table. Or perhaps he saw only the starburst of erupting energy as the blade that parted his flesh and severed the skeins of the Cast that flowed outward through him.

Nobody was probably listening, but Dek shouted "Bullseye!" anyway. That's just the kind of guy he was.

Issak was carried backward on the crest of the expelled power, hand tearing from the blade. The Cast that held Dek prisoner unraveled and he was free. He surged out of the chair, tearing the sword out of his brother's perfect table.

Well, perhaps 'surged' was the wrong word. The chair flew back, but Dek came up at the wrong angle. His body didn't work the way he told it to. By the time he was supposed to be really getting into the slaughter, he was still trying to keep from falling over. The spark-chill from Issak's Cast still crawled across his skin. The demons rushed in. Monkey crap!

His mind flew along as quick as ever, only now he was using all his faculties to compensate for his new physical limitations. By the time the first demon was in range, he had figured that he was now moving perhaps only as fast as the legendary Bruce Lee, which was to say 'Wayyyy slower'. One of his pressing problems was that the nine demons surrounding him were moving with the speed of the also-legendary Jet Li—which was just a bit faster.

Well, you gotta make do. His mind still worked at the speed of modern supercomputers, so choreography wasn't a problem... and he did have a really boss sword.

"It is mine!" A dry whisper-scream filled the air. No one's lips had moved... or at least not to make words. Great. Now he was faced with an enemy subtle enough for ventriloquism. All hope was lost.

His lips hadn't completed the smile by the time the sword passed through the forearms of the first rushing attacker. As the blade bit through the attacker's modified flesh, sparks and ripples erupted from the wounds. Forged flesh?

Without pause, the newly armless demon altered his trajectory, bringing his knee up for a low kick. Dek saw it, but didn't have the speed to get his leg into position to deflect it and still be able to deal with the next attacker.

His groin took one for the team as his blade cut through the demon to his left, then riposted across the neck of the armless demon. Two down, seven to go. Ouch... that was going to hurt later.

His back was to the refrigerator; the other seven were giving him the same toothy grimace just outside the range of his blade.

"You hear me." The whisper voice said from everywhere. Still, he couldn't see anyone's lips move.

"You know, that devil's ventriloquist thing would really be scarier with a little evil dummy." Dek said, eyes shifting from enemy to enemy.

"You hear, Meat." The last word was derogatory.

"I here meet?" Dek asked innocently, "Perhaps you should have said 'we met here', or maybe 'meet me here', and the whole thing was barely more than a fragment… care to clarify?"

"Let us in, Meat. We will not prolong it. You are the key." The nowhere voice hissed.

"Listen, it's nice to 'meet' you, but I tell you what, you have your little puppies here hop on the elevator right quick and I won't have to introduce them to Judaism. Ok?" He gave the blade a small shake for emphasis.

"You are the puppy, Meat." The voice seethed hatred.

"You are the puppy?" Dek parroted with theatric nonchalance, "You know, attempting insult by induction isn't as straightforward as it might seem. Look, you're obviously new in town, so I'm gonna let you off easy…"

"You will die slowly!"

"Don't we all?" Dek's jaw set. This was it.

Issak groaned. Dek had to move fast now. If Issak regained consciousness before Dek either killed him or was long gone, it would all be over. Hobbled nearly down to human speed, there wouldn't be much Dek could do to defend himself against one of the most powerful Savants left in the world. Issak's overconfidence, distraction and intoxication had left Dek the opportunity to 'hand' him a little surprise, but nothing would save him if Issak woke up now.

Around Dek's thoughts swirled loaded memories: Ivo and Roy eating breakfast at the table now covered with Issak's blood. Roy gripping the severed steering wheel, Ivo in the back seat on the floor. Nine monsters saying, 'I killed them' in perfect lockstep.

Looking at Issak unconscious on the floor, Dek realized it was decision time. Would he try to kill Issak, or try to keep the power he carried away from The Outsider? He was pretty sure he could kill Issak before these monsters got him, but if he stayed to kill his last remaining father, they would definitely get him. Would he fight for revenge, or for a chance to save the washroom—the whole wide washroom. His gut pulled him one way, but his heart was free.

"Okay. Make it quick." He said, lowering the sword. He feigned a sob of despair... yeah, it was a bit over the top, but he just couldn't resist. He was rubbing imaginary tears from his eyes when they made their move.

They weren't taking any chances. Three dove in low, two came in high, the remaining two rushed to cover the exit to the foyer and elevator. Not bothering with a counterattack, Dek dove to the left, toward the unguarded hall to the bedrooms.

Most of the demons slammed into each other and the refrigerator, having fully committed to their attacks. Dek landed in a roll and came up running. He was through the doorway and several steps down the hall before the first pursuers were underway.

Still, in his weakened state, they were faster than he was. When he was halfway down the hall, they swarmed through the archway from the kitchen in a tight formation that would make the most team-oriented school of fish jealous. Dek poured on what speed he had left.

They were within two meters as he passed the last doorway, approaching the floor-to-ceiling window at the end of the hall. He was going to have to time this just right.

He left the ground a meter and a half before the window, already twisting to the left, swinging the sword across the window. The blade sliced through the glass, leaving a nearly horizontal line across the industrial glass. Cracks began to radiate away from the blade's path. His spin took the window out of his field of view and replaced it with seven slobbering monsters, close enough to reach out and touch. His legs came up to his chest as he ducked his head and hunched his shoulders. He made himself as small and inflexible a projectile as he could, hoping to transfer enough kinetic energy to finish shattering the glass.

His back struck the glass with what would have seemed like jarring impact if his perception of time weren't so dilated. The pressure built between him and the glass, compressing his flesh, straining his bones. Then they were on him, grabbing for purchase. One grabbed an ankle and another caught a corner of his coat.

His feet drove out even as he was surrounded with the slow waterfall sound of shattering glass. One foot caught the demon holding his ankle in the chest, driving him off his feet and into the others. His coat tore from the hands of the other demon as he exited the building amid the cloud of shattered glass.

As the demons disappeared into the clouds with the rest of the 82nd floor, Dek's thoughts turned to his next desperate move.

LIGHT

BURNING TO BEAUTY

*And it shall come to pass, that instead of sweet smell
there shall be stink;
and instead of a girdle, a rent;
and instead of well set hair, baldness;
and instead of a stomacher, a girding of sackcloth;
and burning instead of beauty.*

– Isaiah 3:24

Screams, darkness, blood, remorse, hope, and through it all the ringing of a dead man's blade.

Rae's scream was like nothing Ping had heard before. It had started with a word, but now was only the sound of denial. The lights went out and some kind of unseen turbulence snapped through the air like a puff of wind. The lights flickered back on and the door burst open, admitting a concerned-looking nurse of about fifty. The sword's ringing was muted by Alex's chest as it snapped back into the hilt.

Blood pooled on the floor beneath the new hole in the bottom of the bed. Rae was breathless at the end of a scream she still seemed intent at continuing. Her mouth was open and silent. She staggered, then fell in a heap and didn't move.

The nurse who'd burst in to investigate the cause of the silent alarm paused, unsure whether to proceed to the bed, or try to help the woman who had seemingly fallen dead. She looked from Alex to Rae, then back again before finally looking to Ping for assistance. He hooked a thumb at Alex's fresh chest wound. She rushed to the bed with her medkit and was joined seconds later by the floor doctor. Together, they worked feverishly to staunch the bleeding, then to reinflate his collapsed lung.

While they worked, they asked him questions, but Ping didn't hear. Amid bright lights and the crisp smell of fall, he sat in darkness that no coma therapy could breach. He turned the sword over in his hands. Spattered blood covered the end and spread with the motion to cover his fingers and hands. He didn't know to who or what, but he was praying for mercy, for undeserved providence.

* * *

Rae's tears were defocused here. Head in her hands. Solitude.

"So, you'll marry me, right?" Her dead man across the table said around a mouthful of cheeseburger.

"That's not funny." She moaned into her hands.

"Whew. I'm glad to hear that," he said reaching for his drink, "I was a bit worried you might laugh."

She cried harder, sobs crashing around her as the weight of her loneliness became clearer with the ghost's words.

Then his arms were around her, holding her tight. Sweet lies filled the air, "It's gonna be all right. Let it all out, you're not gonna need it."

She was lying on Roy's couch with Alex wrapped around her. Outside the window, the storm gathered as night and death approached. Lightning came and went but the thunder seemed to roll on and on. Time passed, or didn't. She lay curled on a dead man's couch with another dead man wrapped around her. He'd been talking, but she really hadn't been paying attention.

"…not a ghost you know… really." Alex finished.

"All ghosts say that." She said weakly.

"No way. Look at *A Christmas Carol*, each ghost was pretty frank about his nature… except possibly for the silent, pointy one. Anyway, I'm sure you can think of plenty of other examples."

"Look. All the jokes in the world won't make me hope this ain't a dream. Just a second ago we were in our booth at Nell's and now we're on Roy's couch."

He chuckled. "You're beautiful when you're deductive. But I didn't say this wasn't a dream… I just said I wasn't a ghost."

"Lawyer."

"You're also beautiful when you're cynical… just so spunky. See? You're the perfect woman. I really wasn't kidding about gettin' hitched."

She was too weary for anything but easy conversation, so more sobs were out. "Ok then lover… wait! There's a snag… you're dead and I'm either unconscious or dead from a broken heart."

"Broken heart? Now that's just sweet." He patted her hand from across the table. "So, if I can work these little problems out... the wedding's on?" He said from across the food-littered table of their favorite booth. "Remember? This is where I proposed to you the first time."

"You are such a geek... always wanting to get married in any world but the one we're currently in... I still think you're gay."

"But I *am* in denial."

"Still gay."

"Then maybe you're a man trapped in a woman's body? I sure am sweet on you, sugar."

"Flattery will get you nowhere, Zombikens."

"Listen, Scoobylicious, technically you're not here from a broken heart... I kinda knocked you out before you could start kicking the Detective's butt... you'd regret that later, by the way. Plus I haven't been able to talk to you much more than the odd word wedged around 'seek medical attention' for two days now—I thought we could spend some quality time together."

She looked up and into his eyes for the first time and instantly the world changed. She knew. She screamed and surged across the table into his arms.

* * *

Working together, the doctor and floor nurse had gotten the major blood vessels sealed after two minutes of struggle using only the doctor's portable kit. The trauma nurse arrived shortly thereafter with more comprehensive equipment. Now she and the doctor were working to stabilize the patient for transport to the OR.

No longer needed, the floor nurse stepped away from the wounded John Doe. She glanced at the patient still mumbling to himself in the wheelchair. He had a postoperative dressing on his head, so she wrote his behavior off to some serious brain trauma. She turned her attention to the female cop out cold on the floor.

The nurse had heard her scream as she'd entered the room, so she was surprised to find a beatific smile frozen on the unconscious woman's face. Though the paths of tears were fresh on her face, she looked like she was dreaming of Caribbean romance.

Her preliminary scan came up clean. She seemed to be sleeping... deep REM.

"Officer?" She looked at the holographic nametag at the bottom of the woman's badge, "Officer Woods?" She shook the fallen officer gently, then slightly less so.

"Yeah. Ok, but just one more, 'kay?" Woods slurred out sleepily. The sentence terminated in the puckering of imaginary kisses. In mid-pucker, the officer's eyes fluttered open. Pucker frozen on her face, her eyes shifted about, finally settling on the floor nurse's confused face. The pucker dissolved into a self-conscious smile. "Hi." She said.

"Hi." The nurse gave the quick nod most reserve to ease the pressure of awkward meetings.

"So, now that my nap's out of the way... back on the job, eh?" the officer wiped at her tear-streaked face. "Whoo! Sure was tired!"

"Uh… what's happening here?"

"You tell me, I just woke up." The officer sat up and looked around.

"Less than five minutes ago you were screaming like your foot was stuck in a blender."

"You sure that was me? I really feel much better now." She stood up in one graceful move that looked like it was cut from the middle of a Russian ballet.

"Whoa!" the nurse fell out of her crouch and onto her posterior.

"Oh, sorry!" The officer said, offering her a hand up.

"You know these folks?" The nurse asked, regaining her feet.

"Well, that sweet guy over there with the sucking chest wound is my fiancé." She giggled like a junior invited to senior prom. She seemed to realize this was less than appropriate and cleared her throat before continuing. "The muttering guy over there stabbed him just now… Boy, I'm so going to bust him for that… stabbing is a serious offense." She said, elbowing the confused nurse conspiratorially.

"Uh…" the nurse waited uncertainly for the punch line, not sure if she'd just heard it. "That wasn't funny."

"Yep. Sure wasn't funny before I got my nap. I was screaming like my foot was stuck in a blender." Her smile was dazzling.

"Are you sure you're ok?" the nurse said, looking down at her scanner again.

The doctor and trauma nurse stumbled away from the bed where they were working on the John Doe. "You see that?!" the doctor shouted.

The trauma nurse nodded. They took another step back amid a shocked intake of breath. The floor nurse followed their stares back to the bed.

"What?" Alex said, sitting up in the bed, prodding the closing wound in his chest with a finger.

Minutes passed and eventually the door to the semiprivate opened and the doctor and two nurses sauntered into the hall.

"Nope, those were not the droids we were looking for." The floor nurse said as the door swung closed behind them.

The doctor concurred, "Yep, not those droids at all—it was about time for us to move along." His head moved through a slow, thoughtful shake.

The trauma nurse was less sure. "Yeah... but what's a droid?"

"Well, obviously not those!" the doctor gave the short laugh that often accompanies blatantly obvious assertions.

"Why were we looking for droids?" The floor nurse wondered.

"What are droids?!" the trauma nurse demanded, shaking her head harder.

"I'm hungry." The doctor said, rubbing his neck. They all shuffled toward the break room.

"So, what's a droid?" Rae said into Alex's ear.

"Uhhg! Chest wound!"

"Oh." Rae disengaged the bear hug, feeling a bit self-conscious. "Sorry."

Alex sat back on the bed, concentrating. He swayed a bit, so Rae sat down next to him. She put an arm around his shoulders to steady him."

"That your work, too?" Rae nodded toward Ping, who was now snoring in his wheelchair.

Alex nodded, "We owe him our lives again... what's this, like three times?"

Rae thought for a moment. "I think we all owe each other a lot. He is pretty amazing, though... you know he started out as a family counselor?"

One of Alex's eyes popped open. "Nah... really?"

Rae nodded, "It's actually a really sad story."

Alex shook his head as if to clear it. "Tell me later... it's gonna take me about forty minutes to finish patching the two of us up.

She looked surprised. "You are getting better, Mr. Potter. It took you forever to fix him the first time."

"Well, he was a lot worse then. Shhh, now. I'm probably being a bit too optimistic. What I really meant was that we've got about forty minutes before they make another try for us."

"What?!"

"How do you get this metal diaper off? It's really beginning to chafe."

CONVERGENCE

The buzzer sounded and Chase looked up from the current edition of *Hypercar Quarterly*. "Whoa!"

Before the camera outside the door was the most beautiful federal agent he'd ever seen. Of course, that cop had been a different kind of hot, but this woman was something special. Porcelain skin, straight red hair, swimmer's body… he could tell these things even through the suit. He went through the motions of verifying the FBI ID that she presented before the camera then buzzed her in.

"Bio-terror." He pronounced as she entered the security room, trying to get his flirt on.

"Sorry?" She said, pocketing her badge.

"Aliens then?" he raised his eyebrows.

"What?"

"You are going to tell me what's going on, right?"

"Oh!" She laughed. "Sorry… no. I'm here to relieve you."

"Aw… come on. I can't leave my post."

"Sorry." She said. The firmness didn't drive the friend-liness out of her voice, but it threatened to if he didn't cooperate. "This is a federal matter now. Have you been debriefed?"

"Uh…" he hesitated, suddenly feeling uncomfortable. "Maybe?"

"You're going to cooperate, right? I'm assuming you're not wanting to toy with obstruction."

"I'm not obstructin'. There was this Fed, came in right after the commotion… but I don't remember much else. Nice guy though. Looked like he'd been skiing lately."

"He had a bad tan?"

"Nope… stat cast had him immobilized between neck and wrist," Chase grabbed his own wrist, "I didn't say he looked like a *good* skier."

"What did you see of this 'commotion'?" She pulled out her tablet.

"I saw the whole…" He paused, like a man realizing he was lost and perhaps naked. "There was this… It was in the ER. A fight maybe?"

"You don't know?"

He shook his head. "Weird."

"Indeed." She made a few scratches on her tablet. "I'll need you to wait in the reception room and help the other guard keep people out."

His chances of a date were fading fast. "You got secret Fed business here, eh?" he leaned toward her as if she might impart more knowledge if she could speak it quietly.

"Something like that." She smiled and gestured to the monitor bank. "Besides it looks like your pal could use the help."

"Jeez Clint!" On the monitor, Clint was apparently sleeping, slumped over the small security desk.

* * *

Less than a minute after the addled security officer left, Miranda Todd buzzed her companions into the security room. Derry entered first, looking like a tourist in Kauai. "Ow. Derry, turn down that shirt, okay?"

"Now that just hurts. Here I come a' running when you call me in the middle of the night and all you do is give me the fashion debrief." He threw an assault gun toward her. She caught it without conscious thought and restowed it under her jacket.

"Look Derry, this isn't my show…"

"Get me a look inside OR-3." Elena Mendez said as the door closed behind her.

"Comin' up boss." Miranda's fingers flew across the security console. An overhead view of the operating theatre opened in the center of the display. Two surgeons and a tech surrounded the coffin-like operating bed.

"That your man?" Derry asked, his eyes shifting to Elena.

Miranda nodded. "Operating theatre's supposed to go available in thirty minutes, so they should be finishing any minute now… triage records look positive." Miranda looked up from the console with an encouraging smile.

Elena's brown eyes remained fixed on the display. A shadow passed through them. Her face softened, but the focus didn't leave her eyes. "How long to link into the security net?"

"Done." Miranda said as her fingers stopped moving again.

Elena opened her tablet, configured an alpha encrypter, and called Hawthorne. She got a failure buzz. She checked the crypto, then the tablet, then the connection. "Net's down."

"In a hospital?" Derry looked surprised.

She configured the tablet for a point-to-point connection, got another buzz. "I can't get RF through either."

"Nonsense!" Miranda's fingers flew over the console. "There she is right there... four floors up, in the observation room above the OR... you shouldn't have any trouble getting microband through to her. Hey! Who's that with her?"

They all leaned in for a better look just as the monitor filled with electric snow. The lights flickered—flickered again. Static filled the security screens.

"Wha?" Miranda began diagnostics, or tried to. The computer console accepted none of her commands. It was completely dead.

"That felt targeted." Elena said, "Lets get out of here. Derry, you've got point."

Three assault guns came up in unison. They moved to the doorway, hard and ready for anything—or so they thought.

* * *

The lights flickered, flickered again and the lights from the city outside blazed briefly through Ping's dark reflection. It was his turn to stare into the window's black glass and wait. Behind him in the semitransparent vista of reflection, Alex lay on the hospital bed, healing himself presumably. Rae paced around the far end of the room. From time to time, he could see her stealing glances at him.

His head was no longer bandaged. Alex had finished what work had been left undone by the medkit and surgeons. He felt strong, steady. Fortunately Rae had been wrong, and the only evidence of his head wound now was a terrible case of bed-head. He wore clothes packed before their flight from Roy's house on Lake Geneva. Apparently the same clothes that Rae had dressed him in for their trip to the hospital. This was definitely his week for being stripped and dressed by strangers. Of course, it was also the week of being beaten senseless and then healed miraculously. Was his glass half empty or half full?

Roy's sword was in his pocket, Roy's twin pistols slung beneath a hard composite jacket most people would probably use for riding motorcycles. He couldn't imagine what Roy had used it for... air skiing behind suborbital transports, perhaps.

He looked up from his borrowed and aliased tablet, his gaze shifted to Rae's nervous pacing, then back to his own reflection. He wore a dead man's clothes, carried a dead man's weapons. His face was expressionless, his eyes soft and dark. Through his reflection swam the shifting lights of the night city. He couldn't meet Rae's gaze, couldn't speak. He didn't deserve to be alive. Sure his little gambit had worked, but what kind of person would try something like that? Certainly a desperate one, but he didn't feel like letting himself off so easy.

Rae stopped pacing and took a deep breath. She walked toward Ping's window, her reflection growing behind him as she approached. She came to a halt behind him. Though he wanted to look down, wanted to just go away, he returned her reflected stare. Man of ashes poured into another's urn.

"How did you know?" She said.

"I didn't."

"Not good enough."

"No, it wasn't… I was playing God again."

"You know, I could just surf to guiltypleasure.org if all I wanted was self recrimination."

"Net's down, so you're lucky I'm here."

"Look…" she paused, "The net's down? Here?"

He gave her a grim nod, "Anyone having a library flashback?" he held the collapsed tablet over his shoulder for her to see. "It went down when the lights flickered off just now. They're getting close."

"I'm getting tired of being almost dead." she shrugged.

"Tell me 'bout it." Ping's smile was a surprise to him.

"How'd you know how to free Alex?"

He took a moment to consider. "I thought it was the most likely thing that he'd been… whatevered… spellified. He checked out in the middle of our escape with no wounds. Then the kit and the doctors couldn't find anything wrong with him. I couldn't see any other way we could free him, he obviously wasn't going to come around again on his own… at least not before we were discovered here."

"How'd you know the blade would break the spell?"

"I didn't for sure, but I'd seen Dek use one like it to shred Garvey's spell in the library. He cut clean through it… knocked Garvey off his feet with whatever backlash it caused. Afterward, the blade was traced with some kind of glowing pattern. Later, Dek told me my sword would cut through anything the Loom could weave."

"Why didn't you tell me?"

He couldn't read her expression. Concern? Hurt? Anger. "What if it didn't work? I've already killed good people with my poor judgment…" He broke off; tried again. "I'm as damned as I'm gonna get."

The silence lengthened between them.

"You know Detective, before a couple days ago, I hadn't killed anyone. The library, that really hurt, you know?"

He nodded. He knew.

"But you know what? Over the last two days of lying low, I've had a lot of time to think."

He made no indications he'd heard, so she continued, "I didn't kill to make my life easier, not even to make it longer… I killed to save Alex, to save you." She paused again, "I didn't do the work of death. I did the work of life, Detective. So did you."

His smile was bitter. "Nice speech, Rae."

"Did it work?"

"What was it trying to do?"

"Get you to stop missing the point."

"And what point is that?"

"The one on top of your head."

"Wha?" he turned to look at her over his shoulder.

She smiled that beautiful smile that Alex had helped him see. "Only suckers waste time hating themselves for doin' what's right." Her hand snapped out quickly, smacking him painfully in the shoulder. "Even when bad stuff happens."

"Man, that was beautiful." Alex groaned from the bed.

They both turned to face him. "Now what, chief?" Ping asked, looking sideways at Rae and rubbing his bruised shoulder.

"Check this out!" Alex said, holding out his arms. After a few seconds, he raised perhaps ten centimeters off the floor. He smiled like a kid with a new toy, floating around the room. Like a slow-motion superman, he made his favorite man-of-steel poses.

Watching the spectacle, Rae turned to Ping, "Geeks should *not* have superpowers."

"Evildoers beware." Ping muttered.

Finished for the time being, Alex touched down on the floor and gave a small bow. If he was expecting applause— and he was—he ended up disappointed. After a pause to allow them to change their minds about the adulation, he moved on. "We don't have long. They'll be in the building any minute. Once they get here, they'll probably knock down the hospital's net and head straight for us."

Ping and Rae exchanged glances. "What?" Alex said.

"Babe… the net went down maybe five minutes ago now."

The blood drained out of Alex's face. "Why didn't you tell me?"

"You were too busy showin' off!"

"How did you know they were coming? That they'd kill the net?" Ping asked, subconsciously checking the positioning of his holsters.

"Elfin magic… didn't think it would be so soon."

"So you did your little flying demo before you warned us?"

Alex looked guilty. He smiled sheepishly, "It was pretty cool… no?"

They were not impressed.

"Time to go." Alex moved toward the door.

"Wait!" Rae said. "Why did you bring us to this hospital? Why not the three others closer to where we were hiding out?"

"Dek's here. The tracker stopped moving earlier tonight, so I used a little power from your cameo to hack Ping's medkit." He turned and ran for the door with Ping and Rae close behind.

"You're saying you've been aware all this time?" Rae said as they sprinted down the hall toward the elevator banks.

"Sensible underwear." Alex said, hitting the call button.

Rae winced. Alex smiled.

* * *

Hawthorne gripped Mendez's empty operating bed with one hand while the other wavered in the general direction of the broken observation window above. In that hand she held her pistol, covering the window above.

Behind her, Anne stood facing the gaggle of… well, she didn't have a description better than 'party demons'. Her vision was still skipping from the arduous trip from window to floor, her hands still shook, her teeth still clenched. She was still uncertain about being very, very sick. The demons' deranged chuckling seemed to dance around the jitters in her overtaxed mind.

"How many bullets you got in that gun, Hawthorne?" Anne asked quietly.

"Call me Sarah… and there'll be plenty left when we're dead."

"Ok, Sarah. Can I ask you a favor?"

"No."

"Fair enough."

"There it is!" The monstrous visitors all hissed at once. "Hiding in briars, but here it will be."

"That make any sense to you?" Anne whispered sideways.

"Nope."

Anne nodded. "Right. Thought not." Then raising her voice to be heard, she said, "You are on the road to destruction! All your base are belong to us!"

Hawthorne glanced over her shoulder, "Wha?"

Anne sniggered. The demons seemed unsure of what they should do now. Not so much thinking as just awaiting instructions. The surgeons had joined the OR tech behind Anne. Jeremy was still frozen four meters before her, perhaps two meters from the closest demons.

"Jeremy!" Anne hissed.

In the slow motion of the shell-shocked, Jeremy's head turned slowly to point his sheet-white face and bulging eyes in her direction. "Onh?" He may have said.

Anne jerked her head and motioned with her eyes for him to skeedaddle behind her with the rest of the non-monsters. He gave a tick with his head that Anne read as a nod, but then his head turned back to the demons and he didn't move another muscle. Well, that wasn't entirely true—at least one sphincter muscle moved, and it was not to Jeremy's great advantage. "Oops." Anne whispered as Jeremy's pants darkened.

As if they were attuned to the scent of urine like sharks are to blood, the demons exploded forward. A demon wearing the color-traced black of a neo-goth grabbed Jeremy around the throat, or would have about three hundred milliseconds later if he had not instead received a face full of Anne Kelley's fist.

With her left hand, she yanks Jeremy back toward the others, perhaps a little too hard she thinks, since she sees his feet exiting her peripheral vision about a meter off the ground. At the same time, her right hand streaks forward, tearing through the toothy grin of the goth-demon. Teeth and blood disengage themselves from his face, but her fist is already gone. Her left leg lashes out low and the demon leaves the ground, smashing into one of the demons behind him.

Anne bores forward, whirling-jumping around another assailant, using the demon's head as a lever to throw it into another demon. Around her, two others turn in perfect sync to press attacks from both sides—one aims a kick to her side, the other levels a punch at her head. Neither connects as Anne dodges the punch while sweeping up the kicking leg. She wraps her arm around the knee and pulls up hard with the leg locked in her elbow. The hip joint dislocates under the pressure just before her kick destroys the knee of the supporting leg.

Gunfire fills the air as she pivots slightly, sliding her elbow backwards under the other demon's still-extending punch. At least three ribs shatter and the heart collapses behind them. The demon with the dislocated hip and hyperextended knee has just begun to fall as her right hand returns to shatter his skull.

The sound of screaming is punctuated by the frequent sounds of violent impact, but never interrupted. The hospital staff may be screaming behind her. She hopes not, but can't really tell. The only scream that she hears is her own. This may prove she's weak, but she can't contain her revulsion. Like a catheterized drunk after a big night out, the horror just flows out of its own shrill volition.

The world is now coming as a series of flash photos that break over her like the waves of violence she now slogs through. Each flash is worse than the last. Here's Anne in mid headbutt with a bloody halo spreading away, here's Anne getting kicked in the face, here's Anne tearing off someone's arm… NO!

The screaming goes on until she doesn't have any more air for it, then there is a pause where only gunfire and the harsh clash of fists compete with the sound of her ragged inhalation. She wants this to stop, wants to run away... can run away. But she knows she won't run. She is the only hope for Hawthorne, poor unconscious Mendez, poor wet Jeremy, and the surgeons. She's done with fear, and now she's done with failure. With a shock that is eighty percent guilt, twenty percent enlightenment, she realizes that she would rather be here than sitting at home with a good book.

Here she matters. Here she can help.

Her scream rips out again amid the melee, fractionally harder this time.

Hawthorne stumbled partially as she pulled the trigger and her shot went wild. The three round burst tore into the wall and ceiling above the observation window. She didn't hit either of the gunmen that had appeared there, but the burst was enough to make them duck back out of view. She stumbled again and went down on her knees painfully behind a waist-high rack of monitoring equipment. Ignoring her bruised knees, she steadied her arms on the rack and continued to cover the window.

Another killer popped up, already firing. Hawthorne sent another burst through the window, but she couldn't tell if she had hit him. She snapped a quick look over her shoulder, to where Anne was screaming like she was being torn apart. She fired a few more shots through the window and tried to decipher what she'd seen behind her. First, her eye had settled on Anne's face amidst a whirling sea of violence, covered in blood, screaming desperately. She'd looked horrified, lost—angry. The monsters were all around her, moving so fast—at least one of them had been in the air—others were laid out on the ground.

Two assault guns poked over the lower lip of the window and began firing. This wasn't the random noise of suppressing fire. Bullets rained down around Hawthorne, striking the equipment rack in front of her, tearing through her left arm and chest. There was a flash of light inside her head, heat from her damaged body. Then she was on the floor with her eyes fluttering open.

She knew this would happen. She'd never had any hope of winning a gun battle with multiple opponents firing assault guns from cover. It had only been a matter of seconds before they'd realized she was shooting back and used their integrated gun cameras to fire from complete cover.

So, time did seem to dilate when you were dying. This was a bar-bet that Mendez would never get a chance to collect on.

Around her on the white floor was a deep red pattern of her blood. Closer in was the slick of blood oozing from her chest and back. Farther out was the spatter from the initial impacts. Perhaps a meter away, her gun lay on the floor. Looking down, she saw the ragged hole in her upper chest, white broken collarbone protruding through the hole. This sight almost drove the light from her eyes, but through will alone, she held on to her last moments of life like… well, like they were all she had left.

The corners of her mouth twitched with an abortive smile. She was really glad that the shock kept her from feeling much… spoke too soon. Her moan came out through gritted teeth.

Above her, she could see the guns pointed toward where she'd last seen Anne by the doorway. They had not yet fired. Perhaps they were waiting for the fight to end before deciding if they would shoot the victor. Perhaps they were waiting for a clear shot.

Anne's screaming continued, but Hawthorne now realized that all other sounds had stopped. No gunfire, no sounds of hand-to-hand combat, no demonic laughter. She really didn't want to look to see what was happening to Anne. The end of her own life was depressing enough without being exposed to someone else's. Yet in the end, curiosity won out and she craned her head back to see whatever terrible fate had led to those forlorn wails.

It seemed to take forever to bring her head into the correct position. She used the seconds to steel herself for whatever tragedy she would see. But when the vista finally crept into view, she was still shocked.

It looked like a bomb had exploded where Anne was standing—but this bomb only affected flesh and bone. The floor was not cratered, the surrounding walls were intact except for one roughly torso-sized impact crater about two meters up. Yet littered around her were the bodies of her previous enemies, some thrown completely across the room. All were dead, many horribly broken, several in pieces. And at the center of the departed blast Anne stood, covered in blood, holding the disembodied arm of one of the demons before her. She was trembling, she was screaming.

Her eyes were darting about looking for help. They first settled on the other members of the hospital staff cowering together against the far wall of the OR. Presumably, they knew Anne from their time shared at work, but the stare that they returned was horror well beyond the panic end of the scale. Anne's eyes darted to the window with it's waiting guns, then quickly away, finally settling on Hawthorne.

Despite the pain and the hopeless situation, Hawthorne knew what was necessary. With great effort, she flashed Anne a smile, and gave her a thumbs-up sign with the hand that still responded to her will. She was tired, but this was almost over.

Across the room, the screaming stopped.

At the end of an oddly placed instant of harmony and mutual empathy, someone yelled "Freeze!" from above, but there was no pause before gunfire erupted.

* * *

As they passed the sixth floor, gunfire punctuated an all banjo and tambourine rendition of Metallica's classic *One*... what was it with modern elevator music? Screams and more gunfire greeted them as the elevator doors opened. Without an instant of uncertainty, Ping bolted into the hall. Rae ran after him, and Alex stumbled out last. It was going to take him a while to work the stiffness out of his muscles. Ironically, this was a much harder problem to solve with the Loom than a sucking chest wound. Not exactly an intuitive distinction.

Ping sprinted down the hallway with reckless speed. Rae was torn between trying to keep up with him and trying to avoid being ambushed. She hissed at him to slow down, but he wasn't listening, frustrating man that he was.

Ping was being driven forward by perhaps the most desperate series of shrieks he'd ever heard. He'd heard desperate before, even hopeless, but this screaming was bottom-of-the-eternal-lake-of-fire bad. It was the wail of the hopeless damned. Only feelings and other pre-thoughts filled his mind and heart... empathy for the screamer, rage for the cause, memories and the supposition of a little girl's scream—he had to get there... Right Now.

He approached the door of an operating theatre, with steps near the door leading up to an observation room. The sounds of gunfire came from the observation room above. He vaulted the railing and took the steps two at a time, but by the time he was halfway up, the gunfire stopped. The screaming continued, and new sounds emerged, the sounds of an intense physical conflict. Twice, the walls rattled with heavy impacts.

He continued his ascent. He reached the door, and paused to check his assault gun: Unlocked, safety off, plenty of rounds left... the shrieking came to an abrupt halt. Too late!

Empathy evaporated, leaving only fury behind. He kicked the already broken door inward. "Freeze!" he shouted.

The room was small, perhaps four meters on a side, there were some chairs and a coffee table filled with quite a few empty drink containers and a lot of empty snack packages. Three people crouched near the shattered window into the operating room below. Two were wearing link goggles and holding their weapons over the lip of the window, using their gun cameras to target while remaining under full cover. The thought flitted through his head that this would have been a better strategy for him as well, but hey, he'd been in a hurry.

The third person in the room was dropping his hand from a communicator at his throat and using the other hand to bring an assault gun to bear on Ping. All three wore no uniform, preferring instead dark, sturdy-looking street clothes. They wore no badges, they didn't seem like cops or SWAT. Their overall impression was military, perhaps mercenaries. They looked a lot like the nice folks from the library archive.

One of the two at the window batted his goggles off his face and dropped into a roll trying to bring his gun to bear on Ping. No one had paid the slightest attention to Ping's 'Freeze', except the woman who kept her weapon covering the OR below, though Ping was pretty sure she was covering, not complying.

Oh well.

Ping fired a five round burst into the one on his feet, four toward the roller, four more, then three more after he stopped moving just to be sure. The one by the window was definitely not complying now. Merciless face set like stone, her rifle left the lip of the window and tracked toward him, already firing. A line of holes appeared in the wall to his right, tearing toward him. Ping jumped left and fired another burst. The last attacker was knocked into the wall. She slumped to the floor.

"Share how *that* makes you feel." He said, disgust in his voice. Internally, revulsion and the warm feeling of a job well done warred for possession of his heart. He tossed both feelings aside… work to do.

He might not have been the most effective counselor, but he was smoking good at this. Maybe his dad was right… stay close to your talents.

* * *

Hawthorne's eyes spasmed shut at the sound of what she was sure was that "final gunfire" everyone in law enforcement fears. She was marginally surprised that she heard more than the first burst, but it did make sense that they would go for Anne first. There were six overlapping bursts, then silence.

After another few seconds, she opened her eyes again. The world had stayed essentially the same as when she'd closed them. The hospital staff still huddled, Anne still looked dazed, Hawthorne's own blood continued to pool around her. There was one difference though—the assault guns that had been covering them from the window above were gone.

Then two things happened essentially at once. A little Asian guy in a biker jacket appeared in the window above with an assault gun at the ready, and the OR doors burst open to reveal a very appealing uniformed cop. What were the chances that this was an actual cop? Not the pawn-in-a-vast-conspiracy-type, but just someone here to serve and/or protect them like real cops would. Looking at the cop's non-issue fletcher, Hawthorne didn't feel hopeful.

Anne's head snapped back and forth from the window to the door with the speed of a parakeet on amphetamines, but then she made no further moves. She had a look somewhere between expectation and resignation.

"Everyone okay here?" The man from above shouted down in a friendly but uncertain voice.

Hawthorne wasn't sure she hadn't imagined that last part. The world went black.

The perky little cop with the fletcher eyed Anne with clear uncertainty. Her gaze started out hard, like shoot-you-or-not hard, eyes moving from Anne's face to the severed arm she carried and back. Finally, the cop's eyes lapsed back into caution tempered by empathy. At this point, Anne realized that she was still crying. No more screaming, but the water works had not disengaged.

"You okay, Ma'am?" Rae asked without lowering the fletcher. She was really hoping she didn't have to put this woman down... she just looked so sad. She wondered if she was the source of the terrible screaming she'd heard from the hall. She didn't dare take her eyes off the big woman with the hard eyes and sad face, but her peripheral vision slowly began to process the rest of the scene. Radiating away from the woman was a blast pattern of corpses. It looked like an explosion had gone off right where she stood. Behind her about four meters away on a monitor table lay an unconscious patient in post-operative isolation wrap. Behind him, against the far wall, four hospital staffers huddled behind equipment that wasn't large enough to cover them all.

"Do I look okay to you?" The woman said shakily, exasperation breaking through her misery. She gave what may have started as a bitter laugh, but terminated in sobs.

Her left hand went to her face. Her right hand held a severed arm like a club.

Rae shook her head. "But I don't need to shoot you though, right?"

"You think it would do you any good?" As she spoke, the big woman waved the disembodied arm she held for emphasis, "Besides, you'd probably need a wooden stake or silver bullets."

As Anne gave the severed arm a final shake for emphasis, a little skinny guy with shiny chrome hair limped around the corner behind the cop. His eyes flashed around the room, taking in the scene. "Wow." He said.

"Just a sec." Anne said, not breaking eye contact with the cop. Still giving her the 'don't shoot me' look, she turned her head extra slowly to one side so she could speak over her shoulder. "Hey Sean!" she shouted.

Behind her, one of the huddling hospital workers poked his head up from behind the operating bed on the other side of the room.

"You are a trauma doc, right?"

"Ah… sure… yeah." he said, not knowing where she was going with this line of questions.

"Ok… just wanted to make sure." Without turning fully away from the visitors at the door, Anne raised her arm slowly to point at Hawthorne's sprawled body.

After a few seconds of pointing and confused silence, the doctor had a flash of inspiration and jumped to his feet. "Right! Stella!" He clapped the other surgeon on the shoulder and rushed to help the fallen woman. Two of the other three came to his side, leaving only poor damp Jeremy on the ground by the wall.

"Told you Dek was here." The little guy at the door said to the cop. He gestured to the carnage with a told-you-so look. He then put his hand on his head, like he was thinking hard.

The cop nodded, then addressed Anne, "You seen a really fast guy with spiky hair and a wicked sword round these parts?"

Anne looked confused.

"Well, who…" The cop's eyes glanced around at the destruction.

"Oh!" The little guy startled the cop, his eyes widened with surprise, then settled on Anne.

"Oh… no… this is…" Chrome-top stammered.

Anne felt a familiar tingle across her skin, more satin sheets this time than caffeinated eels, but unmistakably the same thing. "Don't you even start with me you little pipsqueak!" she leveled her finger at him.

"Pipsqueak?" He looked confused, "…you felt that?"

Anne continued what she hoped was a menacing stare. She didn't think she could beat both the magic whammy the little guy was wielding and the cop's fletcher, so she was left with bravado.

"No. Wait!" The little guy shouted, sensing impending tragedy, "We're not here to hurt you. You don't… Ping! Get down here!"

Anne lowered in her stance, she'd forgotten about the guy above with the assault gun. This was about to get ugly. Sensing Anne's plans, the cop got more serious with her aim, her face hardened.

The little guy held up a hand. "Stop!" he pleaded, "Please, both of you." His glance flitted from Anne to the cop. "We're on your side… I think we are anyway. We can always duke it out later if we find out you're evil… you're not evil, right?"

Anne's laugh was perhaps one-third whimper. "That's the question, isn't it? I mean just look around!" Her three arms gestured to include the perhaps eight corpses. "Supergirl or Bride of Dracula?" She threw the severed arm to the ground with the rest of the carnage.

"Speaking of evil…" the Asian guy in the observation room called down, "The guys up here were bad guys, right?"

Anne sobbed.

"Right?" He repeated, a little more concerned.

"Sure… They gunned down a federal agent," she glanced over her shoulder to where the doctors worked on Hawthorne. "…tried to kill me too, but then everybody's been trying that lately."

The kid put a hand on the cop's weapon, pressed down slowly. The cop looked at him inquisitively, but allowed him to lower her weapon.

"That's Dek." The kid pointed to Anne.

* * *

"Right this way, gentlemen." Agent Vega said. He opened the door to the first-floor conference room and stepped aside. The six confused officers passed through for their debriefing. Rather than following them inside, the agent closed the door. He and his two companions waited in silence. All faces were hard, inscrutable.

From the other side of the door, they heard the sound of two doors opening into other rooms. Shouts, then screams erupted from the other side of the closed door. A burst of gunfire sounded as at least one of the officers had the presence of mind to draw his weapon. The screams were intense, punctuated by crashing violence and the sound of rending flesh. It was over in perhaps twenty seconds, except for the ripples of black laughter and the sound of feeding… these lasted significantly longer.

Do they really have time for that? Vega wondered mostly to distract his imagination from painting the picture of events as they unfolded on the other side of the door.

They were hard men. They were servants of an ancient and proud order, experienced soldiers and assassins. Yet they were still men—they were still afraid. Vega couldn't shake the feeling that the Savants he served had made a horrible mistake that would likely leave them as dead as many of the other clans.

This was supposed to be the turning point for Asado—their ascension to dominance, but Vega didn't think so. He feared that this… thing, and its ever-increasing horde of progressively more disturbing flesh puppets would be the bloody screaming end of everything, including Asado.

But then it wasn't his job to think. It certainly wasn't his job to fear. He made sure his weapons were ready. His men anxiously followed suit. This thing had really poured on the effort to get its hands on this key. Amazingly enough, it had already suffered two defeats tonight from this woman: one in the ER, and most recently in one of the operating rooms. Asado had also taken the beatdown once upstairs in the doctors' lounge, then again at the OR, if the gunfire that terminated the last communication from the other team was any indication.

Their enemy was tough, but easy to underestimate. Vega had seen their quarry's picture during the briefing in the whispercraft on the way here. There had been a significant amount of laughter and even more disbelief. Yet here they were, regrouping while their all-powerful ally collected some firearms, and enjoyed a serendipitous snack, apparently.

It was getting pretty serious about its quarry. This was the first time it had ever asked for weapons. Until now, it had always been a hands-on kind of killer.

"Gruumen au korgst prada Asado!" The monophonic chorus of perhaps ten voices from the darkness behind the door shouted.

Vega was not impressed by its use of the old tongue. Its lack of four more weapons was not his problem. "Aruta kovan – noch plataanos." He called back.

Silence.

The three killers glanced at each other, then back to the door. There was a click, and the door swung slowly open. Muscles tensed, knuckles turned white around pistol grips.

Only one of the thing's Avatars appeared, resolving slowly from the darkness of the room beyond. It eased into the light like someone might ease into a very hot bath. Its mouth and hands were dark and glistening around curved teeth and claws.

Harms had always been disturbing enough, but as this thing got a better hold on their flesh, Vega had learned just how much headroom was left in disturbing.

"Asado plataan... bucha." The words slithered out of it slowly for emphasis. Maybe it was his problem after all.

"No!" He moved as fast as he could. The pistol was already in his hand, all he had to do was point it at the flesh puppet before him and pull the trigger. He never had a chance.

His pistol discharged, but the thing had already broken his wrist and pointed the gun toward Murphy's abdomen. Murphy went down amid a red aerosol induced by the three high velocity needles. He made no sound as he died, which was more than Vega could say for himself right now.

Behind him, Li fired, but Vega felt the shells tear through him as the puppet shoved him backwards. Li tried to shoulder him aside to get a shot at the thing, but it was already moving around him. Vega hit the floor before Li's shout ended in a gurgle. His last volley went into the ceiling, showering dust down on them all. Vega could only groan as the flesh puppet entered his narrowing field of vision slowly... almost playfully.

In its right hand was Li's pistol, in its left hand was Li's severed right hand. As the world seemed to darken a few shades, the puppet bit the three middle fingers from Li's hand. As it swallowed, the lock indicator on the gun went green.

"Gaff togg gruumen, Asado." It said, smiling as it bent over him. Vega's fondest hope was that it would use the gun on him, but there was no mercy in this creature.

It bent lower, the world darkened, its teeth tore into him.

* * *

"So, let me guess: you're Ping, and you're Alex, right?" Anne pointed to the cute little Asian guy first, and the slightly littler chrome-haired kid next.

They looked a bit surprised.

* * *

"But they're gone now, and if I ever see them again, it'll be in the next minute or two." The kid with the coke-bottle glasses said. "We don't have much time."

"Time for what?" Anne asked, as the rolling violence of the car crash continued around them.

"For anything really," the kid said with a thoughtful grin. "But you've got to get out of here right away. If you want to live… if you want anyone to live, you've got to get away before they get down here."

"Down here? Are we in the ocean?" Anne must have looked confused because the kid held up his hands for patience. "Now, whatever you do, don't freak out and run away from me again… wait till you wake up, then you can run like everyone's life depends on it, ok?"

Anne felt fuzzy, distracted. "You're a plucky little guy," she said, tussling the kid's hair. The way he'd said 'freak out' was just so cute.

"Now quit that!" He batted her hand away. "You really have some issues with focus, don't you?"

"My issue bin is large and unorganized… focus may be in there somewhere." They both laughed, but then the kid got assertive again.

"Now listen! I wasn't kidding when I said the fate of the world was at stake here…"

"You never said that."

"Ok, I just said it then… and I wasn't kidding."

"So precocious!" She tried to tussle his hair again, but he was way too quick this time. He grabbed her hand and didn't let go. "Hey!" she complained.

"Listen!" He said, getting a bit testy. "Here's what you need to do: There's some people who will find you soon. There're some important things you need to tell them."

"How are they going to find me?"

"Long story, but there's something I have… like a harmless radio tracker kind of thing a friend tagged me with. I'm hoping that's being transferred to you along with most of my power…"

"I'm hungry. Can we go back to that donut shop?"

The kid was done being distracted from his point. "Thing one: Don't trust Kaspari… He's in bed with the bad guys."

Anne nodded. "Gotcha, Kaspari's got low love standards."

The kid shrugged that off, "Thing two: There are two types of bad guys, one is Asado... an ancient clan of Savants and killers. I hope Alex knows Asado... Anyway, the other is... well like... I don't really know. Sort of like a puppet master, except his puppets are somewhere between ninjas and zombies."

"Ninja zombies... yep that sounds serious." Anne wrinkled her forehead in mock concern. Her neck hurt. She rubbed it slowly, but the pain seemed only to intensify. "What to do... ninja zombies... Hmmm..."

"Believe me... it's scarier than it sounds... they don't wear those silly masks or tabby socks, for one thing..." he shook his head as if to clear the irrelevancy from the conversation, "Anyway, you see, about six months ago Kaspari actually cracked the Loom, and this... *thing*... it's trying to force its way into our world. For this, it needs me... now it will need you."

"You're saying I'm you now?" Anne held up a finger in inspiration, "Hey, are you my inner child?" Had she been drinking? She felt punchy.

"Saints preserve us! No, I'm not saying that you're me, but you're going to be a lot more like me when you wake up, I think."

"...because I'm sleeping now." She waved her finger of discovery about. Her neck was really starting to smart. Maybe she'd cut it in the minivan crash.

His face hardened. "Right now you're at the beginning of a transformation, and I am at the end of my life. Right now you're lying in rain and glass and our blood with my teeth buried in your neck and a channel of power flowing between us."

Anne's hand froze on her neck. She took a step back. She remembered now. She realized who this kid was. It was like someone had turned on all the lights, but her finger was still in one of the sockets.

The kid's face softened into sadness tinged with compassion. Resignation settled into his eyes. "If they don't find you, do your best to find them. The guy you really need to tell this to is a silly-looking kid named Alexander Ahmed, formerly of Rosemont College. The people traveling with him are Rae Jackson and Ping Bannon, both of the CPD. All nice folks. They'll probably end up just as dead as me... just as dead as you."

She was still thinking about that when she noticed that the kid seemed to be getting smaller. She looked a little harder, just to be sure. Not smaller, lower. He was sinking down through the dark waters in which they now floated. She had no idea when the car crash had ended, and no idea how they had gotten here, but he was leaving and soon she would be alone in these frightening depths.

"Don't go!" She shouted, grabbing his shirt at the shoulder and pulling him into an awkward bear hug.

"What are you doing, Anne?" he asked as if she were drinking mustard straight from the bottle at Denny's. But though there was mocking in his tone, his arms wrapped desperately around her waist.

"You're not getting away that easily, Junior!" She adjusted her grip and got an arm under one of his shoulders, "I'll take you seriously, okay? Besides, it looks mighty dark down there." Even in her panic and confusion, she had some compassion to spare for the little stranger who had shared her dream.

"Hey, at least I don't see any flaming pits or pitchforks," he said, craning his head to the side, "this was actually a fair-sized concern—I've been on a bit of a murdering spree lately..." He broke off as their grip slipped and he slid a few centimeters down. "You can't stop this, Anne. I'm done cheating death, now it's your turn for a while. Savor it."

"I'm not letting go! You just need to hold on a little longer and we'll find a way out of here!"

"You can still help, Anne." He said with resignation in his voice, "You just can't help me."

EPIPHANY

"… and then I woke up on top of him, and I ran away as fast as I could—which wasn't actually that fast." Anne concluded. It had taken less than two minutes recount her confusing story, including the rest of the dream that had just come back to her like an epiphany.

The others were silent, staring at nothing in particular, lost in private thought. From time to time, the silence was broken by urgent instructions between the surgeons as they worked behind her.

The cop looked like she was going to cry.

Ping looked from Anne back to Alex. "So, what are we supposed to do now?"

"Uh… he didn't mention anything about that." Anne said, shaking her head.

Alex looked up, startled out of his thoughts. "Run… we run! Now!"

"What?" Ping's eyes darted to the exit; to the shattered observation window.

"Kaspari's here! Come on!" Alex took a step toward the exit, but Anne caught his shoulder.

"What about them?" She waved her hand toward the two unconscious Feds. "We leave them, they're dead, right?"

"We can't fight him... you don't understan..." Then he checked himself, set his jaw. "You're right. We can't leave them."

Anne turned to the doctors. "Sean!"

The surgeons looked up from their work on Hawthorne.

"How long for you to stabilize her enough for us to take her?"

He looked reluctant, "Maybe two hours for prep and... but Anne, you know you can't take..."

"Now listen, Sean," She interrupted with a hard voice she'd picked up somewhere, "There's more of those disco zombies on their way, and I'm pretty sure anyone who's still here is on the buffet, if you get my drift."

The surgeons glanced quickly at each other. "Five minutes." Sean concluded. They went back to work.

"We got five?" Anne looked to Alex. He didn't think long before giving his head a slow shake. This was going to end badly.

Rae and Ping checked their remaining ammo. Ping discarded his assault gun onto a nearby cabinet. He limbered his pistols in their holsters, adjusted his sword in his jacket pocket. He then straightened his jacket, making sure the weapons were out of sight. Rae ejected the drum from her fletcher, slammed another into the port.

Ping looked at their small company. "Maybe I should head back up to the observ..."

"Crap!" Alex shouted, squeezing his eyes shut and raising his arms before him as if to ward off a blow. There was a sharp, wet sound and he was blown off his feet as if hit by a car. Rae screamed, but brought her fletcher up as quick as any hero in an action video. Anne's head snapped around, looking for an attacker. Ping stood perfectly still, one hand in his jacket pocket, eyes moving to the doorway. Alex slammed into the wall at the far side of the OR. He fell limp to the floor, leaving a crater in the tiled wall.

The double doors from the hallway opened inward and a woman in a rich brown suit strode in as if she were on a catwalk, exuding confidence. Her fingers sparkled with bright metal and rubies. Her smooth skin was only a few shades lighter than her suit. "Hey, how 'bout I just kill…"

Anne was moving before the newcomer finished speaking. She was into the slipstream of relative velocity, three steps toward the newcomer when she left the ground. Force tingled across her skin. She raised perhaps twenty centimeters into the air, peddling her feet like a cartoon character before a big exit.

Her wrists and ankles stretched out painfully. Every joint strained to the point of breaking under the unseen force. A short cry escaped her lips before she squeezed them shut.

The woman in brown laughed. She didn't flinch as four explosions rattled off with no discernable time between them. The air before the woman filled with sparks as she deflected the fletchettes. Rae's weapon flew from her hands and into the brown woman's ready hand. "Thanks honey!" She smiled without warmth.

The woman brought up her right hand with a theatrical flourish. She snapped her fingers like a commanding debutante and both Ping and Rae were struck in the face. They both went down hard, their legs above them as they hit the floor.

"Stay!" the woman commanded with an outstretched finger and an inward-directed chuckle. Shiva was ever playful at work. She returned to regard Anne, floating and stretched taught by invisible bonds. "Now you've been quite bad!" She had a flash of inspiration. "You know, something's missing." Her smile broadened.

Anne didn't scream as the holes opened in her outstretched palms, the blood flowed onto the floor. "Lets play charades—your turn." Anne's ankles snapped together. "Wait! I know this one…"

Then their eyes met. Shiva had expected the most satisfying form of terror. She'd expected despair. After four hundred years, only despair still warmed her jaded heart. But here, in this disgustingly fat woman, in that swollen bag of a face, Shiva saw no fear. Where by all rights she'd expected a blank bovine gaze, she saw the dark eyes of the predator, of the patient shark. She saw her own death with confidence. Here was a woman totally helpless, yet able to make Shiva's bravado falter with only a glance.

She looked away, shaken. She'd fought Torpedoes before, but this was different. She'd forgotten what she was saying…

Another shot ricocheted off her shield at ankle level. The cop had managed to wrestle her service pistol out and she was seeing if Shiva's shield went all the way to the floor. A few more shots flew away harmlessly as Shiva examined the fallen cop. She was still on the ground next to the Asian guy who had apparently been knocked unconscious. Her nose was broken and one eye was well on its way to swelling closed. Again, no satisfying despair. What was wrong with these people?

Disappointed, Shiva realized she might as well just kill her. With a mental shrug, her hand came up, her smile broadened. She paused, waiting... Hopefully, when the cop realized, she'd get just a taste of satisfaction.

The cop must have understood the look in Shiva's eyes, because she held her trigger down, releasing a stream of ineffective hypersonic needles at her. Still, it was frustrating determination behind the cop's eyes. Maybe once the evisceration began...

The fear emerged first from the bruised and broken landscape of Alex's senses. Shots filled the air, desperate and pointless, their rapid snaps crested over the ringing in his ears. Blood filled his mouth, covered the dusty floor beneath him. Not far away, he could hear the urgent and hushed pleas of one of the doctors to a God it was clear he wasn't that familiar with. He heard a woman's mocking, confident laughter.

He was about to lose everything. Before he saw it, he knew.

No strength left, yet somehow Alex managed to get a hand beneath him and press away from the floor enough to see the scene at the other end of the room. Rae was on the floor, her legs sprawled out, both hands holding her gun firmly, pumping out shots that ricocheted harmlessly away from the laughing woman. Rae's broken and bloody face was set in grim determination, but Alex knew her well enough to understand that she knew that this was the end.

The laughing woman's hand stretched out toward Ray, "My turn." she snarled.

Slower. Alex could see eddies of the Loom's power responding to the woman's dark will—but that power, though substantial, was a clunky, clumsy thing. Alex wondered briefly if it was a blessing or a curse that time seemed to be lengthening for his last few seconds with Rae.

Weaker. He has no power left, every template and weaving had been swept away by the woman's initial attack. Though he seemed to remain connected to the workings of the Underworld somehow, it was now like standing in a desert. Some of the mental speed remained, but he had no power to act. She was too strong and he was too weak to do anything but watch as everything that mattered to him was wiped away by this arrogant, careless woman. Rae's eyes were hard and filled with angry, hopeless tears, but Alex didn't even have the time to weep.

Closer. Through the skeins and currents of the Underworld, his consciousness drifted closer to Rae, letting her desperation and fear fill his vision until he could almost taste the tears. Loss surrounded him, but his pain was only her pain, his frustration became hers, and he was empty and alone, only wanting somehow to help her. Around him, the music of the Loom resonated with his compassion.

Then there was a moment of clarity that he felt before he understood—Coldness, a spark of fire, then an ocean of warmth surrounded him. He was alone then realized he wasn't, that nobody ever was. Hope touched briefly on anger then he was afloat in a love as boundless as the sea.

That was when Alex realized what Ivo had been trying to teach him—the magic behind the science of the Loom.

Shiva almost didn't feel it in time. Distracted as she often got while killing, the tingle of warning came almost too late. As it was, she barely had time to temper her shield before the current of power struck. She was knocked off her feet, through the wall into the hall, through another wall into a bathroom, through three stalls but only two toilets, through the exterior wall, tumbling and spinning through the air above the street— shattering impact—and she fell to the cracked concrete floor halfway through the parking structure across from the hospital. Behind her, the cracked support column that had finally stopped her flight groaned and the building around her rumbled as it adjusted to the structural damage.

Alex pushed himself off the floor. The world was still spinning, but he wasn't that interested in the world. He settled back onto his heels, kneeling, focusing— accumulating power. That had gone far better than he could have hoped, but it wasn't over yet.

Focus… he had to focus, but the love kept trying to make him laugh and cry, and the fury kept trying to push all thought from his mind. He'd almost lost Rae.

He didn't want to squelch the emotions, just subdue them enough to think somewhat clearly. He remembered Ivo telling him that the Loom responds to focus and passion. Looking at the patch of night sky through the three walls before him, he had to agree. Right now, he had all the passion he could handle. He had to close his eyes… across the room, Rae's battered face evoked the hottest and darkest feelings.

Shaking with fury, stretched taught with focus, Alex knelt and accumulated power for the next round.

Fortunately, Shiva's shield had mostly held. Her left arm was shattered below the elbow, missing below the forearm. Her suit was ruined. That second toilet she'd blown through must have had a broken flusher. After about twenty seconds, she'd stopped the worst of the bleeding and blocked the most excruciating pain. There was nothing to do about the smell.

Feeling rather put off and looking and smelling much more like crap than she would prefer, Shiva rose into the air. She crossed the street and reentered the ragged two-meter hole in the fifth floor of the Hospital.

No more games. She deeply wished she had the time to really make this hurt. She hated to admit it, but it wasn't time she lacked, it was confidence. The kid had surprised her. The briefing in the whispercraft had said he'd been in the Loom for less than two years, but that simply couldn't be true. Ether Lutine had been an amazing teacher or this kid was the Mozart of the Loom.

She was no longer sure she would be able to win if she kept playing with her prey. This admission was hard on her pride. After four hundred years, she'd thought that she'd be able to handle an unarmed and inexperienced Torpedo, an inexperienced Savant, and two grunt cops. Now it was time to finish this quickly.

She touched down on the floor and moved back through the destroyed bathroom. Water on the destroyed bathroom floor mixed with her blood to complete the destruction of her expensive shoes. The kid tried to bring a part of the building's superstructure down on her, but her shield held. She invoked the Cast of Turbulence. It began to stir the currents of power in the Underworld around the kid and the weave he'd been constructing dissolved as the storm around him intensified.

She'd just moved from scowl to smile when the Underworld seemed to blur around her.

Around Alex, the currents of power grew wild. They tore through his Collection Cast before he could compensate. They tried to buffet him back out of the Underworld, away from the Loom. But too much was riding on this conflict for him to fail. He used the small amount of power he'd already collected to weave a loose Obscuring. He used it to distract the Savant long enough to try an ill-conceived counterattack.

While she was making short work of his Obscuring, he managed to anchor himself to her Turbulence Cast. He used her Cast's order as a shield against the storm it was causing. Then, with no energy left to launch his own counter-Cast, he improvised again. He tunneled through the outer weave of her Cast, patching in a weave of his own. Just as he added the tripwire to her Cast, she cleared his Obscuring. He disengaged from her Cast, hoping she wouldn't notice his work until it was too late.

Shiva swept the child's Obscuring aside. While she'd been distracted, the kid had managed to mostly disable her Turbulence Cast. It was still causing distortions around him, but it was now only an inconvenience. She recalled her crippled Cast back into the Loom, and transferred its power into another template she kept ready. As soon as her Hellfire was powered, she'd burn him slowly into cinders—or maybe quickly. Yes, as quickly as possible.

She never got the chance. As the power began to flow out of her crippled Turbulence Cast, the weave exploded. The kid had grafted a rider into her Cast! He was casting without templates, modifying both of their weaves at will.

A lesser Savant would have been destroyed, or at least incapacitated. Even Shiva was knocked to the ground. The energy that blew from her sabotaged Cast was mostly twisted around her closest shields, but her grip on the Loom had been shaken. She scrambled to reinforce her defenses, to get them back together before the kid made his next move.

She wanted to pretend that this was exciting, that it was great to finally have a real challenge, but like most of the cruel, she was a coward. She hated this struggle, and would have fled if she dared—if she weren't more afraid of reprisals from her masters at Asado, not to mention their hungry, playful ally. She shuddered at the thought of what it would do to her if she failed to acquire its precious key.

She had mostly rigged her defenses, but the kid just kept plunking away at them. He might be some kind of prodigy with the Loom, but he hadn't been able to accumulate much power before she knocked down his collector. He was again accumulating power, but he was using it as fast as it came in with a quick series of small and ineffective attacks. He was still young, still foolish. He had to realize that his attacks weren't doing much more than keeping her occupied.

This thought led to a suspicion that never came to the point of realization before Shiva was surrounded by excruciating light, then final darkness.

The mostly unheard explosion blossomed around Ping as Roy's blade shattered shield, warp, and other defenses. It moved through the woman's brown's suit and the body it enclosed without resistance. Both parts of her body fell to the ground.

Across the room, Alex slumped forward onto all fours. He looked like a man who had just completed a triathlon after an all night drinking binge. He was laughing and crying, but mostly moaning in complete exhaustion, rolling his head from side to side on the floor near the burrito-wrapped Fed.

"Help me up." Rae said, trying to press up from the ground on one arm.

Ping moved to her quickly, lifting her by the elbow. She stood shakily for a moment, then gave him a bloody smile. "Nice moves, karate man."

"You too." He said returning her smile.

"Didn't even see you moving 'till she was dead."

"Neither did she… had to wait until she was distracted." He said, snapping his sword back into its hilt.

"Admit it, you got the ninja mask at home." Rae said with a teasing smile.

"I'm Chinese, not Japanese."

"I thought you were Irish."

Ping's short bark of laughter caught him by surprise. He chucked Rae on the shoulder and looked to Alex. "That Kaspari lady wasn't so bad!" He shouted across the room.

Alex pulled his head up. His lips twisted into a tragic smile. "That wasn't Kaspari."

"Yeah," Ping shrugged, "Figured as much."

"Next to Kaspari, she was an amateur." Alex said, trying to get to his feet, but failing and rolling to his side.

"Swell." Ping looked at Anne, who was crouching on the floor examining her wounded hands. Ping moved to her side.

"You okay?"

She sniffed, "Yeah, wouldn't have really been a full day without a little crucifixion."

"Let me see." Ping said, holding out his hands. She straightened and held out her hands, palms up. He took her hands in his, looked at the wounds in the palms. "It's not as bad as it looks." He said with his most reassuring bedside manner. "Look at the bright side, we're in a hospital."

"Yeah, we'd all be dead if I still worked at Arby's."

This time his laughter caught both of them by surprise. It seemed incongruous in a scene of such violence and sorrow. "You're pretty funny for someone so covered in the blood of others." He gave her an inquisitive look.

She looked up, and their eyes met briefly. He found humor and strength in her face… and a lot of other people's blood. He smiled. She reminded him a bit of his mother, only bigger and redder.

She flexed her hands, "They'll heal." She said.

"Yeah, let's get something on them…"

"No, I mean they'll heal right now." She flipped her hands over. The backs held the same holes as the palms, but the flesh between had already closed. Ping did a double take, flipped her hands back over. Yep, he could actually see the wounds closing. Perhaps another five minutes and they'd be gone. "Wow."

She nodded. "Yeah. I may be one of Hell's evil minions, but there are some perks like an awesome medical plan."

Ping was confused. "Hell's minions?"

"Yeah, you know. Your vampire friend bit me, didn't I make that clear?"

"Vampire?" Ping gave her a dubious look, but then he got it. "Dek wasn't a vampire, he was more like a Replicant."

"You mean like in *Blade Runner*?"

"You know the movie?" Ping asked, pleasantly surprised.

"Yeah, but the director's cut is the only version worth seeing more than ten times."

"I think I love you." He laughed, she laughed, she blushed, he lapsed into an amused smile. She pulled her hands away self-consciously. She was now looking only at her shoes. She must be new to banter.

"Oh… I get the name now." She said from behind a sheltering hand and a painful looking blush. "Dek, like Deckard—I should have recognized the haircut."

Ping chuckled silently. "He was also a fan. Hey, you haven't been drinking anyone's blood, have you? Because that would be hilarious."

"I've thought about it a few times," she said, flexing her hands.

Behind her, the doctor stepped away from the monitor table where they'd been using a portable kit to get Hawthorne stabilized. "Ok. She's as ready as I can get her quickly… especially with all the distractions." He said, looking at the crater Alex had made in the wall. "Please be careful with her… and she'll need to keep the medkit on to monitor the shoulder."

After a few seconds of indecisive silence, the doctor spoke again, "So, now you can GET OUT OF MY OPERATING ROOM!"

Like a ragged exclamation point, gunfire from another part of the building punctuated his shout.

* * *

They'd taken the stairs, thinking to avoid unwanted attention.

They spiraled upward through the deserted stairwell. On the third floor, Derry rotated from point and was covering the door. His gray eyes scanned the hall through the small window set in the stairwell door at face level. As the others passed quickly behind him, a door was thrown open halfway down the hall. A shrieking woman in a nurse's uniform bolted into the hallway. She turned away from them, heading toward the elevator bank at the other end of the hall.

The woman's white uniform was spattered with blood, and the flash he caught of her face before she turned away was sheer, hopeless horror. "Hold it!" Derry hissed to his companions as they continued up the stairs behind him.

His hand was already on the door handle when a dark figure moved out of the still open door and sauntered after the woman. It was moving quickly, but easily, obviously enjoying the hunt.

Not being the kind of person to do a lot of thinking is situations such as these, Derry pushed through the door, bringing his assault gun up. "Hold it right there!" He shouted.

The dark man complied. He turned around slowly. Derry's first impression was of a Halloween mask. The mask was half werewolf, half flesh-eating zombie. The worst part though was the smile. The teeth were slanted toward the carnivorous end of the scale and covered with blood like the rest of the thing. But the teeth and blood weren't the worst part of the smile, which was stretched unnaturally wide, exposing seemingly all the teeth. The lips were cracked to accommodate the breadth of the grimace, the muscles of the face were taught and shivering.

"Whoa!" Derry said to himself. Hawthorne hadn't been kidding about being off in the weeds here. Well, he wasn't going to take any chances, he trained his aim on the thing's forehead... he hoped he wouldn't need silver bullets.

The sound of gunfire wasn't his. The creature was gone, replaced by the suspended ceiling above the hallway and a light that was just way too bright. There was no pain yet, but he had a distinct feeling that something was very wrong with his body. With a monumental effort, his neck craned up a few degrees and the creature reentered his field of vision. It was standing much as before but now it held out a police-issue pistol. Quick draw.

Laughing as if at some dark and private joke, the thing turned and began walking in the direction of the fleeing nurse. Derry tried to raise his weapon, but it was no use. Blood and air gurgled from the wounds in his chest with each of his labored breaths.

He couldn't bring his weapon on target, but he pulled the trigger anyway, hoping to distract the thing from its prey. Maybe he could buy the nurse a few moments to complete her escape. Bullets blew through the floor and walls. The thing turned around, brought its pistol up.

Derry was still trying to bring his weapon on target when the gunfire sounded. The thing went down in a spray of dark aerosol as more holes than he could count opened in its jerking body.

Derry's head hit the floor with a whoosh of expelled breath. He angled his head so he could see the door to the stairs. Sure enough, there were Elena and Miranda, looking assertive. Miranda kept her weapon covering the hallway while Elena rushed to Derry's side.

"I said hold it!" She said, checking his wounds.

"When?" He smiled.

"Just now, back in the…" she broke off, noticing his smile.

"Sorry chief." He winced as she hit a sensitive spot.

"Well, this doesn't look that bad." She lied.

His laughter came out as wracking coughs. "Ow, chief."

Her hard face softened. It broke his heart to see it. Some people you just hate to see sad.

"We'll get you out of here…" She motioned for Miranda to come.

"Whoa, now. I'm three times your weight and you don't look like no ant."

"We'll find a stretcher, you idiot." Her smile was warm though the rest of her face was hard with expediency.

"Shot again, eh?" Miranda said, crouching near them, her weapon trained to cover the hall ahead.

"Everybody… knows that… zombies ain't supposed t'… be packin' heat." Derry gasped in four short bursts of words. His breath was getting short. And then it was gone.

"Derry!" Elena shouted from the deepening mists around him. Sorry boss, He thought. He was going to have to disappoint her.

A desperate scream came from down the hall. The blood-spattered nurse came bolting back around a corner, screaming with each exhale.

Miranda Todd could tell she was a bit tense because she almost shot the nurse reflexively when she burst around the corner. She glanced quickly at Elena, who was still staring at Derry. Her eyes seemed glazed.

"Boss?" No reply. "Boss!"

At last, Elena's eyes refocused. The nurse was rapidly approaching. Miranda could feel something bad coming, really bad. In the convex mirror at the corner, she could make out dark shapes, moving like syncopated sharks… this didn't look good for them. Keeping her weapon trained down the hallway, she glanced at Elena again. Her face was hardening. She was looking down the hallway too, but Miranda knew that look. "Elena!" she shouted, hoping to shake her back to reality, "Kyle! Remember?"

Her words seemed to have the desired effect. The fury in Elena's eyes took a half step back. Life was back on the scale with vengeance. "Let's go." She said. They turned and fled, not far behind the screaming nurse.

At the stairwell, Miranda looked back. Nothing. Their pursuers hadn't yet rounded the corner. She quickly brought her glasses out and linked them to her gun's address. She then used the gun's sight to zoom in on the convex mirror at the corner. She was just in time to see the last few things move into an elevator. "I think they're heading up, boss."

Elena didn't think long. "We've gotta hurry. I've got a feeling we're going to see them again." As the door closed behind them, Elena spared another look at Derry's fallen form. This wasn't real. She'd see him again at work tomorrow, just like yesterday and the day before. Not real.

The door closed.

* * *

Two gurneys with two Feds on them, two cops pushing them, with Alex and Anne in the lead, they moved from the OR into the hallway. The surgeons and techs had partially revived Jeremy and were long gone, heading for the street.

"You still feel that disturbance in the Force?" Ping asked.

"Eh?" Alex said.

"You know, that feeling you've not felt since…" Ping said, laying on the irony, but Alex still didn't understand. "Is Kaspari still here?"

Alex nodded, "Oh, right. Nice joke, by the way… I'm just a bit distracted. Can't tell where Kaspari might be, but he's definitely here. Quite frankly, I'm surprised we're still alive if what she said is true." He looked sideways at Anne. "I'm putting most of my energy into hiding us, but I can't believe it's gonna work with Kaspari."

"Well, lets not stick around to test that theory." Rae said as they arrived at the elevator bank. Anne pushed the down call-button.

Seconds later, the first elevator arrived, but the signal light indicated that it was going up. The doors slid slowly aside.

* * *

As they passed the landing for the fourth floor, four people in scrubs came barreling down the stairs. Two were still wearing white surgical smocks that were stained with blood.

The blood registered as odd to Elena, though it took her a second to understand why. Only triage nurses and doctors would be treating patients outside of hermetically sealed operating beds, but these folks definitely weren't coming from the first-floor ER.

To say the medical types were concerned with personal safety was a bit of an understatement. Every face was deformed by fear, every eye locked on the two women's weapons. By the taint in the air, Elena surmised that one of them had a bladder control problem.

As the two groups rounded the spirals of the stairs to face one another, they both stopped. One out of fear, the other out of curiosity. The hospital staff tried to flatten themselves against the wall, hoping that the heavily armed women would just pass by.

They were in a hurry, but Elena decided to invest a few seconds in information gathering. "What's the trouble?"

"You tell me!" One of the smocked men said with a tinge of desperation in his voice. He seemed to be relieved to be talking… probably a surgeon.

"What's with the blood?" Miranda gestured with her weapon.

There was a moment of indecision, filled with tension and exchanged glances. Finally, the only woman moaned. "We don't even know them… don't care what's going on! Please, just let us go!"

Elena lowered the barrel of her weapon and presented her FBI badge. "Don't worry, we're the good guys. Where's the trouble?"

"OR-3." The surgeon said, "But you *do not* want to go there!"

Miranda and Elena exchanged a glance. They both knew that was Kyle's operating room. "We can take care of ourselves." Elena gave her weapon an unconscious shake. The woman shook her head, seemingly ready to laugh and cry. "No. You can't."

"What's up there?" Miranda asked.

"Corpses. Lots of corpses." One of the men said.

"Cops, monsters, witches…" the surgeon said.

"And one really scary phlebotomist," the woman added with a confused shake of her head, "I didn't see that coming at all."

The hospital workers seemed to all guess that it was time to bolt. They moved quickly past the armed women.

"Witches?" Miranda was skeptical.

"Corpses." Elena said, face darkening.

After a quick exchange of uncertain glances, Elena and Miranda resumed their ascent. Halfway up the final flight of stairs, Miranda asked, "What's a flebotomist?"

"Down!" someone shouted from behind the door to the fifth floor. An explosion cut off the shout; then it deepened into an earthquake.

Elena's vision blurred as an ephemeral cloud seemed to flit through the stairwell. The floor shuddered. The building creaked. Dust fell from cracking sheet rock.

Miranda almost lost her footing as the building seemed to swim around her. She grabbed the handrail with both hands, saving herself from a fall down the stairs. Her eyes were pressed shut against intense vertigo. She felt as if she were tumbling through the air like Dorothy on her way to Oz. When she could finally open her eyes, she found Elena on all fours, resting her head on the stairs. Her gun had fallen on the stairs beneath her.

"Wha?" Miranda stammered, blinking dust from her eyes.

Still swaying, Elena grabbed her assault gun and wobbled up the last few stairs. "Come on!"

* * *

Of course, the big woman with the all-blood makeover moved first, but Alex wasn't far behind.

He was already in the Loom strengthening his Obscuring, so he had a speed advantage over Ping and Rae. When the doors opened into the elevator whose last stop had obviously been the more fiery pits of hell, he'd quickly picked up the Cast he'd last used on the Savant in the OR. Its pattern was still constituted, so it was just a matter of redirecting power from the Obscuring to activate it.

Ping was in mid shout. He was either yelling 'down', or perhaps 'doubt' or 'dowry'. It would be a bit more time before Alex could be sure. The big lady was already moving toward the elevator, hostile intentions out for all to see. Ping's pistols were halfway out already... man, he was fast! Rae's hands had left the gurney she'd been pushing and were in the process of finding their proper places on her fletcher. She was entering a crouch and moving to the right to get a better shot around Ping.

With a shock, Alex realized that the demons were also in mid-draw. Each had a pistol; most looked like Rae's work pistol, but a couple had more expensive looking weapons. They were fast too… faster than Ping and Rae, but not faster than Dek—not faster than the woman who now wielded his power. No matter though… in a few hundred milliseconds they'd all be grinning demonic barbeque.

The Cast was in place. The energy focused, leapt out toward the targets packed into the elevator. But then something went very wrong.

Even before the energy touched the demons, the power grew unruly and the weave began to strain, then fray at the edges. Alex tried to compensate, but his weapon dissolved when it touched the first target. The Underworld seemed to contort and the air filled with light and explosive fury.

Alex was surprised he was still conscious. He did his best to defend himself from the backlash that came next. The explosion tore his weave apart, tore his Obscuring away; crashed over him like a tsunami. He was in the air, stretched tight on the swell of power with only the simplest shield sputtering around him. It took all his focus to cling to the Loom, to keep his hastily-erected shield working.

Then he had an idea. It was a rather desperate and foolish idea, but as he flew through the air with Rae and the others about to be exposed to a lot of hot demon lead, he felt both desperate and foolish.

He embellished the patterns in the interior folds of his shield extending them into a replica of his first extemporaneous Cast. He packed the Warping close around him inside his faltering shield.

Then he dropped the shield, or more accurately, he let the storm around him rip it away. His Warping burned brilliant in the avalanche of power, then exploded outward. Then it was gone and Alex was defenseless before the onslaught. The speed of the Loom was gone. He struck the wall on the other side of the hall about a meter up. The sound of crushing destruction filled his ears. A blinding light stole his vision.

* * *

"Down!" Ping shouted. He was done with his draw before the word was out.

Then his guns exploded, or he thought they did. What he initially attributed to near-fatal misfire was actually something else—less fatal, but weirder. The world seemed to end for an instant, leaving him off-balance, but tranquil in a bright and pleasant place. Into this peace, flashes of some disturbing thing that could perhaps be called 'reality' intruded. There were flashes of rushing bodies, a quickly approaching floor, falling dust, flickering light. This all seemed familiar.

Yeah, reality.

He hit the floor with a sobering shock. His twice-healed noggin took the brunt of the impact… this was just not his head's week. Perhaps because of some inherited cephalic fortitude, he didn't black out. Ol' Grandpa Sean O'Bannon was still legendary at the family school for his hard head. One time he'd taken a full-power hit on the forehead with a wooden fighting pole during a ranking test and had still gone on to win the match. According to the legend, he'd even taken a cast iron crock pot in the head from Grandma Yao during a bit of premarital sparring, though he hadn't won that match. Or maybe he had—they'd gotten married less than a month later.

Long line of hardheads... Ping's dad had been so happy when Ping finally "woke up and joined the force". When he started with family counseling, dad had been so "secretly" disappointed that his little Tian Fu had "squandered his gift" and moved into a profession so "obviously full of crap". Dad was subtle in disappointment.

Ping was smiling as he came off the floor; dizzy, but determined. The guns in his hands were so warped that they looked like cartoon caricatures of pistols. The hole in the barrel of one was deformed into an oval and bent about ten degrees off center. Alex had saved his bacon again. He'd known the demons had the drop on him as soon as he saw them... they were too ready, too fast.

As he rose to his feet, he saw Alex sprawled out about a meter below another body-sized imprint in the wall. Ouch. He wondered fleetingly if this was their lot in life—Ping taking the head trauma, Alex trying to make it through wall after wall. He hoped not, though that was a significantly brighter future than the most likely one right now. Right now any future where he didn't end up with an apple in his mouth on the demon smorgasbord seemed rosy.

On his feet, though not entirely stable, he turned to the elevator. The demons were struggling to their feet, some of their clothes seemed to be smoldering. There was a step down of perhaps five centimeters where the elevator had fallen down slightly before wedging into place. Cracks covered walls of the hallway at regular intervals where the metallic supports behind the sheetrock had deformed.

Anne was already up. She spared him a quick glance then bolted toward the warped elevator doors. Two demons had made it into the hallway, but now they were dealing with the phlebotomist… true to form, she'd already drawn blood. One of them was already on the floor and looking even more dead than it did when it stepped off the elevator. She was really pouring on the destruction, moving faster at times than he could follow. Wow.

His smile broadened. His blade came out.

* * *

"Freeze!" Miranda yelled as they burst into the hallway.

Though she was pretty sure they'd done it correctly, nobody listened. They'd displayed their weapons prominently and aggressively. She'd used an authoritative voice and the 'on the edge of shooting' face. She willed them to comply… but the fight raged on.

To call it a pitched battle would convey intensity, but not form. It was complete chaos. Maybe ten of the things that killed Derry were brawling with a uniformed cop using a fletcher like a club, some guy with a sword who looked and acted not unlike Jet Li, and a large red-skinned alien from fast-forward planet.

They glanced at each other. Elena shrugged.

As they stood there indecisively, the guy with the sword bisected one of the demons from shoulder to opposite hip. Elena winced.

The big red alien took a very painful looking blow from one of the demons—pistol to the back of the head. Perhaps its alien physiology had a different home for the brain because the blow didn't slow it down much.

The alien whirled around, looking somewhat miffed. With two or possibly three blurring-fast moves, it trapped the arm that held the pistol. The arm broke at the elbow and the gun flew from the demon's hand. The alien drove its elbow into the demon's head with a sound that was more shattering than breaking. The demon's pistol ricocheted off the ceiling and landed about two meters in front of Miranda as the demon who'd held it landed in a heap at the alien's feet.

"You think that's a flebotomist?" Miranda asked, clearly amazed.

"Don't whack it on the head." Elena replied.

The cop took a kick to the gut, then a fist to the face as she doubled over. To Elena's surprise, the cop didn't go down. Hands on the barrel of her weapon, she swung it into the demon's right knee, then slid one hand to near the pistol grip as she stepped forward, bringing the weapon up, connecting with the thing's chin. As the thing stumbled backward, she swept its arms aside with the barrel end of the gun then twisted the gun so that the barrel controlled the thing's arms while she broke the folding stock on its face. Without stopping, she gripped the barrel with both hands again and struck another demon in the face with the pistol grip. She turned back to the fallen demon. The high tech club raised and fell three times as she insured the thing wouldn't get back up.

Elena wondered why with so many firearms in the fray they were all being used as clubs. It was like watching a second-rate action film, only with no slow motion or hokey spinning head kicks.

The guy with the sword swept a demon's arm off, and the big alien leapt a full meter into the air, spun through about 270 degrees, and kicked the demon in the head so hard that its feet flew over its head before it hit the ground.

Well, no slow motion anyway.

"Did you see that?!" Miranda shouted, eyes wide.

"Don't shoot the humans or the flebotomist." Elena said, aiming at a demon rushing toward the guy with the sword. She pulled the trigger. There was a click, but nothing else. "Jammed!" she yelled.

"Me too." Miranda said. They both examined their weapons. The electronic diagnostics were offline, but it was obvious there was a mechanical jam.

"Check this out." Miranda held up her gun so Elena could see the length of the barrel. It was warped slightly. Elena examined her own weapon. She noticed similar deformities in the metal. With a little more inspection, they discovered that their pistols hadn't been spared either.

"Great." Elena shook her head.

It was then that she noticed Kyle. He was swaddled on a gurney near the center of the fight, looking like a new resident of the maternity ward. With this realization, her eyes went to the other gurney. She saw blonde hair, dark suit cut to allow surgical access, she saw blood, saw Hawthorne.

She flipped her weapon over, grabbed the barrel with both hands and rushed forward. "Come on!"

* * *

"All fighting breaks down to resolve and geometry, Tian Fu." His Dad used to say, usually right after compromising Ping's geometry and giving him a friendly fist in the face.

Good ol' Leung O'Bannon, now Leung Bannon (Americanized), was known internationally as a great teacher, but that's just because most folks didn't know how good a father he was. Sometimes you become well known for things other than what you're best at. Ping was familiar with this phenomenon.

Ping spent his childhood in "Gun Fu", the Hong Kong Wing Chun Kwoon Granpa Sean and Grandma Yao opened when his dad was little. He spent his adolescence in the Chicago extension Dad opened. To add to the all-important Asian mystique such establishments require outside Asia, they'd called the Chicago branch "Chong Fu"—"Gun Fu" in Chinese.

When dad found out the name of the school had to sound mysteriously Chinese, he'd initially come up with "Bu Xue Wu Shu Dao", or "The Way of the Gomer". Good humor and hard heads—it might as well be the O'Bannon family credo.

Life was simple growing up in the Kwoon. He'd been happy, surrounded by stimulating activity, plenty of exercise, and family. His Dad was the biggest influence in his life. He'd taught him to think, taught him to meditate, to explore. He'd taught him to fight.

Ping had broken with two generations of tradition on his father's side and eight generations of tradition on his mother's side to pursue a career outside the Kwoon. It's not that he didn't like his world, but he loved to listen to the students talk about their work. The students that Ping respected most were cops. When Ping had gone to college, he started out in Criminal Psychology. Of course, he didn't expend a lot of energy advertising his law-enforcement intentions to his parents.

His parents never had any problems with his educational choices. "Life is education." Mom said twice daily. Their concern had started when he had switched to the Marriage and Family Counseling program in his second year of school and started talking about taking it up as a career. Ping had to admit now that they were right to be concerned. He'd been happy at first, but the stakes for counseling were just too high. Ping preferred the simple things now, problems you could touch—evil you didn't have to talk out into the open.

He just wasn't tough enough for the high stakes game of family counseling, he had to admit it and move on. Now, he preferred to deal with problems he could solve with resolve and geometry.

"Resolve is the commitment to victory. Geometry is the path to it." Ol' Leung was fond of saying. Ping's father had taught him to drink from the deepest well of resolve. Most people fight out of rage, which is the puddle from which all bullies lap. Others fight for hate, which is the baby-pool in which the vengeful splash. But Leung had taught him to fight for the same thing as all good cops: the commitment to serve and protect. "To fight for others is to always win, boyo."

His geometry had always been spot-on—it was a gift.

He advanced on the demons with the sword positioned before him to gauge distance and angled to maintain a minimum distance from each of the defensive positions the creature's more likely attacks would require. He advanced steadily as the demons tried to shoot him with their disabled weapons. When they realized that shooting wasn't their path to victory, they exploded from the elevator in perfect synchronization.

To his right, Anne took the brunt of the attack, weighing in against three attackers. Ping got two. They tried to rush around his blade from both sides at once, forcing him to attack one and be killed by the other... he chose option C. He faded backwards, moving the blade fractionally to lop the left hand off of the demon coming in on his left. The backwards lunge bought him enough time to dodge left and cut the right leg out from under the attacker on his right.

He realigned his geometry and drove his left elbow into the face of the left-handless but unwavering demon. The demon on his right went down with one missing and one horribly wounded leg. The one on his left stumbled back with Ping's elbow still in its face. Ping moved forward to maintain the same close distance with the handless demon as he dropped the tip of his blade downward and came across with his right elbow. The demon's toothy grin diverged somewhat as the jaw broke.

The thing was fast! Without missing the normal hand-chopped-off-double-elbow-to-the-head-broken-jaw beat, it jerked back enough to club at him with the gun in its remaining hand. The demon was faster, but Ping had better geometry. Ping's left elbow was already in position to guard against most attacks coming from that side, so he only had to change the positioning of his arm slightly to deflect the attack. Ping used the opportunity to move back, just enough to reenter sword range. The blade moved through a tight arc, cutting through the demon's neck. He pivoted back to put the blade through the leg-less demon as it grabbed at him from the floor.

"Nice... moves." Anne said, taking a fist in the face between the words.

Rae had moved into position guarding Alex's motionless form and was engaging two of the demons. Two more of the demons were trying to move around Ping to get to Alex. Feeling a little slighted, Ping moved to intercept them.

Somewhere behind them, someone yelled "Freeze!" in the Law Enforcement Voice. Yeah, right.

Though the demon dodged quite effectively, Ping's first slash was mostly intended to get it to compromise its geometry. His second attack bisected it from right shoulder to left hip.

"When you gonna start flying around on wires?" Anne said around the sound of three quick impacts. She'd hit a demon with her right fist, its head slammed into the wall, then she'd hit it with her left fist so hard that she drove its head through the wall. She finished with a knee that drove the thing all the way through the wall, leaving only its feet in the hallway.

"I left my wires at home. That fancy spinning high kick stuff only works in the movies anyway." He said, keeping his weapon trained on the demon still trying to get around him. "The secret's to move as little as possible."

"Really?" He could hear the smile in her voice. The demon rushed right. He moved the blade perhaps twenty centimeters and removed its arm.

He was about to get all told-you-so when Anne leapt over a meter into the air, crouching so that her head didn't go through the ceiling. Her spinning thrust kick hit the Demon in the head so hard that its feet left the floor. It flipped backwards, landing on its shattered head. Its feet hit the floor behind it.

"*Mostly* doesn't work." He snorted.

"Yeah…" Anne grabbed a handful of another demon's romance-novel-stud hair. She used it to twist the thing's head sideways and down. The thing used the opportunity to hit her with a fist that hooked around her arms. Anne shrugged off the hit and threw a cut-kick that knocked the thing's legs out from under it. Using the demon's long hair, she controlled the fall then broke its neck. "It wouldn't have worked for me before yesterday, either."

Ping nodded. Before them were only corpses and a broken elevator. They turned to see how many demons had made it past them. To their surprise, there were two women using assault guns like clubs to help Rae fight off two remaining demons. One of the newcomers was almost painfully beautiful, with lustrous red hair. The other was a Latina with a determined look on her face.

As they watched, Rae slammed her fletcher into a demon's head. The redhead took a painful-looking straight fist to the face from the other demon. Its other hand now held the woman's gun, which it flipped around so that it now held the barrel. It raised the gun high in preparation to bludgeon her with the butt. The Latina brought her gun down on the demon's head from behind. There was a crunch. The thing hit the floor.

The Latina spared a look for her fallen companion who was already struggling to regain her feet. Satisfied that the redhead wasn't on death's door, she turned quickly and hit the demon fighting with Rae in the back of the head like a baseball pro.

The redhead had regained her feet and her high-tech club. She joined her companion, holding the club somewhat shakily before her. A meter away, Rae hadn't lowered her club. Perhaps three meters away, Ping and Anne stood. For a time, nobody moved.

Finally, Ping retracted his sword and stowed it in his jacked pocket. The ringing blade caught the two newcomers by surprise, but they didn't jump much. He gave them a reassuring smile.

Elena spoke first. "Ok, I'm assuming we're not fighting, then."

Rae didn't immediately lower her guard. "For the moment anyway... today's been full of surprises."

"You guys do that?" Miranda used her club to indicate the matching two-meter holes in the walls from OR to hall and from hall to bathroom.

"That was him." The Asian guy inclined his head toward a little silver-haired kid lying unconscious beneath another body-sized impact crater in the wall.

"So he ran through both walls, but that last one was too hard eh?" Miranda was skeptical. "He looks kinda small for all that damage."

"Long story." Ping said, "He's big on the inside."

Rae dropped her broken and bloody fletcher. She knelt by Alex on the floor.

"Now the kissing and slapping starts." Ping whispered with a sidelong glance at Anne.

"I heard that!" Rae said, checking the slap, but not the kiss. "Baby... Alex baby." She smoothed his hair, kissed his head.

Elena lowered her weapon and moved toward Kyle's bed.

Suddenly the flebotomist was before her, close enough that Elena could feel her breath. She was unsuccessful at restraining the cry of alarm.

"Hold it right there, sweetie..." Anne said, "These folks've had a long day and visiting hours ended at eleven."

"That's my husband." Elena said with an uncomfortable amount of emotion.

The flebotomist's face touched surprise lightly on its way to sympathy. "Sorry." She said, stepping out of Elena's way. That's when Elena had a revelation: the flebotomist wasn't an alien from the larger and more frenetic planet of flebotoma. She was just a rather large woman, covered in blood and gypsum dust. Her even features were partially obscured by the layered coats of blood, but there was symmetry there, natural beauty. Her gaze was direct and uncomfortably bright, yet she broke eye contact when Elena matched her stare.

She struck Elena as two people. Heavy yet starving, bright yet ashamed, beautiful but filled with doubt... determined but unsure. Elena was afraid this woman was going to rip her limb from limb, but the flebotomist looked like she was afraid she wasn't cool enough to be Elena's friend.

Her torn and stained clothes were those of a nurse. The cracked nametag that still hung on her chest said "Lab" on top and "Kelley" in a different font at the bottom.

"He saved us, Hawthorne and me." Anne said, looking at Mendez, "He was already down, but he saved us both."

Elena had so many questions. But instead of asking them, she took the final steps to her husband's bed. He lay swaddled in plastic and cloth with only his face visible. He looked funny, like the centerpiece in an elaborate practical joke. These light thoughts didn't help. They only served to free the sob she'd kept bottled in her throat.

Alex's eyes fluttered open. "Gotta..." he croaked, struggling against Rae.

"Shhh now baby... we won."

"Gotta get...out." He continued to struggle as he spoke. "Kaspari... stairwell!"

"Stairwell, my butt." The cop said hopelessly.

"Wha?" Alex shook his head as if to clear it then stopped, wincing in pain. "He's on ten… coming down."

Miranda was surprised how quickly everyone moved.

* * *

Issak Kaspari walked down the empty hall, the sound of his footsteps his only companion. His pace was deliberate, measured. Haste was for the careless.

The entrance to the stairwell was about ten meters distant when the door burst open.

Though the Simulacra he'd constructed appeared now to be on the ninth floor, Issak could only see the first three floors of the hospital clearly. He'd seen the four fleeing hospital workers long before they burst from the stairwell and into the hall. They shouted for him to get out, that there was danger here, but they didn't slow down as they passed him on their way to the exit.

Yes, danger here.

About four meters ahead, behind a closed door, Issak's Vision showed him two security guards. One was unconscious; the other clutched a stunner with fervor you could only call desperation.

It wasn't in Issak's nature to allow this kind of unquantified threat to complicate the coming confrontation. The easiest thing to do would be to simply inform the guards that it was safe to leave, and let them scramble away. He checked his shield again, feeling a little more obsessive-compulsive than cautious. Even if this frightened guard were clutching a small nuclear weapon, he wouldn't be a serious threat to Issak.

Issak grabbed the knob and pulled the door outward.

There was a strangled cry and a shot in the darkness of the supply closet. The stunner shot didn't surprise Issak… the guard had looked pretty jumpy. What did surprise him was the target. The guard had obviously panicked when the door opened and shot himself in the neck.

Poor guy. All indications were that it had been a spooky night at the hospital.

With a small shake of his head, Issak closed the door. He'd let them sleep it off in peace. He turned to the first-floor stairwell. This was as good a place to wait as any.

The Road To Hell

Issak struggled upward through the static, through the pain. He struggled for consciousness through a shadowland of inky black and phantom light. He struggled to regain the Loom. That kid was full of surprises.

Careless… stupid. Maybe it wasn't too late. He struggled harder. Then there it was… warmth at first, then light—light that burned his left hand. The Loom resolved from the static that coursed over him. He slipped around it, engaged himself in its mesh of creation. As he did so, what remained of his left hand felt like it was being eaten by a flaming tiger.

Full of surprises. Maybe it wasn't too late. Maybe he wasn't completely alone, not yet damned beyond all redemption. Maybe the Outsider had caught him… maybe his plan had worked. Maybe it hadn't had time to hurt Dek before…

He spent a few seconds staunching the blood that flowed from his ruined hand then a few more to put the pieces back together again.

Head throbbing, he rose to his feet, flexing his reconstructed hand. Ouch.

On the floor by the refrigerator were two dead puppets. Both had been killed with the sword Issak had made with his own hands over seventy years ago. The table had been turned over and the chairs were strewn across the floor. There were several large dents in the stainless steel door of the refrigerator. He didn't see any trace of Dek... perhaps he got away... full of surprises, that kid.

His smile was banished by the breeze that moved through the room from the hallway that led from kitchen to the bedrooms. It was refreshing, damp, scented of rain. A peal of thunder followed on the heels of a brilliant flash. Though the hallway was filled with light and sound, the living room windows reduced the effects through the other archway to a flicker and a rumble. The lightning cast stark shadows in the hallway. He could make out the silhouettes of at least three figures standing by the window at the other end of the hallway.

He began to accumulate power. As his consciousness expanded out through the Underworld, he felt the deformities that the puppets caused. A cluster of seven puppets stood around that corner near the shattered window. He struggled with all his might to see through the distortions. After a few seconds he was sure Dek wasn't at the end of the hall with them.

The implications broke over him. They had lived, Dek had not. Thanks to him, Dek no longer had the ability to survive a fall from this height. The destruction around him took on new significance. Here his boy had met his final challenge, made his final moves. He'd done so alone, betrayed by the only person he had left to trust.

The grief crashed in, so loud he couldn't hear it. The rage burnt inward, so hot he couldn't feel it. Alone. The world seemed to slip past him, like it would until he eventually died... a slipstream of minutes and seconds, eons and millennia. He would remain; burning, untouched, alone.

He stumbled toward the elevator. Inside, he hit the button for the lobby. He had an umbrella in his hand... raining outside, but he didn't remember picking it up. The feeling of sinking inevitability filled the elevator as it dropped slowly though the surrounding building.

It would be a relief if somehow he missed his floor and the elevator continued downward until the doors finally opened onto a flaming hellscape. There amongst the cavorting demons, under the distraction of their loving torture, perhaps he could forget who he was, what he'd done.

He'd been prepared. But sometimes preparation isn't enough. He'd had a plan, but plans fail. He had to make this right. For this empty world of ashes, he had to make it right.

Downward at the slow speed of inevitability, umbrella in his hand. The road to hell was paved with his intentions.

A soft tone sounded. The doors slid apart to reveal the familiar lobby. Here the ghosts of his dead family walked, surrounded by the sound of furious rain that seemed to cover the earth. He was separated from the downpour by windows and doors, but that was the illusion. Here with the ghosts, the storm boiled within him.

He crossed the lobby, deployed his umbrella and stepped into the distracting relief of the downpour.

Near a destroyed car, in a field of glass and water, his boy lay. Then he stood amid the destruction. Glass pierced Issak's knees, the umbrella rolled to a stop on its side, tears in the rain.

It's not too late. Not too late at all. His hand still burned as he reached out through the Loom. Bones knitted, organs resumed proper operation, flesh healed. Finally, he knelt before his only son's unblemished body. With only a little coaxing, blood flowed through the repaired veins. Breath went in and out.

Sleeping. This was what sleeping looked like. Sometimes you can make it right. Sometimes, against all odds, it's not too late. But he was old enough to know better.

He shouted into the purging sky: sound and fury, but no words he could remember. He drove his damaged fist into the concrete. Bones snapped, blood flowed. He struck again and again until the pain nearly knocked him out. Then he knelt there, clutching his ruined hand, screaming in the pouring rain.

* * *

They moved down the stairs as quickly as they could. Ping and Miranda carried Hawthorne's gurney; Rae and Elena carried Mendez's. Alex and Anne came last, guarding the rear. Alex's focus was on his Obscuring, Anne's was on restraining the urge to look over her shoulder for the hundredth time.

The going got easier the farther they got away from the fifth floor because the stairs became less warped. As they passed the fourth floor, Alex tripped on an uneven step. He didn't get a chance to fall down the stairs, bowling through the others carrying the gurneys below him. Anne caught his arm milliseconds into the fall.

"Thanks." He said.

"No prob." She said. "So, you folks live in Wonderland long?"

"About a year and a half," Alex gave a weak smile, "Didn't do much more than hang with the Mad Hatter before this week though. Maybe five months for Rae there. Ping's been here only a little longer than you."

"He's adjusting well." She said with a nod.

"So are you."

"This is adjusting?"

"Continuing to breathe is adjusting." Elena said from just ahead of them. "I've only been down the rabbit hole for half an hour and I'm already sure 'bout that."

"Good point." Anne said, "What about Mendez and Hawthorne?"

"I had lunch with Kyle and Sarah today… no Wonderland." Elena said.

"Recent arrivals, then." Alex said. "Welcome all!"

* * *

Despair is for the weak, Issak thought, shoving the blackness away for the thousandth time.

After the millennia he had been alive, he didn't have a lot of room left under his skin for weakness. Yet, weakness or no, he couldn't keep the rage away. Even when he couldn't feel its fire, its smoke filled his vision, its fingers searched over his skin, feeling for any gap in his defenses.

The worst memories were the oldest and newest. Beginnings and endings: memories of Dek's childhood and his... end. Teeth clenched, he pushed away another dear and unwanted memory. This one was of Ivo and Roy: their first trip to a movie house sometime in the nineteenth century. Roy had been so excited he'd kept getting out of his seat to examine the screen. They'd been thrown out of the theatre. They'd laughed all the way home. Three people who together could have laid waste to all the armies of Europe—ejected from a movie house by a self-important usher.

The rage wouldn't leave him, largely because he was its target. Some mistakes you're just not supposed to walk away from.

* * *

Ping pushed the door open and navigated the gurney forward. The way Alex had sounded, he hadn't expected to get this far.

Trying to balance caution with haste, he looked down the hallway to the left... nothing. He pushed the rest of the way through the doorframe with the door sliding down the right side of the gurney. Boy, if they could avoid another pack of disco zombies, hit men, and a powerful wizard for just a few more minutes, they might actually get…

As he moved beyond the edge of the door, Ping saw him. Bald with a well-groomed fringe of gray hair, he looked more like an urbane spokesman for European coffee than the engine of their final destruction. He leaned against the wall about five meters away as if waiting for a friend. Nothing about his appearance or body language indicated a threat, but Ping *knew*. Issak Kaspari, and the end of their little adventure waited in this hallway.

"Hi." Ping said as casually as he could, willing the tension out of his muscles. "Could you point us toward an exit?"

A smile spread across the stranger's even features. He pointed to the exit sign directly above his head.

"Oh. Right." Ping tried to recover from the strain in his contrived conversation with a self-conscious smile. "You know, its dangerous here… you should probably get out."

"Yes." The Kaspari suspect said thoughtfully, "Dangerous here."

Ping still couldn't read him at all. Perhaps it was his imagination, but he could feel the power in the air. It seemed to press in on him like wet Alabama sunshine. Where was Alex anyway? Was he blind? Was he already dead? The only thing he knew for sure was that he hadn't run away.

Family. Ping realized that from the heat and pressure of conflict, the diamond of a new family had been born. He trusted Alex and Rae with his life. He trusted Anne with his life, even though he'd met her fifteen minutes ago. Weird.

The psychologist in him wanted to dissect this phenomenon for a second, but then the urge passed. Studying hydrogen and oxygen was far less satisfying than simply drinking fresh water. Here in the third 'last moments' of his life in as many days, he deployed the telescoping wheels beneath the gurney and continued forward. Karl Marx had said that religion is the opiate of the masses. One of his professors at the University had asserted that family was the opiate of little clumps of the masses… but he was a sucker. Granny Yao knew better.

When he was thirteen, he'd gone through this odd phase where he resented the life of the school. Always surrounded by relatives with 'helpful advice', he'd craved a little freedom. Visiting from Hong Kong, Grandma had set him straight. "You're lucky Tian Fu," she'd told him, "Some people move through life without family." Ping had nodded and gave her his 'humoring the idiot' smile. She'd smiled right back. "But being alone ain't bein' free, it's just being empty." She'd poked him in the chest, over his heart… not too softly either. "Family's the framework of your freedom, like the bones in your flesh. Take the bones away and the flesh doesn't get more free."

At the time, Ping had endured her words as he endured so many of her other fortune cookie sermons. But over time her words returned to him. He was lucky.

Part of the reason he'd moved from Criminal Psychology to Marriage and Family Counseling was that misguided professor and old Granny Yao. He'd wanted to make a difference.

Ping was now almost within range of Kaspari. Two more steps. The second gurney was almost through the archway with Rae at the head of it. Ping's left hand directed his gurney, his right hand slipped into his jacket pocket.

FINISHING TOUCHES

The fire of the Loom shimmered about him like currents shifting through deep and troubled waters. He checked and rechecked his weave. He made a tweak here, shored up the pattern there. The devil was always in the details.

Eight floors up and five floors above ground, Dek waited, feet swinging over the edge of the exam table, oblivious. Two floors above his adopted son, the Outsider's flesh puppets shuffled aimlessly around each other in some kind of demonic holding pattern. Here, as far as he could get underground, Issak prepared.

He hadn't been alone for months now. The Outsider was his constant companion, seeing all he did, lurking always at the edges of his perception. He hoped it didn't understand the subtleties of the Loom well enough to decipher the true intent of the Cast he currently wove, but he was far from sure this was the case.

His son was bait. There was no other way to look at it. Hard choices—if nothing else, his new pact with the Outsider bought them time. In exchange for his help, the

Outsider would leave his family alone for now. Of course, when it got what it wanted, all deals would be off. What it wanted was the only power it lacked—power over the Loom. The idiot Savants of Asado couldn't grant this power to it, though they'd tried. Of course, it would never get its little ephemeral hands on the Loom. No matter what Issak promised, he knew it wasn't possible. The Loom was order and that thing was chaos.

Until recently, Issak hadn't known that the Outsider had followed him back from below. He'd felt the darkness around him sometimes, but it would retreat before any examination. He'd assumed he'd been damaged by his journey Outside. Then things started to happen. Entire clans were destroyed, and little petulant Asado began to emerge as a power to be reckoned with. Ivo had discovered the Outsider's dirty little secret, and then Issak had discovered the shadow that walked with him.

With any luck, Issak would be able to seal the breach he'd made to the Outside, to push this murderous thing back into the darkness where it belonged.

Issak hoped that the Outsider would live by its word at least temporarily. He hoped that Ivo and Roy would be safe for now. He hoped that both he and Dek would come through the danger of the next few moments. He hoped his desperate plan would work. He clung to this hope as he stood and moved to the door. But hope can be a dangerous thing.

Moments later, with the tapestry of his elaborate Cast around him, he entered the examination room where Dek supposedly waited.

He was greeted by fresh air and broken glass.

* * *

Kaspari regarded Ping with clear eyes and a small but un-wavering smile as Ping took the final step into striking range.

Ping pressed the activating stud as the collapsed sword came out of his pocket. He released the rolling gurney and his arms moved the sword in a cross-body slash meant to cut Kaspari in half. At the end of the slash, he was surprised to still be alive. He really hadn't expected his surprise attack to be a surprise. He certainly hadn't expected it to work.

Kaspari's smile didn't waver, his eyes lost no clarity, and he certainly didn't separate into two pieces. In fact, he looked much more amused than dying. Kaspari's eyes flitted to Ping's hands, then back to his face. "So, I guess this means you're not just happy to see me." His smile widened slightly.

Ping became aware that the sword felt odd… he didn't re-member hearing the lock tone or the ringing of the blade. His eyes darted to his hands, which now held a partially squished banana. His right thumb had broken through the skin where the activating stud would have been on the sword.

He gave Kaspari the quick nod of casual greeting.

He looked from his… banana… back to Kaspari. Kaspari balanced the collapsed sword on his outstretched palm. "Now, how did you get this?"

"Dek gave it to me." Ping held out the mauled banana, as if he were ready to trade. "Actually I was just about to ask you the same thing." He tried for a light grin, but wasn't sure his game face was holding. He hoped this wouldn't hurt too much. A lot of his conversational energy was spent preventing the pre-death wince.

Issak stared at the ancient weapon. He remembered Forging it for Ivo when Roy was ready for it… happier times. He shifted his gaze from the weapon to its new owner. The wielder of the banana returned his stare with clear, determined eyes. He was either completely stupid or extremely cool under fire. Either way, Dek had chosen well when he'd entrusted Roy's blade to this man.

"You!" Anne shouted as she entered the hallway with Alex.

"You look like you've had a long day." Kaspari said, shifting his gaze from Ping to her. Ping followed Kaspari's gaze back to Anne. Her expression was hard, but otherwise unreadable.

Ping bounced off the far wall of the hallway upside down, then landed on his back at Kaspari's feet. His kick at Kaspari's knee had gone about as well as he could have hoped. His guess had been more along the lines of exploding into flames, but then he'd always been lucky in combat.

"You're a decisive little guy," Kaspari said from above. "I respect that. It used to serve me well." Hiding beneath Kaspari's intended air of amusement, Ping thought he heard an edge of sorrow.

Roy's collapsed sword landed on Ping's chest. Kaspari stepped past him. "Please, Mr. Ahmed, lets not have any unnecessary… fisticuffs, shall we?"

Alex stood slightly behind Anne. He gave no response, made no moves. The look on his face was thoughtful tension. His eyes darted about, probably more panic than planning. Rae had moved to Alex's side. Miranda Todd and Elena Mendez stood between Kaspari and the gurneys.

Kaspari stopped perhaps two meters before Anne. "And speaking of fisticuffs…" He wagged his finger before her—shook his head slightly. "Don't."

"Why don't you just take her and let us go?" Alex whined, "There's nothing we have that you could possibly…." Then he interrupted himself with an attack.

Down in the underworld, away from the eyes of the others, Alex threw himself at Kaspari. He knew he didn't have the energy for a direct attack, so he opted for a probing attack and hoped for a miracle. His first attack was intended to destabilize one of the many currents of power from which Issak's ready Casts fed.

His attack was partially successful, it caused one of the seemingly thousands of Casts in Kaspari's quiver to shimmer and go dark. Alex hoped that was something vital, but it really was just a means to provoke a hopefully overconfident response. Meanwhile, Alex spent most of his effort weaving something for Kaspari's counterattack.

Kaspari's attack came in. It made Alex think of a large flyswatter, seen from the perspective of a very small fly.

Subtlety— surprising to find in one so young. Issak didn't try to stop the attack that darkened one of the minor Casts he kept ready. Hopefully he wouldn't need to use the Loom to hack into the global network soon, because now he'd have to spend a few microseconds repowering that Cast first. This was obviously a probing attack, so

Issak responded with the equivalent of a large feather pillow in response. He waited to see how Ivo's apprentice responded.

At the last instant, Alex activated his Cast. It was basically a needle within a disposable energy collector. As Issak's flyswatter crashed over it, the energy collector stole some of its power, and used it to drive the needle through the Cast at an angle. Alex's Cast defended him by threading him through Issak's attack after the needle. Along his path through Issak's Cast, Alex left the Weave of Collection. The refined power of Issak's disrupted Cast flowed through the collector, replenishing Alex's energy reserves.

Nice! The incredible thing about watching Ivo's apprentice work was the way he was using no standard Casts. If he was using Templates, Issak couldn't tell. He had been in combat with perhaps a hundred other now-dead Savants, so Issak knew this was not the norm for combat. Usually, combat in the Underworld was done with prepared Casts, like a game of poker, or (shudder) pokemon; you played what was in your hand. Only the oldest and most powerful Savants could modify their Casts during battle. Perhaps only five Savants in the world could actually create in combat. Ivo would be proud.

Another wave of sadness and guilt crested over his mental discipline, almost breaking it. He wanted this kid to kill him in the worst way. He deserved it. Of all the people who had died recently, he deserved it most, but not yet.

Issak reclaimed perhaps half of the power in his ruptured Cast. He'd have normally taken more back, but he was concerned this little prodigy might have the subtlety to attack him through the compromised Cast.

From Ping's perspective, it seemed that the world was straining from the clash of unseen forces. The distortion was subtle—the vibration from a nuclear conflict on the other side of the world. It only affected his peripheral vision and the workings of his inner ear. Blurry and dizzy, he grabbed the collapsed sword off his chest and struggled to his feet. Anne was way ahead of him.

Anne could feel the energies tearing around her like excited Piranhas in a river of beef stew. It was disorienting, buffeting her through sight and sound and skin and bone. Behind Kaspari, Ping was struggling to his feet.

Another surge of power burst over her, Kaspari staggered, and she exploded forward, feeling just a whisper of hope.

Kaspari dodged the tendril of force that lashed out of his own Cast. The kid had actually been able to infiltrate his Cast so deeply that his counterattack came from out of the energy Issak had reclaimed. The tendril was inside his defenses, but he could still deal with it. He pulled his shields across the distance between Alex's attack and his interface with the Loom. He was again protected, but he wasn't the target. Alex's Cast instead struck at the terminals of three of his major power feeds. The resulting explosion tore down perhaps half of his prepared

Casts and scattered nearly all of the Templates he kept ready.

Things were looking worse up in the Overworld, though. As he staggered under Mr. Ahmed's quite unexpected effectiveness, the Cop with Roy's blade was struggling back to his feet and looking assertive. The woman with Dek's power was arcing toward him like a more determined version of lightening. To add insult to injury, the cop standing by Ivo's protégé was hurling a warped pistol fairly accurately at his head. With the eyes of the Loom, Issak could see the Cast around her, guiding her actions, linking mind and body. There was something else in the patterns around her. It was like guide wires for perception, instructing the eye in how and where to look to see her. Fascinating... what could the purpose of those be?

With an effort, he forced his curious mind away from the Forge emanating from the woman's necklace. He needed to focus on the problems at hand. At last he saw how these upstarts had managed to take Shiva down. She'd been the third-ranked Savant in Asado... the veritable cream of the crap.

No more games.

Alex struck again, and another swath of Kaspari's ready Casts went dark. He knew this couldn't last, but that wasn't the plan. Though his Cast was still wreaking havoc just outside Kaspari's interface with the Loom, Alex's focus was now on arming the bomb he was constructing inside the largest remaining power conduit at Kaspari's interface. He knew that Kaspari would evict him within milliseconds, but he hoped the bomb would go off after

Kaspari had expanded his shields to again encompass the conduit.

The texture of the Underworld changed. It took a few ticks of the atomic clock for Alex to realize what had changed: his shields were gone. There was an incision through them that he hadn't seen or felt. Through the incision, Kaspari's power had come. Now Alex was completely defenseless. He tried to put the finishing touches on his bomb before the end. He knew it was already too late for him.

Anne left the ground for her final leap, but didn't go the right direction. The disturbances she felt around her resolved into a resonant harmony, like the inside of a very large engine or perhaps a dragon's growl, heard from within its belly.

She moved backwards halfway between floor and ceiling, equidistant from both walls. Unseen forces pressed in on her, locking her limbs in place. She had no other struggle to make, so she satisfied herself with futile resistance to the crushing power of the engine all around her.

Roy's sword came out, but a fraction of a second later Ping took Rae's thrown pistol in the forehead. It didn't knock him down, but it did knock him out—then gravity knocked him down.

Rae never saw Anne's altered flight plan. One instant Anne was racing Rae's pistol toward Kaspari and the next there was a flash of light as Anne slammed into her, knocking her off her feet. They both fell in a heap on the floor a couple of meters back. Anne landed on top.

Kaspari's Cast was all around him. It was moving so fast that even the speed of the Loom couldn't resolve its blur into individual actions. Alex had lost track of the bomb he had been arming. Now he was completely on the defensive, if you could call it that. All his energy and focus was consumed with token resistance to the decimation that Kaspari wrought on his interface to the Loom. Kaspari now had complete control over the Overworld around Alex. This meant that he could turn Alex into any kind of corpse he desired—charcoal corpse, shredded corpse, eaten by weasels corpse… the possibilities were limited only by imagination.

He was in the dark, the power and speed of the Loom lost to him. Then he was in the deeper black of the Overworld.

He opened his eyes and saw Kaspari about two meters away. "Had to try…" he said with a shrug.

"Yeah." Kaspari nodded.

They both looked around at the destruction. Behind Kaspari, Ping lay on the floor. The extended sword was close to his hand. Between Kaspari and Alex, the two Feds stood braced but indecisive before their friends on the gurneys. They both looked like they were really missing their weapons. Elena pulled out her badge. "Federal Agents… freeze?" They all had a good laugh. It was strange how good it felt.

Alex turned to Rae, only to find her gone. He turned and saw one of her legs protruding from under Anne's sprawled form. "Rae!" He shouted, and stretched down into the Loom. As its heat and light enveloped him, he was already organizing a weave to get Anne off of her.

Alex shouted like he'd been burned. He fell to his hands and knees, breathing heavily.

Kaspari wagged a finger at him, shaking his head slightly. But then he rolled his eyes as Alex crawled toward the two women. "Hey!" he shouted. Alex looked back over his shoulder.

"Excuse me," Kaspari said, somewhat annoyed.

With obvious effort, Alex pressed to his feet. He turned to face Kaspari, but his eyes moved again to Rae's protruding foot.

"Fine." Issak said, exasperated. Though he made no external sign of concentration, wiggled no fingers in magical sigils and spoke no rhymes or Latin, several things happened almost at once.

Free, Anne leapt to her feet. She turned with the lithe motion of a hunting panther toward Kaspari.

The blood stopped flowing down Ping's face and the wound on his head closed. His eyes fluttered open. His left hand went to his head and came away red. "More head trauma... figures." he muttered to himself, looking at the blood. His right hand wrapped around his sword. He struggled into a sitting position.

Rae coughed and sat up. "Sorry." Anne said with a small shrug and a self-conscious grin.

Alex took two steps and extended his hands. Rae took them and pulled herself up. "What I miss?" She said, rubbing her head.

"Me taking the beat-down again."

She moved into his arms. "But you won, right?" Then she saw Kaspari over his shoulder and stiffened slightly.

"Does 'beat-down' mean something else to you?" He tried a reassuring smile as she moved back to look into his face.

On her gurney, Hawthorne stirred. Kyle Mendez groaned and shifted in his isolation wrap. Elena turned as his eyes opened. "Hey." He croaked.

She smiled back. Emotion made her voice unreliable, so she didn't use it.

Kyle's eyes widened slightly as he remembered more. "Honey, what are you doing here?"

"Rescuing you." She covered the catch in her voice with a smile.

"So I'm not dead?"

"Not for at least another few minutes," she glanced around quickly, but her eyes returned to him and lingered.

"You know," he said with a dreamy smile, "I heard that angels come to you in the form of those you love most."

"Yeah, that's how we first met." Elena's hand went to his cheek.

"Just to be clear… not dead? I'm pretty sure angels aren't supposed to use even the white lies."

She shook her head and leaned in close. Behind Elena, words floated, hanging briefly in the air before winking out like stars at sunrise. They were the soft sounds of falling rain outside the warm shelter of their reunion.

"Chief?" Miranda turned her head, still keeping an eye on Kaspari.

"Hey, Mira… I just had the weirdest dream."

"Me too, boss." Miranda put a hand on Hawthorne's shoulder, "Me too."

"Whoo… I feel like I've been shot twice and left for dead…"

"Don't be silly boss. We'd never leave you for dead."

"Where's Derry?" Hawthorne asked. Miranda's face darkened.

Anne's stare was unwavering, determined. Kaspari returned an even gaze. All traces of his earlier grin were gone.

Issak was taking her measure, trying to decide… Through the eyes of the Loom, he examined Dek's Forge. It hadn't just wrapped itself around her, it had fused to her—become her.

There would be no later. If he was going to act, it had to be now. He knew from his experience with Dek that he could sever this woman from the Loom. He knew from harsh experience why he might need to. To give another power is to be responsible for their use of it.

Issak was sure about Ivo's prodigy because Ivo had been sure. He was sure about the policeman who now carried

Roy's blade because he trusted Dek. But what about this unlikely heroine who now stood before him? Dek had given her this gift, but the gift had been out of desperation.

Could she be trusted with this power? Would she use it when she needed to? Would she use it well?

* * *

Awkward.

Beneath the curly wreckage of her first and only permanent, Anne fidgeted in a brown and orange holiday dress that, though it was the largest in the store, was still a size too small. More than usual, she felt fat. Here, surrounded by family, she felt most alone. Here where she should feel most safe, she felt most inadequate.

Around her at the portable table, children older and younger spoke of their interests: acting, music, sports— the rest of her family was talented and engaged in the unknowable dream of life.

Sometimes as she hid in the mechanics of eating, she tried to lose herself in their words like she would in a good book: here's Anne scoring the big goal, here's Anne bouncing lightly on the shoulders of the jubilant team, here's Anne upside down and perfectly poised on the balance beam. She imagined she lived with their courage. She dreamed that she could dream like them, but she was awake and blinking into the morning sunlight of her limitations.

Since this year's gathering was at Aunt Simone's, the kids' table was within earshot of the adult's table. There, up in the big leagues, she could hear her mom badgering Clara, the oldest of the three Kelley girls. Today's topic was the kind and quantity of food on Clara's plate. Mom had stopped badgering Anne about the same thing two years ago when she was six.

She was right in the middle of the warm feeling of gratitude when her mother managed to reach across the five meters separating them, around the corner from the dining room, and punch Anne straight through the heart. "It's too late for her."

In frustration, Clara had said that Anne already had seconds. "It's too late for her.", her mother snapped back.

At first Anne had interpreted the change in her mother's strategy as reverse psychology, or perhaps the tardy but needed onslaught of parental compassion. But now, listening to the familiar stream of fear and warning that poured from mother to sister, Anne had an epiphany. Her mother hadn't changed her tactics—she'd changed her opinion. Anne's mother had given up on her. She would always be fat and useless—she'd always lose life's game.

This realization was a big burden for an eight-year-old to carry, especially since it felt like it had been dropped on her from the tenth floor balcony. At eight years old, her mom already knew it was too late for her.

Around her, the Thanksgiving revelers laughed and talked and ate, but before Anne was a plate of ashes. Fragile hope crumbled and fell, but no tears.

* * *

His icy-blue eyes hadn't moved. His stare was that of a statue... the statue of a surgeon deciding where to make the first cut.

In the back of her mind, Anne heard Ol' God Fear yammering something about immanent destruction and how she probably deserved it anyway.

Whatever. She had questions... Kaspari better have answers. "How could you?" she said, maintaining her stare. Issak didn't flinch, but Anne thought something subtle changed. Perhaps there was a thawing, a softening of the eyes.

"He trusted you." She said, trying to keep most of the fury out of her voice.

"What do you know of me?" Issak asked in measured tones.

"Enough. He told me about you."

He looked skeptical. "Told you?"

"Through whatever you did to him—however that bound us—we were together in my head. He told me about the devil and your deal with him."

"My deal with the devil." Issak's words were almost inaudible, but in their understatement burned both guilt and frustration.

Ping understood the texture of Kaspari's words. This was familiar territory for him; this was his kind of guilt. Not guilt for inaction, not guilt for selfish deeds—this was guilt for noble but misguided efforts repaid with tragedy.

"What were you trying to do?" He asked from behind Kaspari.

Issak disengaged from Anne's stare and turned to the guy with Roy's sword. "Exploring," he paused, his jaw set as if resisting some unseen force, "Under this reality, there is another world, and in that world are the keys to power in this one. I found a way to explore the world below the Underworld, but there was only chaos... and something very old." He gestured expansively, "All this is my fault."

Kaspari had taken the plunge into irrelevant exposition, but Ping wasn't deterred. "What were you trying to do when Dek died?"

"No way back." Kaspari said so quietly that only Anne heard.

"What were you trying to do when Dek died?" Anne asked, fractionally softer than she thought she would.

Issak turned back to Anne, but this time his eyes didn't hold the inquisitor's torch. This time his eyes were semi opaque windows into a very dark place.

"Trying to make it right." He said.

"How?" Alex asked.

"When I came back from underneath, this thing followed me back. I didn't know at first, but it's the thing controlling the meat puppets you fought upstairs. It is the darkness inside the Harms—it's the wave that will cover the earth if I can't stop it."

Kaspari paused. They waited. At last, "It's aligned itself with one of the Clans—a previously minor one called Asado. I believe you've met them on several occasions.

Asado thinks they can use their alliance with The Outsider to gain power, but they'll end up on the buffet table sooner or later. Still, Asado's Savants couldn't give it what it really wanted. When I found out, I made a deal with it... It leaves my family alone, and I give it access to the Loom."

"No!" Alex took half a step forward.

Ping held up a finger for Alex to shut up. He gave him a quick 'Right Now' look.

"What it wanted wasn't possible." Kaspari glanced sideways at Alex. "You can't align a beast like that. Even if you tried it on one of its puppets, the Outsider's presence would disrupt the Cast. The Loom is order, but this thing is chaos. You felt it when you touched them."

Alex nodded. Issak glanced at Anne quickly. "I thought I could use Dek's Forge to trap it. I thought that his Forge would bind to the Outsider and encapsulate its distortions enough for me to get a hold of it. I hoped the Forge would hold it long enough for me to force it back to where it came from."

Issak gave a pained smile, "Luckily, I didn't get a chance to try my little plan."

"It surprised you? Turned on you?" Ping prompted when Issak paused again.

"No," Issak said, "Dek did."

They all waited out another pause.

"He surprised me. I was so focused on making sure I managed it carefully, making sure the Outsider didn't catch on... I never saw it coming." He looked to Anne.

"Even though I thought I held him tight, even though I'd separated him from his speed and power..."

A smile like fatherly pride spread across his face, sweet and painful. "He took me out and killed a couple of the flesh puppets. He thought he was saving the world when he went out the window of Ivo's penthouse. As it turned out, he only saved me."

"Saved you?" Ping asked.

Kaspari realized he was smiling and it looked like that realization nearly killed him. "It couldn't have worked. My big plan—it never had a chance." He gave a bitter smile. "When Dek disrupted my plans, he saved me."

"Why are you so sure your plan would have failed?" Alex asked.

"Because I know something now that then I didn't: *I'm* the anchor that holds The Outsider in this world. It latched onto me when I was underneath. I brought it back with me. It's the link between us that holds the door between our worlds open."

"So the only thing holding this Outsider in our world is you?" Alex asked.

"For now," Kaspari nodded. "I've tried everything, but I can't break its hold on me... if Dek hadn't escaped, hadn't transferred his gift to you," Kaspari looked at Anne, "then my plan would have failed and it would have discovered my deception. It would have realized that it didn't need my cooperation and it would have taken me."

"You mean it would've killed you?" Anne asked.

"No," Issak said, looking tired, "not yet."

"Why not?" The newly sitting Hawthorne entered the conversation.

"If I'm dead, the tether won't hold. It's nettled into my soul, not my flesh."

"So if anyone offs you, this thing's history?" Elena Mendez said, helping her husband to unsteady feet.

Kaspari nodded. "Maybe."

"Maybe?" Alex said.

"I don't know how powerful this thing has become." Kaspari looked around, "Past some point, it will be so established in this reality that it won't need me. I've got to act fast."

"Act… fast?" Anne knew what that sounded like.

Kaspari gave her a black look. Confirmation flowed between them. "When you met Dek—when he died, he was trying to save the world."

"So now you're going to do the same thing." Anne said.

Issak set his face. Hard. Finished. He looked at Anne. "I have something of yours." He brought something out of his pocket and walked to her. He held out his hand.

"Does this mean we're going steady?" she said, taking the ring from his hand.

"It was Dek's."

She tried three fingers before she finally found one that would allow the ring around it. She examined the shiny, featureless metal. She could sense the arcs of power that were forged into the ring… she could almost see the shimmering tracings that wound around the band. "What does it do?"

"It's a key." Kaspari held out his other hand. Anne took what she thought looked like a flashlight, or perhaps a stunner.

Anne touched the activating stud on the object with her thumb. The blade rang from the end of the collapsed sword. The blade shimmered with energy only she and the Savants could see. It was beautiful, like lightning stretched into smooth, even arcs. It seemed familiar in her hand, like she'd held it for years. Reluctantly, she looked from the shimmering blade to Kaspari's face. "King of England." She muttered, holding the sword before her.

Kaspari looked confused, but decided not to pursue the issue. "I'm pretty sure he wanted you to have that."

* * *

They both woke with a start. In his disoriented state, he clawed at the alarm clock. He'd pressed every button his clumsy fingers could find and slammed his fist into the top of the clock twice before he noticed the clock's display. 5:22am—too early.

By the time he realized his mistake, his wife was already out of bed and rushing toward the door. The shrieking that woke them was coming from Scott's room. Sleep vanished like morning mist in the blazing daylight of fear. It sounded like Scott was being eaten alive.

He fought his way out of the covers and rushed around the bed, slamming into a bookshelf, then a dresser in the near dark of the room. He entered the hallway at an uncoordinated sprint. His wife was already at Scott's door, banging on it with her fist and calling to him. He couldn't make out her words among their boy's shrieks.

While her right hand pounded, her left wrestled with the locked knob.

"Move!" he shouted, not slowing from his sprint down the hallway. His wife jumped right and he plowed into the door with his right shoulder.

The flimsy interior door crumpled where his shoulder struck it, but more importantly the lock plate flew off of the doorjamb, leaving a splintered crater. The door swung open into darkness and shifting colored light.

The room's light was off, so darkness largely prevailed, resisted only by a sense lamp Scott had bought when he started hanging out with the wrong kids earlier this year. The lamp had been on a dresser near Scott's bed, but it now lay on its side on the floor. It spilled its shifting patterns of psychedelic light across a wall covered in intricate posters, and part of the ceiling. Behind the lamp, Scott's bed was shrouded in darkness.

Something had changed as he burst into the room. It took him a second to notice, but the room was silent except for their labored breathing and the slow click-click of the rocking lamp as it settled on the floor. "Scott?" His wife said, uncertain.

He thought he saw movement on the dark bed. Not looking away from the bed, his hand reached for the light switch by the door. As his hand found the switch plate, he heard a slow guttural growl from across the room. As unnerving as it was, it only became more so when he realized that it wasn't a growl… it was a laugh.

He slid his hand up the wall and the lights snapped on. Thankfully, what happened next was so fast that there was room for the mind to be convinced that it was misperception.

Crouched on Scott's bed. Black eyes and wicked grin. Sheets and mattress slashed through by black claws. Staring directly at them with eyes the color of slugs. Blood from broken lips. Hissing roar, part lion, part lizard— then gone. Blur of motion and shattering glass.

His wife screamed, both hands over her mouth. He felt like he'd been punched in the face. The thing that had just smashed out their fifth floor window was wearing Scott's favorite T-Shirt.

Wearing his boy's clothes…

He rushed to the window and thrust his head out into the chill night air. Dawn was still perhaps an hour away, though he could see the first hints of morning in the sky. About fifteen meters down, on the street, he saw the thing in his son's clothes streaking into the darkness with unbelievable speed. There were other sprinters on the street. He counted five—no, seven—all streaking southward, toward downtown.

From this height he couldn't make out many details, but most of the runners seemed to be in sleepwear. Others looked like they were at the end of a hot night out, but all were running faster than traffic usually flowed. As he watched, other sprinters came around corners and from other buildings, joining the lemming run to the south.

He followed their path with his eyes, but didn't see anything special… no strange lights or hovering spaceships, no beckoning devil atop the flaming pit of hell's newest extension campus.

A little over two kilometers to the south, the taller buildings thrust themselves toward the predawn sky. Unnoticed among them was the smaller brown stone structure of Mercy Memorial hospital.

* * *

"So, if this thing is everywhere you go… you're saying it's here now?" Alex's eyes moved to survey the hallway's few shadows.

"Ah… too correct. Not its power, but its presence." Issak said.

"So, didn't you just spill the beans?" Alex looked around, "Doesn't it know your plans now… wait—*I* don't know your plans now. What were they again?"

Kaspari smiled. "I'm going back, but this time, I'm going to drag that thing with me."

"That's suicide." Anne said.

"That's life." Issak said, returning to his dry butler irony. "Maybe not mine, but it's everyone else's."

"Isn't it going to try to stop you now?" Alex said, still looking around nervously.

"It's got a choice," Kaspari said, "It can try to get more backup from Asado, it can try to stop me in person, so to speak, or it can sit idly by and hope I fail."

"You hear that?" Kaspari shouted to no one in particular, then he lowered his voice again and continued, "None of its options are good. Asado is probably too far away, and if not, their efforts are rather laughable from my point of view. They don't have any time for sneak attacks or back-stabbing. If it brings its puppets, it will succeed if it can get close enough in time. However, the closer it gets, the more likely that my Cast will succeed. If it does nothing, I'll probably still succeed."

"No." Anne said, "There's another way."

"Now you sound just like Dek," Kaspari said, "…and what is that other way?"

"I didn't say I knew what it was," Anne snapped, "just that it exists."

"Look, this thing's power is growing. Now it can hold onto hundreds of puppets at a time. When it tried for Ivo, it could control only about fifteen puppets." As he spoke he looked at each person in the group. "I don't think there is a limit for it. After its hold on this world is strong enough, it won't need me anymore, and then we'll have lost our only hope of stopping it. Once its power is great enough, it won't only be the mentally defenseless it will remake… soon it will be able to take anyone, anytime. Then it will start remaking the world."

"What if you're wrong again?" Hawthorne asked, still sitting unsteadily on the edge of her gurney. "What if this is just a trick to get you out of the way?"

Issak nodded. "Power I've got. But against this thing, this is my only weapon. If it fails, I won't be much more use in a fight with it."

"This is a bad plan." Ping shook his head.

Issak continued as if he hadn't heard. "When I'm gone, there's still the problem of Asado... they're already on their way to gaining dominance among the clans. If this happens, the world would be a much darker place. You've already met Shiva... she was a lot sweeter than most of them."

"Shiva?" Ping looked confused.

"Really nice Indian girl; looks a lot younger than she is. Loves platinum, rubies, and the suffering of others."

Rae shivered. "Yeah... we've had the pleasure."

"I didn't see it, but I was close enough to feel her death through the Underworld. I must say, I didn't see how that was possible until you folks tried the same thing on me..." his smile was cold, "She's been ducking me for years now... though even if I'd found her, it wouldn't have been easy."

"Right!" Alex snorted.

"Well, it wouldn't have been trivial." Issak smiled, then turned toward the ER.

"Hey!" Anne yelled, "Where are you going?"

"Deep as I can get." He said without turning back. "It's time... and they'll be coming."

* * *

The crowd piled out of "We-Oui!", a near-north-side nightclub frequented by the Link set. Some of the runners moved like antelope, others stumbled and fell, but they were all smiling. As much as their various levels of the change allowed, they moved in harmony.

Rodriguez had never seen anything like it before. On other raids, he'd seen the somewhat spooky syncopation of link dancing, but this was different. It was like watching the end of a marathon burst from the nightclub's doors. The shock of the human explosion was intensified because the runners seemed to move like low-budget digital extras in a video—all controlled by the same program.

The sprinters were really hauling too. The first and fastest were already out of sight. Others fell by the wayside, lost in convulsions. At first Rodriguez thought the crowd was heading for the van he shared with the other officers and detectives preparing for tonight's vice raid. There was a tense moment as the human wave crashed toward their unmarked van before turning left like a school of fish and heading off down the road.

This spooked him way more than he hoped he showed… O'Flannahan was still being a jerk about bullet hole in that overpass. The next guy that jumped out and yelled "Boo!" down at the station was going to be paying for it in teeth.

"Don't shoot, Junior!" Malloy O'Flannahan hissed from the back seat as they began to realize they weren't the targets of a drug-crazed riot.

Everyone laughed. Paying in teeth, Rodriguez mused, as he 'ha ha ha'-ed along with his friends. "You notice my weapon's the only one not out, old man?"

The other officers had a self-conscious laugh as they looked down at their pistols and white knuckles. "You can't hold me accountable for my superior reflexes, sonny." Malloy said.

"Hey, at least that 'asthma' is back under control, hey chief?" Rodriguez glanced back to appropriately relish his partner's consternation.

"Yeah, maybe all those inhalers you got in your locker this morning did some good after all?" Ashok from vice said as he jumped out the door and looked toward the fleeing partygoers.

Rodriguez radioed the disturbance to the dispatcher while the others piled out of the van. He hoped that the mass exodus wasn't caused by anything grisly inside. Hopefully, it wasn't another Harm on a killing spree... maybe someone just tipped the crowd off about the raid.

Detective Ashok Brown was really beginning to despise his job. Now it was only the camaraderie of his fellow officers that kept him going... that kept him together.

There was a time when Vice held a certain black charm in his mind. He had to admit, moving like a hidden torpedo through the darkness of the city's party scene seemed a little cool in concept, but now he saw too clearly the sadness and desperation. Vice was about irony—it was the shortcut to joy that led to destruction. Vice was the domain of lost children of all ages, a dark Neverland of warping corruption.

He dropped from the driver's seat of the van and into the familiar streets of the night. The perhaps thirty sprinters were long gone. He'd never seen anyone move like that. Before him were perhaps seven people who looked like they were in the process of not surviving a chemical weapons attack. One man swayed on his feet, hands on his knees as he coughed and wretched. A scantily clad woman in her early twenties screamed incoherently as she used her arms to ward off unseen attackers. Another man seemed to be trying to flee on his hands and knees, but his shaking limbs eventually deserted him and he curled into a fetal position on the sidewalk.

The worst part of the desperate scene was the screaming. It was unhindered by pride, ego, or any other check—it was elemental and unrestrained. These men and women screamed like children alone and in desperate trouble.

Behind him, he heard the van's other doors open and the other officers pile out.

"Do you ever get used to this?" Rodriguez asked from his left side.

"Never… but maybe that's because it's getting worse."

Empathy added speed to his steps as he moved toward the victims of tonight's good time. He wished he could help them, but he knew he couldn't and it made him angry—angry enough to shoot the next dealer he saw. He wanted to reach out and hold these people until the ambulances came. He wanted to tell them it was going to be all right. But since this wasn't his world and things didn't work the way he wanted, he reached for the riot cuffs.

He used two of the riot cuffs to secure the screaming woman's wrists and elbows together. He used another two pairs to bind her knees and ankles together. He hated his job.

Then the screaming stopped so abruptly he thought he'd been deafened. Before he could be reassured by the return of the thousand small sounds of the night, seven voices bellowed out a single word… or maybe just sound, "Gruumen!"

Ashok jumped. The girl whose ankles he was now binding had participated in the shout. He looked up into her face, but was unprepared for what he found there.

Her eyes had gone completely dark, with only a thin rim of white visible around the edges when her eyes shifted to the side. Her fear had evaporated, along with every other sign of humanity. She looked dead but for the fact that she was still moving. Her waxy skin looked like it would crack with every motion as a smile spread across her face. The smile didn't stop when it should, but kept growing, showing seemingly all her clenched teeth, splitting her lips.

"Release me!" She shouted in a voice that sounded like the devil's proctologist.

"Sure." He said, backing away. To his dismay, he noticed that the clear plastic riot cuffs binding her elbows were turning white under the strain of her shaking limbs. This was a feature designed into the cuffs to provide warning before they broke. Of course, nobody was supposed to be able to break these cuffs. They met the more stringent requirements for Harms, but Ashok had a feeling that those standards needed to be upgraded again.

His fascination with the changes in the bone structure of her face finally yielded somewhat to the demands of his experience and his pistol came out. He pointed it at the girl struggling against his riot cuffs. Her black eyes fixed on the gun like a starving man might look at the last cocktail wiener. "Gruumen!" She shrieked in that same grinding voice. The riot cuffs binding her elbows snapped.

Shouts and gunfire erupted around him. From the corner of his eye, Ashok saw Malloy take a step back and Rodriguez claw at his holster. Then the riot cuffs around the black-eyed girl's wrists snapped. Ashok held the trigger down and the pistol jumped repeatedly in his hands.

* * *

"Have I said enough that this is a bad idea?" Ping said as their party pulled to a halt in the middle of the lowest level of the hospital's parking structure.

"Nope, but we don't have enough time for you to really do that job right." Anne said.

If Kaspari heard, he didn't respond. He was talking to Alex. "You've got to keep them away long enough for me to finish. If they make it within three meters or so, they'll shred my Cast and this is all for nothing."

"Sure. Maybe we can buy you a few seconds if they slip on our blood…" Rae's face didn't match her light tone.

Alex nodded, "I won't be able to Cast when they get close and we don't have a working gun between us."

"You haven't seen her work yet, have you?" Kaspari inclined his head toward where Anne and Ping were moving up the ramp. They stopped about twenty meters away and were engaged in some easy pre-death banter.

Alex thought for a few seconds, then shook his head. Kaspari continued, "You ever see Dek or Roy work?" Alex's head kept shaking.

"We've actually got a really good chance, unless we get attacked by an army. Now, pay attention, if this doesn't work, I'm going to need you to kill me."

"Your confidence is contagious." Alex shook his head.

Kaspari looked distracted for a moment, like a particularly troublesome thought had occurred to him. "They're coming… you feel it?"

Alex closed his eyes. He stretched down, then outward from the Loom. Around him, he could see the complexities of a large and intricate Cast that Kaspari was in the process of configuring. It was like nothing he'd seen before in terms of subtlety and sheer ambition. This was his final Cast.

Reluctantly, he pulled his mind away from the study of Kaspari's work and pressed his Vision outward. He felt them almost immediately, like angry blurred hornets through the arteries of the Underworld. Though he couldn't focus to see them through all of their chaotic noise, he could fix their position by the location of the gaps in his Vision. "Three minutes?"

"Two, more likely." Kaspari said from behind closed eyes. This is going to be close."

"Two minutes what?" Anne shouted toward them with a look of great concern.

"Two minutes to live probably." Issak yelled back, "They're inbound fast."

"How many?" Ping waved his collapsed sword through small circles, warming the tendons of his wrists.

"I lost count around seventy." Alex looked from Rae to Kaspari.

"I got to a hundred and twenty before I gave up." Kaspari said with a shrug.

They waited in silence for the moment.

Ping glanced sideways at Anne. Her face was set with determination. Her eyes scanned the expanse of the garage ahead. Ping knew the ground they needed to hold was indefensible. There were no choke points that could be more easily defended against a superior force. Their task was hopeless and they both knew it.

Anne was smiling.

Ping had been taught the value of such smiles from his early youth. He'd been taught to value the courage they implied. Her blue eyes shifted to regard him then jerked away when she saw he was looking at her. Probably childhood issues. He smiled, laughing softly.

"What?" she asked, becoming more flustered.

"You are without a doubt the most bashful killing machine I've ever met." That got him a smile and a small shake of her head.

"You know," he said gesturing with his collapsed sword, "I was just about to ask you how you could keep it together in the face of our impending horrible death… but I suppose I'm really more interested to know why you're having trouble with the banter."

He spent a second in an open smile to help her realize he wasn't all that serious before continuing. "You know, it's really standard procedure for folks in our position to exchange a few polite jabs at each other—you know, to brace our courage up, laugh in the face of danger—that kind of thing."

She laughed. "Sorry, I'm new to the whole killing machine thing. You been at it long?"

"Fighting? I was punching before I could crawl. Mom says I learned to walk by stringing kicks together." He shifted his gaze to the rising incline of the underground parking structure they were going to die defending. "Killing, though…" He trailed off.

"I hear you." Anne said, following Ping's gaze. There was a moment of silence, then Anne broke it. "Hey, you related to the Bannons of Chong Fu?"

Ping looked surprised. "Yeah. Clairvoyance part of your sparkly little magical package?"

"Yes." She said with a look of grave irony, "I have sensed it."

She paused for the joke to take hold then smiled. "Nah, I think I saw your mom on Oxygen-2 once."

Ping winced, "You remember O2's short-lived *Sisters, Find Your Strength* series eh? You know dad will pay you to forget about that."

"You're the less female spitting image… I still remember the aerobics episode. Didn't she pretty much spend the whole episode whaling on some guy and saying, 'feel the burn, my sisters!'"

"Dad was sore for weeks. You should have seen the look on his face when mom got cancelled… like he'd been pardoned." Ping laughed, remembering. "Of course, mom saw this look. They had an impromptu training session right there in the kitchen. Mom threw dad over the counter... broke grandma's table."

Anne looked concerned. "That must have been terrible!"

Ping snorted. "Nah. You've gotta understand. It was training, not fighting. Neither was ever angry. It was like watching puppies wrestle. They'd always do the trash talk like in an old Kung Fu movie, 'your kung fu is for kittens', that kind of thing. Then they'd get into an epic battle. Things always got broken, but there were never any bad feelings. It's been a family tradition going back two generations. Grandma Yao and Grandpa Sean had some battles that were legendary."

"Your mom sure was funny." Anne said with a warm smile.

"Hey, if we live through this, you should come to the school, meet the folks."

She turned the color of a ripe tomato and began to fidget. Ping got the distinct impression she was hoping she wouldn't live so she wouldn't have to worry about the social situation. Definitely childhood issues.

"You know, if you come both mom and dad are going to want a crack at you."

She laughed, losing a few shades of red. "It's their funeral."

Ping's sword came out. "You have dishonored mommy! Them's fighting words!" He waved the sword between them. "I will feast on your entrails!"

Anne was game. Her sword joined his in the air between them. "Then there will be no doggy bag big enough for your leftovers!" Their swords clashed perhaps ten times as Ping made an increasingly earnest but futile effort to find a way past Anne's inexpertly wielded but blinding fast blade.

"Is that the best you can do?" Ping yelled breathlessly. They both smiled.

This little guy was good, Anne thought as she swatted his varied attacks away. It was like she had all the time in the world to move her blade to intercept his. Sometimes she had to correct her positioning after their blades met to effectively deflect his attack. She'd definitely have a hard time surviving an attack from anyone nearly as fast as she was. She tried to pay attention to the moves he made, tried to mimic them. She was thankful both for the diversion, and the lesson.

In Rae's stolen microvan, the four Feds watched the swordplay.

"I know, but that's too fast to be sparring." Miranda responded.

"You're only saying that because you haven't seen her work before." Kyle said.

Miranda turned around in the passenger seat. "I saw her work while you were taking your nap... but I see your point."

"Oh yeah?" Kyle said, "she run up any walls for you?"

"She knocked a guy through one..." Elena interrupted herself, "*Up* the wall?"

Hawthorne and Kyle both nodded. "Yeah." Hawthorne said, "And none of you were yanked out a window, then spun like a pizza all the way to the ground."

All eyes turned to her. "Now that's gotta be a joke." Kyle finally said.

Hawthorne shook her head slowly, remembering. "I've still got to shoot her about that sometime." Then she smiled and smacked the steering wheel with one hand, "Man! What a night!"

Alex and Rae stood, hand in hand at Kaspari's side. Kaspari was sitting cross-legged on the ground, looking like a Yogi working on his levitation. He hadn't moved in about two minutes.

"How's it going down there?" Rae asked.

"I have no idea." Alex said without opening his eyes. "It's definitely the biggest Cast I've ever seen. It's beautiful, you know. It's massive, yet modular... there's no chaos in its complexity."

"Sounds like you're about to write a haiku 'bout it babe."

One of Alex's eyes popped open. "You know, I'm going to miss that sharp wit."

"Right, like death's gonna save you. I thought we were in this for the long haul. Hey, weren't you already kinda dead once?"

He moved into her arms. "Wasn't really dead then."

"Well, you sure weren't much of a talker."

Closer. Now only a whisper away from her lips. "Seek medical atten..." he started, but then their lips met.

Impossible children. Issak Kaspari thought as he tried to work.

Fortunately he was up to the challenge of working even surrounded by three flavors of distraction. About twenty meters away, Ping and Anne played Roy and Dek's favorite game. In the microvan about the same distance in the other direction the four Feds laughed and jabbed at each other. And, last but not least, about one meter away, Alex and Rae shared what really should have been a much more private moment. In a moment of bittersweet memory, he thought how much he missed Roy and Dek's knack for playful distraction.

Without the training provided by Dek's constant interruptions, Issak might not have been able to work under these conditions. As it was, he put the finishing touches on his Cast just as the fourth distraction vied for his attention.

One floor up, the leading edge of a horde of no less than three hundred demons raced downward.

Anne swatted away Ping's most earnest attack and stepped back, turning to face the ramp up to the next level. "They're coming!" she shouted. She could feel it coming like the wind ahead of a tidal wave—chaotic power, unseen but close.

Alex stepped back from Rae, the laughter in the van drained away, Kaspari didn't move. The air filled with the thick funk of final judgment.

Ping shoved his dread aside and tried some distraction. "Nice try!" He shouted, leaping toward Anne, sword flashing.

There were two ringing clashes of steel, and one less metallic impact followed by Ping landing firmly on his butt. "Didn't you hear the terror in my voice?!" Anne shouted.

"Actually, yeah." Ping said with a slow smile.

Her frustration seemed to increase to the point where she might explode. But then she seemed to deflate, tension spilling out into the air. "You're nuts." She said extending a hand.

"Yep." He took her hand and was whisked too quickly to his feet.

"And possibly stupid." She shook her head, bemused.

"Now that's the pre-fight spirit!" He gave her a quick thumbs-up.

They turned to face their foes together. Their blades extended before them—nearly parallel and steady as those wielded by ancient statues. They waited, listening to the rising clamor from above.

Then the Harms broke like flood waters around the two sides of the downward ramp ahead. The howling ranks of the mob quickly filled the entire opening, which was perhaps eight meters across. They were so thick that the far wall of the parking structure was quickly lost to view. They swarmed like Piranhas, rushing forward so fast that it took them less than five seconds to reach Anne and Ping's position.

Hawthorne's right foot hovered above the accelerator. Her hands turned white on the wheel. The van was pointed directly at Kaspari as he continued his apparent meditation on the ground not far away. They were plan B, and unless something changed very drastically very quickly, they'd be needed.

"What I wouldn't give for my guns." Kyle said from the back seat.

"Yeah, because they would do a lot of good, baby." Elena said as the onslaught passed Ping and Anne's resistance. For a few seconds, they saw them both fading back before the attack, hacking away frenetically. But the area was too wide and the enemy wasn't interested in engaging them. The demons flowed around them like water. Anne managed to stay in front of the line briefly, killing everything that came in reach, but finally she too was lost behind the sea of attackers.

Hawthorne jammed her foot down and the van skittered ahead, riding the ragged edge between torque and traction. She hoped that Kaspari had been right and that his death would be enough. He obviously wasn't going to be able to get his magical doohickey together in time.

"Wait!" Miranda shouted from the passenger seat, but Hawthorne knew what she had to do.

The big Irish cop took a painful fist in the face and went down hard. His partner twisted toward him, gun tracking through a tight arc, but before he could get a bead on the wreck that had hit his partner, what used to be a bouncer from the club tackled him, knocking him from his feet. Ashok brought his gun up, but couldn't help

Rodriguez, who was now wrestling with the bouncer on the concrete.

Repeated clicking drew his attention to the Harm who, now holding Malloy's weapon was trying to use it to kill him—thank heaven for lock rings. Ashok swung his gun and fired twice, but the creature was gone, lunging toward Malloy, open mouth full of what looked like dragon's teeth. Ashok's third shot found the leaping creature's leg, and the monstrosity's stride broke and it tumbled and rolled like a wounded tiger before lunging again at Malloy's unconscious body.

Ashok breathed out, settling further into his shooter's stance, and drew a bead on the back of the creature's head as it raised Malloy's right hand to its mouth. He pulled the trigger and the night sky filled with stars and a wounded peace he shouldn't be feeling. Ashok's vision narrowed to a short, dark corridor looking up into the starry night sky, partially occluded by the devil reaching over him for his gun. He'd never seen the thing behind him until it was too late… until now.

Alex and Rae had moved in front of Kaspari for no reason beyond stubborn resolve not to be completely useless. Rae was holding a tire iron like a baseball bat. The act was futile, but not in matters of the spirit, where the only victory is over fear. As always, she was his inspiration. He raised his inexpert fists, hoping maybe to give one of these monstrosities a bloody nose or maybe even a blacker eye before the end.

Here in their last stand, Alex's mind lingered on Rae as she stood blazing bright beside him. Not enough time. If this was the end, then it was way too soon. If they died of old age on their one-hundredth anniversary, it still wouldn't be enough time. This dream was sweet, but it would end too soon.

Just on the other side of Kaspari, Rae stepped away from Alex and raised her tire-iron like a baseball bat. Hawthorne hoped she could miss them after she killed Kaspari, but she didn't think so.

Then something big changed.

It was like reality had received a sucker punch on the nose and saw stars. There may have been a flash, followed by blurry turbulence that filled all the senses from touch to taste. When Hawthorne was next aware, it was of another shock as the microvan plowed into a support pillar several meters to the right of Kaspari's position. She wasn't so much aware of the collision with the pillar as she was of the harsh embrace of the airbag that exploded out of the steering wheel. It forced her arms apart, shoved her back into her seat and drove her backward into darkness.

Ashok was punching the creature dead in the face as hard as he could and as fast as he could with his right hand. He was using his left forearm against the thing's neck to keep its teeth away. He'd used his left hand to shove the thing back as it tried to bite his right index finger off, and had lost a tablespoon-sized chunk of flesh from his left hand for his efforts.

The air around him was full of screams: anger, pain, terror—but the scream Ashok could hear the best was his own. He'd never wanted to be eaten alive, and his first taste of the experience had confirmed all the earlier aversion. The creature on top of him was laughing, almost casually, like the world's grimiest cowboy might laugh in his first hot bath—it was enjoying every second of this.

They both knew that Ashok had already lost this fight, but Ashok kept pounding away on the thing's face anyway... his big goal right now was making sure the bite marks that would eventually cover his corpse had as many gaps as possible.

Then there was a pulse of some kind—maybe a sound, but he would never be sure—and the grinning, laughing thing convulsed once, like it had been hit by a defibrillator and went limp on top of him.

Alex's eyes were still on Rae when the world seemed to turn inside out.

Alex managed to keep his head enough to follow Kaspari's advice. He managed to check his reflexes and didn't leap into the Loom. As bad as this explosion was here, it was probably a couple orders of magnitude worse in the currents of the Underworld.

The explosion seemed to twist them, and everything else, inside out and backwards. Alex never lost consciousness, but the brownout ended with him on his face perhaps a meter ahead of where he'd been, bleeding from mouth and nose. Groggy but resolute, he struggled to his feet.

He and Rae had been blown forward, landing among the first wave of demons. Rae was pressing to her hands and knees, but none of the demons moved more than random twitching.

While he and Rae had been blown away from Kaspari, the demons seemed to have been sucked in closer. All of the demons were laid out like a fallen forest after a volcanic eruption. They were all aligned, bodies radiating away with heads pointing toward Kaspari. Whatever he'd done, it looked like it had worked.

In the middle distance, Anne stood holding her sword like a samurai after a great battle. Spattered with a new coat of wet blood, she looked like she was very ready to hit the showers. She surveyed the sea of bodies, searching. Ping was nowhere in sight.

Then she moved. Alex doubted he would ever get used to just how suddenly or how fast she could move. There was no perceptible acceleration or deceleration. One second she was standing still, the next she was standing still somewhere else, and his eye was left with a tracer-like impression of motion between the two points.

About five meters from her initial position, she threw aside two fallen bodies. The first landed about three meters to the right. The second hit the ceiling above her, then fell back, forcing her to dodge away, covering her head with her arms.

She reached down and helped Ping to his feet. He was shaky and bloody, though there was no way to tell how much of the blood was his own. His face was puffy, his nose clearly broken. He smiled somewhat self-consciously as Anne supported him on unsteady feet. He stowed his sword and focused on standing.

Then Ping seemed to notice Alex and the others and he began to struggle toward them. Anne compensated and began to help him over the bodies.

"Babe…" Rae said, "Look."

Alex turned to see what she meant. She was staring at Kaspari. He was unmoved, still sitting cross-legged. Now though, he looked as if he were about to explode from internal pressure. His face was hard with struggle. His teeth bared, his muscles taut, he shook with the strain of his labor. Veins stood out on arms and his forehead, sweat dampened his face and head. Though he was still avoiding the Loom, Alex could feel the immense powers at play down in the plumbing for this part of the real world. The roiling power tugged at him from the center, an itch-tingle through both flesh and mind.

Though Issak had cautioned him not to, Alex needed to at least try to help. In the new silence that covered the garage he sank to the ground, crossed his legs and closed his eyes.

"What'cha doin?" Rae asked in her 'you're doing something stupid and need to stop Right Now' voice.

Alex smiled without opening his eyes. "I need to help. This really matters… end-of-the-world-or-not time here."

"I've still got a tire iron…" she threatened.

"I've still got a head for you to whack." His smile didn't waver.

"Be careful."

After a few seconds to calm his mind, he put a toe in the water of the Underworld. The flames exploded around him, nuclear hot, nuclear bright.

As Ping and Anne hobbled up, Alex screamed and jerked out of his sitting position, landing on his back.

Both he and Kaspari shared the look of desperate struggle.

"That's not careful!" Rae shouted, dropping the tire iron and falling to her knees beside Alex. She lifted his head onto her lap and stroked his face, whispering encouragement and threats.

In a sea of fire and lightning, Alex saw Kaspari's struggle. At the base of a huge funnel of energy, channeled by the ground surrounding the underground garage, he fought in the doorway to somewhere else. He fought with a formless black squid with uncountable tentacles. The thing had him, its tendrils wrapped through his essence. He seemed to have given up the struggle to sever the thing's connection to him and was focusing his efforts on forcing the thing back through the door into darkness.

The thing's tentacles flailed at Kaspari, trying to find purchase on something to halt its backward slide. At times, the thing mounted enough resistance to halt Kaspari's advance, but it seemed to be able to hold onto little besides Kaspari and whatever was hidden in the black on the other side of the doorway.

Then the creature passed the dark threshold and everything changed. The creature lost its hold and it and Kaspari fell downward. Kaspari sent out anchoring tendrils of force, trying to remain on this side of the darkness, but it seemed hopeless. He was caught in the vortex of his Cast, buffeted by currents of power too hot and strong to be resisted for long.

Alex realized he had to act quickly. He anchored himself as best he could and then plunged into the vortex. As he approached Kaspari's position, moving slower now, reinforcing his hold on this world with every move forward, Alex noticed the real problem. The Outsider had not released its hold on Kaspari. His flagging strength seemed entirely focused on holding on, so he had none left to try to disengage the creature.

Close enough now, Alex began to work on the tendrils that seemed to wind though Kaspari's essence. He tried to cut, pry, dissolve, warp… nothing worked. About this time, Kaspari noticed him. The fountain of fire that was Kaspari's form here turned partially on him. Alex got the impression of tired acceptance as Issak swatted him aside, forcing him out of the downward current. Then Kaspari let go.

As Issak fell into the darkness, Alex streaked forward. He caught Kaspari, and was immediately pulled forward himself. There was a jarring as Alex's tethers stopped their fall for the moment. The shock was almost enough to make him let go of Issak—almost. As he solidified his grip on Issak, he got a clear impression from him. Something like 'What are you, stupid?' This was the point when the first of his tethers ruptured. Stupid indeed. He really didn't have much of a plan other than "hold on and hope for the best". Only one thing was clear to him. He wasn't letting go.

Below, the darkness began to take on texture. It shifted like ebony sand in slow wind. He could see a distributed intelligence at work in the ebb and flow of the black particles. As he focused, or perhaps came closer, the shifting darkness became clearer, more detailed. They were creatures, numberless as the sands of all seas. His first thought was the black shimmering carapace of roaches—wet, hairy spider legs—black desiccated jellyfish.

The Outsider was not a single organism, but a slow trickle of these linked creatures that had been leaking into the world. Below him, Kaspari fought against the chains that bound them to him. Desperate yet hopeless, he alternately clung to Alex, and tried to push him away. But Alex would not let go. Together they sank toward the sea of insect sewage.

This was it. Alex spared a fraction of his energy and focus to push a tendril of Vision up into the Overworld. He wanted to see her just one last time. Maybe he even had enough juice left to tell her goodbye.

After microseconds that felt like minutes here in the fringes of the Underworld, he could just make out the blurry outlines of the four people around his body. His vision was dim and dominated by the milky static of Kaspari's Cast. He didn't have enough energy to punch his Vision completely into the Overworld, so he saw mostly the constructs of the Loom, with only phantoms and ghosts to show him those in the "real" world.

Kaspari's body was at the nexus of dizzying patterns of energy. Anne was there, too; he could see her clearly because of the Forging of her flesh. In his vision, she shone like an angel, vibrant with heavenly power. So that's what she looked like without all the blood—beautiful.

A dim shadow leaned on Anne for support. Alex could only tell it was Ping because of the brightly burning sword in his jacket pocket and the fire-traced ring that unlocked it. On closer inspection, he could also see the vestiges of the Casts Alex had worked on him earlier. The signature of the Obscuring he'd worked to fix his mind on the antique keys was gone, but the remnants of his last Healing still smoldered with the consistency of slowly dissipating smoke.

Near the shimmering power surrounding his own body was the only person he really wanted to see. She was kneeling, his head in her lap. Thankfully, he could see her clearly. He toyed with the idea that it was because he loved her so much that he'd made it happen somehow, but he knew the real culprit was the cameo hanging from her neck as she bent over him, alternately sobbing and breathing out threats.

He didn't have time to relish his last look at her. Even now, she was darkening, fading, like the rest of his Vision. Below, where the lion's share of his effort was focused on clinging to Kaspari and holding on to this world, things continued to get worse. They were now past the event horizon and the blackness was closing about them. The tendril of his presence in the Overworld was faltering, fraying under the strain.

Maybe he had enough time for one last message. He'd just completed the preparations, when inspiration struck him. With a new sense of hope, he sent his message. But before he could be sure the message had been received, his eyes to the Overworld were closed.

Time passed. Light faded. Their desperate struggle continued.

Then, below him, in the midst of his struggle, Kaspari seemed to explode.

Rae screamed as the blade thrust into Kaspari's chest. The entry wound was clean, there was no spattering blood, but her ears popped as a familiar pressure wave seemed to rock the forge of creation.

Alex was not letting go. The supernova that had engulfed Kaspari blew over and through him, tore him apart, tore the pieces apart. Not letting go. He couldn't really tell anymore if he was holding Kaspari, but he was holding on to something.

The fire burnt him black, scattered the ashes. Not... letting... go!

"Don't you ever get tired of doing that?!" Rae screamed in disbelief, but Ping didn't move the blade. Anne was insensate from the tornado of power erupting from Kaspari. She fell sideways, not seeming to notice when her head cracked the cement. Her arms covered her face, her knees pulled up to her stomach.

Hawthorne emerged from shadows into a blurred and swimming reality. Her first thought was that the microvan had gone off a bridge and they were drowning in a fast moving river. After a few panicked seconds, she cleared the deflating airbag from her face. Her awareness increased and the wet electricity that seemed to rush over her subsided somewhat.

Still alive. After a few seconds, she managed to wrestle the driver's door open. She tried to step out, but was stopped by her seatbelt. It took her a few ticks of the clock to figure out the problem, longer to fumble the seatbelt's catch open. Somewhere not too far off, Rae screamed in exasperation. Hawthorne turned to see, but only saw the ceiling, with its bank of oddly flickering lights.

Operating at peak efficiency, she thought, lying on her back on the too-hard ground. The river of energy again filled her senses as she dimmed toward unconsciousness.

The flames were so bright now that they were no longer flames; no longer hot. Alex was in a white room with no perceptible boundaries. Though he supposed that made it a 'place' and not a 'room', he couldn't shake that roomy feeling.

Then it hit him, as he saw Kaspari sprawled out before him. "Aw crap!" he said without lips or mouth, "I'm dead!"

Kaspari was slowly getting to his feet. "I told you not to help, didn't I?"

"Sure, that's helpful now!" Alex said, frustrated. "Besides, without my help, you'd be getting the all-roach enema right about now."

Kaspari looked very tired, but he managed a wry grin. "Thanks… and thanks for that image, too."

"What happened?" Alex looked around—white.

"My guess is something very white." Issak said.

"You always were an observant man." Ivo said.

At the center of the silence that followed his conversational mushroom cloud, Ivo Lutine stood smiling. His clothes were simple; they seemed to be made of the same elemental white that was the substance of this place. As they watched, another form began to resolve from the brightness. "You need to know that we're all right Issak." Roy said with great feeling. Then he glanced sideways, "Oh. Hi, Alex."

"Hi Roy." Alex said, rather enjoying his dream.

"Dad." Dek said from behind Issak, "Remember that I love you… and sorry 'bout the hand—I missed the wink."

Issak turned to his adopted son. He couldn't laugh or cry here, though the feelings that drive both actions were with him, applying pressure.

"I am so sorry." Issak said quietly.

"Don't die for it. Don't die for us." Dek said. "Live for us."

"Yeah," Roy said, "we always did."

"We'll see you soon enough, Dad." Dek said, "But not too soon." Then a sly smile crossed his lips, "You know, we're not really dead as long as you remember us."

"What kind of crap is that, Dek?" Roy said. "If I'm dead—and I'm going to have to assert that I am… why do I care who remembers me? Like someone's coming to pronounce me 'really dead' when the last guy who knew me takes a frying pan in the head?"

Dek was smiling too. "Wait… what if the last guy forgets us, but then someone reads about something we did… are we back to partially dead then?"

"You'd really have to say 'mostly dead.'" Roy said.

"I don't know, I feel pretty dead right now." Dek shook his head slowly in the attitude of deep thought.

Through the familiar interchange between their insufferable children, Ivo and Issak shared a familiar stare of consternation.

"Pretty dead then," Dek concluded, "but when you're remembered, you're in the enviable state of being just memorably dead."

"Memorably dead!" Roy pronounced with arms outstretched. "Feel the love!"

"How do you stand these guys without being able to laugh?" Issak said, still looking at Ivo.

Ivo nodded. "The feeling turns to love... give it a minute."

"Like they've got a minute." Roy said, giving Ivo the look usually used by the patient in their dealings with the foolish.

"Right." Ivo said as Alex and Issak fell back into the black of pain and almost forgotten turmoil.

Alex's eyes opened.

"Take! It! Out!!" Rae screamed, her voice hard and ragged. From the sound of it, she was about to shoot someone if they didn't comply.

Around him, he could feel the slow tickle of eddies in the Underworld but the storm was over. Rae didn't notice he was awake until he sat up. "Baby!" she screamed, relief cresting over her current wave of frustration. "Are you okay? Tell him…" She pointed to Alex's left with the energy of a woman made mute by exasperation.

Alex turned to see, and found Ping with Roy's sword though Kaspari's chest.

Ping looked a bit self-conscious, "I thought I better not pull it out until you were ready to do your thing."

"Right!" Alex reached out for the Loom, and then for Issak's wounded body.

DOWN TO ONE

Elena and Kyle Mendez sat in a small booth as far from lights of the dance floor as they could find. They'd left the others at the larger banquet tables soon after dinner.

"I still don't feel right being here." Kyle said, looking uncomfortable in his suit. "You know—celebrating."

"I keep expecting to turn around and see Derry and that annoying party high-five of his." Elena nodded. She slipped her arm around Kyle's shoulders.

"Maybe because I didn't see... it just doesn't feel real."

"Believe me honey," Elena said, staring across the sea of reveling college kids and off-duty cops, "Seeing didn't help."

After a thoughtful pause, Kyle asked, "Are we going to be all right?"

Elena turned to him. She felt the urge to say something profound, but then she saw him. He just looked so earnest. She smiled just like she loved him—big and stupid. "Well, we did save the world, which aint too shabby." Their lips met.

Across the room, Issak stood apart, at the intersection of the bar and the wall of the reception hall. He felt alone, or at least like he should be. Anne had been by just a few minutes ago for what seemed like her hundredth check on him. She took her new body-guarding quite seriously. That, or she rightly feared that he would bug out of here the first time she wasn't looking. She was desperately focused on making him comfortable.

"And how are we doing?" She asked brightly from over his shoulder. He'd lived far too long with Dek to be surprised by these little ninja surprise moments. Bittersweet memories closed in on him.

"Anne. What a pleasant surprise." He said with British butler irony.

"So frumpy." She gave his shoulder a smack. "You know, there's dancing to be done."

"Anne, I am the oldest man in this room by well over a thousand years. You'd probably have better luck with Ping's grandad… wheelchair and oxygen tank notwithstanding."

Anne made no response other than a finger imperiously leveled at the dance floor. At first he thought she was ordering him to boogie, but then she flicked her eyes to follow her finger and he got the message. Reluctantly, Issak turned from the isolation of the drink he'd been nursing and let his gaze follow her finger to the dance floor.

As he'd feared, there was Sean O'Bannon, standing shakily behind his walker, shuffling slowly around the dance floor, shaking his hundred-year-old butt. Near him, looking much better preserved, his wife risked all by dancing over and giving his unstable frame a playful bump with her hip.

"See Issak?" Anne said in mock awe, "They fear not even the booty bump! What's your hang-up?"

Though he tried to hold on to it until it turned to love, he couldn't help the laughter that spilled out of him.

In the middle of the banquet tables, Miranda Todd smiled and shook her head. "That your old man?" Miranda pointed to the old man shuffling across the dance floor in the wake of his walker.

Ping shook his head. "Nope. That's Grandpa Sean. Dad's around here somewhere… probably hitting the food line again."

"Boys! Look!" a middle-aged detective one table away shouted. All eyes moved to the bandstand, where the newlyweds had finally appeared. The groom looked uncomfortable in his tux, but the bride was radiant in a shimmering white gown. "Can you believe that's our little Rae?"

"All growed up." A hard woman of about forty said, "Now don't start getting misty on her big day, Cliff."

"Aw… Let's fill her locker with shaving cream." Cliff said.

"Cops." Miranda said in disgust. "You ever considered applying at the Bureau?"

"They don't know I already filled it with marbles." Ping smiled back.

"Gotta steal you for a dance, babe." Miranda's husband interrupted from behind.

"I'm pretty sure there's some kind of federal requisition you need to fill out in triplicate to get that kind of thing." Ping said.

Miranda's eyes sparkled as she departed into the crowd.

Ping turned to his right, and to more weighty matters. "So, Jerry, I need further assurances of my privacy." Ping said with his most grave face.

Jerry's wife giggled.

"I assure you Detective," Jerry's smile ruined his intended air of gravity. "I applied your diaper with complete professionalism."

"So, I'm not going to be seeing any diaper-related pictures on the net?" Ping asked.

"Don't worry, Detective." Jerry's wife said, "I'll never let them out of my sight."

"It's been the cause of much marital strife." Jerry gave a solemn nod.

Ping rolled his eyes.

"Tell us about the demon fight again, Uncle Ping!" the younger of Jerry's kids pleaded from his seat across the table.

"Which one?" Ping replied, preparing for yet another rendition.

"Library of doom!" the older boy said in ominous tones.

"Hellevator surprise!" the younger boy shouted.

"Care for another dance?" Anne said from over Ping's shoulder.

"This time, I lead." Ping said assertively.

"Get used to disappointment." her eyes sparkled... that cute dimple flashed with her smile.

As they re-entered the dance-floor, Rae heard her twelfth "Right on dude!" from a twenty-something student. This one had the meticulously messy hair of the coffee hourse crowd, and had opted for shaking Alex's hand—most of the others had gone for either the high or low five. She smiled as the kid disappeared into the crowd. "You know, if you were a vocabulary TA, I'd say you were a miserable failure... dude."

Alex didn't respond. He just kept up the disturbingly direct stare he'd been giving her all night. "What?" She said for the twelfth time tonight.

His smile broadened. "You look absolutely gorgeous."

"Aw stop."

"Ravishing... Sensational."

"Ok, more."

He let his eyes wander across her, savoring the experience. Her dress was white with scintillant thread woven through. It was simple, elegant, and hung on her at all the right places. Her earrings were simple titanium studs. Her necklace was an elegant titanium weave. Her new ring was a simple titanium band. The jewels were in her smile, in her eyes. She shone like daybreak in Antarctica.

"You are the love of my life."

Unconsciously, her hand went to her necklace. Alex watched her do it.

She noticed him noticing and smiled. "I still miss it." She admitted with one of her dazzling smiles. "It was a real confidence booster."

"You look the same to me."

"Yeah, but you've always been weird."

"And now it's gone," Alex looked at the crowd around them, "what do they see?"

She thought a moment as they resumed the slow spiral of their dance.

"I guess they see what they want," she said, lips near his ear. "But I'm still gonna miss it the next time I need to fight off a mess of disco zombies."

"No you won't" Alex said, stepping back and taking her hand. He brought her hand to his lips and kissed it just above the knuckles.

"Oh yes I will." She said with a playful grin.

Alex kissed her wedding ring then gave her that unnerving stare. "No," he said, lips brushing across the cool metal of the ring, "You won't."

Her smile broadened with understanding.

"I had a feeling you'd still want the Amp," he said, moving in closer, "and no one gets to mess with my baby." Their arms slipped around each other.

"You know the best thing though..." He said, looking into her eyes.

She dropped her eyelids slightly, giving him a suspicious look. "The ring makes me fly, too?"

"We're down to one rule now." His smile stretched slowly across his face.

She felt the heat spread across her face. "And which one is that?" she said, wondering how much longer before they could leave the party.

"Yes, now we get to lie... I've been waiting so long." Alex said with a mostly straight face, "I may even be open to the idea of hanging out in the bedroom now and again."

"You're a sick man, Ahmed."

"And you're a beautiful woman, Ahmed." He laughed, "But now is the time for dancing!" Alex seemed distracted for a moment, as if he'd heard his name mentioned close at hand, then the music stopped and their song started.

"Show-off."

"Impressed?"

"Eh." She shrugged, but then they were dancing and the world seemed to fade until it was only them and Frank Sinatra, spinning through the faceless crowd in slow circles.

Every now and then, their reverie was broached by a 'Right on dude/bro'/man' from Alex's friends, or a threatening 'Now you take care of her' from Rae's friends.

"Get a room." Hawthorne shouted above the music as she danced by in the embrace of an immense tattooed cop with a boss scar on his neck.

Indeed.

* * *

It was late. The last rays of sun had long since deserted the entranceway to the Kwoon. Ping's parents had been defeated for the third time and were upstairs licking their wounds. This thought brought the most disturbing image to Anne's mind.

"What?" Ping said, noticing her shudder.

"Nothing." She raised the pink plastic sword with the worn padding and arched her eyebrows. "Your chit-chat will not save you from my copious annihilation."

"Why? Are your guts going to splash on me or something?" Ping asked with an arched brow.

"No, I mean my copious annihilation… uh, of you." Anne shifted her feet, fidgeted a bit with her hair with her left hand, bit her lip.

"Ah." Ping said, allowing a grin to pull at the corners of his mouth. "You are a killing machine, Miss Kelley, but we have ground to cover with your bantering skills. And besides—It is your suffering that will be copious!" Ping shouted, lunging in for the attack, and the melodramatic battle was on.

She parried his fierce purple sword and compensated as he tried to pivot his "blade" around hers. She forced him to parry a slow motion counterattack, watching his technique. She compensated again as he tried to break the geometry of her attack.

She made the mistake of focusing too much on his blade work, so the kick to her knee caught her by surprise. She readjusted her weight and kicked his retreating leg crossbody. The kick compromised his geometry by twisting him off the line of the fight between them. He compensated by leaping in the direction of the twist. He pivoted to face her again, slashing downward, trying to catch her leg.

"Let your kneecap be the first installment in the payment schedule of your demise!" He shouted, shaking his sword for emphasis.

That got him a laugh. "It is *your* doom that is amortized across these payments, pal!"

"You only laugh because you realize not how little of that payment was principle!" He tried to use her laughter to cover his next attack, but her sword thunked off his head three times, leaving him confused. Thinking back, he was pretty sure one of those hits came out of the air directly above him. For such a big girl, she sure could catch air.

"Your kung fu is for kittens." She said playfully from behind him, her plastic sword tapping him on the shoulder with each word.

"Man, that's annoying." He sighed, rubbing his head.

CPSIA information can be obtained at www.ICGtesting.com
Printed in the USA
BVOW010957170613

323508BV00016B/376/P